# THE WRATH OF GOD

## Whispers of Atlantis

by Jay Penner

**In this anthology:**

*To my wife, for her support, and my daughter, for her endless curiosity.*

Jay Penner (https://www.jaypenner.com), cover designed by Jay Penner. Printed in the United States of America

First printing: Jun 2019 / Updated May 2020

7 2024-08-10
Produced using publishquickly
https://publishquickly.com

# ANACHRONISMS

**an act of attributing customs, events, or objects to a period to which they do not belong**

Writing in the ancient past sometimes makes it difficult to explain everyday terms. Therefore, I have taken certain liberties so that the reading is not burdened by linguistic gymnastics or forcing a reader to do mental math (how far is 60 stadia again?). My usage is meant to convey the meaning behind the term, rather than striving for historical accuracy. I hope that you, reader, will come along for the ride, even as you notice that certain concepts may not have existed during the period of the book. For example:

*Directions*—North, South, East, West.

*Time*—Years, Minutes, Hours…

*Distance*—Miles.

*Other concepts*—Imperial, Stoic.

# Historical Basis

---◇---

I have a short section titled "Notes" at the end of this book. If you are a history buff, stop by and spend a few minutes to explore the connection between the book and known history. I publish a blog covering topics that may be of interest, and I would love for you to visit!

It is also worth remembering that when we say "*Upper Egypt*," we actually refer to Southern Egypt, while "*Lower Egypt*" denotes Northern Egypt. The terms *Upper* and *Lower* are anchored to the origin and direction of the Nile River.

# ATALANNI

Hannuruk—King / Apsara—Queen

Nimmuruk—Crown Prince

Khaia—the Oracle of the Atalanni

Rishwa—Prime Minister

Minos—Governor of Kaftu

Teber—General


# EGYPT

Ahmose—Pharaoh / Ahmose-Nefertari—Queen

Wadjmose—General

Khamudi—King of the *Hyk-Khase*

Iben-Har—Captain of the *Hyk-Khase*

KALLISTU

KAFTU

SAIS    NUTWARET

MEMPHIS

Sand Sea

AEGYPTOS

THEBES

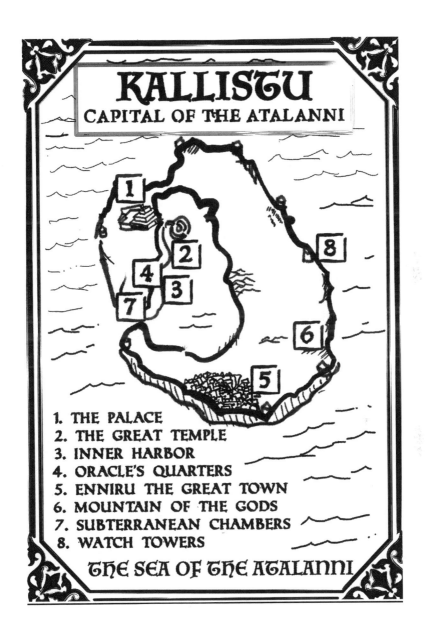

# KALLISTU
## CAPITAL OF THE ATALANNI

1. THE PALACE
2. THE GREAT TEMPLE
3. INNER HARBOR
4. ORACLE'S QUARTERS
5. ENNIRU THE GREAT TOWN
6. MOUNTAIN OF THE GODS
7. SUBTERRANEAN CHAMBERS
8. WATCH TOWERS

## THE SEA OF THE ATALANNI

# PART I
# A LONG TIME AGO

*"The gods have imbued this world with wondrous properties—
earth, water, fire, air. Our role is to understand the world,
interpret its behavior, and bend it to our will..."*

**DAIVOSHASTRA CH. VII: "NATURE"**

# CHAPTER 1

## KALLISTU

The rumblings begin soon after the afternoon prayers and supplications to the holy *Trikaia*—the three principal gods of the Atalanni: the Great God of the Seas, the Goddess Mother of Earth, and the Sky Father. First, the earth shakes gently, like a mother's loving cradling of her infant, but as the minutes wear on, that kindness gives way to anger, and the beautiful, patterned floor cracks. The priests look on in horror as one of the two thirty-foot bronze statues of the sacred bull, positioned at the side of the inner sanctum, topples and crashes into the limestone column next to it, bringing the column down and crushing an altar boy who frantically tries to make his way out. The blue-orange frescoes of the chamber—bulls, dancers, warriors, trees, birds, boats, and deer—crack, and their glory dims as if a young woman's face has aged in an instant.

But the most wondrous scene is that there is now a gaping hole in the earth near the fallen bull. Bright orange liquid oozes from it, burning the ceremonial garments draped around the fallen statue.

"Run!" the head priest screams, and he, along with two men and two women, makes swift strides across the polished basalt causeway that connects the temple to the mainland.

It is a mile to safety.

Few are on the causeway today, for it is the day of prayers, and royalty, nobles, and warriors fill the temple. Commoners are forbidden from visiting the temple complex and the holy island. The men and women run as fast as they can as cracks open beneath their feet. The sea churns, splashing foamy water on them. One man screams as a wave rises from the side and grabs him.

It is as if the sea and earth are locked in a ferocious wrestling match.

In the holding pens in the back corner of the complex, sacrificial bulls and goats create a ruckus and bellow in fear. The crashing waves and shaking earth drown the panic and pleading of the prisoners destined to be sacrificed along with the animals. Manacled and shackled, the condemned shout for the guards and pull on their metal cuffs until their skin rips and bleeds raw. Their pleas go unheard as waves come crashing through their cell windows.

The roof collapses, ending their lives before their blood is spilled before the gods of the Atalanni.

The head priest glances behind him as he runs. The glorious one-thousand-column colonnade still holds, even though some of the proud fifty-foot-tall columns groan as the ground beneath them continues to shake and shift. The colonnade roof has cracked, and the head priest prays that it will not come crashing down. They reach the end of the causeway within minutes, gasping for breath, with soldiers and other concerned citizens ushering them on.

The head priest is the first to arrive at the rock-cut steps. As he springs up, he hears the screams of his acolytes and the crashing of a column.

King Hannuruk looks at the destruction with despair. He wonders what has caused the earth to shake and fire to ooze from the ground, especially on this sacred day of prayers! Hannuruk's leathery, pock-marked face twitches uncontrollably. He turns to Rishwa, his long-serving advisor and Prime Minister. "None of my ancestors suffered such devastation!"

"Yes, Your Majesty."

"This is not the first time that the ground has displayed anger. The last time the earth rumbled a few summers ago, I even built new shrines and decorated the temple complex with breathtaking opulence," he bemoans.

"That is true, Your Majesty," Rishwa replies, allowing the King to vent his frustration.

"I have offered sacrifices of deer, birds, and bulls. Even people!" Hannuruk exclaims, slapping the windowsill.

Rishwa nods. He knows that the King had gone against the advice of his priests when he turned to human sacrifice.

But today, the signs are far more distressing. Hannuruk has heard tales of the Kingdom's ancient past; long ago, the earth had shaken too, and great plumes of ash and fire had been ejected from the ground. This happened when the Atalanni angered the gods by building palaces and towns but no monuments of worship. Since then, the Kings had constructed many temples, and finally, Hannuruk's grandfather had spent many summers constructing the most magnificent temple complex in all the world—the temple of the *Trikaia*—the Great God of the Seas, the Goddess Mother of Earth, and the Sky Father—and Hannuruk's father had further increased its magnificence.

What gods would not appreciate what the Atalanni had built for them?

What about the magnificent central temple with the giant bronze statues of the gods?

And what about the ringed canals that channeled the surrounding sea into teal and green glory, encircling the temple?

What of the greatest inner harbor in all the earth?

Now this?

The causeway, the colonnade, the curved outer walls, the circular canals, the central chambers, the many masterpieces of wall art and statues, and the inner sanctum—all bear wounds from the violence inflicted upon them just hours ago. He can still see dark smoke rising from the inner sanctum, a result of what the head priest claims was molten rock from the bowels of the earth. It all makes little sense, for the only structure damaged in this shaking of the earth is the most sacred complex and the holy island. There is barely a hint of the quake anywhere else, except for some fallen rocks and small portions of collapsed cliffs.

How should he interpret these signs?

"The gods send us a message," Hannuruk says, looking up at the sky. "We should seek guidance."

"Yes, Your Majesty."

The King turns to an attendant. "Tell Khaia I wish to consult."

# CHAPTER 2

## KALLISTU

Khaia stands on the balcony overlooking the bay.

*What a glorious sight.*

The towering cliffs rise from the sea in a graceful arc, surrounding the remarkable temple complex with its statues, frescoes, boat-width canals, colonnade, and glimmering basalt sculptures and flooring. Yet that complex is now a smoking wreck—not destroyed, but damaged enough that it would take many summers of work to restore it to its former magnificence. She fiddles with her bracelet—her favorite piece of jewelry, which she has worn since she was twelve. Her predecessor gave it to her. The bracelet is made of the finest gold from Egypt—on it, the Atalanni craftsmen have engraved a griffin, a lion, a bull, the tree of the island, and symbols that signify the sacred Oracle's position. She touches it gently; it comforts her.

She knows that King Hannuruk would be enraged.

He would seek answers, for what end had he commissioned all the enhancements and accouterments to the great temple, only to watch it shake and break, and that too on an auspicious day?

The old man is known for his fits and outbursts.

Some are no doubt caused by his age.

Some arise from his inflamed tooth, which he refuses to have extracted due to a belief that it would weaken his virility.

Besides, His Majesty was never of sound mind, unlike his highly revered father.

Her eyes drift to her young daughter, Akhi, only one harvest of age, cooing in the arms of a nurse. In two harvests, she will leave her mother and become one of the palace wards. The Atalanni law forbids the members of the Divine Council from rearing children. The boys eventually join the military, while the girls become singers, dancers, courtesans, or attendants to the gods.

A sadness passes over Khaia.

This would be her second child to lose.

The father, a soldier of the army and ritually allowed to lie with her, vanished beneath the waves in a battle against the bloodthirsty Mycenaeans from the North.

A knock on the door brings Khaia out of her thoughts.

"My respects, sacred Khaia. His Majesty King Hannuruk requests to see the Divine Council," says the attendant, peering through the crack.

"Does he not know that it is forbidden for royalty to summon divinity today?" she asks, fully aware that protocol is something Hannuruk only pays lip service to so long as it suits his purposes.

The attendant bows. "His Majesty only asked me to convey his wishes, sacred Khaia. I am merely a messenger," he says, wringing his hands.

"Very well, then. I will meet the King in the throne room."

Khaia prepares herself for the meeting. She disrobes and dons a shimmering blue gown that she secures at the waist with an elegant gold and silver cord. She paints her nails orange and ties a red ribbon around her temple. Her hair falls in curls around her stern, imperial face. She looks at herself in the obsidian mirror and is pleased with what she sees. At thirty-five, she is still healthy; her face shows little sign of age, her breasts remain proud, and her stomach has not yet descended into the folds of the garment around her waist.

She knows men still lust after her.

Is it because of her forbidden stature or her beauty? She is unsure. She may be the Oracle of the Atalanni, but men's desires remain a mystery to her.

Khaia makes her way from her quarters to the palace, walking along the edge of the inner cliffs. It is a beautiful day, the disaster notwithstanding. Her attendant fans her along the way to alleviate the heat of the sun's afternoon rays. On one side lies the green pathway and fences of the royal quarters, while on the other is the magnificent inlet with the temple complex. Gods have bestowed this beauty upon them, she thinks, and yet she feels a chill even in the warm afternoon. Khaia hurries and reaches the palace. After traversing the labyrinthine halls, she arrives at the wide-open throne room. She has made this journey twice each year, every year, for the last twenty since she was nominated the Oracle of the Atalanni. The opulence that surrounds her in this room—where decisions of life, death, and the future of the Kingdom are made—still impresses her.

The room descends into hush as she enters.

The audience bows in respect. The members of her Divine Council kneel in obeisance, and a messenger proclaims loudly, "His Majesty, King Hannuruk, welcomes sacred Khaia, the Oracle of the Atalanni."

Khaia looks around and bows to the King and the Queen. She then walks to her seat, an elegant stool made of Egyptian papyrus.

The room is calm, but she knows a tempest looms.

"You honor us with your visit, sacred Khaia," says Hannuruk as he clutches his graying beard and smoothes it.

"And you with your invitation, Your Majesty," she replies.

They exchange pleasantries and settle down to discuss the matter for which the King summoned the group.

Hannuruk starts, "We have all—"

Khaia cuts him off mid-sentence. "Today was not the day to summon the Council, Your Majesty."

Hannuruk bristles but keeps his composure. She can see his color darken. She continues, "And yet the hour demands that laws be set aside when great danger confronts us."

Hannuruk relaxes, his ego soothed by her concession. He leans forward. "This was not supposed to happen."

Khaia recognizes the accusation in the King's tone. To him, the Oracle is accountable for keeping the gods content, regardless of whether his own actions offend or please the divine.

"We bring the gods' messages to the people, Your Majesty; we do not read the gods' minds."

"But how could you not see this, Khaia?" Hannuruk asks, dropping the 'sacred' formality.

"There were no signs, and the *Trikaia* have not conversed with me this month, Your Majesty. We do not know—"

"You are supposed to know! You are the Oracle!" Hannuruk's voice rises. The members in the room fidget. Conflict between the two great powers of the Atalanni empire does not bode well for those around them.

Khaia does not flinch. She looks at the King and holds his gaze. "Your Majesty, we do not guess the gods' minds. We do not yet know if our gods caused this, or if other forces are at work."

It is then that Hannuruk's son, Nimmuruk, raises his voice. "It then begs the question of how close the gods are to you, sacred Khaia," he begins, looking to his father for approval as he always does.

"Be quiet!" Hannuruk admonishes his son, who, mortified, bends his head and sucks in his breath. Khaia knows it is especially humiliating to be chastised in front of the senior officers of the army and the young Queen, who suppresses a smile.

The King turns to Khaia. "Well, Khaia, what do you think is the message from the gods? What should we do?"

Khaia takes a deep breath and addresses the Prince first. "The moment I realize that the gods no longer favor me, Prince Nimmuruk, I will relinquish the seat of the Oracle."

She holds his stare until the Prince turns away.

Khaia turns to the King. "There is a dense energy about me, Your Majesty," she says, gently slapping her palms to her cheeks. "And I need two days to return with a message. I must attempt to have the gods speak to me."

"What if there is another disaster before the two days?" This time, the soft voice belongs to the Queen, an enigma to many of the Atalanni. She is spellbinding, and at only seventeen summers of age, this foreign-born princess now sits beside the throne of the Atalanni ruler.

Hannuruk shoots a disapproving look at her. It is not customary for the Queen to speak in the presence of the Divine Council.

Khaia knows that the relationship between the royal couple is not one of happiness.

"I do not foresee such an occurrence, Your Highness. If the gods wanted complete destruction, we would have perished by now. It is a sign; the gods, whether they mean harm or wish to warn us, have always given us time to consider our actions and beg them for more information. I ask you to grant me two days."

Hannuruk looks around, and none of his men speak. The Prince has not lifted his head since his father's chastisement. Khaia briefly feels sorry for the man but buries it as she remembers his behaviors of the past.

"Do you think Kaftu has received a similar warning?" Hannuruk asks, referring to the large island to the south that the Egyptians call Keftiu.

"We do not know yet. We should send a vessel to inquire about their situation."

"Could it be that the Egyptian gods are casting their baleful eyes upon us?" Hannuruk presses.

Khaia hesitates. "I request two days, Your Highness. I am confident that our gods will reveal the source of this anger—whether it is the Egyptians, the Shepherd Kings, the Mitanni, the Mycenaeans of the North, or something else entirely."

"The gods of the Mitanni have no quarrel with the Atalanni, sacred Khaia," says the Queen, her lips tight and eyes conveying displeasure. "Indra and Varuna bless this land as their own."

Khaia turns to the Queen. "Forgive me, Your Highness; I do not list the gods of kingdoms with malice, and the Mitanni have blessed us with their friendship and a magnificent Queen," she says, though she refrains from voicing her true thoughts—a girl who sits beside the throne because of me. Khaia is also surprised at how quickly the Queen has picked up their language and becomes comfortable conversing in simple, yet complete sentences, even if with a lilting Mitanni accent.

The Queen nods and speaks no more, twirling her dark, luxurious hair by her ear. Hannuruk sighs loudly and mutters, "I have done all I can to please them. What more do they need from me?"

He then stands, signaling his readiness to leave.

The Prince continues to stare at Khaia.

Something about him makes her skin crawl.

She feels anxious.

But she also knows her time has come.

# CHAPTER 3

## KALLISTU

Khaia meditates in the sacred room of her quarters and emerges long after the sun sinks beneath the waves.

A nurse hands Khaia's baby back to her arms, and she cradles her little daughter. It is Khaia's dream that Akhi would grow to be more like her and find a place within the Divine Council. Life outside for the offspring of the priestly class is not kind.

The baby clutches at her mother's hair and tries to eat it.

Khaia smiles.

Her daughter's birth was heralded as a miracle, for it is extraordinary for a woman of her age to bear a child and live. Yet, Khaia survived the ordeal. That event further cemented the people's views that Khaia was a special messenger of the gods, even greater than her fifty predecessors.

"I will always watch over your wellbeing, my little jewel," she says, lifting the perfumed baby closer to her face and kissing her cheeks. She then puts the baby in a cradle and sits by the lamp in the center of her austere living room.

"It is time," she says to herself as her mind wanders to the relationship between royalty and the council. She remembers her speech to new recruits about the role of the gods. She straightens her back and breathes deeply to relieve the stress.

"Hannuruk thinks I look at the moon, like the wolves at night, and howl at the gods for them to respond," she laughs, speaking to no one in particular.

It is time.

# CHAPTER 4

## ATALANNI SEAS

Our war boats are magnificent. Each is a sleek war machine adorned with the intricate art of dolphins and spears on its side. The tides have turned after five hours of maneuvering and attacking the Mycenaean flotilla.

They are now trapped within an arc of the Atalanni Navy.

We are the greatest navy on this earth!

These denizens of Mycenae, a backward citadel in the lands far north, have been an irritation for two summers now. They desperately try to turn and run, but that is useless, for our arc extends from the northeast to the southwest. We tighten the noose, pushing the Mycenaean fleet toward the cliffs of a small island.

I inhale the heady smell of sea salt and floating seaweed. We will soon mix that with the metallic scent of the blood of these barbarians.

"No one escapes!" I shout.

Men raise a dolphin-patterned flag—bright yellow and distinct against the deep blue skies and water. The oarsmen, aided by the wind on the sails, propel the boats ever closer to the enemy, who now turn pointlessly and collide with one another.

My thirty-foot-long boat slices through the Atalanni waters and races toward the enemy leader's vessel—a poor imitation of our designs.

The men shout their war cries and ready their spears. I must focus on the battle ahead, for my mind sometimes strays to someone back home. Someone I desire more than anyone else, and someone with whom I wish to run away—

Our archers unleash three-headed, bronze-tipped arrows that rip through the enemy as they stand beside their boat in false bravery. Within minutes, the long, shining bronze spike mounted at the front of my boat rams into the enemy's broadside, shattering the wooden boards and embedding deep into the innards of the foe.

"Attack!" Holding my sword and bronze shield, I leap onto the enemy boat. My men have jumped aboard as well, and the Mycenaean soldiers assume defensive positions, trying to fend off the attack.

I target a large bearded man, naked from the waist up and wielding a crude spear. His eyes brim with fury and fear as he thrusts his spear to impale me.

I dodge and step aside.

I swing my sword as he turns and sever his spear arm at the elbow. He screams, his arm dangling by its tendons, but he is not subdued. He tries to push me off the boat, but I slacken and thrust my sword through his belly, twisting it. The Mycenaean grunts and falls, almost faint from his injuries. I kick his head and swing my sword again, cutting his neck to the spine.

I turn my attention to the others.

The scene is frantic and soon devolves into a massacre, with every enemy on the boat impaled or decapitated. The light brown wooden floor is soaked with blood, which sloshes like thick wine as the boat sways.

I assess the situation and pull a conch from my belt. I blow into it loudly, hoping many will hear it over the din of battle.

Soon, other captains blow their horns as well, indicating that the Atalanni troops should attempt to subdue the enemy and hold them.

The enemy surrenders, and the battle gradually subsides. It takes hours for us to extricate ourselves from the mass of tangled boats and avoid being crushed against the cliffs. At my command, the men secure the remaining Mycenaeans, tying them in groups and hauling them onto our boats. These wretched men will be flogged and sold into slavery on Kallistu and Kaftu.

The troops secure the captives and gather fallen weapons. We scuttle the Mycenaean boats and set many aflame to ensure that none return to their wretched citadel. Those not dead scream and flail about as they burn, some leaping into the sea and drowning as we watch.

I turn to Bansabira, one of my trusted lieutenants. "These fools do not learn. They die in these waters yet do not give up. This has been the largest invasion thus far. To what end?"

"I do not know, sir. Perhaps they are so enamored by our riches and beauty that they wish to claim it all for themselves."

"They are brutes—uncultured, with no art to speak of, no skill worthy of worship, just bloodthirsty and ambitious. Perhaps we should mount an invasion on their land and finish them once and for all."

"The elders and the Divine Council are unlikely to sanction that, sir," he replies, "but it is certainly a fine idea. One day the King will tire of defending ourselves and instead send us to attack."

"That is yet to be seen, and you are right. It seems our restraint is being taken advantage of," I say, surveying the watery carnage.

The men turn their attention to the matters at hand. The Atalanni dead, as many as could be gathered, are spread among several boats. We will consecrate them to the Great God of the Sea after due honors.

We wait a day for the winds to take us back home and eventually make our way to the magnificent crescent harbor of Kallistu, the capital of the Atalanni—our home. All I can think of on my way is finding the next opportunity to hold her.

*She is so beautiful! And funny.*

But I must exercise extraordinary caution in how I arrange my escape with her. The remote deserts of Assyria are an ideal place, away from this conflict.

As the boats navigate the single narrow passage that allows us into the inner harbor of the ringed island capital, I notice smoke and fire from the smaller central island. Cracks mar the central temple walls, and fallen columns litter the causeway of the gods.

"What happened here?" Itaja wonders.

"We will find out soon," I reply as we near the harbor and prepare to disembark. On the ground, many officers and the King's Guard wait. I finally disembark and salute Rishwa, the Prime Minister to the King.

*What makes this high-ranked man wait for me?*

"What of the Mycenaeans?" asks Rishwa. The deep creases on his gaunt face reveal his seventy summers of life. With his wise eyes and bushy eyebrows, he has always struck me as the wisest of men.

"Defeated. We have captured about fifty slaves. The rest are dead, and their boats have been burned. What happened here?"

"Very good," he replies. He pauses. "The gods grumble. The King awaits you, Captain Teber."

# CHAPTER 5

## KALLISTU

The King's Supreme Council is seated when I enter the throne room. I have never attended a Supreme Council before, for my rank and position do not meet the requirements for attendance. It is extraordinarily rare for the Supreme Council, which comprises the Royals, the Generals, the Engineers, and the Divines, to convene. The last time it happened was two summers ago when Idukhipa Apsara, then the fifteen-year-old Mitanni princess, wed King Hannuruk.

And yet, I have been asked to attend, along with the most elite of the Atalanni.

"Captain Teber of the Navy," the usher announces, and I nervously follow a royal guard who leads me to a chair behind Unamur, the General of the Atalanni. I salute the General, who turns and looks surprised by my presence. Members are still settling in—the Royals and the Oracle are absent.

"King Minos of Kaftu," the usher announces, and silence fills the room as the attendees stand and bow to the entrant. The colorful governor of Kaftu, a hirsute giant of a man with a mass of silver beard and a head full of unruly hair, walks in surrounded by ceremonial guards. Minos is a spectacle—he wears a white loincloth held by golden cords. Around his ample girth is a thick waistband made of gold and bronze plates, adorned with various gems. Around his neck hangs a golden chain with miniature bells. He holds a bronze scepter and walks barefoot.

Minos is no king; he is the governor of the Island, but the Atalanni rulers have bestowed this title upon him, for he governs the largest of the Atalanni islands. Many stories circulate about Minos, most of them unsavory, but he has proved to be a worthy governor and is fiercely loyal to the Atalanni ruler. He is the latest in the extensive line of Atalanni Governors, all called Minos, who have served the Atalanni kings.

Minos has served King Hannuruk's father and now serves Hannuruk.

Minos is seated beside the platform where the Atalanni royalty sit. As the men and women wait, I survey the room. The seating arrangement forms three concentric circles, with the royal platform as the focal point around which the semi-circular rings originate. The inner circle seats the highest nobility, followed by the other two, each of diminishing rank and status.

I sit in the third ring and recognize a few to whom I gesture with respect.

A loud ringing of bells sounds, and we all stand. The usher announces, "The Supreme Ruler of the Atalanni, The Lord of the Hundred Islands, The Supreme King of Kaftu, Patron of knowledge, art, and armament. His Glorious Majesty, Son of Hannuruk, beloved Son of the Gods of Skies, Earth, and Water, His Majesty King Hannuruk!"

Ceremonial guards fan the King as he walks toward the throne. Hannuruk is an average man, now nearing sixty-five summers, and has gained weight from the decadence of royal living. He wears a gem-studded crown of the bull, its horns embroidered with veins of blue lapis-lazuli. A fine bright white-and-blue skirt is held by golden cords. He wears exquisitely embroidered sandals, with securing threads reaching up to his ankles. Beside him walks the stunningly beautiful Queen Apsara, who looks straight ahead, dressed in the traditional attire of an Atalanni Queen. She wears a luxurious full-length orange-and-brown gown open at the breasts. Her long silver earrings and curled hair frame her face and accentuate her beauty. I, like most others, cannot take my eyes off her. I restrain myself from unabashed admiration, for who knows if the King's spies are watching everyone. Few know I had been in the Queen's contingent of bodyguards for a brief period after her wedding. The Queen's shining black eyes briefly connect with mine, and an electric thrill courses through me. Behind Apsara is Aranare, the Queen's maid.

Prince Nimmuruk follows in his father's footsteps, dressed much like his father but without a full crown. He wears a diadem signifying his position as Crown Prince. He is short and stout, his face smooth without a hint of hair.

Once on his high pedestal, Hannuruk leans and embraces Minos. He guides the Queen to sit on his right and the Prince to his left. The audience takes their seats once the King has settled.

The rest of the members now wait for the last arrival—the Oracle and the senior members of the Divine Council. The shadow of the large sun dial, an ingenious device that measures the passage of time, moves slowly as the Supreme Council waits.

Soon, Khaia enters the chamber. Today I finally see at close quarters the performance of the most powerful woman in the Atalanni empire, perhaps even exceeding the Queen. I have heard that the Oracle is formidable and possesses authority over all that connects the divine world to ours. I am struck by her fearless hazel eyes, accentuated by luxurious liners.

Her entrance is theatrical and mesmerizing. She wears a crisp white-and-blue gown with saffron embroidery. Around her neck hangs an elegant necklace made of precious stones and silver thread. Her earrings are large. Attached to her shoulders are two striking wings—fashioned to resemble that of a griffin.

It is as if she is a goddess floating in the arena.

Behind her are two almost naked priestesses. They wear diaphanous fabric, barely hiding their oiled bodies and distracting firm breasts.

My face warms, and guilt floods my heart.

These are holy women.

*I hope my carnal thoughts do not draw the anger of the gods!*

One priestess holds a polished bronze double-ax with a deep red leather handle cover, and the other drapes a slithering brown-spotted snake around her shoulders. They look straight ahead, ignoring the gaping mouths and hungry eyes, their straight and delicate noses pointed to the Oracle's back.

Once again, the chamber rises in respect, and the usher announces the titles of the Divine Council. Khaia, looking straight ahead, bows to the King and takes her seat in the first ring. The priestesses take their seats in the third ring, and her two senior advisors sit in the first. I have heard of the great power the Divine Council wields in all matters of importance, and this is the first time I see them in such a momentous setting.

I remain unsure about why I am here, for I am of the lowest rank in this room. I am told that the Oracle is here to bring the message of the gods.

The Supreme Council is now in session. After customary pleasantries, respects, and prayers for blessings, the King rises to address the audience. "Three days ago, the earth shook, and we saw fire rise from the ground. We had no warning of the gods' displeasure, and the Oracle herself," he says, looking accusatorially at Khaia, "did not know why, for the gods kept their intentions hidden even from our Divine Council. The Oracle promised us an answer, and we are here today to discover what the gods tell us."

Khaia stands and bows to the audience, who bow to her in return. She does not respond to the King's accusatory statement. "I have spent the last two days looking to the skies, earth, and seas, for the messages do not come in torrents but in small nudges and hints. The gods wish for us to understand them, and they view us not as children who must be told what they think."

"So, you have been receiving messages, then?" asks Prince Nimmuruk, glancing at his father for approval. The King offers no acknowledgment but waits for Khaia's response.

"Yes, I have, Your Majesty," she replies.

A murmur ripples through the Council. It is rare for the Oracle to claim that she received messages directly from the gods, for it is said that the gods send their signs through various manifestations of earth, air, water, and fire.

"And what do they say?" The King asks, leaning back and smoothing his beard, a sign of his nervousness.

Khaia straightens and surveys everyone in the room.

She looks down at her feet and sighs loudly.

Then she addresses the King. "They say we have grown too lazy and that we have diminished their stature in the eyes of the world."

A hush falls over the room.

I suck in my breath. Her words, spoken in a quiet tone of authority, reverberate in the throne room.

"What do you mean, sacred Khaia?" asks Hannuruk, leaning forward and staring.

Khaia continues as all eyes are upon her. "Our gods are growing impatient with our restraint," she says, looking at each member slowly and deliberately. We are immobile. "They say we have looked inward for too long, and that while other empires flourish, our reticence to conquer the world beyond Kaftu and the other little islands is a betrayal of our superiority."

Her tone mocks the phrase 'little islands.'

The Council holds its breath, unsure how to react or what to make of the Oracle's vague statements. Khaia takes a deep breath and slowly rubs her hands together. The silver bangles on her wrists make gentle tinkling sounds that carry in the quiet room.

"What are you implying, sacred Khaia?" The voice, devoid of its usual mirth, belongs to King Minos.

"The gods seek expansion of their dominion; the King's sacrifices no longer satiate their desires," Khaia states, looking at Minos. There are murmurs all around.

"Sacred Khaia," the King begins, his voice trembling, "Every message in the past has focused on enriching the lives of our citizens, building our defenses, expanding our trade, ruling the seas, and advancing our superior knowledge and glorious art. The gods have never demanded an expansion of dominion!"

"Are you suggesting I am no longer capable of interpreting their messages?" she retorts sharply.

*The power this woman exudes!*

"That is not what my father meant," the Prince intervenes. "He merely suggests that these new messages mark a monumental departure from the past."

Hannuruk shoots a glance of irritation at his son, yet does not object. I am surprised that the Prince is capable of saying something sensible.

Khaia maintains silence for an entire minute, icily looking at us one by one, locking eyes with each of us.

There is much fidgeting and discomfort.

She allows the moment to linger until we submit to her completely.

*Masterful.*

The Oracle finally speaks. "Very well, Your Majesty. We do not read the minds of gods, and we do not question their motives. They are gods, and we are mortals. We do their bidding. The *Trikaia* express their displeasure at the state of affairs. That is why the earth shook, fire erupted, and the birds that chirped happily flew in terror. Our gods view us as a lazy empire that enjoys their blessings yet incurs no pain to secure the future of our peoples or expand their glory."

"What do they mean by expanding their dominion, sacred Khaia? Do we not already control all the surrounding islands, including Kaftu, which is as great as a continent? Are we not the masters of the sea and lords of all trade channels in the surrounding waters?" asks Minos.

Khaia smiles wryly. She straightens her back, raises her arm, and opens her palm. "What we control is a speck in this vast Earth, King Minos. We have been battling the Mycenaeans who invade us from the North. They were once in awe and admiration of us, learning our arts and enriching their understanding of our script; yet, they now attack us. The Mitanni gave us their princess but pay no heed to our power or offer annual tributes. The Egyptians see us as dancers, bull acrobats, and painters. The Assyrians pretend we do not exist. What gods would not be insulted by that?"

"Is that your interpretation or the gods'?" asks Hannuruk, his voice now as cold as the bronze left out in the winter evening. I surmise that the King's reticence stems from his advanced age and the pleasures he has enjoyed throughout his life. He has no appetite for a large conflict or other violent excursions.

"The gods speak through me," Khaia says testily, "and they ask the great King to rise to their desires."

"It appears the gods are asking me to conquer one of the great kingdoms that surround us," Hannuruk replies finally, his expression one of disbelief, for there has never been a moment in their history when it has come to this.

There are many murmurs. Okoninos the builder, famed throughout the land for his magnificent constructions, grumbles loudly enough to be heard. "We do not need a war when we live in prosperity and peace." His colleague, Rhaistos, a well-regarded trader, concurs.

Khaia stares at them.

The bright minds in the Council are undoubtedly guessing, wondering, and coming to terms with what they are hearing.

The King speaks again. "As if all our mastery of the sea, our magnificent temples, our sacrifices, our rule over the hundred islands, our powerful trade, and our elegant towns are not enough…" His voice trails off.

Finally, King Minos speaks, "Is that the message, sacred Khaia?"

"It is," she replies. "And not just any kingdom."

I sit, befuddled.

Why am I here?

What is the Oracle telling us?

What do the gods want from us?

# CHAPTER 6

## KALLISTU

"...And not just any kingdom," Khaia says, a chill coursing through my bones. The Prince leans forward and clasps his hands, while the King watches without a word.

"What do they—" begins Minos, but Khaia cuts him off.

"Egypt," she states.

After a breathless moment, King Minos exclaims, "By the balls of mighty bulls!"

King Hannuruk, who seems dumbstruck, asks again, "Egypt? The gods ask that we conquer Egypt?"

"Yes, Your Majesty. They seek dominion over Egypt."

Several exclamations ripple through the room, and a buzz fills the air. Auscetas, an influential trader, slaps his head and sighs loudly. An usher rings a bell to silence the group. The King speaks again, "How do you know it is Egypt?"

Khaia turns and signals to a priestess, who wordlessly walks out of the room, all eyes on her. After several suspenseful minutes, the great doors open, and she re-enters.

On the priestess's shoulder is a magnificent falcon. The bird sits proudly, its dark and white patterned wings flexing gently as its inquisitive eyes scan the room. When the priestess nears the Oracle, the falcon rises to its feet, its talons digging into the priestess's flesh, and it spreads its glorious wings. The impressive flutter elicits audible gasps from the audience.

Khaia points to the falcon and turns to the royal podium. "These are the signs, Your Majesty. I dreamed of a falcon swooping over the seas and standing atop our bronze bulls. I dreamed of jackals surrounding our terrified people and advancing on them menacingly. I dreamed of a shining black cobra encircling the statue of the Great God of the Seas and unfurling its hood upon his head."

She pauses for effect. Every ear hangs on her every word. Khaia continues. "The falcon is the symbol of Horus, the jackal that of Anubis, and the cobra that of Wadjet—all Egyptian gods. These were just the first of my dreams and messages, which became increasingly violent in their depiction of control over us. The falcons carried away the bulls, the jackals ripped our people's bellies, and the cobra stung our gods, causing them to bleed," Khaia explains. Most of us bow our heads and pray urgently in fear of these words.

Khaia continues, "As if to remind me again, this falcon landed on my balcony this evening. It is unmistakably Egyptian."

Hannuruk's voice rises, "But sacred Khaia, just three summers ago you said the trembles meant we should prepare for life outside our islands! We have toiled to build a hidden enclave in the miserable desert as the seed for our future, and now you say the gods meant something else!"

I know what the King is referring to. Three summers ago, there were tremors. Not as severe as this time, yet bad enough for the King to confer with the Oracle. What he had been told then was that the tremors served as a warning to the Atalanni, urging them to expand beyond the Islands and create space for citizens in the desolate Syrian lands. The Divine Council resisted all suggestions to find a place in Kaftu and insisted instead on a space in the vast lands of Asia. Significant plans were made on this basis; a spectacular hollow dome in an enormous mountain near the Levant was chosen to build a hidden conclave capable of housing the first citizens of Atalanni outside the capital and Kaftu. The plan involved seeding this enclave with riches, weapons, and tomes from our secret library, using it as a staging ground for gradual outward expansion, focusing on defense with limited offense. The Oracle had warned that deliberate expansions would attract the attention of surrounding empires and jeopardize the plans. The King executed this mission but shed significant blood through his cruelty. Now, suddenly, the entire narrative has transformed to demand an invasion.

Khaia sighs deeply, exasperated by the King's hesitation. "The gods change their minds as they wish, Your Majesty, seeking no permission from us mortals. They appreciate what you have accomplished, and that is why the gods have spared our houses and palaces this time and shaken their own abode! Their kindness is evident in their actions and omens."

Many in the audience nod. I reflect on Khaia's statement; it is true—most of the damage is to the central temple complex and the causeway. The rest of the island remains almost untouched. It is as if the gods have split their own skin and shed blood, rather than that of their children. Hannuruk adjusts the bull crown on his head and tugs on his beard.

"But why Egypt?" This time Prime Minister Rishwa poses a question that burns in my mind as well.

"There is no greater empire than Egypt and no land of greater prestige. The gods seek nothing less," Khaia asserts. "The Mitanni are a new and rising power, but it is Egypt that the gods desire."

I look at Queen Apsara, who sits stoically. She says nothing at the mention of her homeland.

"The only thing the Mitanni possess that is worth having is the space beside me," Hannuruk states, "and they relinquished that eagerly. I have no doubt there are far greater riches in Egypt, including those that can bear me an heir, unlike the barren Syrian deserts."

The insult is apparent to all, and my eyes, like every other member's, turn to the Queen, whose face reddens. My chest tightens, imagining her pain. She stares straight ahead, making no acknowledgment of these sharp words.

*To ram my fist through the King's teeth would be joyous!*

Minos opens his mouth to say something but checks himself. The Governor's salacious mind is on the Queen, and I have seen Minos glance at her many times. To comment on matters of royal marriage may be a step too far, even for a flagrant rule-breaker like Minos.

The Ambassador of Nations, Umarru, breaks the uncomfortable silence in the room. "We have maintained cordial relations with the Egyptians—"

"To the depths of deep seas with cordial relations. The gods have asked, and we shall deliver!" Minos shouts, his eyes wide open in strange excitement. It is apparent that Minos is aroused and does not hide it.

King Hannuruk, stupefied yet coming to his senses, rises and requests silence from the audience. He puffs up his chest and addresses the council. "The gods are right. They are merciful, delivering an obvious message. Here we are, with our mighty navy hidden in our harbors, our spectacular weapons tried but never tested, our ambitions suppressed by our own laws and the Divine Council's advice. The gods will have no more of it!"

Khaia does not react to the King's pointed reference to the Council. She clasps her hands and gazes ahead.

"We will be a true empire!" shouts Prince Nimmuruk, waving his sword in the air, now working himself up along with the others.

"What else did the gods say, sacred Khaia?" the King inquires. I watch as the leaders beat the drums of war. The general in front of me mutters, "Fighting Egypt is nothing like defeating the backward Mycenaeans who venture into our seas."

Khaia now commands everyone's undivided attention. I fleetingly wonder if such opportunities allow the Oracle to fabricate whatever she desires, and then I chastise myself for such sacrilegious thoughts.

"The gods ask that we demonstrate the superiority of our people, our arms, our knowledge, and take the Pharaoh and his people as slaves," Khaia declares.

Minos waves his hand in the air, gaining everyone's attention. "Egypt is weak. They have not controlled their northern borders and harbors for many summers now, and they still fight the Asiatics. We will subdue them as one might overpower a reluctant maiden," he says, his voice a higher pitch with excitement.

"No, Governor Minos. Just because the deer sleep does not mean the lioness ceases to hunt. Egypt is rising again," Rishwa counters. Behind that slender frame lies a wise voice that commands attention. "The Asiatics no longer maintain a firm grip on their lands and are losing against the new dynasty. Pharaoh Sekhenenre has weakened them, Kamose has pillaged them, and the new Pharaoh Ahmose inflicts great pain upon them. Our messengers suggest it will not be long before the Egyptians rout their invaders and reclaim their homes."

"So you say, Prime Minister. They marry their sisters; one of their gods sleeps with his parent and sibling. The populace resides in squalor and slums with open sewers, while the royals occupy magnificent palaces. Such a kingdom will vanish into nothingness," Minos asserts.

"That may be so, King Minos. But let us not forget that they have sustained this way of life for thousands of harvests, and their gods have not abandoned them. That is their tradition. They are a great empire as well and possess knowledge of the world—perhaps not as much as we do, and we risk looking down upon them at our peril."

Minos scoffs and adjusts his loincloth, glancing around to make his irritation known to all.

Khaia smooths the creases of her garment and takes a sip of water. Clearing her throat, she continues, "But the gods are merciful. They know Egypt is no minnow, and the great land's tribulations in the recent past against the Asiatics must not be interpreted as a sign that the Pharaoh is weak. We must prepare."

"You speak like a general, sacred Khaia," Minos remarks, grinning. He adjusts the gold necklace and rubs his hirsute chest.

Khaia smiles. "You forget, King Minos, that the Divine Council opines on matters of peace and war."

"Well, we have heard from the Oracle and our garrulous governor," Hannuruk says, slapping Minos' shoulder, "but we must hear from our warriors." The King's gaze wanders to my section. I wait for the King to call on the general, who now sits stiffly. But Hannuruk's eyes lock directly onto mine.

Unsure and nervous, I scramble to my feet.

General Unamur, confused as well, stands. However, Hannuruk dismissively waves him back down. I remain standing, my face growing warm, like a clay tablet held near a gentle fire. All eyes—the most important eyes in the Atalanni empire—are fixed upon me.

"Rishwa tells us you have defeated the Mycenaeans a seventh time," he states.

I stand straight and bow to the King, still unsure of the protocol. "Yes, Your Majesty."

"They say you are a formidable commander."

"I am honored, Your Majesty."

"Have you fought them on land, Teber?"

"Only once, Your Majesty, when they landed on the northern shores of Kaftu."

"What transpired then?"

"We routed them. We killed one hundred and eighty and took fifty as slaves."

"How many did we lose?"

"Two hundred, Your Majesty," I respond uneasily.

"Why?"

"We had little experience on land, Your Majesty. The planners proposed bold ideas, but the terrain held surprises."

General Unamur rises to his feet. "If I may add, Your Majesty—"

"Did I ask you to speak?" Hannuruk interrupts.

"No, Your Majesty—"

"When was the last time you raised a sword and stabbed an enemy?"

"Your Majesty, I—"

"When did you last defeat anyone?"

"My role, Your Majesty—"

Hannuruk spits at the man and shouts, "We have invited the scorn of our gods because feckless men like you possess no strength in their bellies to go out and fight!"

I know the General is blameless, for he has merely obeyed the rules and laws of the Atalanni, aimed at defense rather than offense. Yet no one could raise a voice against the King, except the Oracle and Governor Minos.

"You are old, lazy, and useless. You have no role to play in the future of this empire. I should have you flogged and drowned, but I will let you live. Get out."

The embarrassed man bows and leaves the hall in a hurry, and everyone holds their breath. It is as if a glowing star extinguishes in the blink of an eye—the man who rose to generalship becomes a nobody in an instant; such are the surprises of life.

Hannuruk turns to me again. "Governor Minos here thinks you would make a fine general."

I am surprised. "I am honored, Your Majesty. King Minos."

"He wants you as his apprentice. Apparently, we have no wiser men in all our forces."

"I am sure—"

Hannuruk scoffs and waves dismissively. "The Oracle did not seem very excited about the prospect of bringing you here; is that not the case, Khaia?"

"He is young, Your Majesty. We have had generals that have led our men—"

"How many have fought invaders as much as this young man has?"

She hesitates. "None."

"Is not the Pharaoh of Egypt young too?"

"He is, Your Majesty."

"I know I must seek your counsel in matters of war, Khaia, but I prefer to listen to the men who fight rather than women who lecture."

Khaia responds indignantly. "Your preferences have little to do with my opinions, Your Majesty, and my counsel stands that Teber does not have enough experience to—"

"I have heard your counsel, but I am not obliged to act on it. Remember who rules this empire, Khaia. I have one woman by my side to annoy me, and I will not have another. Be quiet and leave matters of war strategy to me."

I hear some chuckles, but the Oracle remains stoic.

Rishwa reaches across and soothes the King. "Every flower may spread its scent. The Oracle has the right to her opinions, Your Majesty. Let us not anger the messengers of the gods. The gods see the immense pressure of a ruler, do they not, sacred Khaia?"

Khaia fixes her gaze on the King. "They do, Prime Minister. But they also expect the King to maintain his decorum. I am not his servant."

Hannuruk locks his eyes on Khaia, and they glare at each other until Minos laughs and breaks the tension.

"Now, now. Shall we all agree that we listen to the Oracle on matters of divine message, but to the King on matters of war strategy?"

Khaia says nothing. I feel uncomfortable in the middle of the quarrel between the Kingdom's two most elevated individuals. I am also skeptical about how the King is better suited to discuss matters of war strategy, for he has never waged war in his entire lifetime. At least the Oracle is brilliant and surely possesses messages of strategy from the gods—after all, if divinity wanted the Atalanni to conquer Egypt, they would have a few ideas for success as well.

But my opinions mean little.

The King turns to me again. "Do you know why you are here, Teber?"

"No, Your Majesty."

"Do you think you can lead us against Egypt?"

# CHAPTER 7

## THEBES – UPPER EGYPT

Pharaoh Ahmose looks behind his chariot with pride. His men are bruised and covered with fine desert dust but victorious in the latest battle against Khamudi, the son of Apepi, the impostor Asiatic ruler who squats over Lower Egypt. The column stretches a great length.

The swordsmen follow the archers.

Mace-handlers walk with ax-men.

The wretched captives walk in the middle, followed by more troops and the baggage train.

The forty-day mission has been a spectacular success. They have destroyed a major garrison near Hutwaret, the capital of the impostors—the *Hyk-Khase*.

Khamudi is weakening. Gone is the fire in the foreigners' bellies, Ahmose thinks—these wretched scum that defile his lands, disrespect his gods, and call themselves Kings of Lower Egypt. Khamudi's father, Apepi, was a thorn in Egypt's side, and Khyan, his father, not only took Egyptian royal titles but also sent ambassadors to far places such as Keftiu, posing himself as king.

*Such a shame. Such disgrace.*

But Ahmose would put an end to it all.

The Pharaoh has proved to his citizens that he is a god, like his brother before him and his father before him. As they enter the magnificent gates of the greatest city known to the world, Thebes, Ahmose looks at the throngs of adoring men, women, and children.

Most gather by the wide granite and limestone royal pathway.

Some stand atop stone platforms, clinging to the obelisks.

Some perch precariously over rooftops.

The rest balance delicately on tree branches.

They shout with joy.

As he passes by, they prostrate themselves on the dusty ground, bowing before their god-King.

"Amun blesses you, Your Majesty, and Ra shines upon you," says Nebhekhufre, the Vizier of Lower Egypt and his uncle by relation. Ahmose likes and respects Nebhekhufre, who understands the ways of gods and the people. The Vizier has governed his areas with care, even when under attack and under the control of the impostors. Nebhekhufre had been at the side of Ahmose's father, Pharaoh Sekhenenre Tao, when an impostor's ax felled the courageous man. Sekhenenre had died fighting, yet in his death, he had heralded a resurgent Egypt that would no longer accept the Asiatic impostors and their backward ways. Ahmose's brave brother, Kamose, too, had sought Nebhekhufre's counsel.

Ahmose smiles and orders the chariot to halt. The Vizier lifts the statue of the bearded Amun high above the kneeling Pharaoh's head.

The Vizier steps down from the chariot and places the miniature statue on a fresh linen pillow adorned with fine silver threads. He then places the pillow on the ground.

As the adoring crowd watches, Pharaoh Ahmose kneels before the god and places both palms firmly on the ground. He bows and touches his head to the feet of the god. Ahmose then stands to great cheers and walks to a specially erected podium in the great quadrangle before the palace. The guards hold back the surging crowds as the Pharaoh prepares to speak.

"I have beaten the impostors like a master beats his disobedient slaves. Glory be to Amun; he shines upon us, and glory be to my father Sekhenenre; he smiles upon us. It will not be long before we destroy the impostor's cities, kill their soldiers, enslave their men, women, and children, and bring the wretched Khamudi's head on a ram's horn!"

A great roar arises from the crowd. On cue, two guards drag one of the captured impostors—a lean and hard-muscled Asiatic with curly dark hair and a knee-length garment. The impostor looks on fearfully as a guard forces him to kneel.

Ahmose moves forward, arches his back, and lifts his bronze and blue-glass striped crook.

He kicks the kneeling captive in the head.

The man topples onto the stone pathway.

As the Asiatic looks on fearfully, a priest wearing the mask of Seth grabs the man's hair and yanks it back, exposing the neck. The man thrashes about, uttering pitiful phrases in his foreign tongue. The priest slices his neck open, letting the ground saturate with blood.

"We will spill the Asiatics' blood until there is a river that rivals the Great River!" Ahmose declares as the crowd cheers.

The dying man's rasps are drowned in the celebration of victory.

The procession proceeds to the palace. The fit and young prisoners will be auctioned off as slaves or quarry workers; the rest will be executed, and their bodies will be hung on the walls. The Pharaoh stops before ascending the steps of his palace and waits for the priests to complete their rituals. They burn fragrant cedarwood incense on a gold plate and utter prayers as they move the plate in a circular motion near the Pharaoh's face. Once completed, they move away respectfully, allowing Ahmose's wife to receive him.

Ahmose's eyes shine at the sight of her.

The lovely Ahmose-Nefertari—a dutiful sister and now royal wife—walks forward shyly, descending the steps like a graceful dancer, and kneels before her husband. Ahmose leans and grasps her shoulders, and she rises to meet his gaze. Ahmose marvels at his wife's delicate features and how much he has missed her.

Then, together, the royal couple turns and faces the multitude before them for one last celebratory cheer before they turn and walk through the massive wooden doors.

Ahmose hurries to the far end of the palace, followed by his wife and attendants. Guards open the door and bow as the Pharaoh enters the spacious room, which opens on one side to a small garden. He approaches the side of a figure lying on a massive oak bed, draped in a linen blanket. The smell of sickness mixes with the sweet fragrance of burning incense. Ahmose gently holds the palm of the man and kneels beside him.

"My brother, I have news," Ahmose whispers near the man's ear. "I have beaten the dirty *Hyk-Khase* again. I have spilled their blood."

Kamose stirs and groans. His face bears a deathly pallor and is covered in sweat.

His left shoulder is swollen and resembles a ripe plum—a sign, they say, that brings a man closer to his end. The royal physicians have placed poultices on his deep wounds, but it has been several moons with no improvement. The co-ruler, known to all as Kamose-the-Strong, is slowly slipping toward the realm of the dead. Ahmose's wife, also Kamose's sister, gently caresses the fallen Pharaoh's hair. She wipes his forehead with a cloth and removes the ceremonial crown, allowing the attendants to fan the matted hair that sticks to the pillows. Kamose's hair still has the luxurious shine of youth, yet the rest of him has aged.

"I will continue my battle until we reclaim our lands, brother," Ahmose continues. "I shall not allow your fight, or our father's, to go in vain."

Kamose breathes hard, and Ahmose feels that his brother has heard him. Ahmose still holds hope that his brother will recover and one day rule by his side in a united Egypt. For this reason, on the advice of the priests, Ahmose has not commissioned a tomb befitting the status of his brother.

The Pharaoh and his wife rise from their positions and return to his chamber. On this occasion, Nefertari will spend the night with him, hoping not just to ignite his passion but also to bear him an heir who will one day rule Egypt.

After disrobing and cleansing themselves, the couple moves to the royal bed. Ahmose-Nefertari places her head on her husband's chest. The Pharaoh reaches for his wife's hand and rubs her fingers. "We will free Egypt soon. The omens say it will not be long before we destroy the impostors. With no one else to challenge us, Amun will lead us to glory."

Just as he finishes speaking, a gust of wind blows through the quiet chambers. The stone statue of Amun, placed on a pedestal by the side of the bed, wobbles and falls to the ground.

# CHAPTER 8

## KALLISTU

He walks quietly along the labyrinthine tunnel under the Palace. The lamps on the walls come to life as he passes, another magical invention of the famed Atalanni Engineers. As he turns, he finally sees her near the far corner—her silhouette revealing her gentle curves beneath the flickering lamp.

They embrace each other with great urgency, their lips meeting with passion and desperate force. It is extraordinarily dangerous, but he is reckless, and she is bold.

They know they do not have much time, for guards patrol the tunnels at predetermined intervals. He knows the schedules, and in his position, he can control access. They have only a few minutes.

"What will become of us?" she asks, her soft voice trembling with fear.

"I am sure that with our power, brilliance, and the gods' blessings, we will be victorious, and I will return soon, my love."

"I cannot endure it much longer; each day is a curse, and I will go mad here."

"Be brave and be bold. Your strength shines brighter than the suns!"

"You are a terrible poet," she says, giggling and breaking the seriousness of the moment. She then runs her finger along his taut muscles, sculpted by battle and rigor.

He pushes her face to his chest and chuckles. He breathes in her aroma and feels the soft curves of her waist. "I mean it. But you must be strong. Once I return, I will take you away. We will vanish."

"I feel so alone. Every day is so tedious. It consists of hours of ceremony in the morning, the prayers, the cleansing. I am forbidden leisure with commoners, and I cannot go outside the Palace. This is a prison! I did not grow up like this. Can you truly take me away? Under the watchful eyes of the King's spies?"

"If I take you away, can you live as a commoner?"

"I can live happily wherever you are."

"Is your life in danger?"

"There are days when he strikes me. But his words cause far greater injury. He speaks ill of my father, my mother, my people. He has threatened to drown me for no fault of mine. But he knows better than to kill me."

A great anger rises within him.

"He accuses me of not bearing a child, yet it is he who is unable to perform on the marital bed," she continues. "Though I retch at the thought of sleeping with him."

"Find ways to keep him at bay. If we are thoughtless in these times, there will be no future. I will free you, even if it means I must kill—"

She places a finger on his lips. "Do not speak of killing him. We do not know how the gods view such acts. They are already angry at the Atalanni. All I wish for is to be free from him, but he must not know I have abandoned him."

He understands her point, though, in his heart, he would have liked nothing more than to kill her husband. But such acts are rare in Atalanni history, and the penalties are severe.

"When do you leave?"

"I do not know. We confer with the King in two days for final orders. The first step is for us to move our weapons and train soldiers from Kaftu. Minos will host us and help build an army until we are ready to sail to the shores of Egypt."

"I am filled with fear," she says, embracing him tightly.

"And I, with hope. I am certain no gods look kindly upon the cruelty he inflicts upon you. We are an enlightened people, my beautiful, and you see the mirth in our women's eyes. They are protected by laws, yet those laws do not extend to royalty."

She nods. He knows there is no escape for her—she would either live condemned or must kill herself if she is to escape her marriage. The only other option is her husband's death or her escape with the man she loves.

He pauses. "Do you want me to take you away now and vanish?"

She shakes her head vigorously. "No! You have a duty to this land. The gods will surely see that as sacrilegious. This is your chance for glory. Come back and take me away."

He kisses her again. She is right. This is his chance for glory, and once that is achieved, he wants to vanish with her. Abandoning his people would surely enrage not just the gods but all those who depend on him. He could never live with that.

She caresses his face. "Your mole," she says.

"What about my mole?" he asks, rubbing the dark patch below his right eye.

"It looks nice on your rugged face. But you should grow your beard, or you will look like a girl."

"I do not look like a girl."

"You have such long hair. Why do young Atalanni men not grow their beards?"

"Because lice grow in them. We do not smell like the men on your side."

"They do not smell."

"They are hairy."

"They are manly."

"Are you saying I am not manly?"

She giggles. "You are the manliest man I know. Grow your beard."

"Military regulations do not allow me."

She pouts. "Stupid soldiers."

"Look at my muscles," he says, flexing his biceps.

She feels them and laughs. "You need to put on more weight. You are lean and strong, but have you seen Urama? Such big muscles!"

He tweaks her nose. "Urama is an oaf. I am a lean, fighting warrior. I am so much taller."

"That you are," she says, hugging him again.

It is time for him to leave. It is too dangerous to remain.

"You must leave. Stay strong. I will find a way for us to meet once before I leave," he says, holding her close for another longing kiss.

And then Teber watches as Apsara, the Queen of the Atalanni, vanishes into the darkness.

# CHAPTER 9

## KALLISTU

I am the first to arrive in the throne room. I wait nervously. Today the King will announce his final orders after several days of deliberations and planning. While he had proclaimed me a general, he has made many decisions without my input.

*Able enough to lead the men into a fate-altering battle, but not considered intelligent enough to make momentous decisions.*

Surely the King knew that I, at fourteen, had been regarded as a capable entrant to the Academy of Engineers—a renowned group operating under the hierarchy of the Divine Council. The Academy is famed for its ability to interpret the signs from the gods and to bend the laws of nature to its will. The Engineers constructed contraptions that felt otherworldly, and no one except the Oracle and her acolytes understood the workings of the Engineers. It was the Academy of Engineers that owned the armory and crafted weapons. In times of peace, the Academy reported to the Oracle, but during times of war, it took directions from the King and his nominee.

The Atalanni have a tradition of nurturing Engineers for many generations—that is what has granted us our extraordinary knowledge of metals, mining, the alignment of stars and planets, the humming of the earth, the signs of the skies, the precision of journey times and directions, and even an extraordinary new method of barter through the use of coins. We could put the famed Egyptians to shame, yet the restraint codified in Atalanni laws has restricted our operations.

Only a few boys and girls pass the tests to join the Academy of Engineers, and I had been one of them. However, before my first month ended, the assessors dismissed me for my unwillingness to follow orders; the exasperated decision-makers, with the Oracle's support, placed me in the military instead of throwing me into prison.

The throne room fills with attendees. The King's Guard, senior men of the military, the Chief of the Engineers, senior members of the Divine Council, King Minos and his advisors, the Royal Secretary, the Prince, the Queen, the King, and finally the Oracle are all present. Today, the King proclaims orders and strategy for the invasion of Egypt.

My eyes fleetingly meet Apsara's. I imagine the smell of lavender on her skin and the sweetness of her breath. My heart palpitates at the thought that I may never see her again.

We are playing a dangerous game.

The assembly falls silent once the King finally rises. The night of orders, as it is called, is conducted with much ceremony. Light from the soft yellow flames of two large lamps reflects off the royal crown. The Queen turns to him and raises her hands in prayer, as does the Prince.

"I will now proclaim orders. As per Atalanni laws, if you disagree, you have the opportunity to question it once without fear of penalty," he states. He dips a bird-feather brush into a bowl of water and sprinkles fragrant water on his wife and son. Khaia steps forward, receives the brush from the King, and walks around the arc, sprinkling water on all the attendees while chanting ancient hymns.

Once the ceremony concludes, King Hannuruk begins. "The gods have spoken, and we march on Egypt. The people stand behind our warriors, and I am confident that our magnificent fighters and our advanced weapons will lead us to a resounding victory."

I nod along with the others. I know the armory holds secrets that seem otherworldly; even so, with a small army, it remains unclear to me how we will conquer land as vast as Egypt.

"Able men from this capital island and those in Kaftu will be drafted to train and serve. Engineers, ship and road builders, healers, cooks, cleaners, priests, planners, messengers, and other support personnel will be identified and sent to accompany the army."

"A few whores—," begins Minos, suppressing his grin as the King casts an irritated glance in his direction. Prince Nimmuruk guffaws.

The King continues. "I have heard your voice, but it is my duty as King to assign the men who act in accordance with the gods' wishes and bring us victory. King Minos will lead the build-up, oversee army recruitment and training, and act as counsel to Prince Hannuruk."

The mention of the Prince's name surprises many.

"Prince Nimmuruk will lead the Atalanni army into Egypt."

Silence envelops the room, and before anyone reacts to the announcement, Minos scrambles to his feet. He dramatically kneels before the King.

"What have I done to displease you, Your Majesty?"

Hannuruk appears taken aback. "You have been a loyal governor, King Minos, and I need you to guard Kaftu and prepare us for success."

"I wish to bring glory to the empire, Your Majesty. I must lead us to Egypt and allow you, and someday your illustrious son, to rule the mighty Atalanni."

"I can bring victory to us, King Minos. Listen to your King," shouts Nimmuruk, his face flushed and half-risen from his seat. Minos does not budge.

"Not now, my son," replies the King, gesturing for the Prince to return to his seat.

"The omens say that the Prince must be the one," declares Khaia.

We turn to the Oracle. Nimmuruk settles back with a smirk upon his face, and Minos rises to his feet. He moves menacingly toward the Oracle, causing several members of the King's Guard to shift on their feet. Khaia remains unflinching as the Governor glares at her—his imposing form looming over her delicate stature. In the flickering flames, it seems as if an angry wild dog is about to bite a fallen baby deer.

"Are the gods so specific with their messages, sacred Khaia? Do they no longer speak to us in riddles?" he asks mockingly.

"They speak as they wish, Governor Minos," Khaia replies, unyielding, her gaze shifting to the King. "As I told you, Your Majesty, I have repeatedly dreamed of a lion cub grasping the throat of a hawk under the watchful eyes of a lion."

Minos, not yet placated, turns again to the Royals. "Your Majesty, if anyone could conquer the Egyptians, it would be me—I possess the power, the strength, the loyalty, the willingness—and yet you choose to trust the Oracle. The Prince has no experience in the theater of war—"

"Enough!" screams Hannuruk, signaling Minos to kneel by flicking his wrists and pointing his index finger to the floor. Minos obeys. The Governor is testing his long-standing relationship with the King.

"I have made my decision, Minos. It is not a surprise that the gods desire the Prince of the Atalanni to carry out their mission and bring glory to our lineage. I command you to do everything in your power to support him. He is your Prince, and you shall according him that respect."

Minos bows again, but he is clearly dissatisfied. Khaia gazes at the ground, but from my position, I can discern her tight-lipped smile.

"Nimmuruk will be the lord of all forces sent to Egypt. Rishwa will aid him in strategy, and you, Teber, will be the commander of the army on the ground, serving the will of the Prince."

I bow to the King and the Prince. I despise the notion that the Prince will be the commander—it does not bode well; nonetheless, the Oracle has made it clear that the gods willed it so.

"The Chief Engineer of armaments will bring his men and women to Kaftu and arrange for supplies, testing, and construction of weapons."

The Chief Engineer, an unassuming man named Alos, bows to the King and the Prince.

"You sail at the first full moon to Kaftu. Bring me Egypt!" commands the King. He sits, and the priestesses begin a chant as they walk around the Royal Couple.

At the conclusion of the chant, they approach the Prince's chair and guide him down from his pedestal. Minos and I are invited to join the Prince by his side, and we kneel before the King. The Oracle picks up a cup and anoints our foreheads with the blood of a sacrificial bull. Khaia's palm gently brushes my hair, and a sense of great calm washes over me.

*Blessed by the Oracle herself.*

With her blessings, I hope we will vanquish the enemy and return home to glory and to Apsara. Next, the Prince taps our heads with his scepter. Eventually, everyone returns to their seats.

Uppiluliuma, Head of the King's Guard, then addresses the room. "The penalty for insubordination or treason is death, not only for the perpetrator but for their families as well. Atalanni law is clear. We conduct peace with honor, and we will conduct war with honor. The Prince will execute our code faithfully and honor the gods and the fallen of the Atalanni."

The Prince sits with his flabby chest pushed forward. He appears entranced.

Finally, the King stands and makes his concluding remarks. "We will reconvene on the day of departure. Make your plans."

As the Royals exit, Apsara's eyes follow me until she passes us. I catch her maid, Aranare, looking at me inquisitively, and I turn away.

# CHAPTER 10

## KALLISTU

Minos lies on the wooden recliner. "You play a dangerous game, Khaia," he says. The sky displays bands of blue, orange, and yellow as the sun sets. The window from Khaia's terrace faces east.

"Only if you say so. I am a servant of the gods, and it is their will I convey," she replies, smiling as she hands a goblet of wine to Minos.

"You have known me for many summers now and know that I am not a man who blindly follows every tradition. Perhaps it is the gods' will that I question your methods?"

"No one confuses you for a man of tradition, King Minos," Khaia retorts, laughing. She smooths her sheer gown and notices Minos eyeing her. Khaia claps for an attendant to fill the wine goblets. Once the attendant finishes his task, Khaia orders him to leave the room and close the doors.

"No one enters," she instructs him.

Minos' eyes lock onto Khaia's. What a strange man, Khaia thinks. Minos is bright, but he is reckless, bloodthirsty, lustful, and possesses no manners befitting a king. He is loud, yet astute in his observations, speaking his opinions freely, regardless of the appropriateness of the forum. But he is an important man, and Khaia must deal with him.

Minos cracks his knuckles. "What do you have against me leading the charge in Egypt?"

"I told you. It was the signs. You doubt my visions. There are penalties for questioning the Oracle," she explains, though the smile on her lips undermines her serious tone.

Minos scoffs and takes a swig. He shakes his head. "I did not rule Kaftu and shape its culture only for you to think I am an idiot. You made up those signs."

Khaia bristles at the remark. "Chasing young Mycenaean boys and girls in your labyrinths and sacrificing them to the gods isn't much of a culture."

Minos throws his head back and laughs, a sound reminiscent of a hungry beast, and his great silvery mane shakes with every guttural sound. Khaia feels a strange attraction to this loutish man. She also knows that he ravishes her with his eyes at every opportunity.

"Culture is what you make of it, Khaia. You might find it offensive, but the people love it. Surely my success means the gods have sanctioned my methods. Have they sent you any messages regarding their displeasure with my customs as well? Dreams of a Minos-like man with a giant phallus running after a maiden, tripping, and dying?"

"No, they have not. Perhaps they agree with your methods. But we are not here to discuss your rituals, penis, and mating habits, are we?"

Khaia smiles at the boldness of this man. No one else in the Kingdom, regardless of their thoughts, would dare speak to her this way. Even the King, no matter how angry, did not cross certain lines. Minos has no concept of boundaries. Khaia walks toward the window and adjusts the curtains— the intense wind dies down.

"Why would you not want me to go to Egypt? Please do not coddle me with that nonsense about lion cubs," Minos says.

"We are venturing into the unknown. We need powerful defenses just in case—"

"Just in case that chubby idiot gets his head chopped off in the deserts of Egypt?"

"Yes, and just because we have our *Daivoshaktis* does not mean we will defeat the Egyptians. It is better for us if you supply our men and act as defense. You can play a larger role depending on what the Prince achieves."

"He will achieve little except to molest Egyptian girls. But the young commander is formidable, and you did not want him there either."

"He is not wise enough. Do you not see? It is one thing to take on swarming galleys and another to confront a Pharaoh. He should have stayed back; we should have sent one of the older generals. We cannot succeed without the right strategy."

"The King sees no value in sending untested generals—most of those old men have never pierced another man's belly. The King is right—Teber is the man for the task at hand."

Khaia walks to Minos' side and sits next to him on an elegant wooden stool.

She places a palm on his shoulder.

Minos' eyes widen.

"Well, then you should know that the Prince has no love for Teber. When they were still children, Teber thoroughly humiliated him in a fight."

Minos arches his eyebrows. "But he is still alive."

"Well, the laws require disclosure before execution, and those who witnessed it were not commoners. What Prince would want to call witnesses to his own embarrassment? Murder would create more questions, and you know that the Divine Council does not take kindly to unlawful killings."

"So you say, beautiful, and yet the King does as he pleases these days," Minos responds, tracing a finger along Khaia's arm. "You surely know that his first wife languishes and goes mad alone in a sparse cell because she gave him a son with limited mental faculties."

"The times have changed."

Khaia is aware of the fate of the first Queen. The King's second son remains hidden from the public eye—he is fourteen summers old but behaves as if he were five. His body is ravaged by various afflictions. The danger to the Kingdom lies in the possibility that one day he could ascend to the throne. Many know that Nimmuruk mistreated his mother, influenced by his father, and had beaten her on more than one occasion. The mother and son languish in a dungeon, forgotten by the world.

Minos reaches up to Khaia's neck and tickles it playfully. "And is there a reason you want the Prince so far away and in danger—"

Khaia places a finger on his lips. "Do not make dangerous accusations. Watch what you say. Nimmuruk is a vicious idiot, and we both know that it is you—not I—who put that young hothead Teber in his current position. It is up to you to ensure he lives and succeeds."

"I will make Teber the best general there can be," Minos declares, his voice hoarse and breath quickening. His great chest rises and falls like waves on a restless sea.

"Does the King think war is easy?" she questions.

"He thinks war is a trivial matter, but the old man is senile. Even his pretty wife does nothing to—"

Khaia leans forward and places her palm on Minos' chest. He grips her hand with his powerful grasp and pulls her closer.

She leans toward his ear and whispers, "He is impotent. There is nothing she can do. But let us leave their marital problems aside, Minos. What is in your mind for the opening gambit?" Khaia smiles as she moves her fingers through the silver strands on his chest.

Minos turns to face Khaia, his face flushed with arousal. "We will first align with the Asiatics. They are becoming weak, but we can bring strength to them and use them as the tip of the spear. Let them take losses as they weaken the Egyptians until it is time for us to take over."

Khaia lifts her face and gazes out. The sky has darkened, and hundreds of seagulls fly.

Workers labor in the harbor to prepare the war boats.

Rows of lamp posts glimmer along the ruined causeway, sparkling like fireflies in the night.

Ceremonial fires still burn brightly in the central temple.

She presses close to Minos. His body radiates heat like a stone under the afternoon sun. "You are a clever man. I had the same thought," she remarks as she moves the curls away from her eyes. Minos cups her breast and pulls her closer.

His breath is raspy. "But do not stand in my way, Khaia, once we achieve glory. I want to rule Egypt from their capital as an extension of the Atalanni empire."

"I have no objections to that, provided you do not question my messages in the courts," she replies as she slides closer. Minos's hands envelop her. She senses his thundering heart and feels him stiffen beneath her. Khaia moves on top of Minos as he watches her, mesmerized.

"What is in your mind, Khaia? I know it is not the gods, but it is you—" Minos begins, but Khaia silences him with her mouth as she positions herself. As Minos enters her, she closes her eyes and imagines herself on a throne.

# CHAPTER 11

## KALLISTU

It is a glorious day. The sky is blue without a speck of cloud as far as the eye can see. Hundreds of warboats stand ready to sail, and the colorful Atalanni flags flutter in the wind. Men stand on each boat, facing the land, placing their hands on their chests, awaiting the arrival of the King and other high-ranking members of society for the farewell.

I stand next to the Prince, who is dressed in a new royal uniform designed for battle. A shimmering red garment covers the Prince from his neck to his knees, crafted from a strange new material obtained from a land far away at the eastern end of the world where the sun rises. His chest is protected by a beautifully carved lion-and-hawk cuirass, held in place by oxhide belts. The pudgy Prince stands awkwardly, out of his element, leading the procession of boats.

The sun warms our bodies, and I watch as the central platform by the harbor fills with dignitaries. Minos whispers, "The Oracle is unhappy that you stand here, young Teber."

"I heard, King Minos. But it is not my place to come between you and her."

"I told her that I would make you a great general and bring you back alive. Show her she is wrong. Oracles are not always right. You know that, do you not?" he says, grinning merrily. I am unsure what to say, for it is surely sacrilegious to question the Oracle's judgment.

"I do not know that, King Minos. The Oracle's words are divine—"

"Oh, you silly fool. The Oracle is divine, that I guarantee. Her words are full of wisdom, but it is her—" He grins and stops before he reveals whatever he is about to say next. "Anyway, we will sail soon. Absorb the glory of this magnificent land, Teber. You never know when you will return."

I bow to Minos, who then uses a plank to board his boat, leaving me with the Prince.

I squint at the platform, hoping to see Apsara. We had met again last night in the darkness of the tunnels. We had embraced as though there were no tomorrow. Her tears had stained my chest, and I had promised to return. I ached for her, but at the same time, my chest burst with pride for what the Kingdom had entrusted to me, even while going against the Oracle's wishes.

I would conquer Egypt, subdue their inferior gods, and bring glory to the Atalanni. When we finished, there would be no empire on all the earth like the Atalanni. Once Egypt fell, I had told King Minos that we should turn to Mycenae and end them once and for all.

*Though the 'we' in that sentence would not include me, for I would be far away in Assyria with Apsara.*

Loud beats of drums and horns announcing Royalty disturb my reverie. King Hannuruk and his entourage walk along the edge of the harbor to the podium, stepping on a flower-bed road. The priests chant loudly, and as the crowd watches, other members of the temple drag an unwilling bull to the center. They tie it to a heavy stone post embedded in the ground and burn lotus flowers around it. I observe as the priests conclude the ceremony by slicing the neck of the bull and letting the blood flow along a gutter into the water.

The King makes a speech, but in the gust of wind and the chatter of crowds, I cannot discern his words. He finishes and picks up the bull's severed head, lifting it high above his head. As the crowd erupts in deafening noise, he throws the head into the water. Prince Nimmuruk and I raise our hands in salute, and I watch as Queen Apsara, along with her husband, lifts glistening gold swords into the air.

On cue, a thousand horns and conches sound on the boats, and men take to their rowing and sailing stations. All my hardened warriors are in the crew, but there are also many other untested men—farmers, shopkeepers, cloth weavers, and other trades—who will now have to be trained as soldiers and sent to battle in a terrain they have never seen in their lives.

Finally, one by one, each boat sails in front of the King, its orange-blue flags high in the air. The officers bow to the King. Prince Nimmuruk walks forward, grips the side of the boat, and stares at the deep blue waters ahead. I take another look at the imposing cliffs and the multitude of colorful people dotting the platforms, multi-storied houses, shops, and cliff overhangs around the harbor.

I bow one last time.

All I can think of is the sad smile of my Apsara.

As the navy makes its way slowly to Kaftu, Nimmuruk summons me to the shade of a linen tent set up on the boat. "Do I have your loyalty, Teber?" he asks, with no greeting. We have spoken only sparingly since his appointment.

I bow. Whatever my misgivings about the Prince, this is not the time for argument. "I have sworn an oath to your father, Prince Nimmuruk, and that loyalty extends to you."

*Until we win, and it is time for me to break away.*

"Trust is earned."

"Yes, Your Highness."

With that, the Prince turns and looks at the sea. I get up and walk to the stern. Minos' boat is close by, and the Governor waves and winks—Minos observes little protocol, and I find it oddly refreshing. I feel a presence beside me, and it is the Prince.

"What is your take on Minos?"

"I am not sure what you mean, Your Highness."

"Do you think he will follow my father's orders?"

"He is a little difficult to control, but he has always been loyal."

"The stakes have never been higher, Teber. Minos is a larger-than-life character. What makes you think he does not eye greater glory?"

"I cannot speak to his motivations, Your Highness," I say. These conversations make me uncomfortable. The ambitions of these men are above my station. I am a fighting man, and politics is not my strength.

"Do you give me your sworn loyalty that you will be by my side, Teber?" the Prince asks. This time, his voice is low and ominous.

As the hazy outline of Kaftu comes into view, I wonder how soon the gods will test my loyalty.

# CHAPTER 12

## KAFTU

We have now been in Kaftu for many days. Minos and his advisors have told Prince Nimmuruk much about Egypt: the Asiatics who invaded the northern part of the Kingdom, the Pharaohs who ruled, and the land and her people. The group has discussed many strategies, even if tempers often flared, especially between the Prince and the Governor, with me having to interfere and calm the two men.

On this day, I walk along the magnificent corridors of Minos' palace. While King Hannuruk's palace is more opulent and intricate, Minos' is larger and more elegant. Every room along the way is painted floor-to-ceiling, with innumerable decorations of fish, dolphins, bulls, dancers, fighters, birds, flowers, plants, sheep, goats, priests and priestesses, princes, high-status women, courtesans, grass, mountains, ships, seagulls, eagles, deer, hawks, and snakes—it is a tapestry of people, flora, and fauna from the island and beyond. The rich colors—deep blue, brilliant orange, soothing green, mesmerizing red, and golden yellow—all bring every room to life. I have dressed for today's occasion—a day of celebration and sacrifice before preparations for war.

"Your palace has been built by the hands of gods, King Minos," I say, admiringly.

Minos slaps my back. The Governor is painted head to toe in an orange dye. He has his hair in a bun. A flimsy linen patch, secured by a silver thread, covers his genitals. With his beard colored red and a garland of lilies around his neck, Minos looks like *Pidangi*, a man-eating demon from the bowels of the earth.

"Built by the brilliant engineers of the Atalanni. Not gods. This palace was constructed hundreds of summers ago by our forefathers, and the kings and governors have continuously built upon it."

"I am honored to be by your side today."

"Enjoy the hospitality. Once the sun sets, we shall talk of war. Let us go to the celebrations. The Prince has never seen a spectacle like this."

"Neither have I."

"You have seen battle. You have seen blood. You have seen the fear in men's eyes. The Prince? He is soft. The only fear he has seen is in the eyes of the unfortunate women presented to him and that of the goats he eats. We will make him a man today."

I wonder what Minos means.

Minos and I look down at a large open quadrangle after walking through a maze of corridors. Throngs of citizens sit on each side of the quadrangle and greet us with loud cheers. A gypsum-bench throne and two stools are placed on the dais, facing the multitude. Minos takes one stool, and I take the other while we wait for Prince Nimmuruk.

Nimmuruk arrives after a wait—ceremoniously dressed in a long brown gown open at the chest. Several bands of blue-dyed ribbons are tied to his forehead. A diadem announces his position as Crown Prince. He carries a scepter in one hand and a gold-and-gem studded sword in the other. Upon arrival, he acknowledges us and approaches his throne. The people roar when they see the Prince. Nimmuruk waves to the crowd. Many trumpets and drums sound, and all the men and women prostrate themselves before their royal. As is customary, Minos and I kneel beside the Prince and extend our hands up to him. After the Prince touches our heads with his scepter, we settle down and wait for the drums to cease.

The Prince has a weak voice that becomes shrill when he is excited. His nervousness is visible—he has never spoken to such a large crowd before. Nimmuruk turns to Minos. "Where is the bugle of the kings?"

"Do you need one, Your Highness?" asks Minos mischievously.

The Prince clenches his jaws.

"Do not be insolent, Minos. Bring me the bugle of the kings."

Minos is a rascal.

Minos claps and whispers to a servant. As the audience waits, Nimmuruk fidgets and bobs his head from time to time, acknowledging them. After what feels like an eternity, two men come forward holding a large bronze bugle—a strange contraption that resembles threaded tubes. It is as tall as a man.

The bugle of the kings is a remarkable display of Atalanni ingenuity—no such thing exists anywhere else. The instrument can amplify the speaker's voice and make it heard at large distances. For men with weak voices like Nimmuruk, the bugle serves to demonstrate that the royals possess the voice of gods.

When Nimmuruk opens his mouth, the people watch, amazed, and some fall to their feet. I know the strict control of information given to common citizens—to them, this is nothing but an act of the gods. Once the noise settles down, the Prince begins. "People of the Kaftu, Great Island of the South, it brings me joy to take part in this celebration before we embark on fulfilling the gods' demands. The Great King of Atalanni, my father Hannuruk, demands this of you: The

Atalanni shall show Egypt our strength, our power, our knowledge! They shall bleed and bow to us!"

The crowd roars in approval. Nimmuruk speaks some more until his voice shakes and his throat tires. He finally makes ominous declarations of death and misery, demanding their loyalty and blood before he ends his speech. Minos is next, and his speech is lively and colorful, just like the man himself, prompting the people to whoop and jump at his words. Finally, after a few more speakers from Minos' court, the audience settles down for the first spectacle.

A giant bull enters the quadrangle. It is decorated in red, orange, and green. Bells adorn its great horns. The bull runs around, causing the bells to jingle. A lithe man dressed in a brief leopard-spotted kilt enters the arena. The man circles, jumps on, somersaults around, plays, and dances with the bull in a breathtaking display of skill and beauty. I stand by the parapet to get a better glimpse of this joyous ritual. Minos comes to my side and whispers. "Now you see why the Egyptians and the Mycenaeans believe we are dancers."

"But this is a wonderful skill, Your Majesty."

Minos only smiles. "Wait for the next one."

Soon, twenty dancers enter the arena. The women are beautiful. Each dancer wears a fine necklace, large circular earrings, bright red lipstick, and a gorgeous multi-layered orange and brown gown. They move sensuously, swaying their hips and tapping their feet to the ground, to the sound of harps and drums.

*You grace us with food from the deep*

*Your mercy keeps us alive*

*O Great God of the Seas*

*Your trident puts fear in the enemy's heart*

*And yet your love is delicate like a flower*

*Your waves rise with grace*

*We sing in joy and seek your blessings*

I enjoy more presentations of dance, acrobatics, singing, prayers, and an enthralling group performance featuring men, women, and monkeys. The din of drums, shouting, trumpets, and animal sounds envelops the air, rising to a crescendo as the act concludes.

The Prince commends the performance with kind words, and Minos thanks them for putting on a grand show for the royal party. People disperse to eat and reconvene for the next act.

A beautiful priestess, holding a double-ended ax and wearing a feathered cap and flimsy ceremonial threads on her oiled body, rises and raises a black-and-red flag.

The crowd falls silent.

They quietly file out of a narrow pathway at the southern end of the quadrangle. I, along with the Prince, Minos, and their retinue, take another path and walk for about an hour along a cobblestone-and-mud road with hills on either side. The sparse vegetation provides no respite from the rising heat as the sun hovers brightly overhead. Sweat already wipes some of Minos' clay covering, and colors run down his back. My officers and I walk behind the Governor, while eight slaves carry a litter with the Prince.

Minos slows beside me. "He probably thinks he can fight the Pharaoh while sitting on a soft pillow. Feather fight."

I suppress a grin and look straight ahead. Minos makes my duties difficult.

We climb another gentle hill and come upon a flat area. In the center, expertly dug into the earth, is a vast, intricately laid-out circular labyrinth with a granite altar in the center. I had heard of Minos' labyrinth and the fantastical stories about it but never had the opportunity to see it or witness the rituals. People sit on stone-cut stepped benches, looking down into the labyrinth. The walls of the labyrinth tower above any man, which means anyone inside cannot see someone else on the other sides of a wall.

Once everyone settles, two priestesses circle the boundaries of the pit, making loud incantations. They sprinkle water on those near the edge, and then finally come to the nobles' section to complete the rituals. I wait curiously to see what happens next.

The crowd goes silent. I look as a priestess, dressed all in red—red paint adorns her almost naked body, a flimsy red headgear crowns her head, and she wields a red-painted double-ended ax—finally shouts, "The first act of the Tears of the Enemy!"

The crowd roars again, and all eyes turn to the labyrinth below. From the far end of the wall, a door opens, and five youths rush out. Dressed only in loincloths, each man holds nothing but a cane in his hand. Their features are Mycenaean, with curly light hair. The terrified youths walk cautiously forward in the labyrinth, each staying close to the other. Then a loud trumpet sounds, followed by gasps from the crowd. I look in great surprise as a giant man, wearing a gold mask of a bull, emerges from the door, holding a mace in his hand.

Minos.

The Prince stands up. He looks both excited by the spectacle unfolding before him and surprised that Minos himself is down in the labyrinth. Minos roars. The men have all reached one corner of the passage, with three having turned a corner and two still with their backs to the corridor that leads to the door.

One man looks back.

Minos charges.

The youth screams in terror and pushes those ahead of him. They quickly become separated—two, two, and one in different sections of the labyrinth.

Minos makes quick strides, turning nimbly around sharp corners. He finally catches up with the man who turns in fear as Minos approaches him. Without a word, Minos raises his mace and smashes it onto the youth's face. Blood spurts from his nose and mouth, and he falls, screaming.

Minos does not stop.

He raises his mace again and brings it down on the youth's head, which explodes like a ripe melon, spilling the brain and shattering the skull onto the stone floor. The crowd roars, and Minos raises his hands in the air in triumph.

As much as this is a display, what is the point of murdering an unarmed man?

Minos charges again. The other youths stumble along the curved walls, and Minos catches up with two of them. The youths turn to face the fearsome apparition in front of them—one falls to his knees, begging for mercy, while the other takes an attacking stance. Minos does not hesitate— with one swing, he lands a powerful blow on the kneeling youth's shoulder and then grabs the cane from the other. After a short tussle, Minos kicks the man in the stomach and slams the mace onto his exposed chest. The struggle ends quickly as they fall dead on the floor, their limbs twisted like grotesque dolls.

It does not take Minos much longer to find the remaining two. While they put up a brave fight, they stand no chance against the Governor's power or his heavy mace. The two are reduced to a mass of red and pink pulp near the altar at the center, which is now drenched with blood.

The crowd roars its approval, and I clap politely, unsure what to make of this spectacle of blatantly unbalanced strength. All my training has emphasized one thing— honorable conduct in battle and the necessity of fighting only armed men who pose a danger. And yet, here, in our own province, there exists a ritual that breaks all those rules. Minos vanishes through the door and reappears on the far side of the labyrinth. He stands on a podium, and two priestesses, on either side, cleanse him of the blood, skin, flesh, and other bodily matter splattered upon him.

Minos' utter lack of protocol becomes clear as he grins and squeezes the buttocks of one priestess. It is sacrilege, but no one bats an eye, and the priestess smiles uncomfortably before walking back to her station.

Minos then strides back to where Nimmuruk and I are sitting. I attempt to speak to him, but Minos raises his hand to silence me. The Governor's expression bears an unreadable look.

Minos addresses the crowd. "We have finished the first act. This is what will happen to our enemies under the Prince's command!"

Nimmuruk smiles at the adulation of the crowd.

"We will render them helpless, weak, frightened, and begging for mercy. We will butcher them if they do not bend their knees!" Minos proclaims.

The crowd cheers on.

"The second act will demonstrate our strength. This will be a remarkable sight, and the Prince will play a momentous part in this ceremony!" says Minos.

The crowd gasps at this revelation. Nimmuruk's surprise shows, but he continues to smile at the people who now all look to him.

I am alarmed but feel helpless without knowledge of what Minos is planning.

# CHAPTER 13
## THEBES – UPPER EGYPT

Pharaoh Ahmose wakes with anxiety. His heart knocks against his ribs with greater force than it did on most days. Today is an important day, a day when he will again consider significant decisions for the future of Egypt itself. His divinity is being tested.

After cleansing in the pool, wrapping his body in untouched white linen, and anointing himself with perfume, the Pharaoh walks to the holy of holies. It is still dark; Ra has not yet risen in the sky. Ahmose removes the bronze key from his belt and unlocks the ornate door made from the finest wood from Syria. He enters the dark sacred chamber. Two senior priests follow him and begin their morning duties. They first burn aromatic incense, filling the room before stepping back to chant mystical prayers to appease Amun and the other great gods of Egypt.

Ahmose approaches the shrouded statuettes of various divinities—Amun, Ma'at, Horus—and uncovers each. He bows before each shining granite idol. The chants increase in pitch as the priests shake the bells in their hands, creating an enthralling environment of smell, sound, and sight. The Pharaoh washes each idol in cool holy water scented with freshly cut, pure white Egyptian Lotus. He prays and places each idol back on its sandstone pedestal. Then, he feeds each divinity spoons of food and drink—barley, beer, and cake. Ahmose lies prostrate on the ground for several minutes, praying for the good of the land and his people. Once the ritual is complete, the Pharaoh washes his hands at a running tap and wipes them in his hair. He steps back to allow his wife, Ahmose-Nefertari, God's Wife of Amun, to enter the chamber. She steps to the side of the statue of Amun and, amidst chants of rebirth and regeneration, touches the phallic representation of the god.

Then, the royal wife kneels before the Pharaoh, allowing him to lift her by her shoulders. Satisfied with the procedure and their reconfirmation of the rebirth of the god and the rise of the sun, the royal couple heads to the throne room to address the most important topic of the day.

The ushers announce the Pharaoh's arrival. Attendees rise and bow as the couple approaches the throne.

Pharaoh Ahmose looks around the vast throne room. He has been here many times since he was ten summers old and ascended the throne through the blessings of Amun. His great brother and co-regent Kamose had shown him the ways of the royal court. Ahmose sits on the throne, a grand granite and limestone-carved seat on a platform that looks out on a hall with massive pillars. Large sphinxes guard the entrance to the throne room.

Today, Ahmose prepares for the next chapter. He has summoned his vizier Nebhekhufre, two high priests from the Temple of Amun, and two of his generals to discuss the path forward regarding the *Hyk-Khase*—the people of the foreign hill country—the dirty Asiatics. Dressed in his crown representing the two lands of Egypt, the Pharaoh receives his subjects and their obeisance and settles on his throne.

"The son of Amun, The Lord of the Sedge and the Bee, Kamose, he who is strong, my great brother, looks as if he will ascend the stairs toward heaven," Ahmose states. Lamentation arises from the audience at this news.

The Pharaoh waits for the audience to settle.

"The Vizier brings news from the North," Ahmose announces.

The Vizier stands before the assembled members in the room. Nebhekhufre is a slight man—his body lean and his face etched deep with lines of worry and administrative pressures. He wears a kilt-and-apron and a large amethyst-and-lapis lazuli-studded necklace made of three distinct layers. His voice carries a deep timbre, making people notice when he speaks.

"Our spies say that Khamudi fears for the future of his land, Your Majesty. The Asiatics seek alliances in the Levant, and we hear they have sent emissaries even to the far east, to the Babylonians, and to the north, to the new Mitanni."

"Have those delegations borne fruit, noble Nebhekhufre?" asks Wadjmose, one of Ahmose's generals instrumental in the successful push against the wretched Asiatics. Wadjmose has risen from humble beginnings to become one of the kingdom's most revered warriors.

"Not that we are aware of, Wadjmose. The Mitanni are new, and they have recently forged an alliance with the Atalanni—the island dwellers in the Great Green Sea. Our great Kingdom sought the hand of Idukhipa Apsara, the princess of the Mitanni, for His Majesty, Lord of the Two Lands. But she had already been promised to King Hannuruk of the Atalanni."

"What of the lands of the East?"

"Samsu-Ditana struggles with revolts on the borders of his kingdom. He has never sought conflict with us. I do not think he possesses the will or the resources to ally with the Asiatics."

As the Pharaoh considers the response, Ahmose-Nefertari, the Queen, speaks. "Does that mean we can plan an invasion of Hutwaret and finish the Asiatics once and for all?"

God's Wife of Amun participates in matters of prayer and administration.

"No, Your Highness," replies Wadjmose. "We are weakened by the poor harvest, and our troops have been depleted by our recent advances against the impostors. We do not yet have the resources to launch a sustained offensive against them."

Ahmose knows that the Kingdom's granaries are low, and many cattle have died. The previous inundation of the Nile has been insufficient and has weakened the Pharaoh's hand. Ahmose has intensified the prayers to the gods and gifts to the temple priests throughout the land, putting further pressure on the treasury.

But these efforts have not yet yielded results.

What the gods are displeased about, he does not understand.

"Then how do you propose we finish them before they regain strength, Wadjmose?" asks Ahmose-Nefertari.

"We should seek an alliance, Your Highness. The Nubians are weak and have shown treachery before. There is another choice."

"The Mitanni?" inquires the Pharaoh. Nebhekhufre nods at Wadjmose. The two men have previously discussed whatever Wadjmose is about to propose.

"No, Your Majesty. The Mitanni, as the noble vizier has said, are too weak and cannot cross the Levant lands to support us. They are a new kingdom. Instead, we propose an alliance with the Atalanni. Together, we can drive out the impostors," Wadjmose asserts.

"That is an interesting proposition, Wadjmose," says the Pharaoh. Ahmose knows from an early age that seeking wisdom and knowledge from his expert advisors is critical to success and his ambitions. "I know little about them, except that they have gifted our ancestors with beautiful pottery, garments, and paints, and they have exceptional dancers and performers. We have traded linen, papyrus, flint, jasper, agate, and gold with them."

Nebhekhufre interrupts Wadjmose. "They are skilled painters, dancers, and traders, Your Majesty. Before your grandfather's time, they also traded olives, figs, and pottery with us. However, they have a formidable navy and a secretive council that creates weaponry through the direct hand of the god."

Ahmose is intrigued. The Pharaoh leans forward and adjusts his onerous crown to prevent it from toppling. He wishes to remove it but knows that such an act would offend the priests and his sharp-tongued wife. The false beard attached to his chin with a strap is another irritation he must endure in the throne room.

"What weapons?"

"We do not know exactly, Your Majesty. They are known not to display or show their creations, but rumors suggest they are unlike anything we have ever seen or heard."

"Why had I not heard of this before?"

"We have had little contact with them since the impostors gained control of Lower Egypt, Your Majesty. And their King, Hannuruk, who ascended the throne during your father's early reign, has instituted a policy of limited engagement with the outside kingdoms except for trade."

"He is a strange king," remarks Ahmose. The attendees chuckle.

The vizier nods. "We have heard rumors that the king is counseled by their priests, who prefer that the Atalanni keep their boundaries to themselves."

"How do you know all this?" asks Ahmose, pointing at Nebhekhufre.

"We have maintained light maritime and trade contact. With the impostors controlling much of the North," the Vizier spits on the ground, "it has been difficult—but we receive steady news from their land. Besides, Your Majesty, we have an ambassador in their court."

"We have an ambassador?" The Pharaoh expresses surprise.

Nebhekhufre smiles apologetically. "I beg your pardon, Your Majesty, but yes—we have a man in their courts to represent our interests. It has been over a harvest, but we expect to see him soon to present his latest report."

"Is he in touch with their king?"

"Not their king, Your Majesty. The Atalanni inhabit two lands where most reside. Their capital, which we have only heard of, is a small island in the middle of the Green Sea. They also possess a large province—a great island called *Keftiu*, ruled by a governor named Minos. Our ambassador lives in the Palace of Minos."

"This governor, is he an influential man?"

"The ambassador says so, Your Majesty. The governor ranks next only to the royals and the Oracle of the Atalanni."

"Why would they help us?"

"We tell them that the *Hyk-Khase* seek dominion over the seas. People of similar stock already control parts of the Levant, and if the impostors conquer Egypt, may Sekhmet strike them to the ground, it is unsurprising that they will turn north to expand their dominion further."

"That is a premise based on fear," states Ahmose. "My brother often said that good negotiation combines fear with incentive."

"The great Kamose, he who is beloved of the gods, is right, Your Majesty," Nebhekhufre replies, his eyes twinkling with pride for his nephew. "We propose a mutually beneficial trade agreement and the development of the ports along the Northern Sea. We will propose attractive terms of trade. The Atalanni are masters of the sea, and access to our harbors and expanded trade will be of great value to them."

Ahmose finds discussions about taxes, grain allocations, trade terms, cattle barters, and other administrative matters tedious. "When does this ambassador come to us?"

"He should arrive here in the next one or two moons, Your Majesty."

"Shall we send him back with our proposal?"

"Yes, Your Majesty."

Ahmose turns to his queen, who now stands and places a hand on the shoulder of the priest who burns incense around the Pharaoh and his queen. Ahmose-Nefertari closes her eyes and holds her husband's hand. The two wait as the priests chant hymns to the gods. A wonderful aroma permeates the room as the royals go deep into prayer.

Once the fire that burned the incense dwindles, Ahmose opens his eyes and looks at the audience beside him.

"A vision came to me, a vision with the blessing of the gods. I saw a falcon over a hot golden desert. It is a graceful creature with silver wings and a golden beak. It flies high in the sky and sees a beautiful blue oasis in the middle of vast dunes of sand. The thirsty falcon then circles the oasis several times and dives to get succor for its parched throat. But just as it nears the water, the color changes to red, then black, and the water evaporates entirely. The falcon has no water to drink, and all around it is only sand."

Ahmose-Nefertari grips her husband's hand. "I dread hearing it, my husband."

Nebhekhufre clears his throat. The Pharaoh looks through the lingering smoke of the incense at the wise old vizier. Ahmose knows that while he is the First Priest of the Temples, he must sometimes defer to his formidable wife, the God's Wife of Amun, or to the wise vizier, who was once the Chief Priest of the Temple of Amun.

"You are wise beyond your years, my Queen. The gods send their messages in mysterious ways. If you will allow me, Your Majesty, may I present my interpretation?"

"I grant you permission," says Ahmose.

"The falcon represents you, who is divinity—Horus and god on earth. The blue water represents our alliance with the Atalanni, those who dwell in the waters. The red represents your domination over the black, which symbolizes the Asiatics. The evaporation is the gods' sign that our land will no longer suffer the scourge of the Asiatics and that all that remains is our sacred sand."

Ahmose is torn between the interpretations of his wife and his vizier. "I have never heard of black representing the Asiatics."

"It is the color of their hair and the darkness of their souls, Your Majesty," Nebhekhufre replies.

Ahmose turns to his wife, whose gentle eyes display great concern. "Your heart remains heavy, my wife."

"The Vizier possesses wisdom and experience, Your Majesty. My heart worries for you and our Kingdom, but the Vizier was once the Priest of Amun and knows the signs of the gods."

Ahmose contemplates the situation. The gods work in strange ways—it is up to him, as the foremost priest of the land, to decide whether a strategy of waiting for an alliance with the Atalanni will yield rewards or lead to the end of his Kingdom.

"I honor your counsel, my beloved wife. But on this occasion, I shall direct our affairs based on what the Vizier sees."

Nebhekhufre bows.

Ahmose continues, "Prepare gifts for the Atalanni. Let us make a grand gesture of friendship. Inform me when the Ambassador arrives."

The attendants prostrate themselves before the Pharaoh and his wife, and Nebhekhufre turns to Wadjmose.

"Guard the secret paths to the Great Green Sea. Send a boat to Keftiu as soon as possible and summon the Ambassador."

As the Vizier walks out of the Palace, Ahmose looks at his Queen and hopes that he has made the right decision.

# CHAPTER 14

## KAFTU

The crowd waits in anticipation. Once again, the priestess repeats her ceremonial actions, and the door at the far end opens again. The curious audience watches as a man tentatively walks out. Gasps of surprise ripple through the crowd—the man is distinctively Egyptian. Most people had only heard of the people of the neighboring empire, and few had seen an Egyptian. He is middle-aged, his head shaved, and his skin darker than that of the Mycenaeans, though not much darker compared to us. His eyes are accentuated by black kohl beneath his eyelids, and he wears a simple tunic embroidered with decorative golden swirls. Gold bracelets adorn his wrists. He takes tentative steps and looks around, holding a club in his hand.

"You see one here, my people! But there are many more, and we shall smite them!" Minos shouts.

The crowd roars, bloodthirsty and invigorated by a sense of conquest. The Egyptian flinches but remains where he is. Teber watches him closely—does the man know what fate awaits him? Minos stays where he is. Prince Nimmuruk walks closer to the edge.

Minos raises his hands to silence the crowd and waits for them to quiet.

"The Egyptian stands proud. He believes no man can challenge him. He thinks his Pharaoh is a god. He believes that his monuments are greater than anyone else's. He claims he can strike anyone with impunity. We will show him fear!"

Cheers erupt again. Minos turns toward Prince Nimmuruk.

A strange smile spreads across Minos' face.

He declares loudly, "As per tradition, the Prince will now descend the labyrinth and strike down the Egyptian."

Minos' announcement startles Nimmuruk. He frantically looks from side to side as the crowd rises to its feet, a great roar of enthusiasm rising to the skies—thrilled at the prospect of their Prince subduing their enemy.

I feel alarmed. "Governor Minos, you should have cleared this with me. We cannot put the Royal in danger," I whisper. The Prince stands speechless, aware that any act resembling backing down from this declaration would be seen as cowardice.

"I need to clear nothing with you, Young Teber. These are our customs. I trust the Prince will faithfully carry out the people's expectations of him," Minos says. "Let us prepare the Prince."

Nimmuruk's face darkens. I approach him to confer, "I will make him pay," he hisses.

Nimmuruk changes into ceremonial attire and receives a sword that is clearly too heavy for him to wield deftly. Once ready, he walks forward to the pit, raising his sword and causing the crowd to cheer once more. Concern gnaws at me, but I find myself powerless—Governor Minos outranks me, and the Prince has committed to the fight in full view of the audience.

"Do you want to delegate the fight to me, Your Majesty?" I ask.

Nimmuruk does not answer. Rage burns in his eyes. "Do you question my ability, Teber?"

"No, Your Majesty, as your loyal servant, I am bound to ask."

"Stay and watch. But whoever surprises me shall pay," he says, leaving the threat vague and open. I bow and step back as the Priestess guides Nimmuruk toward the entrance to the labyrinth. I observe the unsure Prince walk unsteadily, trying to grip his heavy sword. I feel a mix of pity and a sense of glee. The Prince often projected his power over the weak, sitting upon a throne to pass judgment, but now he would face an enemy alone.

As the anxious crowd watches, the Prince steps through the door of the labyrinth. The crowd roars again, and the Prince acknowledges their adulation.

The Egyptian walks ahead, turning a corner, but stands quietly, looking back and forth, eyeing the remains of one of the dead youths.

Nimmuruk advances cautiously, sword held forward, yet his steps lack the confidence of an accomplished warrior.

The Priest signals for silence among the people. I anxiously move to the edge of the labyrinth, straining to see the two men in the corridors.

As the Prince approaches the turn of the corridor, the Egyptian hunches and takes a battling stance, raising his club at an angle.

The Prince closes in on the corner and slows.

The two men are positioned on either side of the wall, waiting for the other to act.

The Prince looks up.

I gesture that the Egyptian is just around the corner.

But the Egyptian sees that as well.

In a flash, the Egyptian jumps around the corner and swings his club forcefully at the Prince. Nimmuruk raises his sword in a defensive posture at the last moment, the impact of the club pushing him back. The Egyptian is taller than the Prince and advances menacingly. Nimmuruk regains his stance and returns to a combat position, but the Egyptian does not hesitate. He swings his club again, striking the sword hard, nearly knocking it from Nimmuruk's grasp. The crowd gasps in horror as I look at Minos for direction.

The Governor's expression remains impassive as he watches the scene unfold before him.

The Egyptian strikes again, and this time, the Prince stumbles and falls to the ground. A great moan rises from the crowd, and Itaja, my lieutenant, taps me on the shoulder.

"What do you want to do, sir?" he asks urgently. As I watch, horrified, the Egyptian strikes the Prince on his shoulder.

The Prince screams.

It is not a scream of valor or aggression—it is the high pitch of a boy struck by fear. But the Egyptian does not strike the Prince again; instead, he curses at him as he looms over the fallen figure, shaking his club.

*Enough.*

"You and Bansabira, cover me if needed," I order Itaja.

I leap across the gap of the labyrinth onto the top of the nearest wall before jumping down, holding onto the ledge before dropping to the floor. The Egyptian, distracted by my sudden movement, steps back from the Prince, who has now shrunk into a corner, his back against the deep-brown hardened clay walls. The Prince's headdress has come loose and fallen to the ground, revealing his thinning hair, a disheveled mop.

I unsheathe my sword.

The Egyptian turns to face me.

Behind him, Prince Nimmuruk is getting back on his feet.

"Stay where you are, Your Majesty," I say, and the Prince halts.

"Why?" the Egyptian asks haltingly. His eyes show no fear, only questions. He is a head taller than I am, and I am tall.

I lower my sword.

Chatter comes from above, the curious faces of people watching the unfolding drama. The Egyptian takes a step forward, but not threateningly. He lowers his club and speaks in a muffled voice, "I am the Ambassador of Egypt. I serve their majesties, Lords of the Two Lands, Beloved of Amun, Pharaoh Kamose and Ahmose. What is my fault?"

*An envoy of Egypt?*

The Egyptian's enunciation is clear, his Atalanni flawless, even if tinged with the accent of his homeland.

I find myself at a loss for words.

The Prince has regained his feet, sword held before him. His face is flushed, and his lower jaw trembles. I raise my hand once more, signaling the Prince to remain still.

"You—"

At that moment, Prince Nimmuruk lunges forward. The Egyptian quickly notices him from the corner of his eye, but it is too late. The blade plunges through the Egyptian's back, the tip re-emerging from the front beside the heart.

"No!" I exclaim, but it is too late. The shocked Egyptian collapses, and the Prince, with a maniacal expression on his face, steps back. He then raises his hands as if in victory, but the rapturous silence that follows shatters the moment.

"Stand back, Your Majesty," I say. "This man may be contaminated by the pestilences of Egypt." It is a lie, but it compels the Prince to step back.

I drop to one knee and support the Egyptian's head. The man chokes on his blood, blinking frantically, his eyes lacking focus. A million questions rage in my mind—this is no honorable conduct! Moreover, this man is an ambassador, a messenger of peace and trade.

"Leave him! Why did you jump here?" screams the Prince. I ignore the instruction and look down at the dying man. Two more officers arrive by my side, while a Prince's aide leads the Prince back to the door.

The Egyptian gasps, blood splattering his lips and teeth, bubbling from his throat. His back arches in pain, hands gripping the earth. I lift him slightly to ease the pressure. He looks up to see people gathered at the edge, peering down. The man turns to me and whispers through the pain, "Why?"

*Such shameful conduct.*

I know the Egyptian will not survive. Warm blood, now spilling forth in great spurts, courses down his chest, soaking my thigh. I reposition him so that his back faces the wall. As his eyes dim, I utter an incantation to the gods and place the man's limp hands on his chest.

A hiss escapes from the ambassador's throat, and he closes his eyes one last time.

# CHAPTER 15

## KAFTU

The retinue returns to the Palace, and no member speaks a word. I have calmed the livid Prince in private, beyond the view of the flabbergasted crowd, and asked the royal guards to escort him. Minos walks quietly beside me, surrounded by his personal guards.

Once we enter the royal quarters, away from everyone, Nimmuruk leaps from his litter and explodes.

"You son of a mangy dog, what do you think you were doing?"

"I was only trying to demonstrate your power to the Islanders," Minos replies, not backing down. However, I know it is a disingenuous answer. If the Prince does not calm down, this will soon turn into a constitutional nightmare.

"You should have warned us beforehand, Lord Minos! You were not to put the Prince at risk," I address Minos calmly. "You—"

"This sewer-dwelling bastard is plotting against me! Do you know the penalty for regicide, Minos?" The Prince screams, red in his face. His guards now fan around the room. I rush to the center, positioning myself between Minos and Nimmuruk, and kneel before the Prince.

"Please, Your Highness, let us pause before we act rashly," I say. Nimmuruk stops. "Success requires all of us to act in consort. That is the King's order and the Oracle's expectation. This must have been a misunderstanding, and with preparation, there is no doubt you would have subdued the Egyptian."

"You should not have jumped there, presumptuous fool!" shouts Nimmuruk, but he no longer advances. Minos remains quiet, which is uncharacteristic of the man.

Once the room settles, the Prince speaks again. "You have to pay for this, Minos. Wait until my father hears of your insolence!"

"Your father did not send you here to act like a spoiled little brat, Prince Nimmuruk, but to fight an empire!"

"How dare you speak back to me, insolent motherfucker!" Nimmuruk rushes at Minos, but I come in between and grab the Prince. With one hand on his shoulder, I extend my sword toward Minos with the other.

"You are becoming too bold for your age, young Teber," Minos says, eyeing me coldly.

"My duty is to the Prince, King Minos," I reply.

Nimmuruk spits in Minos' direction. "You will pay for this! You will pay—"

"He will pay nothing, Prince," a cool, powerful voice cuts through the commotion. I turn in shock to see Khaia, the Oracle herself, standing near the door. With her are the King's Guard, who only follow the command of the King and, in his absence, that of the Oracle, as per Atalanni law.

I bow to the Oracle.

"Do you know what he did, sacred Khaia?" Nimmuruk asks, his voice almost whining, like a boy complaining to his mother.

"I have been told, Prince Nimmuruk. You must administer punishment, but not now. This is not the time for quarrel. The King demands it. The gods demand it."

The Prince's chest heaves, but he quiets. He fears his father; of that, I am certain.

"Sacred Khaia, the Prince—" begins Minos.

"Be quiet, Governor Minos, before you put yourself at risk," she admonishes him. "What you did, while sanctioned by law and convention, was still unconscionable. You should have warned the Prince beforehand."

"How is it sanctioned by law, sacred Khaia? To attempt to kill me?" retorts Nimmuruk.

"Yes, our laws allow Minos' actions, Prince Nimmuruk. At times of war, the kingdom expects a Prince to rise to the unexpected. A Prince must face the enemy with no warning. The ritual signifies surprise, and the enemy, in this case, was not a heavily armed soldier."

Chastised, Nimmuruk sulks. The simmering tension in the room remains, with no one certain of what to do next.

"You did the right thing, General Teber," she says, and I bow. "Let us sit and speak."

The group then walks to the throne room of the Palace. In an unspoken concession, Minos bows to the Prince and invites him to take the throne. Servants scramble to set up an official stool for the Oracle, facing the throne, while others stand aside.

Khaia dismisses all guards from the room. The only ones remaining are Nimmuruk, Minos, a temple priest, the Oracle, and me.

Once the group settles, Khaia chastises us. "You are supposed to initiate preparations for war, and yet you quarrel like children!"

"I assure you I am no child—" begins Minos.

"Watch what you say, Governor. This is no time for your juvenile behavior," she interjects. Her stern tone and flashing eyes put an end to Minos' flippancy.

"You are here to prepare an empire to fight another. Our future is at stake, and the three men here will forge our destiny. The King is a wise man. He knew he could not trust your behavior in the early days, which is why I am here to ensure that you respect the will of the gods and the King. I will not interfere in your preparation for war or your operations on the ground, but I will intervene if the three of you cannot get along."

No one speaks a word.

"If you cannot control your mouth and impulses, Governor Minos, then you will find your days as the King of this Island numbered," she warns, wagging her finger like a teacher scolding a disobedient student.

"I understand, sacred Khaia," Minos responds, his eyes flicking back and forth between the Oracle and me. The Prince sits stonily on the throne.

"Let me make it clear to all. Once we invade Egypt, the Prince will be the supreme commander of our forces. Teber will obey orders but lead the troops on the ground. Minos will supply and defend us. Until then, I will be involved in our strategy."

Whatever misgivings anyone in the room may have had, no one voices a complaint.

A priestess enters the room and chants prayers for peace. Servants bring fruit, clay pots of chilled wine, a preparation of beans and cuttlefish, salted goat meat, and a bowl of grapes. The fine wine cools the tempers. After the servants clear the room, Minos stands and turns to the Prince.

"I apologize for not warning you, Prince Nimmuruk. I ask for your mercy," he says, kneeling. Nimmuruk struggles for a response, still angry. The Oracle nods at the Prince. Placated, he touches the scepter in his hand to Minos' mass of unruly hair—a symbol of the royal's mercy.

Minos returns to his seat, and Khaia smiles.

"Now that we have all calmed down, let us talk strategy. It has been many days now, General Teber. What have you all decided?" Khaia inquires, smoothing her hair.

I clear my throat. "A small delegation will visit the Asiatic King Khamudi when the winds and weather favor us. Meanwhile, we will build and train our army here."

"What if they refuse to align because they suspect our intentions? Surely they wish to control all of Egypt and not play subordinate to us?"

"We will threaten them. The news is that they are struggling. I am certain they would not want to be caught between our anger and the Pharaoh's. They will support us or die resisting."

"You will threaten them when you visit their court with a small delegation?"

"No, sacred Khaia. We will send a messenger after the visit," I reply.

*I am not that foolish.*

"Who is going on this delegation?"

"His Highness Nimmuruk will lead the delegation, and I shall accompany him. Governor Minos will remain near the sea with a force."

"Governor Minos, we had an agreement that you would remain here," Khaia asserts.

"This is the best course of action, sacred Khaia," Minos argues. "It is my duty to be prepared in case of risk—"

"As we have decided, Governor, you will not go," Khaia interrupts, her voice firm.

Minos' temper rises. I predict this. He had forced us to accept his travel, haranguing and harassing us until we had given up. But with a higher authority present, he has no choice.

Minos argues, but Khaia shuts him down. He sulks like a child and finally accepts his role to stay behind and prepare our forces for a large-scale invasion.

Khaia returns to the topic. "When does this delegation leave?"

"Within the next thirty days. We will send a small advance party to inform the Asiatic King and ensure that the path is without surprise," I respond.

"Do you feel confident about this mission? Can you protect the Prince?"

Nimmuruk finally speaks. "Do not speak of me as if I were a child. I must be there to meet the King of the Asiatics, for surely he expects someone of royal rank and not a soldier or a loutish governor."

Minos holds his tongue, and Khaia nods. "Every royal being must be protected, Prince. I say it with no disrespect."

"I am confident that the Prince and I will return victorious with an alliance," I profess, with false confidence. She appraises me without a word and finally nods.

"Be careful and ensure the safety of you both," she advises. "We need you for the war, not lost before the first move."

Minos then reports on preparations and training and summons a minister, who describes logistics, food and weapon production plans, the availability of priests, healers, physicians, engineers, prostitutes, road builders, shipbuilders, menders, and other personnel to prepare or accompany the troops for the invasion.

"Your Highness, our future rests on your shoulders," Khaia states, addressing the Prince.

"I will do my father proud," Nimmuruk responds dismissively. "I do not need everyone to counsel me further.

I hope you realize, Minos and Teber, that I am your lord on the shores of Egypt."

"You are, Your Highness," I reply. Minos remains silent, still smarting from Khaia's reprimand.

"You are the King's son and the heir of the Atalanni," Khaia affirms. "We know you will bring us glory. It is time for us to rest."

With that, the group concludes the evening. As the Oracle exits, I think I see her flick a finger at Minos, beckoning him.

I banish impure thoughts from my head.

# CHAPTER 16

## KAFTU

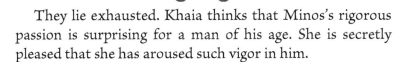

They lie exhausted. Khaia thinks that Minos's rigorous passion is surprising for a man of his age. She is secretly pleased that she has aroused such vigor in him.

"You are a mystery to me, Khaia. I do not know where the gods' will ends, and yours begins."

"That is not for you to know. Why did you put the Prince's life in danger so early?"

Minos sniggers. "He was in no danger. He could use a thrashing or two. The brat screamed like a girl. He surely tucks his penis between his thighs every night and parades in front of the mirrors."

"Every humiliation you heap upon him weakens our hand. He must go to the Asiatics with his head held high, not with anger at his own people. You test me and the King. It will not end well for you if you do not show the Prince due respect," Khaia says, now sitting away from Minos, who sprawls on his bed.

"He must earn his respect. So far, all he has done is threaten us. Where has he lifted his sword? When has he put a man to the ground?"

"Well, you know he has not, but he is the King's son. He is all we have, and the King has ordered so. If you question that, then you risk your future—do you not see it?"

Minos rolls from his bed and stands. He stretches and wipes his genitals with a cloth. He walks to a stand, fills his wine cup, and offers another to Khaia, who declines.

"I see very well. I have not been a governor here for all these summers by being blind. You say the gods wish to expand their dominion, and yet what we have is a weak king and his incompetent, untrained, unworthy son. Who do you think should really be king, Khaia? Who?" Minos says, thumping his chest. The mirth is gone; in its place is a burning ambition.

He continues, "An Egyptian may fuck his sister, and yet he thrives. He has survived thousands of harvests and built an empire while we have sat, because of your Divine Council, and scratched our balls."

"Be careful with your words. You keep raising dangerous questions. The King may be weak, and his son a fool, but he has you and Teber. You have a duty to fulfill. You will never be king, and I hope you entertain no such thoughts," Khaia says as she bends down to wrap her gown around her. Minos reaches and grabs her waist, but she slaps his wrist and pushes him away.

"You have great hopes for the royal asses."

"Asses they may be, but they are still the rulers. And you will obey their braying."

Minos wraps a kilt around his waist and paces around the large room. This room is bare of any paintings, except for a large stuffed bull's head on the wall over the bed, looking down menacingly. Khaia feels a chill.

"When we conquer Egypt, perhaps the people of the Atalanni will crown me king. And you could be my queen," he says, laughing, yet there is no humor in his voice.

"You laugh at your own peril," she says as she moves near the door. Minos's flippancy has made it difficult to understand his commitment to the mission ahead.

Minos turns serious. "I abide by the laws of Atalanni, dear Oracle. I will obey the will of the gods. The Prince is my lord, and I will treat him as such. But the heavens surely seek a powerful leader if we are to be the empire our gods desire."

"Now is not the time for such ambitions. Whatever you seek, you must first prove to us, the King, and the gods that you can bring us victory. Otherwise, your boasts mean nothing—conquering Egypt is not like raping a maiden in your labyrinth, Governor," Khaia says, her voice now chilly like the snow of the far North Lands.

Minos walks close to Khaia and towers over her, his giant head looking down. His eyes are black and devoid of expression. He grips her forearm so strongly that she flinches with pain.

He pulls her toward him. "One day, Oracle, you will stand in the assembly of the commoners and the soldiers and declare that Hannuruk is no longer fit to be king," he says, his voice dripping with threat like a poisonous snake. "And you will make me king."

# CHAPTER 17

## KAFTU

Preparation for war intensifies. Under my training and Minos' threats, a fraction of the army becomes battle-ready and prepares to embark on the arduous journey across the vast sea to Egypt to face the unknown.

Of the three messengers sent to Hutwaret, the capital of the Asiatics and home of Khamudi, their ruler, only one returns. The fate of the other two remains unknown. Khamudi has expressed his interest in receiving the Atalanni delegation, indicating that he would be honored to meet the Prince of the Atalanni. During this time, an Egyptian messenger arrives, seeking the Ambassador of Egypt and bearing news from the Pharaoh. Minos has him imprisoned and executed despite my objections. I never learned the purpose of the Egyptian's visit.

On the thirty-seventh day after the celebration marking the end of the heat of the sun, a delegation of twenty officials, including Prince Nimmuruk and me, supported by three hundred Atalanni forces, finally prepares to leave Kaftu. People celebrate the occasion with festivities that last for two days, and His Majesty King Hannuruk and Queen Idukhipa Apsara grace the event. A magnificent procession of royals, nobles, soldiers, commoners, cattle, and sheep originates from the Palace and makes its way toward the northern harbor, where the boats await.

I wait for the King to deliver his farewell speech.

King Hannuruk appears weary, whether from the excessive drinking of the past two days or from the stress of launching a war and the implications it may hold for him.

Since my earliest memories, I have never seen the King in combat or in conflict. His speech slurs, and his behavior toward those around him is less than royal.

"Tell Khamudi that his survival depends on our support," he says, addressing his senior council.

"Tell him that should he resist our offer, we will begin by ending his kingdom even before the Egyptians do. Tell him I will lay with all his wives and daughters!"

"Yes, Your Majesty," I reply, controlling my urge to glance at the Queen, who sits beside him.

Her eyes are fixed on me.

I sense her sadness.

I also know that I will risk everything if I attempt another tryst with her under these watchful eyes.

"You have a great responsibility, and I expect nothing less than complete victory. Let this empire not perish with you, Nimmuruk," the King says, addressing his son, who stands before him clad in gold-wool regalia. Nimmuruk has recently gained some of my respect. He is unpredictable, his moods swinging wildly like the horses of the Asiatics. I must keep his cruelty in check during training, but he has put effort into improving both his fighting skills and his assessment of the task ahead. I must observe how he will fare in the theater of deceitful diplomacy and war.

Minos stands sullenly. I know the Governor longs to be part of this mission and will hound the King to regain the opportunity to engage in the war.

The King sways where he stands, and his Queen and two attendants strive to balance him. He pushes her away, and drool spills from the corner of his mouth. This man repulses me, and it is a travesty that the woman I love is under his control.

I pray for victory for the Atalanni, and for me to take her away. Finally, amidst great pomp, accompanied by the sounds of drumbeats and trumpets, we board our boats.

As we sail away, Apsara bows her head and weeps. Only the gods know when I can return to wipe her tears.

# PART II

*"Other kingdoms are primitive. They act as if gods sit on a throne and direct man's every affair. The divine has placed us on this earth for a reason and given us the intelligence to understand the world. And that is why, unlike the Egyptians, we do not spend most of our lives in meaningless rituals…"*

**DAIVOSHASTRA CH. IX: "ROLE OF GODS"**

# CHAPTER 18

## HUTWARET

I have never traveled so far on water, and the beauty surrounding me mesmerizes. The days pass peacefully, with little interaction between the Prince and me. He keeps his counsel while I oversee the journey. A few men fall ill along the way, unable to handle the heaving, but they recover as time goes on.

Many days later, we finally arrive near the shores of Egypt. The hazy outline is thrilling to see, for we all desire this land. With us are men who have previously visited Egypt for trade, and they will act as our guides until we connect with King Khamudi's men. We land on an isolated strip of the coast—a marshy wetland not too far from where Egypt's great river's tributaries drain into the sea. We have heard that this river snakes through this vast land, splitting into over fifteen branches that empty into the sea. Our plan is to travel east on foot along the coast until we reach a muddy road marked by two low-lying hills and a temple dedicated to the Asiatics' gods. The guides assure us it is hard to miss, and it is there that we should expect to meet the messenger who will take us to their King.

The weather here is quite humid, and with foul critters and insects harassing us day and night, we finally arrive at the temple in six days. It is a sorry dedication to a god. Made of clay and loose stones bound by brittle mortar, it contains nothing but a bare room with a statue of a man inside. No beauty exists within its walls.

Our instructions are to climb onto the roof, hoist a fire, and leave it burning through the night. The journey has brought sickness to many of the men. I think they are cursed by the local gods, and our physicians tend to men who shiver even in the warm sun.

The early morning after we hoisted the fire, guards wake me, alerting me to several men approaching on horses. A horse is a magnificent beast! These muscular creatures have come from the lands far east, and the Asiatics have learned to domesticate and employ them in war. Minos once told me that he tried to rear them in Kaftu but was unsuccessful. I have even heard rumors that the Atalanni Engineers trained horse traders in the Levant to learn how to build chariots of war and use horses to draw them. We do not have horses, and buying them for the Atalanni army is one topic of our conversation with Khamudi.

The riders approach rapidly, raising dust behind them. I ask my soldiers to take position behind me. The horses slow as they draw near, and the riders stop at a distance. The tall rider in the front dismounts and walks toward me. Once he nears, he extends his arms to show he is unarmed. He summons another man, who I learn is the interpreter.

"Iben-Har," he says as he bows to me. Iben-Har is a strange man—he is dressed like an Egyptian, wearing a kilt and waistband. His body is smooth and hairless. Yet on his head are dark curls like the Asiatics, and he wears a long, carefully manicured thick black beard. Iben-Har states that he is a commander in Khamudi's army. "King Khamudi welcomes the contingent of the Keftiu."

I am surprised by his announcement in our language. I bow to him. "You speak our tongue! I am Teber of the Atalanni. I am here on the orders of King Hannuruk, and I serve Prince Nimmuruk in this delegation."

"We have men from your lands in our palaces, Teber of the Atalanni. I can converse in the basics of your language."

I nod appreciatively. His mastery is better than he reveals. At my signal, two messengers trot toward the Prince, who is in his litter, bringing him to Iben-Har, who kneels in respect.

"King Khamudi looks forward to your visit, Prince Nimmuruk," he says. After the pleasantries, the Prince retires to his tent, and we welcome the Asiatics to my tent, offering them food—salted fish, olives, and water. I then regroup with Iben-Har and his men to plan our travel ahead.

"How far is your King's capital from here?" I ask as we stand inside the tent to escape the heat outside.

"Three days' walk if your men can keep pace," he says, "five otherwise."

I recollect that some of our men are sick, and we have no hurry to arrive a day early. "We will take five days," I say, and he nods. "Tell your advance riders not to draw attention to our arrival and for the King not to plan a grand welcome."

He smirks. "The King has no plans for a great welcome. We have traded with you before, though this arrangement with high-ranking officers and the Prince himself is unusual."

"Do we face a risk from Egyptian forces?"

He gives me a strange look. "We are Egyptian, General Teber. The pathetic weaklings in the far south call us the *Hyk-Khase*, but it is they who are no longer the rightful owners of this land."

I curse myself for having forgotten Minister Rishwa's lectures. The Asiatics had incorporated most of the native Egyptian customs with their own and now saw themselves as the legitimate rulers of the land. "My apologies. I am unfamiliar with this land. But we must keep ourselves careful of any incursions."

"Yes, of course. We know that the boy-Pharaoh and his bandits are growing bolder, but our King will crush them like the insects they are."

I nod. The messages I have received say the Pharaoh is gaining the upper hand, but with our assistance, we hope the Asiatics will defeat the Egyptians before we take over both.

He continues. "There is no danger on these paths. These are well-trodden and patrolled. The Egyptians have no presence in this corner," he says, unconsciously referring to the Pharaoh's people as 'Egyptians.'

I say nothing to the man. We agree to begin our march south at the earliest opportunity once we can prepare the men. It is noon as the sun beats down on us before we can start. Iben-Har and I walk while his men trudge slowly ahead of us on horseback. They caution us to watch out for a strange beast known as the hippopotamus and not to be lulled by its portly form.

The landscape here is greener than at home. Date palms, sycamore, and acacia trees dot the fields. We walk along the meandering river, which, Iben-Har says, eventually merges with the Great River that snakes down to the far unknown to the south. A smattering of villages appears, and the people look on curiously as we march. Poverty is rife in these lands. We have better homes even in our poorest quarters, and we are superior in intellect. The stench of human waste lingers as we cross every village, with the people so meager in their dwellings made of sunburnt brick. Frequently, we pass Egyptian temples—they are impressive and cater to their many gods. It is as if the gods have all the comfort while the peasants have none. The Asiatics call their god Ba'al, but they have few temples in his name. I feel uneasy as I pass every Egyptian god's abode, wondering if they know our purpose and are prepared to strike us dead. But I trust our gods to watch over us.

Iben-Har is condescending. He views my age as worthy of derision. But I have no desire to argue with him, for my purpose lies not with him but with his King. As we march, my mind repeatedly drifts to Apsara—her beautiful eyes, her hair, her nose, her lips, her smile, her fragrant skin, the curve of her—I pull myself from my reverie. It is as if the gods have cursed me. I pray for her safety, for Hannuruk surely is losing his mind. I hope Khaia will protect her.

There is some laughter. I look to my left and see one of my men throwing stones at something. Iben-Har notices it too and shouts, "Tell him to stop!"

Then, suddenly, a dark, lumbering form charges across the grassy embankment toward the stone thrower.

*A Hippopotamus!*

I am amazed at the speed of this animal; it is swift as a horse, despite deceiving us with its girth. The beast opens its extraordinary mouth—I am struck by the large, sharp teeth. It slams into the man, and before our men can react, it clamps its giant jaws around his waist.

With a single snap, it severs the man's torso, rips his entrails, and tosses half of him like a rag doll onto the grassy ground. It then turns upon those trying to attack it. Just then, Iben-Har holds my forearm. "My men will handle it."

The ferocious animal now charges at another group. They harass it with their pathetic swords and spears, but it has a thick hide and brushes off the attackers. It tramples another man as I look in alarm, but by then, Iben-Har's men, equipped with thick nooses and long, curved hook-like spears, surround it. It takes another man's life before the combination of rope around its neck and limbs, along with spears to its belly, fells it. The hippopotamus finally dies after much effort, leaving carnage in its wake. We instruct the men to stay far away when they see these hulking monsters feed or rest by the riverbanks. I complain to Iben-Har that he should have warned me.

"I thought you wise men knew," he smirks, much to my annoyance. "It runs like a horse and swims like a fish."

"We have heard of lions," I say.

"The hippopotamus kills many more than lions, General. People underestimate it, for it looks like a jolly gentle giant. They possess a terrible temper," he replies.

His men deftly chop the carcass—they even eat this animal in these parts. That night, we are given a taste of salted hippopotamus meat, and I am surprised that it tastes acceptable with the local beer. I sternly admonish my men and tell them to avoid mischief.

We march for five days and finally approach the walls of Hutwaret.

"Our city," declares Iben-Har. We can see nothing but the walls, but I assume an impressive city hides behind them. We first cross another tributary of the Great River. The bridge is heavily guarded. We finally reach the massive wooden doors of the city gate. It is our agreement that only our delegation enters the city while our forces will remain behind the tributary.

What lies beyond the gates surprises me.

Ahead stands a large palace. Its roof is low, and the architecture is flat with rectangular sections. It resembles a much larger version of some temples I have seen on the way. Ochre colonnades front every building, and each section has a flower garden in front of it—jasmine, rose, daisy, chrysanthemum. It is beautiful, not as grand as our palaces, but not so backward as I had imagined.

We finally come to a stop at a large quadrangle. The smell of flowers and sycamore trees mixes with the odors of poorer humanity at a distance. Our towns are clean; they have toilets. These barbarians have no belief in the body's cleanliness!

Iben-Har asks us to wait.

After several minutes, the Prince pokes his head out of his litter. "What is the wait?" he asks, irritated. His pudgy face glistens with sweat.

"I do not know, Your Majesty," I reply, and I too bristle at this disrespect shown by the Asiatics.

There is some commotion, and suddenly, many well-armed soldiers jog into the quadrangle. They take positions on both our sides. Iben-Har returns and whispers to me to ask the Prince to dismount from the litter. I hurry to the Prince and request that he dismount and prepare to be greeted. He gets down, and I stand behind him.

Iben-Har then announces loudly, "King Khamudi, Lord of Upper and Lower Egypt, Son of Ba'al, Blessed of Amun, Greatest of the Virile, and Warrior of Warriors."

The King of the Asiatics is a slight man. He is the same height as the Prince, but he is thin and wiry. He moves energetically toward us. He wears bronze chest armor. A bright white gown falls below the knees, tied with a gold-studded belt. His head is shaved, and he wears a false beard—black and curled, hiding specks of gray and white hair underneath. He has a thick black-dyed mustache, and his eyebrows are accentuated with black kohl. His men kneel as he moves along the line. The protocol allows the highest-ranked official from our side to remain standing to greet the king, but the rest must kneel—so I get down and wait for the King to meet the Prince. Interpreters find their places by the royals.

"We welcome you to our glorious land, Prince Nimmuruk," Khamudi says, holding out his hands.

"I am honored by your greeting, King Khamudi," says Nimmuruk. "And I am humbled by your strength and wisdom."

The two men embrace. I wonder how Nimmuruk's ample belly would feel against the warm bronze of Khamudi's armor. I have been told that Khamudi's embrace is reserved only for exceptional circumstances. This is a good start.

I rise to my feet, but the King does not acknowledge me.

They lead our delegation through beautiful colonnaded corridors. The walls are an orange hue. The King stops at one point and whispers to us, "You must see this."

We turn into a small adjacent chamber that is devoid of any furniture or ornamentation and bend to get through a low door. But I am astonished when I rise on the other side—the walls of this room are painted in vibrant colors and spectacular imagery reminiscent of what we have in our palaces! There are deer, lions, dolphins, floral patterns, antelopes, bull dancers, priestesses, dancing girls, bull acrobats, olive trees, and boats—all in blue, red, ochre, orange, and green.

*Beautiful! So far away from home, and yet it is as if I am at home.*

"We have always enjoyed your artists and dancers, Prince Nimmuruk. Their skills surpass what we see in this land. We have people in this court who once lived in your lands," he says as the Prince looks around. I surreptitiously brush my palms over the paintings.

They lead us to a waiting room to rest. Slaves serve clay pots of cooled water infused with honey, and we eat a fulfilling meal of lentils with garlic paste, fish, dates, honey, and bread with beer. Iben-Har informs us we will have an audience with the king after we rest. The Prince and I have spoken at length about our strategy for these discussions, and we have no inkling of how the king would open the conversation.

"He seems friendly and appreciative of our visit, Your Highness," I say. The Prince is not convinced.

"You know little of the high-born, Teber," he smiles, "the greetings mean little. He sees us as weaklings here to trade. His behavior is not one of trust. It feels as if he is humoring us."

I choose not to question him. The food is refreshing and brings energy to the body and clarity to the mind. The Prince is taken to a special room reserved for royals while we rest in the painted room. When I am finally awakened, the sun has set, and I can hear chants from the temples. We wipe our faces to rid ourselves of the effects of deep slumber and arrange our garments to prepare for the audience with the King in his court. Iben-Har arrives and leads us to the throne room.

The throne room is modest. Khamudi sits on a granite throne. There are no magical lighting lamps, and no beautiful priestesses. He is surrounded by rough-looking men in long gowns. Iben-Har stands three positions to the right of his king. Slaves bring a comfortable seat for the Prince to sit opposite the King, but without a supporting platform, the Prince is forced to look up at the ruler of the Asiatics.

*Intentional.*

At first, there is much talk of trade and taxes. Khamudi complains about how our people do not assimilate and how our food pales compared to theirs. He also grumbles about the prices of our wine, vases, and copper. Finally, after the banter, we settle into business.

"So, what is it you seek, Prince Nimmuruk? It appears you care little to speak about trade," Khamudi says, now serious. His piercing eyes focus on the Prince. He twirls his false beard.

"An alliance, King Khamudi. My father seeks to assist you against the Pharaoh."

I am surprised by the Prince's directness. Khamudi leans back and looks at his men as if he has misheard the Prince's words. "Alliance? For what do we need an alliance, Prince Nimmuruk?"

The Prince pauses. I hope he can navigate these treacherous waters of diplomacy deftly.

"You are losing to the Pharaoh," says Nimmuruk. His voice rings in the hollow chambers of the throne room. Khamudi does not react for a moment; then he turns toward Iben-Har and points at him without saying a word.

Iben-Har almost jumps from his seat and prostrates before the king. "I have had no role in this statement, Your Majesty!" he wails.

Khamudi's face tightens with anger. He flicks his finger for Iben-Har to rise and turns to the Prince. "What makes you say so, Prince Nimmuruk?"

"We have our messengers who report the happenings, Your Majesty," says Nimmuruk, his voice at a higher pitch. He is already stressed by the encounter.

"Do you have spies in our kingdom?" Khamudi asks, his voice low and raspy—accusatory. It has lost all its warmth.

"Do not accuse me—" the Prince starts, and I decide it is time to intervene. Nimmuruk's ego can kill any hopes of discussion.

"We have no spies, Your Majesty, but it is in our interest to know what happens in this great kingdom and to understand the impact on our trade."

Khamudi turns toward me. I bow to him.

"We are not losing," he says.

*But you are; you posturing idiot. You just do not want to admit it.*

"We bring an alliance for your consideration, King Khamudi—"

"Who are you?"

"I am a trade advisor and a commander of the Navy," I lie.

"You are too young."

"I have the confidence of the King and the Prince, Your Majesty," I respond.

"Continue," he says, finally.

"Our messengers say Pharaoh Ahmose gains strength, and we worry about the rise of imperial Egypt."

"Ahmose? The boy? Do you know what we did to his father?"

"No, Your Majesty."

"We took an ax to the old fool's head. We split it like a watermelon. He had to be carried off, bleeding his foul blood on our lands!" Khamudi exclaims, his hands chopping the air. His bangles shine in the light. His men join in a chorus of approval.

"Not just that. We hacked his son's shoulder and saw him run away. He will die soon as well."

I infer that Khamudi speaks of Kamose, Ahmose's brother. I was unaware of what had happened to him. Our spies had not reported on his brother's condition. I question the quality of our intelligence. "The tides of fate change, Your Majesty," I say. "We have men, material, and a powerful Navy that controls the seas."

Khamudi leans back on his throne. He is quiet as he sips his beer. Slaves offer us honey-infused water, and we decline.

The Prince signals for me to come to him. He leans and whispers in my ear, "When do we threaten him?" I almost laugh at the stupidity of that comment.

"Not yet, Your Majesty. Your silence is powerful and unnerves him," I claim, lying but sufficient to calm his ego and keep him from jeopardizing this mission. There is more silence.

Finally, Khamudi speaks. "What do you have in mind?"

*Finally!*

I take a few steps forward to be closer to the King. He leans forward to listen.

"We help you capture the Upper Kingdom. In return, you open major harbors by the sea to expand our trade into Egypt."

Khamudi smiles. He slaps his thigh and looks around at his council. "They say they will let their men bleed so we can grant them more access to our harbors," he declares loudly, and they break into laughter. Heat suffuses my cheeks.

Khamudi turns to me. "You take us for backwater idiots," he says, wagging his finger. "No respectable king would offer such a weak excuse."

The astute observation surprises me. The Prince, who held his tongue until now, erupts, "Do not speak of my father in such a manner, King Khamudi. The ruler of the Atalanni does not seek alliance without reason!"

"Well then, he should send an honest delegation and not think of us as swamp barbarians!" roars Khamudi. His raspy voice cracks, missing portions of his words as he screams. "We already have an alliance with the Kush, and I have never heard of a kingdom that offers the blood of its people in return for an expansion of trade."

Suddenly, the court erupts in recriminations, with each side accusing the other of treachery, disdain, disrespect, and stupidity. Khamudi calls us dancers, painters, and idiotic ambassadors. The Prince calls the Asiatics fools blind to reality and blowhards, and the taunts and yelling overtake any attempt at reason. I try in vain to calm everyone, but I feel like a cat chasing many mice at the same time. I realize they have clearly seen through the ruse, and nothing we say will convince them we seek an honorable alliance.

Though, of course, I know that our alliance is anything but honorable.

At one point, several courtiers jump into the arena, and we end up pushing and shoving each other. The crude behavior of these Asiatics is astonishing! One man opens his gown and masturbates in full view, taunting us. Remarkably, no one is stabbed or arrested, and I give Khamudi credit— he would not harm or imprison his visitors. I could not imagine such a scene in King Hannuruk's or even Minos' court. And Minos is a rogue.

Finally, the shouting dies down, and Khamudi settles back into his throne. An attendant strikes a bronze plate with a bell to bring order and silence. The King asks everyone if they need water or wine; the absurdity of the scene is confounding.

Khamudi finally speaks. "It is clear to me that you have other nefarious reasons for seeking an alliance. We have entertained you as guests, and yet you seek to deceive us."

I attempt to speak, but the King holds up his hand.

"We are not fooled so easily. Our warriors are strong, Prince of Atalanni. We cut off the hands of those who attack us!" he proclaims and gestures to a man beside him.

The man walks toward us.

He stops his advance and kneels.

He picks up a wedge of a stone block on the floor. Some blocks have grooves that allow one to remove the stone. He removes the block and gestures for me to come forward.

I lean into the hollow on the floor.

*Severed palms.*

Desiccated palms of grown men.

The bones jut through the dried, broken skin. It is revolting to see human remains in the room, but such is their custom.

"Those are the hands of unfortunate high-ranking fools of the Upper Kingdom who thought it fit to attack us. We can defend ourselves well, Prince Nimmuruk. There is nothing more to hear from you. You may stay here for the night, but you will leave tomorrow morning and return to your land," he says. "If your troops remain, we will kill them and hold you to ransom."

"You cannot threaten a Prince that way!" shouts Nimmuruk, his face red and sweat glistening on his skin.

Khamudi says nothing. Instead, he stares at Nimmuruk and smirks. "We have threatened Pharaohs for a hundred years, Prince Nimmuruk. I am now Pharaoh as well. You are nothing," he says. With that, Khamudi rises and storms out of the room, followed by his officials.

The Prince shakes in anger, but there is not much we can do. Deceit hides beneath the thin veil of our proposition. Khamudi has seen through the ruse, and we must now decide the next course of action. We spend the night with little chatter, and my mind is a cauldron of emotions. It remains unclear to me why Khamudi is so confident that we came in the guise of peace. Our first engagement with the Asiatics has failed spectacularly—and neither the Prince nor I have been able to salvage it.

In the morning, Iben-Har unceremoniously escorts us out of the gate, and Khamudi does not appear to bid us goodbye. The gates shut behind us, and a contingent of heavily armed Asiatics escorts us across the bridge. Khamudi's distrust is plain—his troops line the riverbank on either side. Iben-Har speaks little as we walk. I reckon he fears for his life because of this debacle.

Prince Nimmuruk rages on our way back and sulks in his tent as I think of our next move. I know I must bide my time—so I walk back to Iben-Har and tell him we need until noon to depart; the tents must be packed, soldiers prepared to move, and the ill must be tended to. After some argument, he allows us to delay departure but insists his men will remain where they are.

I return to the tent and approach the Prince. As much as I hate it, he has been designated commander of the forces, so I must consult him. I wonder how the news of this failure will be received back home. How Minos will try to capitalize on the Prince's ineptitude.

"What do we do next, Your Majesty?" I ask. The Prince's pudgy face is red; his eyes are puffy, and the stubble on his chin makes him look ill. He pulls a ceremonial thread from his hair and throws it to the ground, then takes a swig from a beer flask.

"How dare he treat us this way?" he says. "We have to teach him a lesson!"

I know I must tread carefully, but my ultimate loyalty is to my land and its glory, not to Prince Nimmuruk. "We are here to secure their cooperation so we can confront them in battle against the Pharaoh, Your Highness—not to waste our limited resources trying to destroy him."

"We have the skills and weaponry to lay them to waste and force the rest to follow our command."

"We do not have enough weaponry or men to lay them to waste. Besides, to destroy him would only strengthen the hands of the Pharaoh."

Nimmuruk shoots me an irritated look. "How so?"

"We may kill and destroy some here, Your Highness, but what we will leave behind is an insurgency. The Asiatics will turn on us for our actions, and the Egyptians, under their rule, will return to supporting the Pharaoh. Neither of these outcomes is in our interest and will only prolong our effort. We have formidable weapons and men, Your Highness, but we do not have enough of either."

Nimmuruk paces in the tent, having removed most of his garments. His back and chest are sweaty; a slave walks behind the Prince, fanning him.

"My father will be livid," he says. "We have to find a way."

"We will do as your father, His Majesty, commanded."

"What do you propose?" the Prince asks.

"I have an idea."

An idea that requires Iben-Har to listen to me.

# CHAPTER 19

## KALLISTU

Khaia's mind is preoccupied. Governor Minos has been impatient and continues to protest the order that he must defend Kaftu and supply the Atalanni troops in Egypt. His insistence on meeting her to influence the King's decision has become irritating.

But for now, Khaia has other pressing matters to attend to. She hurries through the labyrinthine corridors of the royal palace toward the Queen's quarters.

Khaia wipes her brow. It is hot inside; the westerly breeze has not cooled the palace enough. The Queen's quarters lie deep in the palace, one level below the ground, but with windows opening out of the cliffs onto the ocean. The views are spectacular, but the low roof creates a sensation that is at once beautiful yet claustrophobic.

Slaves fan her and the Queen, but with every pause, the heat envelops them in an instant like a woolen blanket in summer.

Khaia appraises the Queen, who sits on a comfortable blue cushion in front of her. Apsara looks back coolly. Aranare sits beside Apsara, fanning the Queen.

Khaia has asked for this audience. She tells the Queen that it is the Divine Council's responsibility to meet with the royals from time to time to convey messages from the divine and act as counsel if distress arises. They have met only once since the war delegation left for Egypt.

"I am here to inquire after your health, Queen Apsara," says Khaia. "And I thank you for granting me an audience."

Apsara smiles. The dimples enhance her face, and the blue-glass earring reflects the lamp and shines into Khaia's eyes.

"I thank you, sacred Khaia," she says. "Your visit is a breath of fresh air."

"You are the rulers and protectors of this land," says Khaia. "We have just embarked on a perilous path. Your health is of great concern to our gods and to me."

Apsara nods but says nothing. There are questions in her eyes, but her lips remain closed.

"May we speak in private?" Khaia asks, her eyes shifting toward Aranare, who hovers around the Queen like a protective mother. Apsara turns to her maid and gestures for her to leave the room.

"You are calm, Apsara," she says, dropping the formality of royalty. "But like rising mud below a quiet lake, I sense turbulence."

Apsara raises an eyebrow. "It is natural to feel stress when we embark on a course of war, and what you sense is nothing more."

"Call me Khaia, my Queen. Within the confines of this room and between us, I speak to you not as an Oracle but as another woman. We both shoulder great responsibilities."

Apsara nods. But her silence frustrates Khaia. She wonders if the Queen's demeanor is naturally reticent or if she distrusts Khaia's motives.

"I sense a great deal more than natural stress. When you and the King enter my dreams, you are on your bed, and there is always a dead olive tree between you."

Apsara looks up sharply.

*Finally.*

"I do not know what you mean," Apsara says. Her voice is cold. She adjusts the drapery around her neck and pulls it closer over her chest.

Khaia leans forward. "Your marital discord concerns us all."

Apsara blinks. Khaia sees that the Queen struggles to respond to this blatant intrusion into her marital concerns. Khaia continues, "Perhaps such matters are never brought up in front of the Mitanni rulers, my Queen. In kingdoms where the King has a vast harem of wives, like the Egyptians, it does not matter if one wife is in a well of distress. But we are neither Mitanni nor Egyptians."

"What are you saying, Khaia?" Apsara asks. Her body is tense.

"The Atalanni Kings have but one wife. Polygamy is not looked upon kindly by the gods, except where the Queen is no longer of sound mind or body," Khaia states.

"Are you implying I am not of sound mind or body?"

"I said no such thing, my Queen. But tongues wag, and rumors spread when there is no child after three summers of marriage."

Apsara's face reddens at Khaia's words. She grips a cup and struggles to respond. Khaia continues, "The Egyptians lay all blame at the king's feet if there is no child. But the common people of the Atalanni pin that responsibility on the queen."

"The King already has two sons. So why should it concern you or the people that I have no child of my own?"

Khaia appraises Apsara. This is not a woman who would collapse and cry. "One son is incapable of rule, and the other is out fighting a war," Khaia states. What she does not tell Apsara is that a messenger had left the capital just before her declaration of the gods' intent to the Supreme Council to meet Khamudi, the King of the Asiatics, to warn him not to believe any Atalanni delegation that may come through. She had considered the potential outcomes. Yet Khaia had not expected that Teber would be part of the party going to meet Khamudi, for she did not wish him danger; instead, she hoped that the skilled general would find his way out.

Apsara takes a sip. Her eyes fix on Khaia's from behind the rim of the cup. Then she says softly, "A war that you said was necessary."

Khaia leans back and scowls. She then straightens her back, making herself taller and more imposing, and jabs a finger at the Queen. "A war that the gods deemed necessary. I am a messenger. Do not question my intent, Your Highness."

Apsara bristles at the admonition.

"I do not know why you are here, except to find me at fault for something I—"

"I am here to convey the concerns of the Council, as we are also the guardians of the Kingdom's future. We are approaching dangerous times, and you have thus far failed in your duty as Queen," Khaia replies, her voice cold.

Apsara explodes. "What duty do you speak of? Does the King have no duties? The duty to treat his wife with kindness? The duty to perform on the marital bed? The duty to conduct ceremonies without swooning like a drunkard?"

Khaia appraises the Queen. Her nostrils flare in anger, and her face is red.

"He is King. Perhaps he treats you the way you claim, because of your actions. Perhaps he does not perform in the marital bed, for you do nothing to excite him. Perhaps he swoons during ceremonies because his Queen has nothing but disdain for him. The signs do not indicate your innocence," Khaia states slowly and deliberately.

"Then it matters not what I say, for you have no desire to believe me. Hannuruk will never produce an heir, dear Oracle, no matter who the woman is, for he can no longer produce the seed that gives life."

Khaia sighs. "You do not understand, Your Highness. It is not about whose fault it is, but that this coupling will place this empire at risk. And the Atalanni will not cast blame on the King's feet."

Apsara is quiet for a long time. Khaia feels a tinge of pity for the Queen but dismisses the thought. She thinks of her own sacrifices and actions in her rise to becoming the Oracle.

Khaia sees Apsara's tears reflect the soft yellow hues of the room lamps, and the Queen sniffles before she composes herself. "I can divorce the King and allow him to marry someone else."

Khaia laughs, but without mirth. "You are an innocent girl, or you have forgotten your vows. Atalanni queens cannot divorce the King. There is no such provision in our laws. Your wedding is for life—as long as you breathe, Your Highness. Even if the King dies."

Apsara shakes her head. "Then, I shall ask the King to divorce me."

"Please do not take me for a fool, Your Highness. You have surely asked him, and he has surely said no. He is still wedded to you, is he not? No Atalanni King has divorced his queen in the past fifteen generations. Once a King weds, his wife remains in that role until the end of her life. Do not forget that his first wife still lives."

Apsara pulls her knees to her chest and sobs. But Khaia makes no move to console her, for this is the intended direction. Finally, the Queen composes herself.

"Why can he not wed another woman to prove his masculinity, just as he wed me when he was still married?"

Khaia sighs as if responding to a child. "It is only allowed if there is a clear, demonstrable reason, or if the wife is no longer alive. You are young, beautiful, articulate."

"So, as long as I live, this land is in peril?"

Khaia stands and smoothes the creases of her garment. She straightens the curls of her hair and clasps her hands. "Some sacrifices are greater than the preservation of self, Your Highness," she says. Khaia then bows to the Queen and takes slow steps backward until she reaches the door. "And if pain is what you worry about, I have many ways to lessen its sharpness," she adds.

Apsara does not respond. Her eyes have lost their strength and brightness. She slumps against her cushion, her chest heaving. Khaia hopes the message is clear, and that the Queen possesses the strength to do what is necessary.

# CHAPTER 20

## LOWER EGYPT

Pharaoh Ahmose is concerned by the latest developments. He stands with Nebhekhufre and Wadjmose by the west bank of the Pelusiac branch of the Great River, about a day's march from Hutwaret.

The flags of his army flutter behind him; it is a windy day, and powerful gusts bring fine dust from the western deserts, coating the men, trees, and grass. The three men stand on the sandy bank, letting the cool water lap at their feet.

"The ambassador to Keftiu has not returned," Ahmose says.

"He has not, Your Majesty," Wadjmose replies. The General is in his battle gear, and the decorative bronze buttons on his leather corset reflect the sun, distracting the Pharaoh.

"Remove your corset, Wadjmose. It hurts my eye," Ahmose commands. Wadjmose hastily removes it and lays it by his feet.

"And the man who went to fetch the ambassador has not returned either?" Ahmose asks.

"He has not, Your Majesty."

"And you are certain that he departed for Keftiu?"

"Yes, Your Majesty. Our men saw him off at the northern harbor. Neither he nor any of his guards or boatmen have returned."

"How do we know they were not ambushed by the Asiatics at sea?"

"The Asiatics have no fleet to speak of and had no reason to ambush them, Your Majesty."

"Perhaps they were ambushed on land during their return?"

"We have had our lookouts stationed along the western paths, far away from the Asiatics' influence. No one has recorded any visitors from the sea."

Ahmose sighs. He does not like what he hears. He kneels down, washes his hands in the water, and wipes them on a cloth hanging from the belt of his kilt. He turns to the Vizier.

"What do you think, Nebhekhufre?"

The Vizier has aged with worry. His normally leathery face shows deep lines highlighted by the shadows of nearby trees. "I share Wadjmose's observations, Your Majesty. I dislike these developments. There were three other incidents which, when I recall them, now seem to lend credence to our worries."

Ahmose looks at the Vizier questioningly, and it seems that Wadjmose is surprised as well.

"What incidents?"

"Just a few days ago, we learned that on two separate occasions, trading boats were accosted by the Atalanni navy far from their land and forced to turn back. The crews were not killed but were warned not to venture further north toward their territory."

Ahmose stands with arms akimbo, feeling a tingling warning in his neck, as if a large mosquito buzzes close to his ear.

"Did they know it was a trading boat from us?"

Nebhekhufre shields his eyes from the sun. "It would be hard to miss, Your Majesty. Our boats have a distinct appearance. Our men have a distinct look. The signs of Egypt are unmistakable," he replies, with a hint of pride.

"Have our trading boats ever been turned back?"

"Never. We have no records of Atalanni hostility toward Egypt."

Pharaoh Ahmose paces along the rocky beach, sometimes kicking the stones into the water. He is both God and King, yet feels like a boy. He wishes he could sit here all day, throwing pebbles into the water, but he knows matters of far greater gravity demand attention. "What I know from my messages from our gods, and from observing my brother, is that conflicts between empires often begin, not always with armies, but with grain and cloth. Our men have not returned, our trading boats have been turned away, and all this in the same span of time. I do not like this," Ahmose states. "Wadjmose, you served my brother and father. What is your opinion?"

The General looks distressed. "You are the god of this land, Your Majesty. I may be a general, but your divine vision supersedes all my experience. I believe dark forces are at work among the Atalanni, and their intentions toward us are no longer pure."

Ahmose, deeply worried, trudges to the edge of the bank. He scoops up the greenish water and raises it to the sun, seeking blessings from Ra. His belly feels like a hollow pit of worry—a foreboding he cannot shake off.

Ahmose curses under his breath. Have the gods abandoned him? he wonders. The Hyk-Khase still squat on this land, and now another threat looms.

Just then, he hears a servant announce, "A runner comes with an important message, Your Majesty."

Ahmose turns. At a distance, a man comes running—he pants and hobbles, doing his best to cover the last few paces before reaching the Pharaoh. As he nears, Ahmose notices that the messenger's almost naked body is drenched in sweat, and his eyes have lost focus. He collapses a few feet away from the Pharaoh, near the ring of guards.

"Get him water and revive him," Ahmose orders. The guards hold the messenger until his breathing settles and he comes to his senses. He eagerly gulps the water and lets some dribble on his chest. He sees the Pharaoh himself in front and prostrates before his living god; Ahmose receives his obeisance. Finally, the messenger stands up, looks at the Pharaoh, and rubs his hands nervously.

"Speak," says Ahmose.

"The Asiatics, Your Majesty. The Asiatics..." he stutters.

"What about the Asiatics?"

"They have just hosted a military delegation from the Atalanni with their prince and their general."

# CHAPTER 21
## HUTWARET

We wait in the humid weather, sweat running down our backs. I sent Iben-Har back to the fortress with a simple message—tell your King to witness a demonstration of our power that could be turned against them if they did not cooperate. Iben-Har demanded that our troops retreat half a mile and that only I, along with a few of my demonstration personnel, would stay where we were. I refused to listen to Nimmuruk and commit to a foolhardy attack on Hutwaret. The Prince thinks a few magical weapons suffice to break a city's will, and his inexperience has already put us in jeopardy.

Men peek from the top of the fortress walls. Asiatic troops have left their stations and returned to the city. Now it is just us, a bridge over a river, and a formidable fortress behind which Khamudi plots.

"Just send us a few goats and pigs," I told Iben-Har, "and we would show what we had."

Our weapon-bearers stand behind me in a line—ten of them. In their hands, they hold the slingshots of god—*Afastis*—long bronze tubes, about three feet in length. I have seen *Afastis* tested on animals, and the effect is terrifying.

The gates of the fortress open slightly. A few Asiatic soldiers walk out, holding swords and axes, but they stay near the gate.

The gates grind and open further, and suddenly thirty to forty men in loincloths charge at us with swords and maces. Desperation and determination flicker on their faces. I realize I have little time before they charge the gap and reach us, and with my forces half a mile behind, there is no chance for us in hand-to-hand combat against so many men. It also dawns on me that Khamudi has decided to sacrifice men instead of goats.

The Egyptians near us.

I can see the whites of their eyes—only fear and panic remains.

"Go back! Back!" I shout, gesturing frantically at them. But they ignore my warnings.

Condemned men.

Threatened with something I do not know.

I pity them, but I have no choice.

I turn to my men and scream, "Burn them when they near!"

My men use the *Afastis* when the Egyptians are within sixty or seventy feet. I put my fingers in my ears. First, there is a series of clicks, all within the blink of an eye.

Then there is a synchrony of thunderclaps and yellow flames erupting from the barrels.

The heads and chests of many of the charging men explode as if by magic, and chunks of skull, brain, ribs, and spine fly and splatter on others. The remaining men freeze in terror.

I have learned a few Egyptian words, sufficient for greetings, goodbyes, and a few warnings—helpful during our journeys.

I gesture and shout, "Go back! Go back!"

They hesitate, looking back at the fortress, squinting. I understand why these men rush on this suicidal mission— there are children and women at the edge of the walls. Shouting from the ramparts reaches my ears, and I imagine it to be orders for the men to continue.

They turn toward us again and charge, screaming frantically, waving their weapons, and I have no choice but to order another discharge of the *Afastis*. The firing continues until I believe every man is dead—their bodies splattered on the dust. I taste and spit blood and pieces of their flesh.

But one man remains alive.

He looks back, hoping the men on the walls are satisfied with the carnage.

He runs back, arms raised. Imploring.

In that moment, I hear a high-pitched scream of a woman, and a child tumbles down the walls, dropping onto the hard ground like a stone. The man wails loudly but continues to rush toward the gates. He desperately clings to the motionless body and screams at the people above, cursing them. A soldier comes behind the man and stabs him. He crumbles forward. I hear more commotion on the walls as a woman comes flying down.

*The wife?*

The family is dead. There is silence. No one else comes through the gates, and they shut again. Someone gestures from the top of the wall, indicating that we must wait. Finally, the gates open again, and Iben-Har appears. He approaches me and states he wishes to talk to the Prince. We finally walk back to our main contingent. The Prince waits impatiently and jumps to his feet as we enter his tent.

"So, what is the verdict? Does your King wish to ally with us or not?" he asks.

Iben-Har remains cool. "King Khamudi wishes to clarify some questions, Your Majesty."

"What does he need to know?"

"Your bolts of fire. What use is having just ten?"

I panic at the question. Before I can open my mouth, the Prince opines, "We have two hundred and fifty more and another five hundred at Kaftu!" he declares triumphantly.

*Idiot!*

"And thousands more in production," I say, but Iben-Har smirks. It is too late to undo the damage.

"How many troops do you have here, and how many on your island?"

"We have—"

I cut the Prince off. "Our contingent here may be small, Iben-Har, but it is well-trained. And we have over forty thousand waiting for orders to sail."

Iben-Har appraises me, but then turns to the Prince. This is a clever man. He knows he can speak to our foolish Prince and get what he needs. I try again. I curse our inability to converse in our tongue because Iben-Har is conversant with it.

"Iben-Har, the Prince is busy with matters of greater import. It is I you should speak to regarding military arrangements and logistics."

Nimmuruk shoots an angry glance at me, puffing up his chest. "I am the commander. Teber will speak when he is spoken to. What else do you wish to know?"

I see Iben-Har suppressing laughter. This is what happens when you send a man untested in diplomacy, his eyes seem to say. Nimmuruk has forgotten every lesson Rishwa imparted to him, and Minos tried to drill into his head—never reveal your true strength, never disclose our secrets, and always project your strength to be far greater than it is.

And yet here we are.

"Your fire bolts are very impressive. You are blessed by your gods, and your men are blessed by your magnificent leadership, Prince Nimmuruk. Do you have other similar weapons that we may use against the Egyptians?"

I watch in horror as Nimmuruk continues to display his immaturity. "We have fifty boat-mounted missiles that can set fire to nearby towns, and hundreds of clay pots of poisonous liquid that can waft in the air and strike men with sickness. Nothing you have ever seen, Iben-Har. Even your minds would not be able to conjure what we possess."

Iben-Har gently kneads his beard. His sly eyes dart between the Prince and me, and only a fool would not notice the glee in them—a fool like Nimmuruk.

"That is most impressive, Prince Nimmuruk," Iben-Har says. "No doubt it will strike fear into your enemies' hearts! King Khamudi has a proposal."

"King Khamudi should be grateful for our presence. Without us, you will soon—"

Iben-Har cuts the Prince mid-sentence. "King Khamudi will collaborate if you teach us how to build your god-gifted weaponry."

We are speechless.

"Those weapons are gifts from our gods to us. Not for us to reveal the secrets to you Asiatics!" Nimmuruk shouts indignantly.

"You speak of us as if we are barbarians! Yet here you are, begging for our help for whatever nefarious designs you have!" Iben-Har retorts.

I watch quietly and let them argue. There is not much hope here.

Nimmuruk berates Iben-Har. "It is you who act like uncouth bastards, shaking your penis in our faces while arguing. What cultured civilization does that?"

"So says the Prince who wishes to be carried off in a hearse because he eats too much!"

Nimmuruk and Iben-Har hurl insults at each other. I hastily intervene and pull them apart before anything worse occurs. The Prince's chest and his prosperous belly heave. Iben-Har collects himself.

"Your Highness. General Teber," he says coldly, "We have been warned that you are here not with good intentions but with greater designs. You are fortunate that the King has allowed you to leave alive. You clearly have no intention of collaborating, for you have turned down our very fair offer—share your knowledge in return for the blood we will shed alongside you."

*Someone had warned the Asiatics?*

Nimmuruk composes himself. "We will get what we seek, with or without cooperation."

"And so it shall be, Your Highness," Iben-Har replies, unyielding.

It dawns on me that someone had compromised our entire mission from the beginning, and we had no hope even before we stepped into Khamudi's court.

But why?

The only reason Khamudi left us alive could be that somewhere in his reptilian mind, he thinks attacking us would bring great harm to him, given his already precarious position. What his strategy against the Pharaoh is, I do not know.

But for now, we must retreat.

"Does your King guarantee our safety?" I ask.

"He guarantees nothing, General Teber. But if we have no agreement, he promises he will cause no harm on your way back. However, if you face other difficulties, you are on your own."

I am relieved. The villagers pose no alarm, and the only real danger comes from the large, ungodly aggressive hippopotami that roam the lands.

We stand in silence, contemplating what to do next, but I know there is nothing here for us. Without Khamudi's cooperation, we must find a different tactic against Pharaoh Ahmose. Perhaps we should destroy Ahmose, even if it means a significant loss of men on our side, and then turn on the Asiatics, eradicating them from this land. But any such strategy requires discussion with the King himself, for the Prince has proved utterly incompetent.

Iben-Har looks at us shrewdly, and a smile passes over his lips.

"You may have your magical weapons, Prince, but we have men—many men who are willing to die. You will run out of your weapons long before we run out of men. Please remember that."

I bristle at his condescending tone, but I know he is right.

He pauses for our response, but both of us say nothing. Iben-Har then wags his finger at me. "King Khamudi has one last thing to say: if you return and dare to challenge us again, we will kill you all, cut off your hands, and send your palms in baskets to your King. Stay away, and never threaten us again."

With that, Iben-Har rubs his hairless chest and walks out, leaving a fuming Prince who now turns to me.

"My father will be livid!" he screams, spittle flying, squealing like a girl chased by rats.

"Your Highness—"

"You were supposed to make this alliance happen. You were supposed to counsel me as the general," he says, suddenly laying the blame at my feet. I am tempted to point out to the Prince that it would not have mattered what we did, for we were compromised before we even set foot in the Asiatics' court. But this is not a man I can reason with.

"The Asiatics are untrustworthy, Your Highness. You saw that with your own eyes. You tried, but how can you reason with uncouth barbarians who put severed palms inside their royal chambers?"

Nimmuruk splutters and shouts some more, but there is nothing to debate as we are at risk if we do not leave. I finally calm him down. We decide to leave before sunset and camp several miles north of our current location. We hope that we will not be ambushed as we sleep.

We march until the sun finally vanishes beneath the great ledge at the far west, and I order the setting of camp and the establishment of a perimeter. We stay far away from the riverbanks. I place night sentries all along the perimeter and send men further out in a circle, hiding in the bushes and lying low, vigilant for any danger during the night.

But the night is quiet. The sounds of Egypt's nocturnal creatures awaken me from time to time, yet nothing untoward occurs. My mind eases—it seems Khamudi has kept his word and refrained from attacking us, though danger still lurks until we depart the shores of Egypt.

In the morning, we wake early as the sun rises, and we pray. The power of the gods is such that no matter how far we journey from our land, the sun appears the same, bestowing the same heat and rising and setting as it always does. I order the captains to assemble and prepare to march.

It takes an hour before we are ready. We trudge north again through the muddy fields and the low-lying hills on either side. I detest such terrain, as it can easily conceal the enemy and increase the danger of ambush. Thus, I send two scouts on either side of the marching column to walk in parallel along the hilly grasslands beside us.

We decide to rest and eat when we approach noon. Just then, I hear some commotion.

One scout is screaming something and flailing his arms from the higher ground to the right behind me. I cannot hear him, but it seems some troops behind me understand.

Suddenly, an arrow flashes behind the scout.

The tip rips through his back and emerges in front. The man collapses in a heap.

That is when I hear someone scream behind me.

"Pharaoh's forces behind the hills!"

# CHAPTER 22

## LOWER EGYPT

Pharaoh Ahmose watches as the arrow streaks through the sky like a silver bird and strikes the Atalanni scout. He grips his chariot while the charioteer steadies the horses. Ahmose remains amazed by the agility and power of the horse and chariot—a capability that Wadjmose has learned from the Asiatics and brought to Egypt. The horses are magnificent beasts, and the Egyptians have much to learn about taming and utilizing them. So far, only the Pharaoh, his general, and the accompanying vizier ride in chariots. Ahmose believes that, in the not-too-distant future, entire armies may consist of horsemen and their chariots. Wadjmose never tires of stating that the horses are key to the glory of the Egyptian empire.

"Formation!" Wadjmose thunders. Ahmose feels pride for his general—loyal and skilled. It is unfortunate that Wadjmose is childless, for his children would surely bring glory to Egypt. Wadjmose swings his chariot, and the force of six hundred men forms an arc that resembles an open jaw as it moves and angles toward the edge of the low-lying hill behind which the Atalanni walk. This force is a fraction of the army that still waits behind near Hutwaret. The Atalanni know they are under attack.

Ahmose worries about the soldiers' skill—these are not the best, for the messenger was clear that the Atalanni force was small. But Ahmose hopes the losses will not be too great.

It is essential to capture the senior men among the Atalanni and understand their motivations and reasons for conflict.

Twenty horn bearers in the front sound the bugles of battle, and the soldiers trot on the soft, muddy ground. Ahmose's chest swells with pride. The archers are in the front line, prepared to shower the enemy. Lancers, spearmen, and swordsmen are behind and at their sides. The Pharaoh himself is in the center, flanked by the general and his senior men. Vizier Nebhekhufre is on the far left.

As the wide jaw turns, the enemy forces come into view.

They are all on foot. Their soldiers have formed a tight formation, and all hold bronze shields and spears. A few of them in the front wear strange masks and hold shiny pipe-like contraptions in their hands.

There is a tall man in the center, adorned in traditional Atalanni garb and holding a long spear.

Ahmose wonders whether he should parley with them to understand their intentions, but a powerful rage envelops him.

The Atalanni were supposed to be trading partners.

And yet here they were, undermining his authority, attempting to align with the wretched Asiatics, and plotting to take over Egypt.

There is nothing to discuss.

He turns to Wadjmose and nods.

Wadjmose turns to his men and raises his hand.

A great shout arises from the multitude, and the archers let loose their arrows. The bolts slice through the sky and descend upon the enemy.

But the Atalanni seem well prepared. They hunch under their shields and interlock them so that the arrows inflict minor damage. Ahmose is impressed. These mysterious people were not known to be warriors on the land.

Can dancers with shields truly fight?

Within minutes, the curving Egyptian force has the Atalanni men at the center of a wide arc. Ahmose charges the front lines ahead of his running men, and Wadjmose swerves to the side. There is great clamoring. Mud and dust kick up beneath thousands of feet. The Atalanni men are well prepared and armored. Their hair is styled in buns, and their torsos are protected by leather and bronze plates.

The chariot angles toward a cluster of Atalanni men engaged in a tight formation. The Pharaoh's elite bodyguard surrounds him as he disembarks from the wobbling chariot—still not a fine fighting machine—and together they draw their swords against the enemy. A great shout rises as the group engages the Atalanni.

The fighting is swift and vicious.

The Pharaoh's elite force hacks away at the Atalanni men, who, while impressive in their demeanor and physical appearance, are not the best-trained soldiers. Ahmose himself strikes a man and hacks away at his shoulder. Heads and limbs roll onto the wet ground, now saturated with blood, and the air is thick with the smell of bodily fluids as the wind carries sounds of despair and fear. It is clear to the Pharaoh that they are gaining ground—they are greater in number, and their arc is tightening around the Atalanni.

He pauses as his men form a protective ring, and Ahmose gets back on his chariot to survey the scene. Men spar in dense pockets. He spots the Atalanni general not too far away, fighting valiantly and dropping his enemies. The Atalanni general must be captured, the Pharaoh thinks. But just as he is about to issue orders to make a concerted effort to kill the Atalanni soldiers but capture their general, a great sound of terror emanates from the rear. It is the sound of his own men. Ahmose orders his charioteer to move to a location where they see smoke.

He is astonished as they near the location.

Heaps of his men lie dead, many with their faces, chests, and torsos blown off, and some with their hair still burning. Others roll on the ground, screaming as their intestines spill out. In the distance, there is a row of Atalanni men holding the bronze pipes he had seen before. Suddenly, flames erupt from the ends of those pipes, producing great thunderous claps, and several more Egyptian officers, some standing near the Pharaoh, collapse as their flesh explodes and burns. Ahmose panics. The Atalanni soldiers begin to regroup behind the men holding their magical weaponry. Ahmose screams for his men to retreat, and just then, there is another clap, and the Pharaoh feels a streak of heat near his ear as if an invisible bolt of lightning charges the air.

The charioteer's head explodes, showering a mess of brain, blood, and skull across the Pharaoh's face and body. Ahmose stumbles back from the chariot and falls to the ground, terror-stricken.

Someone is shouting his name.

Hands drag him to safety.

There is a din and the sounding of retreat horns. Ahmose thinks he hears Wadjmose, but his ears ring like great temple bells, and images blur as he struggles to make sense. He stumbles back to his feet and sees Wadjmose holding Nebhekhufre in his arms. The old vizier is bleeding profusely, and it appears half his face is missing.

There is a loud impact on the ground beside him, and something hard strikes Ahmose on the head.

Then there is darkness.

# CHAPTER 23

## LOWER EGYPT

We jog from the battlefield as quickly as possible, trying to distance ourselves from the Egyptian troops who have retreated and are now just raising dust in the distance. The Prince is safe—he has been protected at the center. I curse myself. The Egyptians caught us by surprise. I had no time to prepare the *Daivoshaktis*, and by the time we loaded the weapons with the fire powders, we had already lost many men and were in danger of annihilation.

My heart thunders in my chest. It was so close! To see the enemy appear suddenly and cover the gap was terrifying and a learning experience. We should never have been caught unprepared again in hostile territory!

I had seen the Pharaoh clearly before the chariot turned away.

It was true what they said.

Ahmose is still a boy.

He was dressed like a king, and he rode a chariot.

But he is a boy. The crown and the light armor did little to augment the Pharaoh's teenage features. Ahmose is slight in stature; his skin shines in youthful bronze. He has not shirked from his duty to lead his people. Pharaoh Ahmose is no Hannuruk—our King is surely drunk and brooding somewhere.

Ahmose had escaped. We captured thirteen Egyptian soldiers and forced them to march along. I plan to question them and learn as much as possible about the Pharaoh's forces and intentions.

All these developments make me nervous.

Where were our gods?

Why had they forsaken us?

What was their wish?

How did the Asiatics know of our intent?

And now—

How did the Egyptians know where we were?

Did Khamudi decide to do his dirty work through the Pharaoh's forces by leaking news of their arrival?

We travel without a break for hours until nightfall. I decide it is time to rest the troops and confer with the Prince. There has been an unusual silence from Nimmuruk's camp—no orders and no summons.

We set up camp, and I order an extensive perimeter. We take stock of our situation—more than a hundred are missing: dead, captured, or fallen during the march. It is a devastating blow, but it could have been far worse. Many are wounded and barely surviving.

I finally enter Prince Nimmuruk's tent.

The Prince lies under a blanket. He is quiet, and his face bears a deathly pallor. I worry the Prince is mortally injured, but a quick inspection shows that Nimmuruk is in shock or is still too terrified to speak. I spend the next few minutes calling the Prince's name, holding his hand, and finally bringing him back to his senses. Nimmuruk gasps a few times and sits up, shaking and clearing the cobwebs from his mind.

"What happened to the Egyptians?" he asks weakly as he reaches for a cup of water.

"They ran away, Your Highness. We instilled great terror in them," I say, feeling both pity for the Prince and disdain for this weakling.

"They almost—" Nimmuruk says and chokes. I allow the Prince to gather his faculties. Nimmuruk has never been on the battlefield, and it is puzzling that the gods hinted to the Oracle that the King should nominate the Prince for this sensitive mission. Whatever the case, this entire mission has been a disaster. I know the Prince has much to answer upon his return.

So do I.

I change the subject.

"We have captured some of the Egyptians. There is much to learn."

Suddenly, Nimmuruk's eyes light up. This is great news for the Prince—the chance to parade the prisoners and make claims of valor.

"Where are they?"

"They are being held outside."

"I want to speak to them," he says, standing up.

"Do you not want us to prepare them for questioning? This is not something you should concern yourself with, Your Majesty. We will interrogate them."

I am concerned about what Nimmuruk might do. Besides, there is another problem in talking to the Egyptians—the Atalanni contingent has no translators, as the two who came with us are missing. It is too late and too risky to fetch a translator; the only other Atalanni and Egyptian translators are in Khamudi's palace.

I order my officers to bring the prisoners to open ground as the sun slowly sinks beneath the western ledge. The sky is a band of orange and blue as the guards bring the prisoners before us. Each man is tied to the others by a rope around the neck. They look tired, beaten, and many bear marks of blades and fresh wounds. But each man looks defiant, their dark eyes reflecting the campfire around which they are made to assemble.

"Does anyone know our language?" a lieutenant shouts at the group in Atalanni.

No one answers.

I know just a few words—enough to facilitate the most basic communication.

"Understand us?" I ask in Egyptian. I hope my voice is gentle.

There is some murmuring. Finally, one man in the lineup shakes his head. "No."

It is not surprising. Most Egyptians have never seen the Atalanni in their lives, let alone learned the language. After more gesturing and attempts by multiple men to muster whatever Egyptian they know, not a single Egyptian is of any help, making it almost impossible to extract anything meaningful if they have no means of expressing the questions or interpreting the responses.

Nimmuruk grows increasingly angry. He walks toward one of the tied men and delivers a stinging slap. "Speak! Speak, you wretched bastards! Do you think you can kill the great Atalanni?"

Nimmuruk, the brave—brave only when confronting tied, beaten men.

"May I suggest something, Your Majesty?"

"What is it?"

"Let us take them with us. We have interpreters on Kaftu who can speak to them and help us learn more about the Pharaoh and his forces."

Nimmuruk does not respond for a minute as he ponders the situation. His sickly face and moist cheeks reflect the pale yellow of the fire in front of him, yet his eyes reflect little.

"Your Highness?"

"I am thinking, Teber," he says, pacing around. He walks away and confers with some of his adjutants—men loyal only to the Prince and not under my command. Nimmuruk then issues an order. A few soldiers accompany an adjutant and vanish into the darkness.

I worry.

Nimmuruk comes back to me. "I do not think it wise to take them back with us."

"Why not? We have lost many men and still have ample rations. We will have space on our boats."

"It is not about logistics. It is about how we will be perceived back home."

"I do not understand, Your Highness. We go with prisoners who can provide us information for our next mission."

"You are a fool!" Nimmuruk shouts, drenching my face. "These men saw what happened. Who is to say they will not speak of how we almost lost the battle and that we have gained nothing—"

"They know nothing about our mission with the Asiatics, Your Highness—"

"How do you know? What if there are spies in this group? We have no way of finding out. Imagine what my father will do if he learns of what happened here!" Nimmuruk shrieks. His fear is palpable; he thinks his father will turn on him and remove him from any future command.

Fear of shame. Of being the unworthy son. Perhaps even being cast away like his idiot half-brother. "They are just soldiers, Your Highness. They can provide us valuable details, and we can show how we defeated the Pharaoh in our first encounter and captured his troops."

"Well, if they are just soldiers, there is not much they will know, will they?" he asks shrewdly, a strange look in his eyes.

"What they know—"

"I have decided, Teber. We will teach them a lesson for attacking us."

I plead some more, but to no avail. Nimmuruk asks them to wait. After a while, the men who left the group return, and the adjutant nods to Nimmuruk. I turn in the direction they came from and, at a distance, see flames jutting from the ground.

Like from a pit.

Nimmuruk barks orders for the guards to bring the Egyptian captives, and they all walk toward the flames. I follow closely, dreading what might happen, but still hoping that the Prince wants to threaten the Egyptians again. We reach the location quickly—a fire rages in a crude pit filled with dried wood and leaves. Guards stand around the pit in a circle.

"Bring them to the front!" the adjutant yells. Guards drag the tied men closer to the pit.

I realize what this vicious idiot is planning to do.

"Your Highness, it is against our law to execute unarmed captives! Do not—"

"Be quiet, Teber!" Nimmuruk shouts. There is more argument. I tell him repeatedly that there is value in preserving the captives.

"I am warning you, Teber, this is an order. You are to follow it as my general," Nimmuruk hisses. The Prince's bodyguards advance menacingly.

I look at my men, but they are unsure what to do. After all, the Prince outranks their General. I back away, knowing this is not the time for conflict. The guards drag the captives toward the pit, and the Egyptians, realizing what might happen, begin to resist and shout. They are frantic. Some try to run, dragging the others tied to the same rope around their necks. Some fall, causing others to collapse or kneel.

There is much shouting and imploring. One man prostrates himself and grabs onto the feet of his guards, screaming. They kick his face.

I realize the Prince is excited by what he sees. Nimmuruk shouts at the men. "Yes, cry, you bastards! This is what happens when you attack us. Push them!"

The guards club the lying men. They lift the fallen and push the line. Three guards hold the rope in front of the leading captive and drag it like men pulling an unwilling bull. Eventually, the captive line comes parallel to the pit.

Amidst great cries, the guards shove them all into the fire.

The Egyptians tumble one after the other into the flames, flailing and shouting like pigs being slaughtered.

I cannot look. There are heart-rending cries as they burn. The acrid smell of their charred flesh rises with the smoke. A mass of moving and rolling figures fill the bright yellow flames. Some guards laugh and mock. The Prince exhorts the men to throw more wood and leaves into the conflagration.

It takes minutes for the screams to die.

What we witness disturbs me and some men. My training has taught me not to harm unarmed captives, but I have realized that this intent of war brings out the worst in our men.

And I realize what kind of man Nimmuruk is.

Once the din settles, I look at what we have perpetrated on the men who followed their Pharaoh's orders: charred flesh and bones of those who died without valor.

"That will teach them a lesson," Nimmuruk announces loudly. A soldier advances to the edge of the pit and urinates into it, and a few others join in the merriment. The Prince is gleeful. His fearful demeanor has vanished and is replaced by the confident strides of one who has accomplished much.

"What a worthless swine," I swear under my breath, and Bansabira nods in agreement. Depressed, we walk back to our tent. I hope that the rest of the journey will proceed uneventfully.

For the next three days, the force moves north carefully and deliberately, watching for either the Pharaoh's troops or the Asiatics. But we eventually arrive at our departure point, and the boats, hidden in the swamps, remain intact.

But then the augurs and forecasters tell us we must wait for the right winds. In that tense atmosphere, with the Prince and I on barely speaking terms, yet possessing a mutual understanding of what we will convey to the King, we wait.

I wonder what might be happening at home.

About Apsara.

# CHAPTER 24

## KALLISTU

Khaia waits for Minos in her official chamber—a cavernous hollow by the cliff near her living quarters. The room is spartan, specifically designed to echo voices and amplify a sense of serenity and piety. There is only one chair—a bamboo and silver-studded design—and Khaia sits on it. All others must stand or seat themselves on the cold marble floor. The walls are stark, with no paintings or script. Servants fan the Oracle, who wears sheer drapery and no other ornamentation on her body.

Khaia anticipates this will be an unpleasant conversation. Minos is hot-headed, and he is insistent on making his case to her, using their physical intimacy to gain access to her mind.

What a stupid thing to have done!

But it is too late now. Minos is clever; he knows that to influence the temperamental King, he must go through the Oracle.

She hears footsteps in the corridor beyond the door. Every sound echoes.

Khaia signals her guards to stay alert but hidden in the secret chambers along the walls.

Minos charges into the room, taking confident strides like a man sure of the outcome. Two men accompany him— Phaistos, a slim, eagle-eyed commander of Minos' security, and the other's name is unknown. He is a large man who acts as the Governor's bodyguard.

Minos's loud voice booms, "Respects to you, Oracle!"

He kneels, but his face is angled up, and his eyes twinkle mischievously. He is a handsome yet dangerous man. Khaia feels something stir within her but suppresses her emotions.

"Rise, Governor."

"I am surprised you wish to meet me in your official chamber," he says, grinning.

*Idiot!*

"Matters of immense importance are addressed here, not at the temple or the King's throne room," Khaia says, deflecting the conversation. Phaistos' eyes shine with a strange energy.

*What does the brute know?*

"We must speak in private."

Khaia sighs. She dismisses the maids and instructs Minos' men to leave as well.

They hesitate.

Minos gruffly tells them to get out.

The chamber goes quiet. There are only the sounds of two breathing souls. Khaia's guards are hidden deeper and are invisible. Minos gets up and tries to get closer to Khaia. She signals him to maintain his distance.

"State your business," she says coldly. Minos steps back, uncharacteristically, but it seems he realizes this is not like any other day.

"We must speak," he says, folding his massive arms against his chest. On this day, he wears a deep purple waist cloth that comes down to his knees. It is held by a shiny silver band. Otherwise, he is bare, his hirsute chest glistening with oil and sweat.

"I know what you want to discuss," she says.

"Well, then you make no effort to support me!"

"The King has decided, Minos. And I have said this before—we need you as our defense. We cannot have you running around in Egypt."

"You must hear me, Khaia. You know I deserve greater glory than being a transporter and a waiter."

"What is it you really want? Do you think fighting there will somehow make you King of Egypt?"

Minos eyes Khaia shrewdly. "You are clever. But if I am King, then you can be my Queen," he says, dramatically kneeling and raising his hands toward her.

Khaia smiles at the theatrics.

"There is one King. And that is Hannuruk. You have a large island all for yourself. You are important to the King, though you test him at times. Why are you adamant about having him reverse his decision?"

"Because I must make a name for myself, too. Do you not see it? Do you not see my stature and ability? Why must I be confined? His idiot son will achieve nothing, and that young general will get himself killed without me."

"It was you who suggested we elevate him to the rank of general in the first place and had the King nominate him to lead the invasion, not I!" shouts Khaia.

"He is a capable boy, but he needs supervision. He requires someone who can show him how to fight in the theater of war."

"And you are that leader?"

"Yes, I am," retorts Minos. "Teber will be a good military man, but he is no strategist! He is too young. The boy is an idealist and a rule follower. That will not work for an invasion like this. And the Prince is a brainless pig in a royal crown."

Khaia ponders Minos' remarks. His disdain for the Prince is clear. Perhaps Minos sees himself in Teber but is envious that the young general is out facing the Pharaoh while Minos rules an island.

But none of that matters.

"The gods have made their determination. We must wage war, and we must do so carefully. You know that better than anyone here, and you understand the difficulties we face if we are ill-prepared. If every able warrior is out in the sands of Egypt, and we lose due to inadequate backup, we will lose our empire. And with that, Minos, your ambitions and our riches will vanish. Think about it!"

But Minos is impatient. It is in his mind, Khaia realizes, that this is his opportunity for glory. He angles to rule a greater land.

"I have thought long and hard. My place is among the soldiers. Hannuruk listens to you. And you will do this for me, for us, for this empire." His voice is resolute, and he stands like a statue. A gentle breeze wafts into the room, spreading the aroma of daffodils and orchids. Khaia hopes that the calming scent will quiet Minos.

"I will not speak to the King on your behalf. This is settled," she states, standing up, nervous and agitated. This conversation is not going as she hoped.

"That is ridiculous!" Minos shouts. His face is red, and his veins pulse. "I have every right to be in the battlefield, leading our men and bringing glory to the empire. I am not a woman who will sit in my house and watch!"

He paces around the spacious room. It is quite a sight. Minos has a habit of stopping from time to time and stomping his right foot on the ground—like a bull—before he walks again.

"Your rights are determined by the King and by my visions. Those are your rights. Do not claim authority where you have none," Khaia rebukes him.

Minos freezes. It is as if he is controlling the turbulence in his mind. A blood vessel pulsates on his temple. He tugs on his beard. Then he turns towards Khaia, bringing himself close to her.

Towering.

Then he grunts. His lips tremble, and his jowls shake—it is the sign of a man who can no longer control what he wishes to say. He bares his yellow, crooked teeth—a hungry wolf by his meal.

"Your vision?" Minos scoffs. He looks away as he smooths his unruly silver beard and absentmindedly adjusts his genitals. "Your vision is what you make. That is all. What makes you think I believe this Oracle nonsense? It is for the idiot King and the commoners to believe that gods whisper in your ear. The Divine Council is a bunch of scammers— intelligent scammers. Nothing more," he snarls. "And you can all suck my cock!"

Khaia gasps at the raw accusation. Her heart hammers against her chest as she ponders where this is going. Minos stares at her, smirking, unrepentant regarding his words. It is unprecedented that someone would question the Oracle or the Divine Council in such a way.

To question her authority.

Her purpose.

"Watch what you say, Governor. You are crossing all lines laid by our lawmakers and gods—"

"Lines? What lines do you speak of? When you allowed me to fuck you on your sacred bed and moaned my name? Or when you instigated a war on Egypt because you seek power through your subversive means?"

Khaia's cheeks feel hot as molten rock.

*The insolence of this man!*

"Shut up!" she says, just under her breath as she lifts her hand to strike. But Minos is as quick as he is big. With the ease of handling a child, he grabs Khaia's raised arm and spins her around as if she is nothing. He pulls her towards himself, pressing her back to his torso and enveloping her throat with his other hand. She can feel his hot, stinking breath on her neck and his erection against her lower back.

"You harbor grand ambitions, Khaia. What man spurned you to create this fire in your breasts?" he taunts.

"Why do I need a man to be ambitious, Governor? Can a woman not have her own thoughts?" Khaia responds icily.

"You will speak to the King," he whispers in her ear. "Your charade is over. You will speak to him. You will make your divine proclamation that you foresee foreboding and that I must enter the battle."

Khaia is quiet, terrified but letting her mind think what to do next. She breathes and exhales to calm herself.

"You will do as I say from today. Or your secrets will be revealed, and you will be cast away like the whore that you are," he says as he presses himself harder against her.

Khaia is no longer afraid. Minos still needs her.

"Let me go, Minos," she says. Her voice is a hoarse whisper.

He releases her and turns her towards him. "Do you understand?" he hisses. There is a maniacal glint in his large, bloodshot eyes.

"I understand. Do not do something foolish and jeopardize your chances. I will speak to the King," she says. He relaxes.

She continues, "But you must promise me that when you win the lands, you will make me the supreme Oracle of the Atalanni and Egypt. You need me. The people will listen to me. I am a powerful instrument."

Minos pushes his head back and laughs. "You complain about me, yet your ambition is no less!" he exclaims. He holds her by her waist and attempts to kiss her. She pushes him away in mock anger. "Not now, Minos," she says, smiling. "Your anger has parched my throat."

Khaia walks towards a simple rock-cut shelf. On it is a vase of fine wine and clay cups for drinking. She fills two cups and brings them to Minos.

"Let us drink to a heady future. I need to think about how to engage the King," says Khaia. Minos nods and drinks all the wine in one gulp, licking his lips. She brings him another, and he drinks that without pause.

Khaia shakes her head.

"If you are serious about this, then we must speak to the King in four days during lunch," she says. King Hannuruk maintains a very rigid schedule—if they do not meet him by then, he retires to fifteen days of seclusion, a ritual held by generations of kings.

"Of course. Why do you think I rushed here? I know he will retire to seclusion, and the more time we wait, the harder it will be for me to change his mind."

Khaia traces a finger on his chest. "Go back to your quarters, King Minos. It is not worth the risk for us to be seen here when we have a bright future ahead of us," she says, and he grins.

"Let us make it a lunch the King will never forget," she says, smiling.

# CHAPTER 25

## KALLISTU

Khaia has told the Governor that they must align on what they will tell the King at the upcoming lunch. Minos is eager; this is finally his chance to shine. He arrives at the Oracle's chamber at the appointed hour, where Khaia greets him officially. Minos maintains his decorum, knowing the importance of the day.

Together, they pray to the gods—all the *Daivos*—Fire, Water, Earth, and Sky. Khaia asks Minos to relax and project a calm demeanor. They discuss how to reflect each other's arguments to the King in order to convince him to change direction. Finally, just before they are about to leave, Khaia invites the Governor to partake in cups of wine—specially made for important occasions. They drink together, relaxed, allowing the gentle warmth and headiness of the drink to prepare them for the conversation ahead with the mercurial ruler.

They wait for the King's messenger to take them to the banquet hall. This time, it is for a small audience: the King, the Queen, the Oracle, the Governor, Prime Minister Rishwa, Phaistos—Minos' chief of security—and Uppiluliuma, Chief of the King's Guard. The dining hall is tastefully decorated; bright sunlight pours in from the vaulted ceiling, and the silver and gold vessels shine and glint. The dignitaries sit around the King, who is at the head of the table.

Hannuruk looks lucid today—not wobbling or blubbering.

Queen Apsara sits beside him, but Khaia notices a distinct lack of strength in her eyes.

*My words are making a mark,* she thinks.

Finally, after greetings and obeisance, the King turns to Khaia. "So the Governor has a specific topic on his mind. What else is there to discuss except preparation for war?"

Khaia glances at Minos, who is uncharacteristically nervous, and she smiles encouragingly. "There is always something to discuss regarding war, Your Majesty," she replies.

"When Minos is involved, it is never good news, right, Minos?" Hannuruk ribs Minos, and the audience laughs. Minos grins, but when he tries to laugh, some water spurts and dribbles over his beard. He wipes his face and forces a grin, looking annoyed by what has just transpired.

"The Governor is a colorful man," says Rishwa, devoid of malice. The Prime Minister assesses Khaia and raises his eyebrows, as if to ask, *What is it now?*

"We have debated war arrangements and responsibilities, Your Majesty, and Minos is rightly insistent that we be most prepared for the major battles ahead," Khaia states while eyeing Minos.

"Our success hinges on it," Minos adds, his voice raspy and labored. He takes a swig of wine, but Khaia hopes he does not overindulge.

"Of course. But we have already settled all matters of war preparation and accountability, have we not?" insists the King, tapping on the table.

"Yes, Your Majesty," Khaia acknowledges, "but war is a complex subject. Sometimes the gods send messages that direct our affairs."

Hannuruk pauses from taking the next bite of salted fish dipped in olive oil.

"What new messages do they send?"

Khaia hesitates. "Let me not disturb you from your next morsel, Your Majesty," she smiles. Hannuruk nods and takes his bite, savoring the food. They eat quietly until the King is ready. It is a sumptuous meal—salted fish, pomegranates, grapes, bread, honey cakes, lotus water, roasted lamb, land snail delicacies, and many types of dessert.

Khaia observes the sundials and calculates the time elapsed since they have arrived. Lunch is always slow with the King, but today it is warranted.

She takes stock of the room.

Rishwa is intent on his bread.

Apsara has her head down and has barely looked up at anyone, let alone pay attention to the conversation.

Phaistos watches everyone like a hawk.

The King's Guard stands dutifully.

Hannuruk dabs his chin with a fine cloth and picks another piece of fish.

But Minos—he is not the man he usually is.

There is no boisterous Minos.

There is no loud and angry Minos.

There is no clownish Minos.

The Governor is uncharacteristically quiet, and he sweats profusely. He wipes his face with a cloth and gestures to two servants to fan him.

His cheeks glisten, and his face looks unnaturally reddish.

Khaia thinks to herself that the conversation will soon get his heart racing—and it is crucial to get the large man's heart to race.

*Especially today.*

"May I continue, Your Majesty?"

"Yes, go on," Hannuruk says, waving to her. The group listens quietly, awaiting what the Oracle has to say this time. The King dismisses the attendants.

"Recent omens do not bode well, Your Majesty, and as the Oracle, it falls upon me to bring these signs," she states while fixing her gaze on the King.

He grunts. "Go on."

"There are persistent dreams—dreams that show a lion cub practicing its hunting skills, baring its teeth and extending its claws. But as it surveys the vast plains and the gazelles ahead, a larger, angrier male pounces upon it and breaks its neck."

There is sudden silence. Hannuruk fixes his piercing eyes on Khaia. Minos looks perplexed, but the Governor appears as though he might expel the contents of his stomach. A sheen of sweat covers his face, and he groans audibly.

"What does that mean?" the King asks.

"It means only one thing, Your Majesty," Khaia replies, her voice frosty and measured.

"And that thing is?" asks Rishwa, concern etching his face. Khaia reckons that the clever man already knows what comes next.

"As I told you all long ago, the cub represents the Prince—the brave prince who is far away in Egypt, on a mission to make the empire proud and bring glory to his father. The cub of a lion," Khaia explains, and Hannuruk puffs up his sagging chest in fatherly pride.

"But?" the King inquires.

"But the Prince is in danger. There is another lion, bigger, angrier, ambitious," she continues, her eyes slowly tracking toward Minos.

The Governor looks befuddled. His eyes are frantic, and he rises from his chair. "What are you saying—" he begins, but the King shouts at him to be quiet. Minos appears utterly confused, looking around desperately.

Khaia continues as everyone is transfixed by what is happening. "Governor Minos here seeks your throne, Your Majesty," Khaia states evenly, "but the gods told me this morning that they shall strike him to the ground."

Khaia stands and raises her arms as if praying to the powers above.

She then points to the Governor and shouts, "Traitor!"

Minos springs to his feet. "You fucking—" he starts, but his words stutter.

His muscular hands shake.

Copious quantities of saliva drool from his mouth.

He wobbles where he stands, and the large man crashes down on the banquet table as the horrified audience leaps up from their chairs.

No one moves.

The King, livid at what he has just heard, makes no attempt to help Minos.

"Leave him!" Hannuruk orders, and Phaistos, who lunged to assist his master, steps back.

Minos thrashes about on the table, rolling and falling to the floor, creating the heavy sound of a large bull collapsing on a sacrificial platform. Khaia watches as the scene unfolds before her.

Minos' face turns blue.

The Governor clutches at his throat and flops on the floor like a dying fish. He struggles to breathe, and hoarse sounds emanate like fingernails on a stone wall. Foam pours from Minos' mouth, his eyes now red like a demon owl's, and his eyelids fill with blood. The grunting and gasping for air continue for several minutes as his large body thrashes about on the pristine floor.

The Governor is strong.

His life clings to him like an obedient dog to its master, even as he kicks at it in anger. Even in his throes, his hands lash out to grab those around him. The gurgling and gasps abate, and the Governor's body shudders and shakes in its final desperate convulsions. The loose ceremonial garment rips away, leaving him shorn of any dignity. He urinates, and his bowels lose control.

Those around him step back from the stench.

Minos' frantic eyes open, and the bloody red orbs stare into Khaia's eyes. But his mouth forms sounds that no one can hear.

Finally, he expels a great gush of blood mixed with vomit, drenching himself and the floor in filth.

He shudders violently, and finally, the great governor of Kaftu, loved and feared, twitches and takes one last breath. His eyes roll up into his head, and his head flops lifelessly to the floor.

As the audience stands in silence, Khaia walks slowly to Minos' body and kneels before him as if in prayer. She leans close to the tortured, grimacing face and whispers, "The poison in your mind is weaker than the poison in my wine."

She feels a presence beside her head and turns to find Phaistos staring at her with his soulless eyes.

Minos receives a hasty, yet respectful, burial at sea with full honors. King Hannuruk determines, with Rishwa's advice, that it will do no one good to speak of Minos' deception during these times of war. After swearing everyone to secrecy, the news to the people is that the Governor, amidst heavy responsibilities and continuous effort, suffered great pain in his chest and became beloved of the gods. The messengers also convey to the citizens that the Oracle had received warnings of Minos' health and that the gods were pleased with his service and saw no danger with his passing.

In only fifteen days, the empire is calm again. Messengers are dispatched to Kaftu and all other islands, along with the local governors, to quell any unrest and speculation.

Minos is suddenly only a footnote in Atalanni's history, even if remembered in his homeland of Kaftu.

# CHAPTER 26
## KALLISTU

Our journey to Kaftu is mostly uneventful. The winds favor us, and the gods have blessed our return with no untoward surprises.

I wonder if the Atalanni gods hold power outside their dominion and if the gods of Egypt reign supreme in their land. I have made an uneasy peace with the Prince, for both of us stand to lose much, including our lives, if our stories do not portray the mission in a kind light.

The Prince acknowledges that I have saved him more than once during this journey and that I have been loyal despite his misgivings. I recognize that I am alive after the meeting with the Asiatics because of the presence of royalty. We share disdain for each other, but I know we cling to one another for self-preservation.

We share a meal and go over the strategy for facing the King. However, we worry about the Oracle and the Prime Minister; their mental acuity far surpasses that of the aging King.

"You are certain that someone high enough informed the Asiatics about our mission?" asks the Prince.

"Yes, Your Highness. To bring that up would alarm whoever works against our interests. We should stick to our original plan. The Asiatics are distrustful and lack the intelligence to take on our offer."

"And then we iterate their barbarian ways to illustrate the point?"

"Yes. The uncouth behavior in the court, the dried severed palms, the killing of prisoners—"

"You made your point about killing prisoners. Let it go."

"Yes, Your Highness. I speak only of the Asiatics. Of course, we will inform the court that the Asiatics seek absolute supremacy over Egypt and are loath to make any arrangement that creates an obligation."

"No other justification?"

"No. If we keep it simple, we avoid being caught in a lie."

Nimmuruk smiles and nods. The Prince becomes thoughtful.

"Unless we have a mass production of our weapons and a large army, there is little chance of success in Egypt, is there?"

I am surprised by his acceptance. Most of my war strategy comes from education and knowledge shared from our history or from travelers from other kingdoms. But all those tales emphasize the fundamental need for successful wars—people and materials. We are blessed with neither. We possess great intelligence, but we have too few men. It is like a lion being attacked by many wild dogs; no matter how majestic, powerful, or intelligent the lion may be, it cannot withstand the assault of a hundred dogs.

Nimmuruk continues. "We must wait until we are sufficiently prepared."

"Governor Minos will rise to the task and provide us with an unbeatable army."

Nimmuruk scoffs with irritation. "The only thing that bastard will rise to do is rape goats. I will have my father teach him a lesson."

I choose not to respond. The Prince has not forgotten their dispute in Kaftu, where Minos almost got the Prince killed.

"But I agree with your assessment, Your Highness; our invasion cannot be hasty. You have an astute understanding of military matters," I say, hoping to inflate the Prince's ego.

Nimmuruk nods as if he accepts my praise. "The question is whether my father has the patience to wait or if the Oracle has messages that urge no further delay."

"We cannot guess the will of our gods."

"But the events in Egypt give me another reason to believe what the Oracle said," Nimmuruk replies.

"How so?"

Nimmuruk leans against the bench and looks out at the sea. The skies are spotless, and the blue waters calm. The Atalanni vessels move elegantly in formation behind the Prince's boat. It is a scene of tranquility.

"Look around us, Teber. Once we returned to the boat and set sail, we were safe. But Egypt held many unpleasant surprises."

"That is true, Your Highness."

"The Oracle's assertion that our gods are displeased because we have not won them greater dominion is clear; the gods of Egypt hold sway over their land, and our gods are quite helpless."

I am surprised once more—Nimmuruk's thinking is in alignment with mine.

"Perhaps they need our help just as we need their blessing?" Nimmuruk suggests.

"That might be so, but is that not what the Oracle said? That they need us to expand their dominion. Our experience supports the Oracle's messages," I assert. The divine beings work in mysterious ways, and their demands are difficult to explain.

Nimmuruk looks unconvinced. "I should have been more diplomatic," he reflects on his actions in the court.

"We learn from our experiences, Your Highness."

"You gloat over my failure," Nimmuruk replies glumly, avoiding my gaze.

"No, Your Highness; your father has given me his confidence to serve you, and I am your loyal servant. We will win Egypt together," I say. "They will not surprise us the next time."

Nimmuruk looks satisfied with my answer. He stops talking and watches the water as the navy progresses slowly back toward Kaftu, our first stop, before sailing onward to the capital.

I walk to the bow.

The gentle breeze whispers that the days ahead are fraught with peril.

When the navy approaches the harbor in Kaftu, there is no grand welcome party, and Minos is absent. He was to receive the returning force. However, we quickly learn of the Governor's death.

I am shocked, but Nimmuruk snickers, declaring that it is good for everyone that the Governor is dead. I am skeptical about the cause of death. A robust man, full of life, simply collapses and dies?

The army remains in preparation under the command of Phaistos, Minos' security chief, one of the few men with experience in leading the military.

I know little about Phaistos; he is a mystery. But currently, the equations of power and control over the island are unclear. The King has ordered that the governorship of the island be resolved after the Prince returns.

We spend two days inspecting the preparations. What we find is not very reassuring—it has not been long since we departed, and Minos had his mind set on matters other than polishing the sharp edge of the fighting force.

There is much to do.

Eventually, we leave for Kallistu when the winds favor us; the time to face the King has arrived.

# CHAPTER 27

## KALLISTU

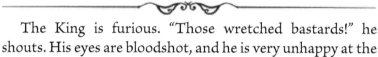

The King is furious. "Those wretched bastards!" he shouts. His eyes are bloodshot, and he is very unhappy at the news from Egypt. Rishwa tries to keep the King calm and attentive. The Supreme Council is in full attendance.

We keep our heads low, and the Prince is happy to let me do all the talking. We have an understanding, and I hope there are no missteps.

"What exactly did Khamudi say, General?" asks Rishwa.

"They believe they have the situation under control, Prime Minister, and refuse to engage with us. We also noticed that they are truly barbarous in their nature—"

Prince Nimmuruk scoffs loudly and rolls his eyes theatrically. "They are disgusting: sewers right beside the palace; severed hands of their enemies inside their houses! They even bury the dead below their living rooms. They are truly wretched."

I nod fervently at the Prince's account. This is all going well, so far. "We believe they lack the intelligence to understand our proposal," I say, feeling confident about how this is progressing.

"Is it due to a lack of intelligence, or are they astute and understand our true intentions? A muddy river may look shallow, but beneath may lie crocodiles," says Rishwa. The Prime Minister's gentle demeanor hides a sharp mind. Rishwa has held his title for over forty summers, indicating his formidable knowledge of palace politics and methods to remain in the good graces of the rulers.

I glance at the Prince, who keeps his mouth shut.

"At no point did they show great intelligence, Prime Minister," I assert. "All we saw were juvenile, immature responses to our proposals."

"Does that mean our assessment of the Pharaoh's rise was inaccurate?" asks the King, directing his attention to Rishwa.

"I do not believe so, Your Majesty. It may just be that the Asiatics are wary of introducing another party into the equation of their ambitions," says the Prime Minister, his eyes still on me.

"You disagree with the general's assessment?"

"Even the hungriest beast suspects unfamiliar feasts. I question the absolute certainty of their assessment. The General and the Prince have been in a foreign court for the first time. The King of the Asiatics is an old hand. His forefathers fought the great Egyptian empire and held their own; they do not always reveal their true intentions."

Hannuruk nods. The Oracle is present, but she is uncharacteristically quiet. She fidgets with her drapery and watches them intently, then finally speaks. "But maybe they are correct, Rishwa," she says, taking our side. The Prince nods appreciatively at Khaia.

"They could be. I am only pointing out that Khamudi has not survived this long against Egypt and maintained peace with the Assyrians and the Mitanni by being foolish."

Hannuruk looks unconvinced. "There are rumors that Khamudi's father picked a fight with the boy Ahmose's father because he did not like the grunts of their strange beast called the Hippopotamus."

"I would lend some credence to fantastical stories, Your Majesty," says Rishwa. "There may be some truth to it, but the genuine reasons may remain unknown."

Hannuruk nods in agreement. The King finally looks intently at his son and asks, "How did we lose our men?"

Nimmuruk looks flustered, and my heart skips a beat. "Disease, Father. We lost many to wretched illnesses in Egypt—their air and water are poison, just like their souls."

The King exchanges glances with the Prime Minister. "If you were not my son, I could put you to death for lying," Hannuruk says, his voice carrying a hard edge.

Now, it is the voice of a King.

Not that of a father.

But that of an angry King.

"No, Father, I—"

"Be quiet," he tells his son and turns to me. "How?"

Blood rushes like a roaring river in my ears. I glance frantically at the Oracle, and she nods imperceptibly.

What is she saying?

"We were ambushed, Your Majesty."

"By whom?"

"By Pharaoh Ahmose himself," I say, feeling defeated.

Hannuruk leans back against the throne and looks accusingly at his son. Nimmuruk shrinks in his seat, and Rishwa nods reassuringly at me.

"We know the challenges of a new mission, General, but let this be a lesson—do not lie to the throne. Trust is like a fragile clay pot; once broken, it can never be repaired. Yes, you feel shame and fear, but you are both home. And you escaped. Tell us the truth," Rishwa says while adjusting himself comfortably on his cushion.

This time, I decide to be truthful and explain the ambush and the escape. I omit the execution of the prisoners, deciding to let them ask questions rather than volunteer information.

Nimmuruk looks almost grateful.

But they do not ask about the prisoners. Instead, the topic shifts quickly to implications.

"We are far from prepared for an invasion without the support of the Asiatics," says Rishwa. Khaia looks irritated but says nothing.

"Our preparations have taken a hit with the loss of the Governor, but we are working with great urgency, Your Majesty," says Phaistos. The new leader is already exerting his influence in the court and making his voice heard.

"What is the latest assessment of our readiness to begin an invasion?" asks Rishwa.

"Six moons at least to have an army of forty thousand ready, Prime Minister," Phaistos replies.

I realize that remaining quiet will lead to a gradual erosion of my authority.

"What is our situation with armaments? And I do not speak of swords and arrows, but the *Daivoshaktis*," I inquire.

Phaistos shoots an irritated glance at me. But before he can respond, Rishwa speaks up. "How important is it for us to have the *Daivoshaktis* deployed in large numbers?"

I take a gamble. "May I speak freely, Your Majesty?"

The King grunts, and Rishwa nods encouragingly.

"Egypt is much larger than our lands. They have a great number of people to deploy. We also do not know if the Asiatics will fight against us or remain defensive. Yet if we are to conquer the empire to satisfy our gods, we must fight both the Asiatics and the Pharaoh," I explain, looking around. I strain not to look at Apsara, who has remained silent and withdrawn.

My beautiful Apsara has lost weight.

Rishwa looks at Hannuruk and nods his agreement. It is important to have the Prime Minister on my side. Feeling confident, I move from my position directly to the front of the throne, facing the King. "There is something else to consider, Your Majesty. Thus far, we have only spoken about the Asiatics and the Pharaoh in Egypt. What we do not know is how the others will react. What about the aggressive Northerners? Will they see this as an opportunity? What about the Mitanni? We must be confident that they will not interfere."

Apsara looks up sharply but does not comment. Rishwa holds up his hand. "Wise words, young General. We have sent word asking them to stay away."

I return to my original concern. "You asked if our *Daivoshaktis* must be deployed in large numbers. Yes, I firmly believe we should. Khamudi made it clear that they have far more men than we have weapons. We also face the logistical problem of moving supplies across the great sea, while they need only fortify their defenses and engage in a battle of attrition. Our invasion will fail if we act with arrogance."

The King turns to Khaia. "You have been quiet. Are there any fresh signs?"

"The hints have changed. The cub has grown his mane. The claws of the attacking hawks grow sharper. And a majestic mountain rumbles louder with each passing day," she says and clasps her hands to her chest.

I think I can interpret the signs but decide to let someone else ask.

"What does that mean to you, Khaia?" asks the King.

"The Prince is becoming a lion. The Pharaoh grows stronger. And the divine expresses impatience."

Rishwa smoothes the fabric on his thigh and leans in. "Egypt grows stronger as we wait, and the gods grow angrier with our delay?"

"You are astute, Prime Minister."

*This is ridiculous!*

Why are the gods nudging us toward disaster? How can we win without adequate preparation? Hannuruk leans toward Rishwa, and the two confer for several minutes in hushed tones.

The Oracle joins them.

The Prince strains to hear their conversation. They discuss animatedly, and eventually, Nimmuruk joins them. Phaistos and I eye each other from across our chairs; I dislike this man, but I have little to go on except a feeling. Perhaps Phaistos is a capable commander.

The King suddenly stands and asks most of the council to leave, except for a few of the most senior members. He then turns to his wife and orders her to exit. Apsara rises and walks by me. She pretends to survey the room, and for a brief second, her gentle, wet eyes land on mine. There is an almost imperceptible smile; it is as if she radiates great affection that is unseen by all except the recipient. I control myself from running to her and sweeping her into my arms.

And then she is gone.

Then, inexplicably, the King orders everyone to enjoy a meal. There are refreshments—bread, beer, wine, olives, meat, pomegranates, watermelon, cool citrus water—and we eat quietly with little conversation. Eventually, after what seems like an hour, the King resumes court.

"I understand the prudence of waiting to equip the army to its fullest and invading when the time is right. But it is clear from the signs that the gods do not reward those who wait, but those who seize their fortunes against seemingly insurmountable odds."

I can guess what is about to happen. Hannuruk looks at each member intently. Nimmuruk sits with a proud expression. Khaia nods. Rishwa shows no expression. Phaistos' eyes reveal crinkles at the sides, hinting at a smile. The King continues. "We will not wait. The longer we train hidden in our lands like cowards, the stronger Egypt becomes. It is our delay that will lead to our failure and dishonor in the eyes of our gods."

Then Hannuruk takes a deep breath, as if reluctant to say the next words. "It is decided. We will attack in three moons. Phaistos, you oversee all efforts to prepare for the invasion. Ensure we run the trade routes quietly to the North and East and have enough supply of tin and copper. Nimmuruk, the gods see you in charge, and you will continue as commander of the forces."

Nimmuruk bows to his father. I hope the Prince possesses more sense and strategic vision this time.

"Teber. The Oracle insists you must remain here, in charge of order and defense of Kallistu and Kaftu, but my son wishes you to join him. The gods do not dictate military assignments," he states, glaring at Khaia, "the King does. You will go with him. And this time do not return with defeat," he warns, his voice stern. Khaia shakes her head.

There is nothing to say, especially when they have decided. That Rishwa did not object means there is little hope of persuading anyone. Besides, what could Rishwa say, as he has never led an invasion either!

And as the council debates preparation and tactics until night, it is not the empire on my mind; it is not invasion and glory on my mind; it is not Ahmose or Khamudi occupying my thoughts; it is not the gods or divine powers weighing on me.

There is just one thing—

Will I be able to see Apsara once before I return to Kaftu in two days?

Circumstances make it impossible for me to contact Apsara. I see her several times over the next two days, always at a distance, speaking to me through her eyes and smiles.

But there is great sadness in those eyes. Once, when no one is looking, she makes a sign by placing her palms together and resting them on her chest—a sign that we share, one of affection and deep longing.

Finally, my last chance to see her up close occurs when the King and his principals come to bid their goodbyes and dispatch last orders. Her eyes never leave me, and my mind struggles to concentrate on the King's words. During every opportunity, we convey our love through our gazes. When I bow to the royals and give my final salute before walking to my boat, Apsara makes a sign that only we share.

*Goodbye, my love, and may the gods bless you if we never see each other again.*

# CHAPTER 28
## LOWER EGYPT

Pharaoh Ahmose is distraught after the ambush. He questions his divinity, for he knows he came close to death. His beloved uncle and vizier of Lower Egypt, Nebhekhufre, is dead. The wise man's face had been blown away by the fiery weapons of the Atalanni. Had it not been for the Egyptian forces' superior numbers, they might all be dead or captured by now.

The savagery did not end with the battle. Two days later, men reported a pit filled with burned soldiers—executed by their captors. One man barely survived, and with the brief words he spoke before he died, he told them how the Atalanni had thrown them into a pit and set them alight, with no chance to plead for their lives.

"Savages. They burned the bodies to rob them of their chance in the second life," Ahmose lamented to his priests. He had ordered special prayers so that the men would be regenerated in their afterlife.

It eludes Ahmose and his generals what the Atalanni seek. The Asiatics have been secretive—they have fortified their defenses and retreated from their offensive positions as if waiting for something. Ahmose has spent the last three days in prayer, along with his wife, paying obeisance and offerings to Amun, seeking his guidance.

Pharaoh Ahmose, his wife Ahmose-Nefertari, Wadjmose, and two of his commanders walk along the palace corridors. With Nebhekhufre gone and the Vizier of the Upper Kingdom far away in Nubia, Chief Priest of the temple of Amun, *hem-netjer-tepi*, the first priest of god, Menkheperre, accompanies them.

"What do they want?" the Pharaoh says loudly.

"They seek Egypt, Your Majesty. Why else would they try to talk to the Asiatics and attack us? Why has our ambassador not returned? May the gods help us, but we must now accept that the Kingdom of the Atalanni and the men of Keftiu seek to wage war."

Ahmose is quiet. He reflects on the recent developments and his own situation. The harvest has not been plentiful. His vizier is dead, the Asiatics are fortifying their positions, and now a grave new threat looms from beyond the Green Sea. To fight two forces would not only strain all their resources and finances; it might doom Egypt.

Besides, there is the confounding question of the almost magical weaponry of the Atalanni.

"What do you make of their weapons, Wadjmose? They spit invisible force; it is as if the Atalanni gods direct them. Their power far exceeds what we possess."

"I have given it much thought, Your Majesty. They may possess a nature we do not understand. But have you not seen that they did not have enough? They also needed time to launch, just like our arrows. While they may inflict great harm, with cunning, observation, and planning, we can withstand their onslaught and even capture their weapons to design our own."

Ahmose appreciates Wadjmose's counsel and assurance. The formidable general is not easily cowed—he has seen much in his battles with the Asiatics when he served the great Kamose. Ahmose pushes thoughts of weaponry aside and returns to a greater question.

"We cannot fight on two fronts. We do not know how long we have before they decide to invade, and we do not know if they are joining forces with the wretched Asiatics."

"You speak like an experienced general, Your Majesty," Wadjmose says, pride and respect for his Pharaoh evident in his voice. "You are right. Our resources are stretched. Our men are not ready for war on two fronts. We must keep the Asiatics at bay if we are to fight the Atalanni."

"But how?" asks the Pharaoh. He has some thoughts, but a satisfactory solution eludes him.

"Deception," Wadjmose replies.

Ahmose raises an eyebrow. "Go ahead, what clever idea grows in your mind, Wadjmose?"

Wadjmose stops and turns towards the royal couple. He wipes his bald head and lowers his voice conspiratorially, even though no one else is around. "We know the Atalanni visited the Asiatics, but they did not stay long. When we engaged them, there were no Asiatics present, and our spies have relayed that there was some sort of conflict between the delegation and the Asiatics."

"Go on."

"If there was no agreement, then the alliance that the Atalanni proposed did not interest the impostors, at least for now."

"What do you think they came with?"

Wadjmose smiles as if he is proud of his theory and confident. "They go to the Asiatics. Why? Because they wish to align with them to fight us as a combined force. But why do they return with their tails tucked between their legs? Khamudi is no fool; he suspects that once battle is over, the Atalanni might turn on him after he has depleted his forces fighting us."

Ahmose nods in agreement. "If Khamudi had no intention of cooperating, then he sees weaknesses in the Atalanni and does not view them as a terrible threat."

"You read my mind, Your Majesty. Amun has blessed you with brilliance," Wadjmose says, and Menkheperre makes gestures of spiritual blessings. Ahmose is pleased by his general's encouragement.

"What is your plan, then?"

Wadjmose rubs the sole of his feet on the sandstone flooring and rocks on his heels.

"We send an emissary to the court of Khamudi. We tell him that the Atalanni have sent us a messenger and asked if we need help to defeat them."

"Clever. You wish to sow seeds of distrust. But will that not make Khamudi return to the Atalanni and secure their cooperation first?"

"My deception does not involve merely sending the message, Your Majesty," Wadjmose says, his eyes smiling even as his lips remain serious. "We tell Khamudi that the Atalanni referred to them as animals and that we have refused the Atalanni overture because Egypt will not accept a third force into our land. We will fight for what is ours as brothers. No neighbor shall have a say in our dispute."

Ahmose briefly bristles at the suggestion that Khamudi could even be called brother, but then sees the cunning in Wadjmose's plan. The Pharaoh laughs and turns to his wife, who smiles and nods her understanding of what is being said.

"We make it seem to Khamudi that we accept his right to this land and that we manage our disputes while treating him as an equal—all while painting the Atalanni as intruders to Egypt—his land!" Ahmose-Nefertari says in her soft voice, and the Pharaoh and his general nod appreciatively.

"The God's Wife of Amun speaks what is in our minds, Your Majesty," Wadjmose says admirably.

"And your plan may yet work, general," Nefertari adds, gently pushing her hair back behind her ears. Ahmose is distracted by his wife's beauty and intelligence. But the Pharaoh is not surprised—after all, his wife is the granddaughter of his formidable grandmother, Tetisheri, and his powerful mother Ahhotep—his father's favorite wife and the woman who raised her two brave sons.

They all stand quietly, contemplating their move. After a while, Ahmose turns towards Menkheperre. "Prepare for three more days of prayer, Chief Priest. I must appeal to our gods with the greatest effort."

The Priest nods in assent and leaves.

Ahmose then turns to Wadjmose. "Send our emissary to Khamudi. Meanwhile, prepare our battalions. Send word to Nubia that they shall send their men in support. Inform the Canaanite tribes that Egypt asks them to remain out of disputes that may arise soon. Come to me with a plan on when we will be ready to face the Atalanni should they invade."

Wadjmose bows. "Anything else, Your Majesty?"

Ahmose ponders. "One more thing: issue a royal decree that there shall be no mention of the Atalanni anywhere. Not in our tales. Not on our walls. Not on our papyrus. Not on our tablets or silver scrolls. Let them not exist until we wipe them out."

Wadjmose kneels before the Pharaoh and the Queen. "As you say, Your Majesty. You are Egypt, Nebpehtire, and your word will be done."

Ahmose touches the kneeling general's shoulder with his scepter. Wadjmose rises and leaves to begin preparations.

It is now just Ahmose and his wife. He reaches for her affectionately and holds her by the waist. The couple walks slowly towards the royal quarters, and Ahmose wonders what stories the walls of temples and tombs will tell about them when they die and ascend the stairs to heaven.

# CHAPTER 29

## KALLISTU

While she mourns Minos' passing, Khaia is certain that his death was necessary. However, the news from Egypt has not been in her best interest—the Prince lives, and now there is a pause until the army is ready to invade.

*Khamudi. That short-sighted fool.*

With Minos dispensed, it is time to visit Apsara again, but this time in the presence of the King. She has already sent word that she must meet the royal couple, and they await her in the throne room. It is a closed audience—only the couple, Rishwa, and Khaia. Prince Nimmuruk has left for Kaftu. The boy fears his father after the last disastrous mission and would rather be anywhere than here.

Once they settle, Khaia broaches the topic directly with the King, avoiding the Queen's eyes.

"The gods have been quiet and appear to be content with your decision, Your Majesty," she says, but her brows furrow in worry. She rubs her temple and holds a finger on the tip of her nose as if in deep thought.

"And yet something bothers you," he replies.

"I worry about the success of their mission. May the gods bestow their divine grace upon the Prince, and I hope he survives and returns with all his strength and faculties intact."

Hannuruk nods. He is somewhat drunk again, and it seems the periods of lucidity are decreasing by the week. The King has gained weight; the rich food, little exercise, and unbounded luxuries are making him soft. A gray stubble covers his aging face, and his eyes droop. When he holds his wine cup, his hands shake, and his words stutter.

"A King needs more than one heir, Your Majesty. These are dangerous times," says Khaia. She hears a sharp intake of breath from Apsara.

"Are you insinuating that my son will die?"

"No, Your Majesty, but war is war. Even the bravest sometimes give their lives for the good of the land, and while we all wish that not a hair on the Prince be harmed, one must be realistic."

Rishwa observes thoughtfully but says nothing.

"My second son is incapable of wiping his own bottom, let alone ruling an empire," Hannuruk states, "and Minos, who might have been a worthy successor..."

Rishwa clears his throat. "We have a great wolf proud of its territory, and yet its pack is missing. Our constitution allowed the King to anoint the governor of Kaftu as successor, but he is gone now," he says, watching Khaia intently.

The King nods, and his eyes wander toward nothing. He sighs loudly and burps.

"We need an heir," Khaia asserts, more forcefully this time. Her eyes lock on the Queen's. If she must poke a beehive, so be it.

"Why is this such a great concern of yours, Khaia?" Apsara asks, her voice shaking as she forces the words.

"You be quiet!" the King admonishes her. "Be quiet! You are a barren ornament! I must consult with the Oracle, and you keep your mouth shut."

"I am your wife and the Queen—"

Hannuruk raises his hand as if to slap her, and she flinches. However, the King's shaking hands fail to strike

Apsara, and he gives up. Her face turns a deep shade of red with humiliation. Khaia feels a fleeting remorse for her actions, but it is necessary. The Atalanni are not known to strike their women, and yet here is the shameful King himself raising his hand, she thinks.

"You be quiet and listen. I am stuck with you, a wife in name!"

"Your Majesty, kindness toward your Queen is needed if you must produce a child. The strength of your seed will overcome her barren womb," Khaia says.

Apsara is about to say something but bites her lip. She tries to control herself, but a tear slides down her cheek. The King turns his face away.

"What are you suggesting, Khaia?" he asks.

"That you or the Queen will do the right thing, Your Majesty," she replies cryptically.

She knows Apsara hears her.

The group falls silent.

"Well, what right thing can I do?" Hannuruk shouts, "This barren heap will give me no child! There is nothing I can do while she eats, sleeps, and grows fatter!"

Tears flow down Apsara's cheeks; she is red and frozen.

"There must be a—" Khaia begins again.

Hannuruk turns his drunken, bloodshot eyes toward his Queen and cuts Khaia off. "Maybe the gods will make her kill herself. Perhaps that is our only salvation."

There is absolute silence in the room, and Rishwa places his hand on the King's shoulder.

Apsara gasps.

She springs to her feet and runs out.

Hannuruk slumps on his throne, mumbling incoherently with wine and food dripping onto his chest, while the Prime Minister calls the aides to clean the King and take him back to his quarters. Rishwa's eyes look accusingly at Khaia as if to question her cruelty at this hour.

Khaia looks back defiantly. The road to ambition is not paved with smooth sandstone.

# CHAPTER 30
## KAFTU AND THE GREAT SEA

On the fourteenth day after prayers to the *Trikaia*, the augurs clear the navy to leave the harbors of Kaftu and begin the invasion. The sun rises in the sky, and the Oracle blesses us. The King speaks of a new era of conquest, victory, and the expansion of the Atalanni empire to all corners of the world.

We have prepared as best we can. Phaistos has done a remarkable job—much to my surprise; he has prepared an expeditionary force of nearly thirty thousand men and seven hundred boats of a size no other Kingdom has ever seen. He has equipped the Navy with enough food and weaponry to last a year, though we are woefully short of our *Daivoshaktis*. He has also secured engineers, mechanics, boat builders, road builders, physicians, augurs, weathermen, healers, singers, cooks, cleaners, sweepers, garbage men, scouts, runners, translators, and caregivers. I am told that the Kingdom's resources are stretched, and yet there is great excitement in the air.

I have been unable to meet Apsara before I left. She stood silent at the final ceremony, and I was afforded no chance to be near her to address her. In the end, as I walked to the plank leading to my boat, Apsara made her sign of love. When the harbor receded from view, all I could think of was her looking at me.

Only the gods know if I will ever see her again.

But my longing is replaced by the monumental task at hand—to lead the force to victory in an ancient land guarded by powerful gods. I hoped that our divinity saw our preparation, willingness, and bold actions in the last few moons as a testament to our loyalty to them and that they would protect us from the gods of Egypt.

The scene behind me is as exhilarating as it is majestic. Hundreds of Atalanni boats follow us in a wide, elegant formation. There are sails, but no flags or markings on the boats. We have detailed plans on what we will do upon our arrival in Egypt—our brilliant planners and I have spent an inordinate amount of time devising various methods to confound and terrorize the Egyptians. The Prince has been sullen for days; it has finally dawned upon him that we are about to wage an actual war from which we may not return. Quiet contemplation has replaced his rudeness, and I let him be.

My trusted lieutenant is Bansabira. He is loyal, attentive, and fanatically brave. Itaja is my second-in-command. There are one hundred commanders in the force, each leading about three hundred into the field. There is a *Upashaktis* for every ten commanders, making ten *Upashaktis* in all. Most of the commanders and soldiers are untested in large-scale war, and I hope that our training, cunning, weaponry, and intelligence will make up for what they lack in hard fighting.

Before this expedition, I had heard many stories about the Egyptians. It is hard to know how much of it is true and how much is exaggerated. The wind remains in our sails.

But on the twelfth day at sea, as we approach Egypt, dark clouds form in the skies, and the wind batters the boats. My stomach tightens—it seems the gods of Egypt are preparing to welcome us.

We are masters of the sea, and our ambassadors have informed us that there is no navy in all the earth like ours. None so powerful, none so nimble, and I am confident that we will face whatever is thrown at us. Our boats are designed to handle unkind winds and enormous waves. We are also the only navy with two-level boats—with oarsmen below deck and soldiers above. It is a design I am told is incomprehensible to others.

My worry is not my boats but the Prince.

He has been on the sea a few times in his life but never in angry waters. Our last visit to Egypt was smooth, and the waters posed no challenge, but this time the welcome is different. Egypt knows we are there to bring it under our dominion, and her gods are not happy. I walk to the Prince's cabin.

"It is about to get rough, Your Highness. The winds show no sign of abating, and clouds grow darker by the hour."

Nimmuruk looks ill. He nods. "What do you suggest I do?"

"Stay where you are. Wear floating vests—"

"Are we going to capsize?" The panic is clear in his high pitch.

"I do not mean that, Your Highness, but we must be prepared. The vests will keep you safe."

He mumbles something about the incompetence of the boat builders.

I turn to the captain of the boat and order him to light the lamps on our masts to signal the navy to prepare for severe weather. Soon, there are twinkling pinpricks all around me. It is like being in a thick forest at night, surrounded by fireflies—except that there is no land beneath our feet and fireflies are boats with thousands of our men.

What if we all drown even before we land in Egypt? I laugh to myself—that would be the most inglorious way for this entire plan to unravel. I pray again that our God of the

Seas keeps us safe. It does not take long for the wind to pick up again, and the waves rock the boat like an angry bully terrorizing a child on a swing. Foam flies around us, and water washes across the floors. We lower our sails quickly to prevent smashing into each other because I have another worry. The fronts of our boats are like battering rams, tipped with bronze, and reinforced by a new metal they call iron—it is hard and turns orange when left in the air. It is a remarkable metal we have recently come to know, and our engineers expect many uses for it.

But if a boat collides with us, then it could be deadly too. We hope that the weather will wear itself out, but it does not.

The wind whistles, and the waves batter the boats. I have seen impatient waters before, but this feels ominous. It reminds me of the tales my tutors told me of a hundred Atalanni boats traveling to the North and vanishing beneath the seas long ago. I hope we will not become another chapter in the vanishing tales.

I wear my floating vest and hunker down—there is little we can do as the rowers fight to keep the boat under control. I know the captain is below, exhorting the crew to remain calm.

And then it happens.

Out of nowhere, like a monster rising from below, one of our boats appears from the stormy darkness and slams into our side.

The impact tosses me like a rag doll.

I strike a post, and my shoulder screams. I scramble to my feet as the entire boat shakes and shudders. I hear the shearing and breaking sounds as the bronze and iron tip ruptures our side, entangling the two boats. Even amid the cacophony of the winds and waves, I hear screams and desperate shouts from below.

"Take stock!" I scream to the scrambling crew—there is not much space on the deck, and the canvas roof of the tent has ripped off. I wobble across to find the Prince; he is sitting in a corner, shaking, his face and body wet from all the splashing water. He is incoherent, and I can barely see his features as the rain drenches us.

The gods of Egypt have the upper hand today, I tell myself, but we will not fail!

I grasp his hand and request assistance from another crew member to help me lift the Prince to his feet. The boat sways perilously now, tilting away from the impact. Waves begin to rise and lap against us, and we tightly grip the banisters. The Prince trembles, and fear consumes me.

I comprehend the peril of being trapped beneath an overturned boat. Chaos reigns supreme. The captain must still be below deck. Several men plunge into the water.

The captain rushes toward us.

His screams are barely audible as he shouts near my ear, spewing water and urging me, "Jump, sir! Jump!"

The Prince gazes at me in panic. I see the whites of his eyes, and without hesitation, I signal the other man on the opposite side of the Prince. Together, we drag him and leap into the water.

The water is frigid, and the waves toss us about as if we are insignificant. However, I cling to Nimmuruk. Our vests assist us in remaining afloat.

After a while, exhaustion sets in.

Screams and shouts fill the air when our heads emerge from the water, and the roaring sounds of the sea engulf us when we submerge.

I offer up a prayer.

This is not how it is meant to conclude.

A glorious death at the hands of a Pharaoh or in the embrace of the woman I adore.

But not death, submerged underwater! Vanished.

Apsara's visage appears before me repeatedly. She reaches out to me.

Her eyes glisten, and her lips form a pout, as if to bestow a kiss.

Yet, suddenly, she extends her hand towards the sky and soars away into the heavens, and darkness descends upon me.

# CHAPTER 31

## KALLISTU

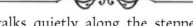

Apsara walks quietly along the stepped granite slope overlooking the magnificent waters. Daffodils bloom on one side of the royal garden, and no one is in sight. She has asked her maids and bodyguards to stay away.

The invasion has finally begun, and Teber is gone.

Her mind is an ocean of sorrow and pain. Growing up under the careful watch of her father and brothers in Washukanni, Apsara dreamed of a happy and meaningful future.

One where her father would give her away to a handsome and kind husband.

One where the people and the nobles admired her intelligence and beauty.

One where the generals and politicians respected her opinions on kingdoms and governments.

Just like how her father would listen to her older brothers.

Like how he never admonished her, even if her opinions were childish. She dreamed of being a great queen—loved, feared, and admired. She had heard that the great empire of Egypt had powerful women.

But her father had betrayed her.

He crushed her blossoming dreams and aspirations. He had married her off to an old and loveless man who sat like a hermit on an island that was nothing more than a beautiful prison. And yet, she had tried to be a good wife. She had tried to cater to his needs and fleeting desires. But none of it had mattered. Hannuruk had no affection for her, and he was revolting.

He had raised his hand against her more than once.

Such insult and ignominy! Her hopes of having a child—nurturing it, becoming a mother, becoming the queen mother of a future king or princess—had been crushed under the oppression of an abusive husband.

To think that there was once a chance to be married to the young Egyptian Pharaoh!

Her eyes sting with tears as the cool but powerful breeze sweeps across the open terrace. She pushes her hair back and walks faster toward the higher platform on the cliff. She clutches her silver necklace and tugs at it nervously. Her heart beats hard against her chest—and her once soft, healthy body has lost weight, with her ribs showing. Her maids have worried about her endlessly, often remarking how her eyes have dulled and her skin has lost its shine.

But one thought consumes her.

Teber.

It was such a dangerous thing to do—to desire a commoner, to lie with him, to plot with him to run away. But she loved him more than anything else in the world. If there was a sparkle of brightness in her world of darkness, it was he. She knows she has gone against every Atalanni law and the rules of the gods. And yet she wonders, was it not a god that put her to this? It is confusing—which god condemned her to this life, and which propelled her to take these risky actions?

And now Teber is gone—away to fight a battle that the Oracle said was the desire of the gods. It feels as if her heart is held in a vice and squeezed when Teber sails away.

Apsara knows that there is scant chance to see him or hold him again. It is as if every force in the universe conspires against her wishes and desires. It is as if the gods no longer have a place for her in this world, discarded from merciful grace and joys.

And then there was the Oracle goading her, and her senile husband treating her increasingly viciously. Apsara has not slept well after those conversations. It is clear what the Oracle implies: as long as she lives, the King will never marry again, and the empire will have no issue if something happens to Nimmuruk—that lecherous prince she despises. It does not matter that it is not her fault—the people see it as such. There is something about her that the King hates but does not reveal. Maybe it is she who throttles his passion.

In the people's eyes, she is to blame.

Tears roll down the Queen's cheeks. There is nowhere to run, no one to protect her. Her glory will be her sacrifice. Khaia alluded to that when she met her again—that Apsara will be remembered as the queen who saved the empire.

The selfless one.

Apsara stands atop the platform. Beneath her, the tranquil blue sea beckons, like a loving mother in a mesmerizing blue apron, opening her arms for her baby to fall from the skies and be embraced in her bosom. Apsara's body shudders, racked with sorrow. She cries and silently begs forgiveness from her father, brothers, and Teber.

Apsara looks ahead and sees the vista through her tear-filled eyes. She turns her face towards the sun in the direction where her home lies. She thinks of her people. She arches her back and extends her slender hands on both sides, as if she were a bird soaring away to her freedom.

The world behind her dissolves as if it never existed.

She feels the footsteps of her father behind her, taking her to the days of her childhood when she ran giggling.

She feels the footsteps of Teber, as he sometimes snuck behind her in darkness and embraced her.

The wind howls in anguish as Apsara, Princess of the Mitanni, Queen of the Atalanni, leans forward toward the void.

# CHAPTER 32
## LOWER EGYPT

Pharaoh Ahmose leads his army, with Wadjmose by his side. The Asiatics have agreed to stay away for now, but Ahmose knows they watch and wait for the first sign of weakness. The preparation has been difficult. Harvests have not been bountiful, and almost non-existent trade with neighboring regions has made Egypt poorer. However, exhortations, threats, punishments, and bribes have helped them raise a considerable army to fight the Atalanni. The Pharaoh knows that the Atalanni Navy must cross the Great Green Sea before it arrives somewhere on the coasts of Egypt, and he hopes that the challenges of transporting large numbers over water will keep the numbers on the Atalanni side low.

He is proud of his men—a mix of hardened veterans from wars with the Asiatics, Syrians, and Nubians, alongside fresh, loyal newcomers who wish to gain glory under their god and Pharaoh and under the capable leadership of an exceptional general. Ahmose knows that many will never return, but that is the nature of war.

His chariot moves slowly across the uneven land, now dry in many areas, as thousands of feet kick up dust for miles behind him. The great army of Egypt advances slowly and purposefully—the archers, mace handlers, swordsmen, spearmen, axmen, and Nubian knifers—followed by hand-pulled food carts, ox-drawn baggage trains, healers, physicians, priests, and planners.

Ahmose has accepted Wadjmose's plan to trace northward across the river delta, far from Asiatic influence and Khamudi's spies, and to set up camp near the Great Sea, north of Sais. He then plans to send scouts along the coast to watch for the Atalanni's arrival. Even with horse riders, the coast requires several days of traversal, but patience is key.

He has advised the army logistics to be prudent with food supplies and to secure meat where they can on the way. They have found gazelles, cranes, and hippopotamuses to kill and eat. Ahmose listens to Wadjmose as the general turns to one of his trusted lieutenants, a man also named Ahmose, Son of Ebana, an experienced soldier who has fought the Asiatics under Pharaohs Kamose and Ahmose.

"Baba, what is the morale of the troops?" Wadjmose asks. Wadjmose prefers to call his lieutenant Ahmose as Baba, for that is Ahmose's father's name, allowing the general to use that sacred name with levity without confusing it with the Pharaoh's.

"Positive, General. They feel a sense of purpose and wish to serve you with honor."

"Death and disease?"

"We have lost forty so far due to stomach ailments and other fevers."

"How far is the rear of the army?"

"About two miles south, but keeping pace."

Baba is one of the few men with horses—he is awkward with his horse but has learned to ride the beast. Wadjmose smiles as the horse grunts and whinnies, while a fearful Baba clings to the reins.

"You are better off fighting on your feet," he says. Baba grins but leans forward, holding on to the horse's neck.

"How do the Asiatics handle these beasts so well?" he mutters.

"Perhaps they are much less clumsy than you!" laughs Wadjmose. Yet, he knows Baba is anything but clumsy—he is a clever and resourceful fighter who has extinguished the ambitions of many a rebel.

"Those wretched savages can do nothing like us," protests Baba. He then casts a quick glance at the Pharaoh, hoping he has not offended him with his coarse language.

Ahmose shakes his head and grins. "Do not forget, Baba, that our army is now powerful because we have learned from those barbarians. Our bows shoot farther, we protect our chests better, and we have learned to tame these magnificent creatures," he says, affectionately patting his horse's neck as it stirs and snorts.

Baba bows in acknowledgment of Ahmose's words, and Wadjmose gently slaps his lieutenant on the head. "You should be ashamed to be lectured by the Pharaoh himself!" Wadjmose says playfully. They all know that the Asiatics' weapons and tactics helped them usurp the land hundreds of harvests ago. About an hour later, the scouts announce that a messenger is on the way back, and soon they watch as the horse kicks up gray earth.

The messenger bows before them.

"Anything new?"

"No, Your Majesty, it is all quiet."

The Pharaoh ponders the news. The march is slow, and it will be at least another twenty days before he can set up camp.

"No signs of any kind?"

"None, Your Highness. I have scoured two days east of our proposed camp, and there is no sign of anyone having arrived or anything on the horizon."

Ahmose wonders if there will ever be an invasion or if their march is a complete waste. It has all been based on guess and instinct, and little else. What if the Atalanni are not ready? What if they take another harvest? Do we sit here and wait? Do we return after this expensive and wasteful trip?

"So, no signs at all?" Wadjmose asks. "None from the gods even?"

The messenger is about to nod his head but then pauses. "Nothing except a great storm far in the Green Sea."

# CHAPTER 33

## THE GREAT SEA

Something tightens around my neck and shoulder, and I spit saltwater, gasping for breath.

Where is Nimmuruk?

It is dark and still raining, and I hear shouts. Suddenly, men appear. Relief washes over me as I realize my men are rescuing me. Someone drags me up to another boat, and I lie there for a long time, recovering.

"The Prince?"

"Safe, sir."

"How did you find us?"

"Spotters saw you," the man says. I know that, as much as the gods of Egypt tried, our God of the Seas has seen to our safety, even as he battles his divine enemy. We endure the night, unable to assess the situation or contact anyone else until the seas calm. When the sun rises, I look around to see the devastation. The Navy is bruised but still floating. The skies brighten, and I signal everyone to wrap up their cleanup and continue sailing. We do not yet know how off-course we are or where we will land. Four days later, we finally arrive on the shores of Egypt. Our advance scouts tell us where it is safe to anchor. The spot is marshy and desolate but perfect for our needs. We spread our boats along the shore and disembark.

We are here.

Egypt.

It is as if the gods directed us to this location. We find a large sweet water lake not too far from the seashore. There are fowl and gazelle in the grassy vegetation.

The land is soft, gray, and marshy, and it takes some effort to find suitable ground along the northern shores. We spend three days setting up camp and supply lines. We raid some local villages, and the prisoners now work in the army camps. The Prince calls for a war council. I gather my *Upashaktis* and arrive at the royal tent. The army is camped in three segments all along the lakeshore, with the advance guard and scouts positioned near the East, West, and center of the southern edge of the lake. So far, there has been no sign of any enemy activity.

The Prince looks better today. He is in an energetic mood as he paces around the tent, wearing just a small patch of loincloth. He has washed and perfumed himself and wears his hair in dreadlocks. We have had little conversation since we landed, as I was away overseeing camping arrangements and protective barriers. We stand around a makeshift wooden table. The prince holds a bronze rod with which he can draw on the soft clay on the table.

"I am glad we all made it through the storms," he says. "Horus and Amun could not stop us."

There are murmurs of assent.

"What are our losses?" he asks.

"We lost forty boats and seven hundred thirty-five men," I reply.

He does not respond. He holds the rod behind his shoulders, clasps the ends with both hands, and twists to crack his back. "Did we lose any of our *Daivoshaktis* or food?"

"Two weapon boats and one grain boat, Your Highness," says Bansabira, who is in charge of logistics.

Nimmuruk turns and spits. "We will break the backs of their gods."

We wait to see if he has anything else to say, but all he does is twist and stare at us.

"Shall we go over the plans, Your Majesty?" I finally ask.

"I was wondering when you would come to that," he replies.

I bristle but continue.

I draw a rough outline of the lake and our locations around it. "We are comfortably camped and recuperating. So far, there is no sign of activity. Our advance scouts are away to the south and should return in three to four days."

"Where are we? How far are we from where we were last time?"

"We are much further west of our last location, Your Highness. But our guides know the terrain."

"Nothing from the Asiatics?"

"None. Villagers say that they have not seen the Asiatics in this region in many harvests."

"Explain your plan to me."

I ask for the bronze stick, and Nimmuruk hands it to me reluctantly. "They say it is about a moon's march to the capital Thebes. And this is assuming there are no surprises on the way."

"A month in this weather," he murmurs. I glance at Bansabira.

*Does the prince think we are on an excursion?*

I ignore his remark. "We will stay on flat, open ground wherever possible. Our chances are best on such terrain."

"Is it mostly open land from here to Thebes?" he asks, clearly not recalling the briefing given before the invasion.

"That is what our scouts and advisors say."

"How confident are you that we will encounter no enemy?"

"Our priests say that they see no signs of the enemy, Your Highness. But they have been wrong in the past," I reply, remembering that one augur claimed our sailing to Egypt would be smooth and without incident.

"But what if?" he presses, but I do not begrudge him; it is the sign of a maturing commander—to always plan for the unexpected.

"We are much better prepared this time. We have advance scouts and a rear guard. Our force is large and well equipped. Three divisions of ten thousand men will march in a wide formation to avoid being boxed in."

I explain our strategy in case of ambush. We do not yet know if there are narrow passageways or canyons, but our advisors tell us that as long as we stay along the river, we will remain on flatlands. Go further west, they say, and you meet desert; go further east, and you encounter rugged mountains. But we will avoid such areas.

"When do we march?"

"In ten days, Your Majesty. We must wait for our advance scouts to return before we move the entire army."

He seems relieved that there is more time before our departure—postponing the inevitable.

"What do we do until then?"

I am tempted to ask him if he listened to any of the briefings before we sailed. "We practice our routines, ensure we are ready for the march, anchor the boats and hide them where we can, and review our plans and directions again," I say, knowing my voice conveys impatience.

Nimmuruk stares at me. "When I ask you a question, general, you answer," he says. The rest of the men shuffle uneasily.

I stare at him.

"Do you understand?"

"Yes, Your Highness," I reply. I have saved this spoiled idiot, and yet he has no gratitude.

"Report to me every morning. You may leave now," he commands. I turn to exit the tent, but then he stops us all. "Remember, all the *Upashaktis* report to me. You are the general until I say otherwise."

The excitement and energy in the room are palpable.

"Are you certain?" I ask the scout.

"Yes, sir! There is no question."

"How big is the army?"

"We think it is at least fifteen to twenty thousand men. They march in a narrow column."

"Have you been spotted?"

The scout bows his head sheepishly. "Yes, sir."

Nimmuruk intervenes. "How many days before they arrive here?"

"If we stay and they march, then less than ten days, Your Highness."

"How many horses do they have?"

"Few, sir. We noticed only a few horse riders and a few on chariots. Otherwise, their army is entirely on foot."

"Composition?"

"It was difficult to tell from the distance, sir. But they most certainly have archers along with swords, maces, and ax-men."

We question the scout further to gain a thorough understanding of the advancing army. It is the Egyptian army, but we do not yet know if the Pharaoh accompanies it, as the scout stated that there were no grand displays anywhere in the column—either at the head or in the middle.

"We will teach them a lesson they will never forget," Nimmuruk says, swinging his short ax.

"Let us not underestimate them, Your Highness. They have had the intelligence to group and march their armies north, which means they have planned this well. Prime Minister Rishwa briefed us that their general, Wadjmose, is a formidable man."

What is remarkable is that the Egyptians have astutely calculated that we might invade. If we had been delayed by weeks, we would have had to face their army just as we landed, which could have been a disaster.

Nimmuruk scoffs. "Our tactics will destroy them," he declares, looking around the room. Most of the senior officers nod vigorously, out of fear or respect. I know that at least three of my *Upashaktis* are fanatically loyal to the Prince. I wonder what tactics the Prince speaks of, for he has had no input on any of it. What is worse is that he has refused to deploy all our *Daivoshaktis*—worried that we will deplete all our weaponry and should hold considerable reserves for future offensives. He ignores my argument that a decisive victory now would put us at a significant advantage.

He is convinced that we can thrash the Egyptians without fully employing our *Daivoshaktis*.

I plead and argue with no success.

The next few days blur together. We declare a rapid march southward, and the army assembles for the journey. I rearrange the march plan—while the terrain is mostly benign, it may not be wise to spread too wide and risk the enemy smashing the center. Every *Upashaktis* leads their unit in blocks two hundred deep and one hundred wide. We finalize our flag semaphores and tactical orders, and at the first crack of dawn, the Atalanni army finally begins its fateful journey.

I pray to the gods for victory, for the well-being of Apsara, and for the glory of the Atalanni over others.

# CHAPTER 34

## KALLISTU

*But why?* Apsara wonders.

The last thing she felt was the wind on her face before strong, wiry arms enveloped her and pulled her back to safety.

Prime Minister Rishwa.

He had saved her life, and she had sobbed uncontrollably while holding him. The old Prime Minister infused strength in her—to hold on, to survive, to face the odds. He told her remarkable stories of valiant queens of the past; those who dealt with unloving husbands or rebellious populations. He explained the need for courage and duty.

He imparted the obligations of a queen—one of which was never to be cowed or run from life.

But the days are hard. Hannuruk's ailment of the mind and his tooth are only worsening. There are days when he screams and rants for hours, especially when the effects of the calming salves on his gums wear off.

Yet, she is resolved to survive.

She thinks of Teber every day, not knowing where he is or if he is still alive.

But no news means there is still hope.

# CHAPTER 35

## NEAR SAIS – EGYPT

My ears still ring from the explosions of the *Dharbastis*. We watch, with utter exhaustion and despair, as the Pharaoh's army retreats, leaving behind the dead. The first major clash has yielded no victory for either side; however, our underestimation of their forces and tactics, combined with lower numbers and insufficient use of *Daivoshaktis*, has led to significant losses on both sides and a stalemate.

We lack the energy and reserves to chase them. I had to convince the Prince to pull back. The Egyptians have an endless supply of men and materials via land, while we do not. My legs wobble, and I collapse from exhaustion. Around me are the corpses: stabbed, bashed, burned, cut, and impaled. Some are still alive and groaning, and we will soon put an end to the misery of those beyond hope. The Prince is alive, but we have lost many.

Bansabira sits beside me and hands me a water skin. I take greedy gulps, my hand shaking. "How bad?" I ask him.

"We have lost battalions, sir. We should have retreated earlier. We will count the losses later tonight."

I lean back and lie flat on the ground, looking up at skies still hazy with dust and smoke.

I am such a failure.

Our first mission to Egypt was a failure.

We barely survived our first ambush.

We just saved ourselves from the first major battle.

"Do you still trust my abilities, Bansabira?" I ask him, feeling anxious.

Bansabira looks at me and grins. His matted hair is styled into a bun, and blood covers his body. "If it were not for you, we would all be dead by now, sir. It is you who keeps us alive, with that clueless idiot dictating tactics."

I sigh. Who said wars were easy to win?

# CHAPTER 36
## THEBES – UPPER EGYPT

Pharaoh Ahmose has called a war council after days of depression and prayer. He feels demoralized but cannot show that to his people. Wadjmose has stood by his side, encouraging him and giving him the power to persevere. His wife has been a constant companion and a fountain of strength during these days of darkness. The council is in full attendance—the Queen, the vizier of Upper Egypt, Wadjmose and his senior officers, Menkheperre the Chief Priest, chieftains of ten nomes under the Pharaoh's control, the Masters of Treasury and Temples, the Minister of Agriculture, and high priests of the temple of Amun—they all wait for the Pharaoh to speak.

As the living god, Ahmose knows he must put on a brave face and yet find a way out of the potential destruction facing his land. Ahmose appreciates Wadjmose's counsel and assurance. The formidable general is not easily cowed; he has seen much in his battles with the Asiatics while serving the great Kamose.

Ahmose makes his opening statements. "The brave soldiers of Egypt have laid down their lives to fight an evil that comes from the Sea. We have fought them and pushed them to the far north, but the pestilence remains."

The council nods in agreement and cheers the Pharaoh.

"But our situation is dire. Our granaries are depleting, and we have lost many young men in our battles with the Atalanni. We must regain strength before engaging them again," he says, surveying those around him. "Once we drive them out of our lands, we will turn on the wretched Asiatic impostors."

Wadjmose rises from his chair. The general looks haggard from worry—his handsome, broad face shows lines of stress, yet his eyes shine brightly. He takes center stage and addresses the Pharaoh and the council.

"You speak like an experienced general, Your Majesty," Wadjmose says. "You are correct. Our resources are stretched. Our men are not ready for a war on two fronts. We must seek a truce if possible, and at a minimum delay another full-scale clash."

"But how?" asks the Pharaoh. He has some thoughts, but the right solution eludes him.

"Perhaps we can trick Khamudi into launching an attack on the Atalanni in exchange for a truce with us?" suggests Menkheperre.

Wadjmose nods appreciatively at the Chief Priest's suggestion. "Except there is a greater risk that they will turn on us instead and try to recruit the Nubians and the weaker among us to fight the Atalanni after they destroy us."

Ahmose agrees with this assessment. "They are quiet. They wait. We must resolve the Atalanni question first." Besides, Ahmose has established a powerful garrison of eighteen thousand men to the south of the Asiatics' capital to discourage any venture southward.

"If we do nothing, the Atalanni will regain their strength, re-supply, and march again," says the Minister of Agriculture. His chief worry is the chance of civil revolt if the temple granaries are empty.

"Can we send emissaries to them and request a truce?" asks Menkheperre. It is an idea that has been on Ahmose's mind, but he waited for someone else to voice it, for it could show signs of weakness.

All eyes turn to the Pharaoh. Ahmose feels hot beneath his skin; this is a test from the gods, and yet a solution eludes him. He prays silently and hopes for a spark in his mind. If he cannot lead the great people of Egypt, he will only be seen as an ineffective boy.

"I have an idea, husband," a gentle voice wafts from the side. Queen Ahmose-Nefertari takes his hand.

"What is it, dear wife?" he asks, knowing that the God's Wife has insightful opinions.

"Direct attempts to reach the Atalanni may not work, for we know they can blockade our boats and may not hesitate to murder our peace emissaries."

The men nod in agreement.

"But the Atalanni King is wedded to the daughter of the Mitanni King. Mitanni is a very new kingdom and desires cordial relations and trade with Egypt."

Ahmose's eyes light up. "We shall send a message to the Atalanni through the Mitanni."

Nefertari smiles. It is a beautiful smile—wide, energetic, and her eyes twinkle with happiness from her husband's appreciation for her idea.

The men examine the proposal further, and it seems like a sound plan. There are paths to the Mitanni capital that can evade the Atalanni's watchful eyes and the Asiatics. Once they reach Sinai, the regions are friendly to Egypt, and there are no quarrels with the governors and chieftains that serve the Mitanni or the Assyrians. Besides, most of the land away from the towns along the seashores is arid and deserted.

Finally, Ahmose decides, "An emissary shall go with gifts to the Atalanni court, with the assistance of the Mitanni. We shall convey that Egypt wishes to make peace."

"Yes, Your Majesty," responds Wadjmose.

"We will wait for the emissary to return to us. Then, an Egyptian delegation will depart for the Atalanni capital."

"It will take many moons for this to happen. It is a risky strategy, but we must be patient," says Menkheperre. The others nod in agreement.

"We have many emissaries to choose from, Your Majesty, but who shall we send as representatives of the Royal house?" asks Wadjmose. Any overture of significance must be presented by someone of high rank.

Ahmose sighs and looks at his wife. It is as if they read each other's minds, for they have someone in mind for this critical mission.

# PART III

*We are superior to all other peoples. Our knowledge greater, our arts richer, our towns cleaner, our men braver, our ships faster, our blades sharper, our ways more right and our gods more able. The Atalanni are rulers and the rest lesser."*

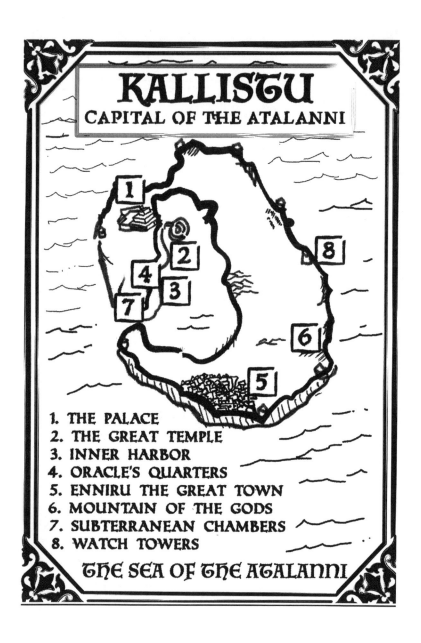

# KALLISTU
## CAPITAL OF THE ATALANNI

1. THE PALACE
2. THE GREAT TEMPLE
3. INNER HARBOR
4. ORACLE'S QUARTERS
5. ENNIRU THE GREAT TOWN
6. MOUNTAIN OF THE GODS
7. SUBTERRANEAN CHAMBERS
8. WATCH TOWERS

## THE SEA OF THE ATALANNI

# CHAPTER 37

## KALLISTU

Much time has passed, and much has happened. The Prince and I have been recalled to Kallistu for this momentous occasion, even as our army remains in Egypt.

I cannot help but marvel at the scene.

Princess Sitkamose, Kamose's daughter, and Prince Binpu, Pharaoh Ahmose's brother, stand proudly before King Hannuruk. It is a scene no one ever predicted—that royalty from Egypt would stand before the Atalanni King seeking a truce.

I have never seen Egyptian royalty up close.

Sitkamose is not beautiful in the way we regard our women—she is tall and resembles a man, but she possesses regal, handsome features. She wears the distinct gold-and-blue wide-patterned headgear with a serpent on top, which they call the Uraeus. Her hair is a dark black wig that falls over both her shoulders. She sparkles in a bright white linen gown with silver-bordered embroidery and a gold-patterned waist belt. In her hand, she holds a curved stick made of gold and adorned with Lapis Lazuli.

She is a striking woman.

Binpu is of slight build and stands beside his older cousin. He too is dressed in the same wide-patterned headgear but also wears a full necklace made of many strings of beads. He is disfigured—his back is bent slightly, giving him the appearance of an older man even though he is less than twenty. Translators and other royal support personnel accompany the Egyptians. Behind the Egyptian Prince and Princess, several Egyptian slaves stand with gifts—gold necklaces, ivory jewelry boxes, lapis-lazuli rings, finely engraved alabaster boxes, amulets, blue glass armbands, turquoise pendants, blue-glazed scarabs, ivory-inlaid swords and daggers with gold hilts, silver scimitars, ingots of precious copper and tin, various luxurious linens, and many other items. This contingent arrived days ago but had been asked to wait for an audience with the King and the Prince, who now holds an elevated position in his father's eyes, for the King sees it is his son who has brought the Egyptians to this state.

King Hannuruk looks ill and obese. The King's speech slurs most of the time, and his eyes are bloodshot. Apsara sits beside him—my beautiful Apsara—she resembles a dancer from the heavens. I hope to meet her soon. She appears healthier—there is color in her cheeks, and her eyes glint every time she glances at me.

The Prime Minister occupies the King's side today. His steady and calming presence is comforting. With the King's condition, it is now Nimmuruk's court. Phaistos sits beside the King; he now assumes the role of Minos, though the King has not yet named him the successor of Kaftu. There are curt introductions and greetings, but the air is hostile, and there is little affection on either side. The Egyptians are stern and unsmiling, while Prince Nimmuruk smirks and sniggers from time to time.

The Prince's behavior is impolite and unwelcome, but such is his personality.

Once the pleasantries end, the treaty begins. The Egyptian royalty is afforded the courtesy of comfortable chairs, though they are seated at a level below that of the King and Prince, thus forcing them to look up. It is no different from how the Asiatics treated us in their court.

This is war. They are here for a truce, and we must secure an upper hand to prevent further bloodshed and loss of Atalanni lives.

"State your reason," says Hannuruk, opening formal discussions. The King, despite looking ill and indisposed, articulates well. He slurs a little, but the words are unmistakable in his low growl.

Sitkamose stands, proud. "Under the guidance of the God of Egypt, He of the Sedge and the Bee, Lord of Upper and Lower Egypt, beloved of Amun, Pharaoh Ahmose, I am instructed to negotiate a peace agreement between the Kingdoms of Egypt and the Atalanni," she declares, her voice loud and clear.

Hannuruk's languid face displays little emotion. "Are you authorized to negotiate on behalf of your Pharaoh?"

"Yes, Your Majesty," replies Sitkamose.

She extends her arms and opens her palms.

An adjutant places a papyrus in her hand.

She then holds it up to display the royal cartouche of Ahmose and the instructions under a wax seal.

She breaks the seal and reads. "Egypt authorizes my beloved sister and brother to negotiate a peace treaty with the King of the Atalanni. I ask that Hannuruk, Father and King of the Atalanni, grant audience and heed this proposition."

Nimmuruk scoffs. "Why does your Pharaoh call my father 'Father'? He is no father of yours!"

Sitkamose regards the Prince coolly, as if appraising an insolent fool. "We address the kings of our neighboring kingdoms as father or brother, Your Highness. It is a mark of respect."

"You are making—"

Hannuruk turns to his son and admonishes him. "Be quiet! This is a peace treaty, not your harem."

"Father—"

"I said be quiet," says Hannuruk. Nimmuruk turns red and bristles under the admonishment, but he keeps his mouth shut. He casts a baleful glance at the Egyptian Princess.

"Princess, what is Egypt's proposition?" asks the King gently.

Khaia straightens and watches Sitkamose.

Princess Sitkamose bows to the King.

"We propose a complete halt to hostilities. In return, Egypt will pay an annual tax of a hundred boats of grain, allow access to our harbors, submit three talents of gold from our mines, and supply the workforce to extract tin from Cyprus. We will also grant you sovereign access to land fifty miles long and fifty miles deep on the coast of Egypt."

Phaistos leans forward, but Hannuruk raises his hand. "I will be the one speaking," he says, "and the rest of you remain silent until I allow you."

Phaistos, chastened, leans back. I will not open my mouth until I am asked, but I am certain the Prince will break the rule eventually.

"And why would we agree to such terms?" asks the King.

"It is a fair agreement, King Hannuruk. You seek more land, and you receive a piece of our sacred earth without further bloodshed. You gain grain to prosper, and Egypt is spared from additional hostility."

"What makes you think you are in a position of strength?"

"Egypt is much stronger than you think, Your Majesty. If we were weak and beaten, you would not have entertained a delegation," she states. It is a smart and respectful response.

Hannuruk smiles. His jowls droop, and he wipes the saliva from the corner of his lips. "And yet it is you who seek the peace conference and not us," he observes.

Sitkamose bows and smiles. "It is thus an acknowledgment that both kingdoms desire truce."

Hannuruk watches her intently, and the Princess maintains her constant eye contact. He finally turns to Rishwa. "What do you say?"

The Prime Minister rubs his chin. "A fool barters his bread for gold, but the wise man barters his bread for seeds. Your Highness, Princess Sitkamose, why do you believe that a hundred boats of grain, some gold, and a small piece of land make a good settlement in return for the safety of your entire population and the preservation of your kingdom?"

Before Princess Sitkamose can respond, the diminutive Egyptian Prince, Binpu, speaks up. He possesses a strong voice—it is deep, soft, and carries the weight of royalty. "No kingdom relinquishes a piece of its land and access to its harbors without serious thought and great sacrifice, Prime Minister," he asserts, continuing, "To cede a piece of Egypt is the greatest sign of respect, peace, and intent for harmony. Would you," he points to the Prime Minister, "ever consider giving a portion of Keftiu to a foreign ruler?"

Rishwa nods. "While we acknowledge the intent, you have so far not convinced us why we should accept so little when we can receive so much more."

There is silence in the room. It is late afternoon, and a persistent heat hangs in the air. Sweat beads upon foreheads, lips, and chests, while the slaves work hard to fan the members of the peace treaty. Nimmuruk snaps his fingers at a servant to come closer and fan him harder.

Finally, Princess Sitkamose speaks. "What is it you seek?"

Rishwa turns to King Hannuruk and the Prince for approval. They then confer among themselves before the Prime Minister addresses the Egyptians. "We demand an annual tribute of one thousand boats of grain and a quarter of all your gold, land two hundred miles wide and one hundred miles deep, and a temple dedicated to our gods to be built in your capital, to be worshipped every year alongside your gods."

I can feel the sting of the response. Curiously, the Oracle sits stone-faced, displaying no expression and uttering not a word so far. Her eyes remain fixed on the Egyptians, and she has barely made eye contact with anyone else.

I wonder what she is thinking.

I glance up to see Apsara, hoping to steal a look while everyone is busy watching the Egyptians. Unfortunately, she too looks ahead curiously. She purses her lips and places her knuckles beneath her chin. The slightest dimple on her chin is maddeningly beautiful.

I wonder if she is reconciled with the King and feels a pang of jealousy. Sitkamose confers with her cousin and refers to something on a papyrus. I wonder if those are instructions to negotiate settlements and how far they can go.

"Six hundred boats of grain, one-tenth of gold, a temple midway between your lands and our capital, and land which is one hundred miles wide and fifty miles deep."

Rishwa laughs appreciatively. "You negotiate well, Princess. You only give us a marginal extension of your original proposals."

I observe Sitkamose's body language. She appears comfortable with the Prime Minister, who resembles a wise father. Besides, I am astonished at the terms—we will have a permanent foothold in Egypt, our gods will tread upon their land, we will spill no more blood, and access to Egyptian harbors will make us the most powerful nation.

In time, we can build our strength on their land and launch a more significant attack. I wonder if they see that.

"You bargain harder, Prime Minister. I know you recognize the benefit of establishing a foothold in Egypt. To obtain such a large piece of land affords you the chance to build your fortifications and establish your divisions. Egypt understands that. However, we believe in an honorable truce."

There are further negotiations, with minor changes to the terms. Phaistos questions whether Egypt plans to ambush and attack us on the dedicated land, and the answers satisfy the assembly. So far, the Oracle has not spoken. Even when the King asked her once, she merely stated, "I obey the terms. I chose this day for the gods commanded me it should be when such matters are discussed."

She is correct. We had to make the Egyptians wait over ten days before convening this audience, all because of the Oracle's instructions to the King.

Hannuruk finally speaks up. "We have discussed much, and the Atalanni recognize your genuine gesture, Princess. But we must deliberate amongst ourselves and make a decision. You will be well taken care of, and we ask you to rest until we reconvene in a few days."

The Egyptians rise and bow to the audience. "We are two great kingdoms, King Hannuruk, and our agreements will usher in an era of prosperity!" declares Sitkamose.

We continue debating once the Egyptians depart.

"Well?" asks Hannuruk.

"We do not know if behind the door lies a hungry lion or an inviting maiden. The question is whether the gods will accept this agreement," replies Rishwa.

"It is a substantial agreement," states Hannuruk. His son looks almost disappointed but remains silent. I harbor my own reservations but prefer to remain quiet until I am asked.

"That it is," says Rishwa. "The gold and grain can be dismissed, but the offer of land on the shores is a significant concession."

"What do you say, Khaia? Do you think this will appease our divinity?" asks the King. Khaia is quiet for a while, and she finally speaks. Her voice is gentle, lacking the usual sharp edge. "Their concessions are significant, Your Majesty. Their intentions sound sincere. It is not for me to say if our gods are pleased by a piece of land in Egypt—perhaps they are. But I have seen no signs either way, and I wish to wait a few days to see if any untoward signs arise after we make our decision."

Nimmuruk interjects. "Surely, there must be some signs. We made them come here for a truce!"

"The absence of expressions of anger and the pleasant weather shows their satisfaction so far, Prince. I cannot foretell the future," she says, turning her attention to the King.

"Should we accept?" the King asks again. This time, he turns to me. "What do you think, Teber? You have seen quite a bit of their land and fought them multiple times already."

I stand up and face them, positioning myself to gain an eyeful of the Queen even as I speak to the King and the Prince.

"They are a clever and resilient people, Your Majesty. Their gods are resourceful. That the Pharaoh concedes so much means they must want peace. When I contemplate the challenges of fighting them on their land, I believe their offer can spare us from further bloodshed."

"Do you not think we can beat them handily?" Rishwa asks.

"Of course, we can. We already beat them!" shouts Prince Nimmuruk, his face flushed because no one has sought his opinion.

"Well, if you beat them handily, then why are we not in their capital?" his father retorts. "Do not think I do not know about losses! Yes, you fought well, but we have not beaten them enough!"

"It is a war, father. Of course, there are losses!" Nimmuruk responds to his father. There is a stunned silence—he has never raised his voice against his father before. Hannuruk glares at his son, and I wonder what comes next.

After several tense moments, the King breaks into a broad grin. "You are right, Khaia. My son has become a lion!" he exclaims, slapping his son on the shoulder. Nimmuruk cannot contain his joy—I have never seen him smile so much, and his malevolent eyes twinkle. "I am the son of an illustrious father," he says, false humility dripping from every word.

Hannuruk turns to me again. "Teber, my son is the supreme commander, but you are the general and the tactician. What do you think?"

I look at the Prince, and his smile has vanished. He wears the same frustrated expression—one of a man whose counsel no one seeks.

"I maintain it will always be challenging, Your Majesty. It is simply the size of their land and population. We will be limited by our nature—island dwellers with a limited population under our command. If we agree to the truce and gain a piece of their land, then we can take the next few summers to build a powerful presence, establish necessary trade routes, shore up our defenses and weaponry, and then make a bold attack. We must grow our population—"

"Minos is dead," deadpans Phaistos. The audience erupts into laughter. Even the serious Oracle cannot help but grin.

Rishwa smiles, and the King nods as well. He turns to Phaistos. "What do you say?"

Phaistos has been quiet, his shifty eyes darting among us. However, I have gained some respect for his abilities. He pauses for a moment. "If General Teber had defeated them conclusively, we would not be having this conversation. But given the current situation, I agree with the General's assessment."

I marvel at his ability to blame and praise me simultaneously. "May I, Your Majesty?" I ask.

The King nods.

"Phaistos was not on the ground fighting and perhaps has little understanding of the complexities of war, but I must admit he has executed commendably as a coach and supplied us with the necessary provisions for the invasion," I say, holding Phaistos' gaze.

Apsara giggles, and the King roars with laughter. "Our men have a new spirit today!" he exclaims, and Phaistos breaks character and smiles as well. There is levity in the room, and we argue a little longer before reaching a consensus that this is a splendid development.

Finally, the King makes his final announcement. "So, it is decided. With our bravery and robust action, we have brought the Egyptians to the bargaining table and gained a foothold on their land!" he declares, and there is great cheer in the room. Khaia remains the only quiet one, and I do not understand why.

Hannuruk turns to his son. "I may be gone one day, my son, but you will launch a bigger war on Egypt and make it ours!"

Nimmuruk bows to his father and pumps his fist. "I will, father, but I hope that glory will come to us long before you are gone!"

More cheers and bows ensue.

I can almost feel my heart lighten. If this development holds and we enter a truce, that would give me ample time and the chance to unite with Apsara.

I will vanish with the woman I love and let greater men fight for what they desire.

As the assembly finally dissolves, I stand aside as the royals make their way out of the throne room. Apsara's eyes connect with mine—joy and laughter dance within those depths.

It feels as though the gods finally smile upon us.

# CHAPTER 38

## KALLISTU

They enter the cavernous chamber and make their way to the rock-hewn stairs that seem to disappear into the darkness below. It is damp, hot, and growing hotter as they descend the steps illuminated by flickering lamps set at intervals of ten to fifteen steps. Their skin is wet and slick with sweat, and it becomes increasingly laborious to breathe with each step.

It feels as if they are approaching the gates of hell.

Far down in the abyss, a golden-red glow emerges, and that is all they can see if they dare to look below instead of focusing on the steps ahead. They tiptoe, breathing harder with each step, sometimes wiping their faces or covering their noses to protect themselves from the noxious fumes and smells that waft up from below. The golden-red glow seems tantalizingly close, but they know it will take hundreds of steps before they reach the rim of the pit where molten rock bubbles and swirls.

"It feels worse than five days ago," one of them says.

"It is. But not to the extent we feared," replies the other.

They continue, passing each flickering lamp, the only other contribution to the otherwise claustrophobic darkness around them, smothering them in a black and ill-smelling blanket.

"Be careful!" one of them warns, gripping the forearm of the other. The stone steps are damp, and without the right grip, it is easy to tumble and vanish below. Many have died here, but today is not the time for accidents.

After what feels like an eternity, they finally arrive on flat ground.

It is sweltering here.

Some others await them. Here, they are level with the pit, and what they see is merely a faint yellow light emanating from beyond the rim. They dare not peer into it yet; it is as if the god's angry eye looks back at them.

"Well?" asks the leader.

The man who has been waiting bows. His face glistens with sweat, and he has draped himself with a sheer fabric, dampened for protection.

"The forces gather strength below us. Molten rock has not yet swelled above our markers. But without question— ten days or less—we will experience major tremors."

"You are confident."

"As confident as I can be. We have rarely been wrong."

"This is not the time to be wrong, even if it is rare, Chief Engineer," the leader asserts.

The Chief Engineer of the Atalanni is known for his fierce intellect and is one of the most revered figures in the Divine Council. At fifty, he knows the deepest secrets of the earth and the skies, the signs and behaviors of metals, and has been instrumental in the discovery and creation of the Atalanni *Daivoshaktis*—one seen as magical and bestowed by the gods, but one that the Oracle and the Chief Engineer know has been forged in the minds of the engineers.

"I understand. For the last month, there has been a steady, unquestionable increase in the activity below us. Our instruments may be crude, but they are sufficient to show changes. The pits in other chambers," he says, pointing to other areas beyond this cavern, "show similar symptoms. When we see such activity, there will be more tremors soon."

"What is soon? You said ten days."

The man bows again. "I stand corrected. Yes, only ten days. It could be as soon as five."

The leader contemplates the situation. The Egyptians wait to hear the King's proclamation, and they have so far been kept in the dark.

"How bad will it be?"

"There should be tremors, nothing more. But they will be felt."

"As bad as last time? Those almost destroyed the central temple."

"Not as bad. We learned from that incident—"

"If you are wrong, I will have your head."

"As you wish, sacred Khaia," the man replies, bowing to the Oracle.

"Is that all?" Khaia asks.

The man shuffles nervously on his feet. His two assistants look equally anxious. Khaia wipes her brow and steps closer to the Chief Engineer.

"You are nervous. What is it?" she inquires.

"I wanted to wait a few days before I told you, Khaia," the Chief Engineer admits. "But you are too astute to ignore my emotions."

One half of the Chief Engineer's face reflects the warm glow from the pit, and he resembles a strange apparition from the otherworld.

"Well, go ahead. I do not want surprises."

"The measurement pits near the central temple and in the two western extremities tell a different story."

"What do you mean?"

"There is much greater violence in the molten rock; it is rising fast, and there is an almost continuously increasing tremor."

Khaia wipes her face again and fans herself. There is a hint of nervousness in her voice. "What does that mean?"

"While the next tremors might be gentle, Oracle, I am afraid we are headed for a far worse eruption."

Silence descends.

Except for the bubbling and soft hiss from the uneasy earth.

The Chief Engineer explains what the signs mean and what the implications are. Khaia listens intently, sometimes asking questions for clarification. When it is over, she swears them all to secrecy under the pain of execution.

There is much to be done and not enough time.

Finally, Khaia walks gingerly to the edge of the pit. Her thick footwear protects her from the heat on the rocks. She peers over the side—the scene is both beautiful and terrifying. The bright orange-red liquid rock swirls beneath—It almost looks delicious to consume, and yet it is nothing but the harbinger of death.

She steps back—now struggling to breathe. She signals to the others that it is time to go and instructs everyone to leave.

As she begins her climb back, her mind becomes a red-hot cauldron of emotions.

# CHAPTER 39

## KALLISTU

The trembling of the ground starts as a gentle vibration beneath our feet and then feels like the heavy breath and grunt of a horse or a bull. The quake lasts for minutes— never too severe, but just enough to compel the multitude out into the open. A hairline crack appears on the barrack wall. Other structures around us, including the palace walls, remain unharmed except for a few cracks. A few loose compounds and decrepit walls come crashing down.

Birds fly in the sky, animals create a great ruckus, and people wait for the trembling to cease. The sea below sways gently, with waves rising higher but never with sufficient intensity to damage the temple causeway beyond its current ruined state.

By the time the tremors end, most people are out in the open. I make my way to the palace alongside a few senior officers and find Phaistos and his contingent climbing up the steps that lead to the palace compound at the edge of the western side of the inner cliffs. The quake subsides after about twenty minutes, and as is customary, assessors fan across the island, lighting large signaling lamps to exchange casualty and damage reports.

We progress to the large open arena, sometimes used for high-level meetings, where the King's Guard directs us to be seated and await the royals. I speculate that these tremors bode ill for our plans with Egypt. We wait for two hours before the King and his entourage finally appear—he looks grim, and Nimmuruk seems angry. The Royals take their seats, with Apsara beside the King, looking sullen and avoiding my gaze. The Prime Minister stands right beside the King.

Soon, the Oracle and her people make their appearance. They are all dressed in their ceremonial garb, each holding a bronze-handled, gilded double axe in one hand and a bronze bell in the other. These instruments are used when the Oracle has anything momentous to declare.

The air is chilly; it is as if a dark force swirls around us.

Everyone sits in the open arena. I am in the front, on the innermost ring of the circular stone benches, close to where the Royals are. It is still hard for me to accept that I am one of the most senior-ranking officers of the Kingdom. The ushers ask the audience to listen.

An announcer takes the stage on the stone podium in the center of the arena.

"We have lost sixty people to crumbling walls and collapsing cliff sides," he says, "and there are cracks on the throne."

Gasps ripple through the audience. An Atalanni throne is a sacred object—it comprises a solid slab of granite, overlaid with marble and sandstone, and is decorated with sacred symbols. It is a beautiful throne, though I have little respect for the man who sits upon it.

"The King will speak," he announces before stepping away. Two men with musical horns sound a note, and Hannuruk stands up. It is evident to anyone observing that the King is in no condition to speak—he sways where he stands, and when he raises his hand, it trembles. After several guttural attempts, he turns to his son and grips his shoulder. "Him," he utters a single word and collapses back into his seat.

Nimmuruk bows to his father and stands up. This is not a favorable development—the King may be a drunkard and losing his faculties, but at least he ruled in peace and considered options before deciding. I can see that Nimmuruk is working himself into a rage, as I have seen so many times before. He huffs and puffs up his chest. His face reddens, and he clenches and relaxes his fist repeatedly.

This is his first full command of the senior audience.

He waits for a moment as all eyes fix upon him. Nimmuruk turns to the Oracle. "Sacred Khaia, tell everyone what you told us," he commands.

Khaia stands and the audience bows. She takes two steps forward, and two of her chief priestesses stand behind her, swinging their double axes. These women are mesmerizing. The blades glint in the evening sun. They then gently ring the bells, and the soft tinkle brings calm to the arena.

"The gods are displeased," she states. A hush falls over the crowd, and I can sense many taking a sharp breath as they intake. "They do not approve of our agreement with Egypt," she says softly, but her words are clear to all. The Prime Minister bends his head down in deep thought, and Phaistos' eyes catch mine. There is a quiet understanding of what this means.

"The rumbles are a warning, but their gentleness is a message that we must stay our original course. A small patch of land is an insult, not an accomplishment," she explains. "The Goddess Mother of Earth appeared in my dreams nights ago, just after our conference with the Egyptians, and she spoke no words as I implored her. All that came of her were sounds of the tremor we all heard just a few hours ago," she continues. The audience, myself included, makes signs of peace and seeks forgiveness from the Goddess. It is no wonder the Goddess sent her message to the Oracle and followed up with the tremors.

"You all know that I asked to wait ten days before we gave our assent to the agreement, and now you know why."

A murmur spreads through the audience. King Hannuruk sways in his chair, and a servant wipes the drool from the corner of the King's mouth.

Khaia resumes, "The desires of the gods are mysterious yet meaningful. The relationships of kingdoms are complicated. The dominion of one over the other is a natural state of the world; the superiority of one people over another must be exercised through their free will. The gods of the Atalanni ask that we demonstrate our worth to them."

The priestesses ring the bells again.

Khaia kneels and raises both her hands to the skies while her priestesses walk around the kneeling Oracle in circles, chanting hymns. The ceremony lasts several minutes. Finally, the Oracle rises and thunders, "This is not the news I wished to impart to this noble audience, but it is my interpretation that the gods expect us to evacuate this capital—"

An uproar erupts. Most of us react with shock. Leave the capital?

After much commotion, the ushers restore silence and allow Khaia to continue.

"Our reluctance to act with urgency and ambition has caused their frustration. That we compromise easily on tough questions is shameful. Today's tremors are but a beginning; the earth will shake in anger again, and not in the too distant future. Why? Because our divine powers wish us to establish a home on the mainland and spread our seed and our power. That hour has come. We must plan for it."

I fidget. Many others hug themselves as if the icy finger of fate has brushed against their necks.

"What that means, as I have explained to their Majesties and the Prime Minister, is that we begin the evacuation of our cherished treasures, divine weaponry, libraries, and symbols of worship, moving them to the secret holdout we have designed in the eastern desert. Moreover, we must conclude our war with Egypt and take possession. Nothing else will bring our gods' mercy back."

With that, Khaia steps back and takes a seat. The priestesses ring the bells again, chanting their hymns as the audience sits in stunned silence.

Okoninos and Pausinur rise from their seats, seeking to ask questions, and they express hostility toward the Oracle. The usher requests their compliance. I harbor numerous questions and emotions, unsure how to react. I am also angered that I had not been privy to this information before the announcement.

I have led a war for them. I saved the Prince multiple times. I brought us back from Egypt. And yet I am denied access to the innermost thoughts of the eminent powers of the land. I wallow in self-pity and self-righteous indignation for a while until Nimmuruk rises again.

We all wonder what comes next.

"Bring them!" Nimmuruk announces.

There is a stir, and from the entry door, the Egyptian Princess Sitkamose and Prince Binpu appear, followed by their bodyguards and our soldiers behind them. They look bewildered, yet they make their way to the center of the arena to face the Royals and other officials. They are only partially dressed in their regalia, and Sitkamose's hair is a messy tangle.

Once they settle in the center, Nimmuruk addresses Khaia again. "Tell them, Oracle," he instructs.

I observe Khaia's annoyance at being ordered around, but she rises and addresses the Egyptians. "Our gods have spoken, Princess Sitkamose and Prince Binpu," she declares, as they watch her intently. "We cannot accept the truce you offer us."

Sitkamose and Binpu glance at each other, and when Sitkamose attempts to speak, the Oracle raises her hand, signaling for silence. "Your offer, while generous at the outset, is not commensurate with the equation of our powers and the prestige of our people," she declares. I wonder if her mind is preoccupied with the momentous announcements just made.

Sitkamose responds, her voice dignified, "We feel great sorrow."

Khaia bows to the Princess and resumes, "I am certain Egypt came to us with good intentions—"

"They came to deceive us!" shouts Nimmuruk, interrupting the Oracle. Khaia turns to him in irritation, but the Prince stands, gesturing excitedly. "Their gods sent them here to fool us and force us into a false sense of accomplishment! Now look at our situation; we will lose our capital, and our gods are angry at our weak response. They tried to turn our gods against us!"

"Your Highness—" Khaia begins, but Nimmuruk disregards her.

"These two came here with malicious intent, and their god, the Pharaoh, is a wily trickster!" he exclaims, spitting at the Egyptians.

Sitkamose retaliates. "This is preposterous! We came in peace, and yet here you are accusing us of—"

Khaia places a hand on the Prince's shoulder. "Your interpretations go too far, Prince," she cautions, as this formal gathering devolves into a spectacle.

"Be quiet, Oracle!" Nimmuruk responds, swatting her hand away and ignoring his father's flailing gesture. "Why is it preposterous?" he shouts, pointing at Sitkamose. "You ugly dog-worshipper! The only thing you have not done so far is try to bribe me!"

Binpu rushes forward, cursing. His bodyguards hold him back as our soldiers surround the Egyptians. Sitkamose maintains her composure, head held high, but I can see intense anger and humiliation mar her features.

I wonder if the translators are performing their duties correctly.

Sitkamose retorts, "Your words are beneath the dignity of our Kingdom, and your gods laugh at your words, Prince Nimmuruk. How do you not realize that these tremors may be your gods advising you not to reject our proposal?"

Nimmuruk is momentarily flummoxed, but then he returns to his rage. "How foolish do you think we are? Have you not heard the Oracle's words? You are on our land, and our gods wield great power over yours—"

"Then why did you flee with your tails between your legs in the last great battle?" Sitkamose counters. "Our gods seek harmony with yours, and yet you spit at their benevolence!"

"We have not laughed at you. Do not make false accusations, Prince!"

Rishwa stands on his feet, and I rush to the center. We both attempt to reason with Nimmuruk, explaining that insulting Egyptian royalty is unwise, as we do not know how our gods view such behavior. Furthermore, the protocol between kingdoms requires respect among royalty.

However, Nimmuruk does not back down. He screams expletives at the delegation and, disregarding all norms, pushes his way through the guards to confront the Egyptians directly. I signal two of my officers to accompany me, asking one of them to fetch a sword. The Egyptian bodyguards remain unarmed—as was the requirement for them to appear at this assembly—but they form a protective cover around their master and mistress. Khaia approaches me, looking anxious. The Prince's guard prevents her from reaching him. "Teber, force Nimmuruk to stand down!" she says urgently, and I nod in response. I move ahead, trying to stay close and defuse the situation before it escalates.

As if by divine intervention, storm clouds gather quickly in the sky, darkening the surroundings while the wind picks up speed.

I am unarmed and frustrated that the man tasked with retrieving a sword has vanished. Nimmuruk now pushes against Binpu, while Sitkamose hugs her cousin protectively.

"We will crush you like cockroaches and burn your land, you lying daughter of a whore!" Nimmuruk screams, stabbing his fingers at Sitkamose. He has worked himself into a dramatic rage—his face is red with exertion and slick with sweat.

"Show respect to my sister, Prince Nimmuruk. You are brave only when surrounded by your armed guards!" shouts Binpu. I push ahead, forming a barrier between the two princes, and ask the translator to instruct Binpu to back down. There is a brief respite, and the two Egyptians look to me for intervention.

"Get back, Teber. Stand back before I cite you for disobedience," Nimmuruk threatens. He is not finished.

"You stand back, Your Highness. This is not the way to conduct our treaty!" I yell back at him. We should be ashamed of our conduct.

*What better are we than the Asiatics?*

The King's Guard pushes me back, and my orders have no effect. I possess no authority over them. Even Khaia is powerless as the King ignores her pleas, and the Prince prevents her from getting close.

"I will come and destroy Egypt and take you all as slaves! Your sister will spend her life chained to my legs, and I will fuck your Pharaoh's wife!" Nimmuruk shouts.

Sitkamose remains steady even as his men restrain Binpu. I admire the tiny Egyptian Prince for standing firm, despite his severely disadvantaged position. He says something, but the translator does not respond. Then Nimmuruk goads the translator. "What did he say? What did your sister-fucking bastard say? Speak it!"

Sitkamose places a protective hand on her cousin while the translator resists.

"Tell me what he said, or I will cut your head off!" screams Nimmuruk. Yet the translator remains mute, and Sitkamose and Binpu look on defiantly.

At that moment, the Atalanni translator steps forward, angered and upset. He exclaims, "The Prince curses that may Amun strike our land, may Horus smite our warriors, may you, Prince, burn to death, and may the wails of our women and children carry through eternity."

Before anyone can react, Nimmuruk pulls his obsidian dagger and stabs Binpu just below his ribcage. I lunge at the Prince and pull him back, but it is too late. Sitkamose screams, grabbing her cousin as his blood sprays onto her. The bodyguards begin to shout and jostle with the soldiers, and I scream at everyone to remain contained. I push the Prince away, and my officers leap into the fray. After some shouting and chaos, the King's Guard steps back. The Prince vanishes among them as my men pull the Egyptian bodyguards back and restrain them while we rush to the collapsed Binpu and the wailing Sitkamose.

I scream for a royal physician as I bend down to support the Egyptian Prince, and Sitkamose glares at me. Fury and sorrow fill her face, but I have no time to address her.

This is the second time Nimmuruk—the cowardly weasel—has attacked someone unarmed and unprepared. If the gods should be angry at anyone, it should be us!

Binpu bleeds profusely; his face turns white, and his eyes grow glassy. The physician attempts to stem the bleeding, but his expressions reveal that there is no hope. The Atalanni obsidian dagger is a fine weapon of exceptional sharpness, and the serrated edges easily slice through flesh as if it were honey. The fallen Prince convulses as blood rises in his throat and oozes from his mouth.

The Egyptians wail mournfully. The Princess cries, holding Binpu to her chest. She speaks to him, but he is unresponsive. Finally, in the arms of Sitkamose, the daughter of the great Kamose, Binpu, brother of the divine Pharaoh of Egypt, dies in the court of the Atalanni.

Sitkamose sits up. Her cheeks are wet with tears and her cousin's blood. Her throat, chest, and royal gown are all drenched in red. Her splendid hair falls across her face, hiding an eye. She raises her right hand and points it at the King on the throne.

She then whispers ominously.

The translator next to me speaks in a faint voice, "Wrath of god. She says the wrath of god will burn our houses and wipe our names from history."

# CHAPTER 40

## KALLISTU

I hold her gently in the darkness and feel her tears run down my chest. She smells of lilac, cinnamon, and sweat. Her soft body exudes a glowing warmth. Disheveled, she finds a rough surface that, while not made for making love to a Queen, is a luxury given the circumstances. Our secret meeting place remains hidden from most, and this is the last time we will meet before I rush back to Kaftu to continue onward to what we believe will be the decisive invasion of Egypt.

She seems to be doing better. She states that the King has moved from treating her with violence to being cold and indifferent. Then the discussion shifts to something else.

"Why do we need this war?" she asks, whispering.

"Because the gods want it. Because our rulers want it. Because the Oracle says so."

"And you believe all that?"

I am surprised by her question. "Do your people not heed the call of your high priests and the signs of your gods?"

She remains quiet for a while. "We do. But our gods have never sought war. The rulers solely make those decisions. Our priests limit themselves to matters of ceremony and righteous living."

"It seems each kingdom and its gods act differently," I say, unsure, but knowing no better. I harbor suspicions and questions, but I do not wish to offend powers I do not understand.

I can feel her breath as she nudges her face into the nook of my neck. I hold her and enjoy the feeling, but she is restless.

"Is there something else on your mind?"

"You can already make out how I feel?" she asks and giggles.

"When you twitch and breathe in that way, it usually means there is something you wish to say," I reply, smiling in the darkness.

"It feels like we are married," she says, squeezing my hand.

"We are, and yet we are not. Tell me, what is it?"

She hesitates.

"You know you can tell me anything. We are way past secrets, Apsara," I encourage.

"I will not anger you?"

"Nothing you say could ever anger me, love. No," I reassure, smoothing her hair. It is soft to the touch.

She remains quiet for a while and then sighs. "What do you think of your Oracle?"

"What do you mean?" I reply, surprised by the question.

"Is she... does she not have too much power over your King?"

"In what way?"

"Hannuruk does what she asks. So far, she has influenced the biggest decisions—the invasion of Egypt and evacuation."

"But is it not based on the signs of the gods?" I ask.

I sense her struggling to respond. "But—what if those signs have nothing to do with what she is asking?"

"How do you know that?"

"How do you know it is not that?" she retorts. I realize that our absolute acceptance of Khaia's words leaves us vulnerable, with nothing to defend ourselves against a messenger of the gods.

*But what if the messenger is lying?*

I feel a chill I have never experienced before, for I have never questioned the Oracle's words and actions. It is blasphemous to the Atalanni, yet Apsara retains the freedom of her mind and the wisdom of her land.

"I do not know, Apsara. We have grown to believe in the Oracle and trust that she watches over the well-being of the Kingdom."

Apsara falls silent. I know she is dissatisfied with my answer; she is sharp.

"Khaia visited me privately when you were away on your mission to Egypt," she reveals. This surprises me. Why would the Oracle visit the Queen privately?

"Why?"

She turns and presses against me. "She is an unpleasant woman," Apsara whispers, her voice low and conspiratorial. "She has taken a great interest in my marital woes."

I am at a loss for words. "Why does that concern her?"

"You are a fool sometimes, Teber," she teases.

"I am a happy fool for having fallen in love with the wife of a King," I reply, hugging her tightly. "Why is she concerned?"

"She speaks incessantly about the lack of issue. She knows it is not I who is the cause for the absence of a child, yet she seeks to place the blame at my feet. She seeks to drive me to—"

I cut her off. "How does that matter to her?" I ask again, for the reason eludes me. What is it that Apsara sees that I do not?

"Do you not see it? Minos died during the lunch she arranged. She sent Nimmuruk—"

A light illuminates the distant corridor. These lamps come to life only when there is movement. I whisper urgently to her, "Get dressed; you must leave!"

"Teber, listen to me—"

I hush her. She scrambles to her feet and arranges her garments. We cannot even say a peaceful goodbye!

I grab her in a hurry and kiss her deeply.

"Come back to me, General," she implores urgently, her sweet breath in my ears.

"I will move mountains, my Queen," I whisper back.

And then, in a flash, she turns and vanishes into the darkness.

# CHAPTER 41

## THE EAST

The flowing wind is cold and caresses Khaia's neck like a lover's gentle fingers as she looks out to the sea. The evening hues of gray and blue entwine in an embrace. The boat sways gently as the easterly winds push her vessel toward the shores of the Levant. This mission has been hurried; over a hundred Atalanni boats, with the King himself at the head of the fleet, are tasked with transferring their greatest possessions to the secret enclave in the desert, the one they call "The Second Atalanni."

Prime Minister Rishwa sits next to her on the bench; his pale, bony face shows no emotion as he intently watches the birds making their way to the island of Cyprus, a hazy outline far away and one of their primary sources of tin.

She knows that his mind, just like hers, cannot find rest. "The Prince is a fool. A court monkey has more intelligence than Nimmuruk," she says.

Rishwa blinks and sighs. "He is the Prince, Oracle. The monkey possesses more legitimacy and authority than any man except his father."

"And his father has no control over the idiot—why have you not persuaded the King to dismiss him from his post, Prime Minister? Killing a royal on our land—this is a shame we will never erase," she replies.

Rishwa smoothes the necklace on his gaunt chest and smiles. "Well, you could not convince him. What makes you think he would listen to my counsel about his only thinking son?"

"I tried. He listens to me when my messages are conveyed by the gods. Otherwise, I am just a woman, and you know that. The gods do not grant me succession plans," she says indignantly.

"Do not test fate, Khaia. The more you attempt to influence his war and administrative strategy, the angrier he becomes. He has already complained to me more than once that you exceed your bounds," he warns. Khaia knows that while the King may heed her counsel on certain matters, he has no desire to listen to her regarding war operations or his son's behavior.

"Our strategy to win Egypt is now in flames. I hoped that once we secured military victories and deposed the Pharaoh, we could promise cleaner towns, greater prosperity, education, and health to the peasants and bring them under control—"

"And if they discover what happened to Binpu, there will be no compromise. This war will endure for a long time, Khaia. Nimmuruk is a short-tempered idiot and has ensured thousands of lives have been lost."

"We must let them know that Binpu died in an accident," she insists. The Atalanni invasion fleet is on its way to Egypt with Teber and Nimmuruk leading the charge. The Egyptian princess is in a comfortable prison, and no one is certain when or if she will be released.

"You hope too much," Rishwa replies. "News always leaks. We are about to face an enraged Egyptian army."

Khaia reaches into a plate in front of her, picks up honey-drenched dates, and sucks on the syrup. It is sweet and sticky, and she loses herself in the sweetness and the fragrant aroma. She licks her fingers clean of honey. Rishwa also partakes in the snack.

"I hope we win," she says, sucking on her finger, her voice trailing away. A large white bird swoops down in an elegant arc to snatch the food, and Khaia screams in surprise. The bird flaps its wings and slaps her face as it unsuccessfully attempts to grab the dates.

They both laugh, and Khaia's cheeks flush with embarrassment.

"Was that a sign from the gods, Khaia? Is the bird slapping you a message from someone?" Rishwa teases. The Prime Minister has his moments.

"Your humor is the greatest in all of Atalanni, Rishwa," Khaia replies with a smile. "Unfortunately, this was merely an unruly bird."

Khaia grows weary of discussing Nimmuruk.

"How long before we reach the shores?" she inquires.

"Two more days at sea and a seven-day trek to the mountains," he answers.

"How long are we staying there?"

"Has the King not informed you? We will be there only briefly. We will first transfer all the treasure and weapons, you will bless the enclave, we will celebrate the seeding of our Kingdom outside the island, and then we will return. It should take only a few days. We must return to catch the winds."

"He only told me to be present for the blessing. The old man has even forgotten where his balls are," she remarks.

"Be careful. Even an oracle can only survive so long on a loose tongue."

"Of course," she replies, her mind drifting to the future. The sun has vanished beneath the waves, and only bands of dark blue streak across the sky, merging with the gentle lapping waters.

But Khaia knows that turbulence lies ahead.

Khaia's mind is preoccupied as she prepares to bless the magnificent enclave carved into the rocks. Apsara and Nimmuruk remain alive, which poses a problem, but the King has become a senile blathering idiot under her firm control, and Minos is dead.

Some of Khaia's plans have already been disrupted, but she would persevere.

One step at a time.

Khaia surveys the assemblage of the elite before her—the King and his advisors, High Priestesses and Senior Engineers, the Prime Minister, the designers and architects of the enclave, and many nobles and high-born individuals staunchly loyal to the King. They had already spent hours touring the incredible facility with its multitude of passageways and chambers. This enclave in the rocks is enormous.

She gazes around the gorgeous dome and marvels at all she has seen so far.

The means of locating the place from outside is ingenious.

The entry passage is almost magical—lamps illuminate as they walk. Colorful paintings of royals and commoners adorn the walls. Intricate statues of their ancestors guard the doors. Those doors lead to passageways that burrow deeper into the mountain, opening into vast chambers that house immense treasures, weapons, living quarters, and the sacred library. High lamps illuminate the otherwise dark cathedral. The weapon rooms hold a robust cache of the *Daivoshaktis*. The walls display fierce and frightening images of Atalanni attacks on Egypt—some based on recent events, others imagined. The paint is fresh—these are recent creations. The libraries, deep within the system, hold immeasurable tomes of Atalanni wisdom. The treasure room contains sarcophagi filled with spectacular artifacts, including loot from Egypt.

She returns to the present and turns to the statues by the passageway doors of the dome. On each statue is a plaque inscribed with the Atalanni sacred writing.

*The gods of the Atalanni*

*Bless this enclave*

*Welcome ambassadors*

*Be awed by our mighty intellect and wisdom*

*Beware, intruder,*

*Of the terrifying power of our anger*

*O kings of lands around*

*The Atalanni shall be your rulers all*

Khaia opens the ceremony with a chant, and her priestesses spread holy water among the attendees. The nobles, governors of smaller islands, and other high-born individuals loyal to the King sit in a semi-circular arrangement. The King, the Prime Minister, and her engineers sit behind her on a temporary platform. The architects and civil engineers, possessing all knowledge of the construction, are among those present.

Once the chants conclude, the Oracle walks around the chamber, touching the head of each attendee to bless them. It is now time for the King to deliver his speech. King Hannuruk appears lucid today. He has maintained a clear mind over the last few days as Khaia slowly poured poison in his ears, but she knows it is his actions that truly matter.

Hannuruk rises to his feet. Apsara is beside him, looking slightly unwell. The voyage across the sea and the trek across the desert in the last month have not been easy for everyone.

The audience bows as the aged King takes the podium. His voice reverberates deep and clear in this large chamber.

"The invasion must have landed in Egypt as we speak. We are here to inaugurate our magnificent hidden city—for the Atalanni plan for our contingencies, and we do it in a manner no other Kingdom can even imagine!"

Great shouts of acceptance follow.

He motions toward the expanse of the chamber in a sweeping arc. "Yes, the deception of the Egyptians has caused us to abandon our beloved capital. We have relocated many of our prized possessions and secret knowledge here. Once we conquer Egypt, we shall seed the Kingdom with what we possess."

Many nod in the crowd.

"What mind on earth, except the Atalanni, could conjure and design this brilliance? Do we not carry the soul of the gods?" he asks as he looks around him. "There is no such place as this. Not in Thebes. Not in Babylon."

"Not in any corner of the Earth, Your Majesty," shouts one of the enthusiastic noblemen.

"Not in the backward citadels of Mycenae. Not among the primitive mud huts of Mitanni," he states, not forgetting to insult his wife's homeland. Khaia notices that Apsara shows no reaction.

"Great work has gone into building what we see. We are here to bless this enclave for eternity and to celebrate those who had a hand in this labor," he exclaims, raising both hands above his head and clenching his fists. The crowd erupts in cheers once more.

"We must eat now," he says, gesturing at the slaves standing by the sides. "The first to eat shall be the nobles, the governors, the builders, and the chiefs of logistics and men who have discovered this place and know their way around it so intimately," he proclaims. There are murmurs in the hall, and many rise from their seats to the cheer of those around them, making their way to a large wooden banquet table that can seat hundreds.

"Not all of you. I will honor specific members first," he adds, and a member of the King's Guard walks around with a scroll, reading off names and asking them to move to the banquet seating. Khaia hears the names called—Kirkos, Umarru, Auscetas, Rhaistos, Pausinur, Okoninos, Ululu— until the seating is complete.

They take their places on the benches as slaves bring sumptuous food and place it all along the table. Khaia watches quietly. The King instructs his adjutants to ask some to leave their seats and return to the stone benches. After offering blessings for lunch, the attendees begin to eat. Cheerful chatter fills the air as the diners feast on quail, eggs, pomegranates, olive oil, excellent bread, wine, salted goat, cakes, grapes, and fragrant honey water. Khaia observes as soldiers from the King's Guard discretely enter the chamber, taking positions behind the stone benches closer to the dome wall.

A guard rings a bell, and all eyes turn back to the podium where the King stands. He is wearing his ceremonial bull crown, and in his right hand is a glistening gold dagger laden with gemstones.

He resumes speaking. "You enjoy my hospitality, eat my food, and live on my grace," he states, a hard edge replacing the softness in his voice. A sudden silence blankets the cavernous dome, and all sounds of cutlery cease. The waiters and waitresses recede into the background.

Khaia clasps her palms and looks down.

Hannuruk continues. "And yet you seek to undermine my rule, thwart our efforts, and tear down everything my ancestors and I have built!"

Murmurs rise from the people on the stone benches, but those at the banquet table remain immobile—the fear palpable on their faces. One of the nobles attempts to rise, "Your Majesty, what are you—"

A King's Guard steps in front of him, commanding him to sit down and be silent.

"It is because of your betrayal that the Asiatics know our original mission. It is because of your plotting that Minos died! I have now learned of a heinous conspiracy to kill me, my wife, my son, and the Oracle so that someone else may usurp the throne—traitors!" he shouts as he points to the banquet table.

Gasps of panic rise from those at the table. The King's Guard swiftly surrounds the banquet and points swords and spears at them. Fear descends on the men and women gathered around the banquet table. A hot heaviness envelops the room with suffocating strength.

One of them shouts, "Your Majesty, you are being lied to! Those around this table are your most ardent supporters and well-wishers!"

"Your Majesty, I held your son in my arms. Why would I seek to harm him?"

"Lord, I reside in the house you gifted. I eat the food you provide and serve at your pleasure. Someone is deceiving you!"

"I have governed the thirty Northern islands for you for fifteen summers with absolute loyalty!"

But Hannuruk remains unmoved. He gestures to a guard who brings forth two tied and beaten men. They are naked, afraid, and shaking. All eyes turn to them, and Hannuruk leans forward in his chair and commands, "Point to those who were in your conspiratorial meetings!"

One man, no older than twenty, with reddish-brown welts visible on every inch of his body, weakly looks at the King and those around him. Khaia's eyes meet his, and she gives the faintest nod.

The man lifts his feeble arm and points to the banquet table.

The King questions the other man, who does the same.

Many gathered around the banquet table cry, while some vomit to the sides. Those remaining seated on the stone benches sit like statues, their eyes darting back and forth on this scene of unfolding terror. "Let the traitors' blood flow and drench the food they eat," he commands, waving his hand at Uppiluliuma, the commander of the King's Guard. At that moment, a great roar of anguish erupts as the heavily armed soldiers begin to hack and stab the people at the banquet table. Some attempt to run, only to be impaled by thrusting spears. Others sit bowed, awaiting the glinting blades that will sever their heads. A few fight valiantly with bare hands, grappling the sharpened edges and metal tips while protesting and shouting their innocence. Khaia looks away, but the wails and screams take minutes to diminish as the efficient soldiers systematically butcher every man and woman around the table.

Soon, silence fills the dome. The shell-shocked spectators on the outer benches sit without a sound, many sobbing quietly, wondering if they will be next. But carnage surrounds the banquet table—bodies litter the floor, many with missing heads, hacked limbs, impalements, stabbings, heads smashed with maces, or torsos sliced away by sharp blades. Blood runs like a river below and on the table, drenching the floor, the wooden surface of the table, the food, and the cups of wine and water. An acrid stench of iron and loose bowels rises in the air, mingled with the scented smoke from the ceremonial lamps. Some still writhe on the floor. Finally, when no sound escapes a throat and no breath comes from a body, Hannuruk orders the soldiers to stop. He collapses into his chair and turns to Khaia. "Do you think this cleans the treasonous filth from my house?"

She nods.

There lies Kirkos' head. And there, Pausinur's hands. Arrogant builder Okonino's legs. And there, Ululu's head. And many more. All these men who, at various times, questioned the Oracle's motives or competency are now dead.

The King turns to those on the side. "You have remained my loyal subjects. Come to the table and eat!" he orders. Some consternation arises among the few remaining.

"What are you waiting for?" Hannuruk roars.

They jump up and walk to the table, each elbowing and trying to outdo the others in a rush to reach the center. They avoid the dead and look fearfully at the guards who stare down at them. Some hyperventilate and cry, thinking they are about to be next. The rest seem resigned to their fate. They stand around the table, unsure, looking at the King and others still on the podium. Khaia feels a tinge of pity but pushes it away, for these are her loyalists, and they will survive.

They will even have a glorious future with her at the helm.

"Eat!" Hannuruk screams, breathing heavily and sweating profusely.

A rush ensues at the table. The men and women pull the corpses, most still oozing blood and other fluids, and dump them aside unceremoniously. They clean the table with their hands—pushing away heads and hands from the surface. Many drain the blood still pooling at the sides by scooping with bare hands. Then they gingerly separate clean plates and food from the contaminated. No sound of protest is heard. Some gag and heave, but no one leaves the banquet.

Eventually, they all settle in their seats and pick at the morsels of food. Relief is evident on their faces as the King's Guard recedes and leaves the chamber. Rishwa sits stone-faced, refusing to look at Khaia. Apsara has left the hall. Phaistos looks confused and anxious.

Hannuruk appears exhausted—he is heaving heavy breaths, and his eyes are closed; the servants fan him vigorously. Someone sprinkles water on his face.

Rishwa abruptly stands and calls for attention. "What must be done has been done," he says. "We have completed what we are here for. Get up, and we will leave. We will return once we receive word from Egypt or if the gods on our island compel us to do so."

Hannuruk is in no state to respond. The guards usher the small number of survivors and ask them to prepare for the return journey. Only one man with knowledge of the return path survives, and most of the servants and baggage carriers wait outside at the base of the mountain. It takes just a few hours for the return party to leave the secret enclave as they walk the cobbled stone paths of the exit route, which is guarded by statues of past kings.

All the bodies lie where they are, leaving the murals and the statues to be mute spectators to the carnage. Khaia wonders what might happen if they never return and if someone else discovers this place.

What would they think?

As she exits the Second Atalanni and walks down the rough path of the mountain, she looks back at the ledge that conceals the entryway. The world around here is serene—the birds chirp, an orange hue suffuses the sky, and the winds whisper gently in their ears. The journey back to the sea will take them through golden-yellow landscapes and lovely canyons, different from the island back home.

She feels a strange sensation in her loins.

Ambition is like a flowing river of molten rock, she thinks, and it burns whatever is in its way.

# CHAPTER 42
## THEBES – UPPER EGYPT

Ahmose stands on a constructed sandstone podium. It is a sultry afternoon—the sun beats down upon them. The dusty air is at a standstill, as if to respect the Pharaoh's wishes. The towering palace of Thebes and the gates of the city form a vague outline behind him, while the nobles, warriors, and masses of his Kingdom stand before him. His heart remains full of grief—it is an overflowing well of poison. His beloved wife stands next to him, her face resolute and dark eyes flashing fire. Wadjmose, Baba, viziers, governors of various nomes, and other senior military officials kneel before the Pharaoh.

Thousands of peasants from the farthest towns gather here today, standing and straining to hear, with men among them relaying the Pharaoh's speech from the front.

It is a momentous time for Egypt.

A time of shame.

A time of resolution.

A time for vengeance.

The Uraeus feels cumbersome on the crowned head, and the solid gold staff weighs heavily on his wrist.

Pharaoh Ahmose takes a deep breath and addresses his people. "The tears of Amun fell upon my head during morning prayers," he declares, "and they scalded my shoulder. There is a rage in those tears."

He pauses for effect. "The Atalanni are cowards. They are low barbarians—their King and his warriors are nothing like their ancestors, who wished for harmony with Egypt.

What ruler kills the Prince of another Kingdom who came in peace?"

A great roar of anger erupts from the crowd. "Destroy them, Pharaoh. Erase their name from existence!"

"I have lost my brother, the great Kamose, who has ascended to the heavens. And now I have lost Binpu, a brave and gentle soul, to the beasts that bared their fangs upon a fowl that meant no harm. My messengers tell me that Binpu was placed in a pit with ten Atalanni warriors and forced to fight. My brave brother slew six before a coward pierced him in the back, attacking from behind!"

The people before him shout—

"Those cowards!"

"May the shame of the world descend upon them!"

"Prince Binpu now lives in happiness in the afterlife!"

Ahmose waits for the lamentations to cease. He thinks of his beloved aunt, Sitkamose, who went willingly and bravely, with noble intentions.

"My aunt—" he says, blinking his eyes to control his tears. As the living god and their Pharaoh, he knows he must keep his emotions in check. His wife weeps silently. The tears of Ahmose-Nefertari, God's Wife of Amun, move the crowd, and they sway, holding their hands on their chests. Ahmose continues, "May Amun and Horus bless the noble Sitkamose in the afterlife. She could not bear the insult of losing her nephew and consecrated herself to the sea."

Another mass expression of sorrow rends the air. Ahmose does not yet know if Sitkamose is alive; all he has are the words of a messenger who heard something from another messenger, who heard it from an escapee of the Atalanni capital. But those details do not matter, for what is needed now is anger and a resolution to strike the Atalanni.

"The wretched Atalanni forces are returning after we have routed them like the diseased dogs they are. But this time, we shall spare no one."

A deafening roar saturates the stifling air in waves.

"But remember. We will wipe them from our memories. May no man mention their name. May we spare no soldier. May no priest tell their story, and no scribe give them life on their papyrus. Evil from the sea shall vanish as if the gods never placed them on this earth."

"Yes, Pharaoh!"

"And if I die—" he pauses.

Another great shout erupts from the multitude. Ahmose-Nefertari drops to her knees and holds the Pharaoh's legs. The general and his men prostrate themselves on the ground, and many in the crowd weep. "Our god shall not leave this earth," chant the priests and others.

Ahmose blinks away his tears. The love of his people moves him. He gently places his palm on his wife's lightly bulging belly. "If I die, you will carry on. May no man surrender. My wife will lead you to glory. After her, my son will. Then, his son. We shall embrace them in eternal war!" he exclaims, raising his staff above his head.

Loud cries and exhortations reverberate for minutes, and as if by cue, the vast columns of the army pour out of the gates and march in full splendor on either side of the Pharaoh, saluting him as they move ahead while the onlookers bless them. Fathers, grandfathers, sons, brothers, nephews, friends, co-workers, uncles, brothers-in-law— every boy and man ready for battle walks for the honor of their land, as those necessary to maintain administration and food production cheer them on. Mothers, daughters, wives, sisters, aunts, grandmothers, and every other relation laugh and weep as they see their men off. They must be strong and fill the shoes of their men. The women throw flowers, grain, pieces of cloth, bread, and dates upon the marching men, blessing them as they go.

Ahmose stands still and watches.

The cowardice of the Atalanni was what was needed to truly bring the Kingdom to its feet.

He hopes that this is the beginning of the new kingdom of Egypt, rising from the shame of the last one hundred harvests.

# CHAPTER 43
## LOWER EGYPT – PERKHURE

Ahmose gazes at the vast assemblage of the enemy before him. They have finally met in a gently undulating field, with low-lying hills on either side. This battle will decide the fate of Egypt, he thinks. They have fought these wretched invaders before, but not in a full-scale conflict.

The surveyors have given their report. The Atalanni forces are arrayed in a grid—they have a large central block of infantry with archers in the front. The emblems suggest that the Prince leads this block. To the left of the Prince is a slightly smaller block, armed similarly, and led by the same general they had faced before. To the right of the Prince is a similar block. On either flank of the forces is a smaller contingent, standing behind. Wadjmose believes they are fast-moving, light-armor forces that will flank from the sides when needed.

Wadjmose has advised the Pharaoh to array Egypt's forces traditionally. They have assembled in a wide, gentle arc. The Pharaoh stands in the center with a block of twenty thousand soldiers. On either side are ten thousand—one led by Wadjmose and the other by Baba. The entire formation is twenty rows deep. The Atalanni are compressed into a much shorter width, about a third of the Egyptians. The formation puzzles Ahmose, for his army can now wrap around the enemy like a noose and strangle them. But the Atalanni possess something he does not — their divine weapons. They are terrifying; however, he has instilled courage in his soldiers. "They may have weapons designed by their gods," he had said, "And yet they have been unable to conquer us. Do not fear them, as they do not have enough of their weapons. We have the numbers." He hopes his men will not flee from battle. Nervousness fills the air, and many wear the look of fear and death, but the living god of Egypt trusts his men to fight with everything they have.

They have a cavalry of thirty horses, while the invaders have none. However, Ahmose does not trust the cavalry—it is only meant to see if they can inflict some damage and support messengers across the battlefield. Wadjmose rides one, for he is a master of it along with a few other experienced men. Ahmose is on a chariot driven by two horses, and he trusts his charioteer. He knows there is great promise in these beasts, but they require time to tame and train.

There is much flag-waving and clamor from the enemy. His forces shout and raise a loud ruckus, while runners carry the war emblems back and forth on the frontline. Finally, when the benevolent Ra reaches the midpoint between the morning and the zenith, stillness falls over the lines.

Piercing sounds of conches and horns rise in the warm air, and the two armies rush at each other amidst great battle cries.

As dust rises from the running soldiers, Ahmose watches as the lines, a mile and a half wide on his side, close the gap with the concentrated enemy. He can see them now, the whites of their treacherous eyes visible behind their bronze helmets. The formation shields Ahmose in the middle, but he is wary of the Atalanni weapons. He can now see the Atalanni Prince's emblem, bright purple and orange, at the center of the block that comes toward him. In no time, the lines clash, and the loud sounds of battle fill the air—the clang of metal swords, the wet squishing sounds of pierced flesh, the cries of the wounded and dying, the hiss and swoosh of swords and flying spears. The Pharaoh's chariot wheels are equipped with sharp blades on the side, and they excel at severing the limbs and heads of any enemy that comes too close. He is also a master archer, and his arrows pierce the Atalanni armor with ease. The twang of the bowstring comforts him, and his years of practice pay off as his bolts meet their targets with unerring accuracy.

Strangely, he has so far not heard the sounds of the explosive weapons of the Atalanni. But his hope is short-lived: suddenly, a few men ahead to his right explode in a spray of blood, and a small piece of flesh flies by the Pharaoh. There are more explosions—he sees the Atalanni soldiers, dressed in heavy armor and carrying large leather bags on their waists—reaching into the pouches and flinging shining orbs at their lines. These orbs explode in great flashes of fire, killing those they contact and setting fire to others nearby. Soon, many soldiers run engulfed in flames, screaming and flailing, setting others on fire as they rush in blind terror. Far to his right, he sees greenish fumes rise into the air, and his men collapse, screaming. The poisonous fumes appear to cause blisters on contact and suffocate the victims.

*What are these weapons?*

"Do not fall back! Stay and fight!" Ahmose screams, and his commanders relay the shouts, but the front line begins to panic. He instructs two of his commanders to run to the far sides and constrict the Atalanni, but the real risk now lies in the heavy infantry of the concentrated enemy punching through their center and fracturing the lines.

Now Ahmose understands why the enemy had concentrated their positions.

*It is the hammer.*

"Do not give up the center and do not break," he commands his men as he rushes forward in his chariot, surrounded by his elite guards. He feels something shoot over his head, and in quick succession, two men to his left fall as their chests erupt in blood.

*The Atalanni fire pipes!*

"Spear men! Target the Atalanni pipe-wielders!" he shouts, and, at his order, the commanders gather some spearmen in the melee to concentrate their missiles on the enemy. The spears cut some down, but the fire pipes continue to wreak havoc. Ahmose defies his bodyguards and orders his charioteer to head straight into the pipe-wielders' lines. They fire at him, but they miss as the Pharaoh deftly avoids the incoming streaks. His body shakes with anger—how dare they fire on a King? But there is not much time to think. He reaches the enemy line and swings the chariot in a tight arc, cutting down several of these demonic weapon wielders to provide an opportunity for his men to recover. However, he quickly realizes that his forces are spread too thin. Chaos reigns for the Egyptians as the concentrated block of armored Atalanni begins to crush the Egyptian center. Ahmose does not yet know where Wadjmose is or how he is faring. Even as he frantically wonders what to do, one of his bodyguard's heads explodes, showering the Pharaoh with pieces of brain and skull.

*No!*

There is mayhem all around. His center is being pushed in as the Atalanni spearmen impale the Egyptian soldiers and hack others to pieces. The commanders struggle to maintain control, and the Pharaoh feels the battle slipping away as he swings his chariot back to safety. His eyes sting from the smoke, and his lungs burn from the sharp, acrid odor of the explosions. The stench of death hangs heavy in the air.

So close, yet so far, Ahmose thinks as he squints.

But his army is now falling apart in the middle; the dense mass of the hoard of invaders thrusts through his lines, and it is clear that if this continues any longer, the battle will be forever lost. He raises his face to the blazing sun and begs for intervention.

That is when he notices for the first time the Atalanni Prince, in an excited motion, ordering something to the surrounding men. Then, he sees the Atalanni middle split like a river.

*What are they doing?*

Ahmose's heart races.

When he turns, he sees Wadjmose rushing towards him; a manic glee spreads across the general's face.

Ahmose knows exactly why. He breaks out into a grin.

*Thank you, glorious Amun!*

# CHAPTER 44
## LOWER EGYPT – PERKHURE

From my vantage point, on the ground that is slightly higher than the center mass, I can see our forces pushing the Egyptians back.

*We are winning!*

If only I had the *Daivoshaktis* with me! I would have made quick work of the Egyptian infantry, but those elite troops with the special weapons accompany the Prince. In the dust, gore, and melee, the powerful center mass of the Prince's battalions slowly pushes through the enemy center—the distinctive pale orange and maroon uniforms of the Atalanni army contrast with the dust-adorned white tunics of the Egyptians and the Nubians. However, I am puzzled that the central mass does not move quickly enough; it appears splintered. The Atalanni center was to function like the head of a hammer—it should ram through the Egyptian center and never split under any circumstance.

A familiar headgear adorned with yellow plumes runs toward me.

Bansabira.

He gasps for breath and takes a moment to recover. I have someone near me offer him a quick drink—we are in a safer zone, surrounded by our units, with the Egyptians on the fringes or in the front, retreating against our steady onslaught.

"What is it?"

"Nimmuruk," he gasps. "The Prince, he—"

"Is he dead?"

"No, no, he split the center!"

I reel from shock. "What do you mean he split the center? We had agreed to never—"

"I know what we agreed to, General," he replies, irritated. "But the Prince decided, just as we were punching through their center, to split our forces on either side and encircle them!"

"But we do not have enough men to encircle a thinner, larger force that is spread wide," I yell, not so much at him but in alarm and frustration.

"Yes! I tried to hold the left branch, but we are getting massacred, and I think Nimmuruk is in danger if you do not intervene," he says, wiping the drool from his lips and tugging on his dark, blood-stained curls that fall across his face.

"That fucking idiot," I curse, and I survey the unfolding chaos. We are making progress, and even amidst the din of battle, I can see my troops inching forward. However, we may be in severe danger if I do not divert some of my resources to protect the center. I decide quickly. I call two of my *Upashaktis* and inform them I must take a third of the men, still waiting to engage, with me to the center. They appear shaken—they know this puts them all in much greater danger. As much as I loathe the Prince, I cannot simply abandon him on the field. We muster the men to join me at the center.

The journey proves perilous—our thinning lines become infiltrated by Egyptian units, and we must fight them. I kill three men on my way to the center, lopping off their heads. At that moment, I realize the precarious position we are in. As expected, we are spread too thin and outnumbered. Our men fight valiantly, but they are falling. The Prince flails about, not fighting anyone, surrounded by a ring of our soldiers striving to keep the enemy at bay. In the distance, I can see the Pharaoh, his golden-hued chariot and headgear melding into the fine yellow dust that reflects the sunlight, urging his troops onward. He remains unreachable, protected by a full contingent of heavily armed Egyptian troops.

My unit plunges into the melee, slashing and piercing enemy flesh, soon restoring a semblance of balance to the battle. I give urgent orders for us to regroup and fall back into a defensive position. I lose all sense of time and place. At some point, my chest burning, my body screaming in pain, and my eyes hurting as if a thousand needles pierce them, I realize both sides are immeasurably exhausted. Many stand and stare at each other without lifting their weapons. Many others lie on the ground, having surrendered. A few circle each other, with each man hoping the other will give up and flee, but neither makes any effort to attack the other. To my relief, I hear the distinct clang of Egyptian cymbals rising above the clamor. It signals retreat, and just in time, for we have also suffered immensely after the Prince's colossal blunder.

The two sides separate, and the battle concludes. It has been a disaster for us—we quickly realize that a sizeable part of our army is dead, with the most significant losses in the central hammer Nimmuruk split.

*What a stupid, worthless commander!*

My unit has also taken significant losses as it broke to save the Prince. We conduct a swift parley with the Egyptian envoys to allow them to collect their dead, and we gather ours. For the next several hours, we set up camp further north of the battlefield while the Egyptians disappear behind the hills in the south. There is no potential for another battle for another moon or more as both sides recover. I look across in sadness, and Bansabira, a battle-hardened commander himself, has tears of frustration in his eyes.

"We were winning," he whispers, pointing to the dead and dying on the blood-drenched, muddy field. "Your strategy was working. We were winning."

# CHAPTER 45

## LOWER EGYPT – PERKHURE

Failure brings out the worst in men. "You stupid son of a sewer-cleaner. How dare you insinuate I put us in danger?" screams Nimmuruk. The Prince is in a rage; his shoulder and waist are still red from the violence of the battle. His fatal mistake turned the tide of the fight against us; every commander in the force knows it. We have lost four of our *Upashaktis*, critical for leadership on the battlefield.

"Bansabira should have stayed and driven through the Egyptian center, but you split the hammer," I say calmly, not backing down.

"No! No, no, no! If he had fought as you claim he did and led his side capably, we would have encircled and destroyed their center and captured their Pharaoh! You should have come faster to the center. You failed," he says, pacing around, shouting, and pointing at me. The others are scared and nervous. Nimmuruk has already put to death one *Upashakti* and two commanders even before I arrived. Their headless bodies lie in front of the tent. The heads are nearby—glassy, lifeless eyes staring into the darkening skies.

"I could not have come to you while we were pushing back their left flank! We were on the cusp of destroying them, and you split the hammer in the center and diverted my men for your safety!" My voice rises. Others shuffle nervously.

Nimmuruk rushes forward to my face and starts screaming, spittle flying into my face. "My safety? I was there slaying the enemy like the swine they are. Your commander is a worthless goat fucker. Not only did he fail to carry out my orders, but he then ran to you like a dog to complain, putting the Crown Prince of the Atalanni in danger, even as I fought far more bravely than you." He looks around, and some of the others nod. I know they do it out of fear because anyone with even a modicum of sense would recognize that the fool Prince was frightened and had committed a terrible mistake.

"He didn't come to complain. Not only did he return to you, Your Highness, but he saved the forces under your command from annihilation by warning me."

He shakes his head and tugs on his thin hair. His chest heaves with anger, and his face, dirty from soot, dust, and sweat, crumples in hate. Then suddenly, Nimmuruk stops.

He returns to calm.

His eyes take on a dark, vacant look.

He stares at me unsmilingly.

"Bansabira," he says flatly. Then he looks at one of his loyalists. "Bring Bansabira to the announcement area."

A flurry of activity ensues as we all head out to a hastily cleared grassy area between the tents and funeral pyres. The stench of the dead and burning bodies fills the air. Hastily constructed pyres surround us, discharging acrid smoke. Hundreds of corpses lie in haphazard ditches, heaped on each other. I dread what is about to happen. I quickly slip away, leading two of my *Upashaktis* to gather some of my most loyal commanders. We run from tent to tent, rousing them. I instruct the bewildered men to don their armor and bring their best weapons.

They follow me.

Soon, I muster a hundred loyal men—hardened, experienced warriors. They share their disdain for the Prince. They know what happened.

We rush back to the Prince's tent. It is dusk, and a large fire burns on one side of the area. I ask my men to spread around in a circle, melding with the others, and to wait for my order if such a command should arise. I part men and reach the inner edge of the ring, and the sight both chills and enrages me.

Bansabira, my most trusted and talented commander, hangs from wrists tied to an overhead pole. He is naked, and his entire body shivers—not from the cold evening weather, but because of the fear and pain coursing through him. There are red welts on his back, a result of lashes from a rough bamboo whip held by a punisher.

"What are you doing?" I ask the Prince. "This man saved you."

He smiles. "Saved me? He disobeyed an order and plotted to have me killed on the battlefield. Did you have something to do with it, General?"

I clench my fists. "You make wild accusations against the men who serve and protect you, Your Highness," I say, as anger wells up within me. I have been obedient to this talentless, vicious idiot for too long. "Why have you said nothing?" I address one of the *Upashaktis*, and he squirms with discomfort.

"Prince's orders, General Teber, how could I—" he stutters.

"Stay where you are, Teber. Let this be a lesson. I have been too lenient with my men for too long," Nimmuruk says, nodding to the punisher.

The man lays down the small bamboo whip and picks up a larger one. It has small barbs, designed to rip flesh and inflict great pain.

He swings it in a high arc, and it makes a sharp crack as it connects with Bansabira's buttocks. He screams, and a long red and bloody gash opens up. Bansabira holds on and does not collapse to his knees. The lash comes down again, this time on his back.

And again.

And again.

Bansabira's back and buttocks become a mass of red as blood oozes from the welts. His legs shake uncontrollably and eventually give out under him.

He dangles, but he has not begged for mercy so far.

"Stand him up!" shouts Nimmuruk, and two men rush to Bansabira.

I run forward as well.

"Not you, Teber. Stay where you are. Make sure this never happens again," he says.

Bansabira lets out a low moan as the men stand him up.

Nimmuruk laughs.

Something snaps within me.

I rush to the center and order the punisher to stand down. He looks confused, unsure of what to do. "Sir, I am—"

"Get back," I tell him.

Nimmuruk is enraged. "How dare you! Now you deliberately disobey me, return to your station," he shouts. A few of his guards shuffle nervously. The *Upashaktis* remain frozen to their feet—and that is when I realize I can turn this to my advantage.

"Men," I say. Suddenly, my officers emerge from the group with their swords drawn and form a protective cover around me in an arc.

"What are you doing?" screams Nimmuruk. I can see his slick, shining face contorted in rage. "Kill him," he shouts.

Suddenly, confusion erupts. Not all his guards rush at us, and the *Upashaktis* stand their ground. We clash with the Prince's guards, but these brutes are not trained for swift close combat. They are better suited to leap upon unarmed men and rape helpless women.

Blades connect with power, and we swing, dance, jab, and strike. I kill two of the rushing guards—my sword slices through their chests even before they have the chance to raise their hands. My men make quick work of the rest, systematically striking them to the ground. In no time, the melee settles—the Prince's guards that rushed us are either dead or writhing on the ground. However, the surrounding scene has changed—many more men encircle us, but they merely watch. Many have their swords drawn.

We regain our defensive posture. I shout at them. "Stand back. Let us not allow this Prince to destroy our honor and murder our valiant forces!"

Murmurs arise. I can hear the Prince shouting, but his words fall on deaf ears.

"Ignore his orders," I say. "You are all under my command now."

"General, is that wise—" begins one of the *Upashaktis*.

"Yes, do you wish to be annihilated under this imbecile?" I ask.

For too long, I have watched from the sidelines while this ungrateful wretch made a mockery of our honor. I realize my actions could lead to my execution, but I have had enough.

The Prince shouts in the background, but with most of his guards dead and others not making a move, I know I must be decisive.

I turn my attention to the Prince. "You are a brave warrior, you claim. How about you face me? Your Highness? Kill me with your own hands?"

Panic fills Nimmuruk's eyes.

"Come, Your Highness, let us discover whether you are a lion or a whimpering swine," I taunt him. I point my sword at him and crouch. Here Nimmuruk stands alone—no longer a sparrow protected by eagles.

Nimmuruk frantically scans the crowd and addresses those around him. "What are you looking at? He is threatening your Prince; get him!" he shouts, but no one moves.

I think they realize their chance for honor or victory lies with me.

Nimmuruk flounders around, but he is now trapped within the ring with me. The wall of men prevents him from escaping.

"Come, coward," I yell. It is as if a great monster has awoken within me, challenging no less than a successor to the Atalanni throne.

"Yes, Your Highness, demonstrate to us your greatness," some brave soul shouts from behind the lines. This has become a mesmerizing contest. Nimmuruk stops attempting to shore support. I sense his fear, and he finally unsheathes his sword from its scabbard. He takes tentative steps forward, but his unsure hands tremble.

I glance at Bansabira.

Someone has untied him.

He lies on his side, raw and bloody, his eyes half-closed, and his tear-streaked yet brave face reflects the firelight.

Flames ignite in my belly.

I lunge forward and strike the Prince on his shoulder with the flat side of my sword. He yelps, like a stricken dog, and staggers back. He flails about, swinging his sword and misses me wildly.

I circle Nimmuruk again.

"What are you doing, Teber? You are under the orders of the King to follow me!" he whines.

I ignore him.

Then I cover the ground swiftly, this time delivering a stinging blade-slap to his exposed side.

He screams in terror.

I hear laughter.

Nimmuruk's eyes dart around in frantic desperation.

"Men, stop him! Kill him! You disloyal cowards!" he howls in a high-pitched voice. Yet no one makes a sound.

Realizing no help is forthcoming, Nimmuruk lunges at me. I am prepared for this lazy, arrogant, honorless fool. I first strike his sword with a powerful blow, knocking it from his grasp. Then I sidestep and trip him, causing him to sprawl upon the muddy ground.

A stream of obscenities escapes his lips as he crawls toward his blade.

I strike his buttocks with the flat side of my blade.

The Prince screams and flips onto his back.

He looks at me with a frightened expression. "Stop it, Teber. What are you doing?"

I have nothing to say to this godless man-child. I turn and point at the lashes lying near Bansabira. The men understand.

Someone throws the smaller lash at me.

Nimmuruk's eyes widen.

I lash him across his stomach. He howls and doubles over, clutching his belly. I whip him across his thighs, and he rolls, crying in anguish. His skin is chafing raw against the muddy, rough grass ground.

All those images flash before my eyes.

The Egyptian ambassador dying in my arms.

The soldiers burning in the pit.

Binpu's eyes as the light within them dimmed.

Thousands dead because of this man's stupidity.

Finally, Bansabira's lashing—an ultimate act of cowardice, heaped upon a warrior who had saved Nimmuruk's life.

I reach down and grab him by the throat.

I pull him up. He frantically grapples with my iron grip, but he is weak. I think of him as an obstinate mule as I drag him to the fire that burns a bright orange.

This time, it is his turn to beg and cry.

Nimmuruk jumps, dances, and fights my grip, but no voice comes from him because of the pressure on his throat. The men look on without a word. He tries to kick me, but I avoid his legs. It is as if a great fire ignites my skin, my bones, my skull, and my mouth. It is as if all the injustices this man and his father have inflicted upon us course through my veins and bleed from every pore.

I heave Nimmuruk into the fire.

His greasy body catches the flames in an instant as he falls onto the logs. Nimmuruk bellows as he springs up like a human torch. He shrieks and stumbles back into the orange-blue tongues of the hungry god. It is not long before his skin and flesh singe in the crackling heat, and all we see is a black and gray apparition whose movements slow with the passage of time.

I wonder if the Egyptian gods possess the power to make their royals' words come true. Binpu had said that the Prince would burn. And now I, the general of the Atalanni, had murdered the crown prince by throwing him to the flames.

There is absolute silence around me as the fire crackles and hums. I sprint towards Bansabira and kneel beside him. He is unresponsive—I shut his eyes and signal the men to fetch a physician. It will take many weeks for him to recover if he is not consumed by fever. I turn to one of the *Upashaktis* and place a hand on his shoulder.

"It had to be done," I say.

"The gods forced your hand, General," he replies. He then turns to the others and announces loudly, "General Teber is now our supreme commander. May no man speak of what happened."

The men quietly raise their hands in response. It is as if a shroud of evil has lifted from them. Perhaps now there will be a victory against the Pharaoh.

But I long for peace.

# CHAPTER 46

## KALLISTU

Khaia sits by the garden overlooking the bay, holding her wiggling little daughter—now over two summers old and with an unruly mind of her own. Khaia's necklace attracts Akhi, and she pulls at it, babbling. "No, you cannot have them," Khaia says, trying to pry the fingers away. "No. No. No," the girl repeats, shaking her head vigorously. Her luxurious hair shimmers in the light. Then Akhi's attention turns to something else, and she wants to get down and run. Khaia holds her tightly, but the toddler squirms and protests her mother's grip. "No, Akhi, you cannot run around here. It is dangerous."

However, Khaia's mind is preoccupied.

It has been over three moons since the declaration of the evacuation of the prized possessions of the Atalanni. Much has happened in these days, and Khaia is pleased. Her journey to the secret enclave and the destruction of the King's loyalists is complete. Although there is no news yet from Egypt, she hopes the invasion is proceeding well. From what she knows, there are no significant fortifications in Egypt, so a long siege is unlikely. She believes Teber has prevailed; she has great affection for the general.

Her grip on power has strengthened. Her loyalists are gaining prominence, though many powerful men protect the King and ensure his constitutional right to the throne. She sometimes misses Minos, but his death was necessary. King Hannuruk is slowly losing his mind—the old monarch alternates between rages and philosophical musings. He speaks of the days gone by, of peace, of harmony, and of the Atalanni's superiority in the arts and architecture.

He bores those around him with his endless monologues and stories of courage, real and mostly conjured. She humors him.

It is only a matter of time.

But Apsara continues to be a concern and a thorn in her side. The girl has proved to be a survivor. She has patrons Khaia does not know of, and gaining access to the Queen has been challenging. Apsara unquestionably resents her, and there have been too few occasions to engage with the Queen. However, Khaia has found someone willing to whisper into her ears about the Queen's life. This woman, a young and impressionable member of the Queen's court, is in awe and fear of the Oracle and is willing to do her bidding. Khaia has been meeting this woman every few days, hoping to gain any information that might be useful.

Today is another day.

The girl approaches with great alacrity, her bosom heaving from the strain of walking uphill to where Khaia sits.

"Greetings, sacred Khaia," she says, bowing to the Oracle.

Khaia hands her daughter over to an attendant nearby and asks him to keep the energetic child busy. Akhi protests and clings to Khaia's tunic with her chubby little fingers until the attendant gently pries them away and hauls off the screaming toddler.

"You are early today, Aranare," Khaia remarks. "Is nothing keeping you busy?"

"I wanted to report something that might greatly interest you, sacred Khaia," she says surreptitiously, her eyes darting back and forth.

"Well, you are alone with me here. Stop behaving as if you are surrounded by the Queen's guards. What is it?" Khaia snaps.

"My apologies, sacred Khaia. You know I risk—"

"Your risks have come with rewards."

The woman bows and steps closer to Khaia. "I cannot be sure," she whispers, "but I am quite confident—"

"What is it?" Khaia rebukes the woman and slaps her arm.

The woman flinches back and apologizes profusely before Khaia admonishes her once again for stalling. "The Queen..."

"Yes, what about her?"

"She might be pregnant!"

# PART IV

*"We seek to find reason and define our actions based on what we see, hear, feel, and smell, and not what we believe the gods tell us in our dreams..."*

**DAIVOSHASTRA CH. XII: "ACTIONS"**

# CHAPTER 47

## KALLISTU

King Hannuruk rages in the chamber. His bloodshot eyes bear a manic appearance, and his face is red, his hair disheveled. The King paces around, pushing lamps and decorative ornaments off their pedestals, kicking and slapping the slaves who cower in terror. From time to time, he grabs his own hair and curses under his breath.

"I have no news from my son, and now this," he shouts, clenching his fists.

Prime Minister Rishwa and Khaia are the only two others in the room—the most senior members of the Kingdom aside from the King. They wait for him to calm down. The topic is too sensitive for anyone else to partake in the conversation.

"This!" the King screams. "Who would have thought it would come to this? She is pregnant, and your priestess tells me I may not be the father!"

He turns to Khaia and stares at her, his chest heaving with exertion. The old King looks every bit a madman, but a dangerous one. "I do not know if I must believe your priestess," he says again.

"It is at your discretion, Your Majesty," Khaia replies, "but a decision must be made soon, before the Queen's belly makes it abundantly clear to all."

"I am not a fool. I have not lain with that whore. She is incapable of arousing desire in me," he asserts, spitting to the side. "It cannot be my child."

Rishwa and Khaia remain silent.

"What should I do, Khaia? Why do the gods punish me so?" he wails. "If I pretend nothing happened, I will raise a child that is not mine. I will not have a bastard child borne of my wife's adultery. I am King!"

"You have an option, Your Majesty," Khaia offers.

Rishwa clears his throat. "No mountain is impassable, and no sea unnavigable. You can divorce her. The constitution states that the King may separate from his wife if there is even a hint of adultery. No shame will come to you, Your Majesty, for that is our law. The Supreme Council will recognize it. You can secretly exile her."

Khaia does not mention execution, nor does Rishwa. She knows the King will choose his path on his own.

"I am not a coward to let her go for what she has done. Tongues will wag, no matter how many I silence as I seek to find her lover," he says, his eyes burning with shame and anger. "I cannot see her. I do not want her presence near me. But as King, I cannot let this go so easily. I could execute her now, but that would be too easy," he says, and a red shroud of cruelty slowly descends on his face.

"Of course, Your Majesty, but—" Rishwa begins.

"I will invoke the *haimskaia*," Hannuruk declares.

Khaia feels as though someone has punched her in the chest. She catches the horror on the Prime Minister's face. "Your Majesty," she says urgently, "the *haimskaia* is to be administered only in extreme cases where a Queen bears a child that is not the King's and also actively plots the King's death."

Hannuruk looks at her with wild eyes. For the first time, Khaia feels fear toward the King. "How do you know she is not plotting for my death? How do we know her lover is not planning a coup? This wretched Mitanni scum shames our Kingdom and me," he rages.

Khaia recoils at the rotten stench emanating from his diseased mouth.

"Your Majesty, no gods will look kindly upon such cruelty. No Queen has ever been subjected to it. It was a law written long ago. Divorce her and let her vanish from our memories. But if you cannot do that, then execute her swiftly and announce that she killed herself," Rishwa urges, his voice almost pleading.

Hannuruk turns to his long-standing advisor and spits on him. Rishwa recoils but remains immobile. "Cruelty? The gods have stopped looking down upon us with kindness. They have abandoned me! The lack of news of my son and these tremors over the last fifty days are signs that our gods are unhappy with what she did and demand justice. Right, Khaia—"

"She is still a child. Let her die quietly, Your Majesty. Show mercy, and the gods will look kindly upon you. Their messages—"

"Enough! Enough of your divine messages! I should have her tortured, but I will not. She has one hundred days to tell me who her lover is and everyone who conspired with her; otherwise, she dies under *haimskaia*. Let the people see the King does not take betrayal lightly. Guard!" he screams and summons Uppiluliuma, the Chief of the King's Guard. "Take your men. Arrest the Queen."

Rishwa and Khaia try in vain to persuade the King toward a swift execution, but he remains unmoved. Uppiluliuma bows to the King and walks away quietly. Hannuruk dismisses them and retreats to his dark chamber, as sullen as his mind.

Khaia stands as still as stone. This was not how she wanted it to be. Rishwa looks at her accusingly. There is anger in those wise eyes. "Did you instruct your priestess to tell the King that Apsara is pregnant?" he asks.

"How dare you accuse me? Did I have to tell—"

Rishwa interrupts and waves his hand dismissively. "Apsara does not deserve such a death," he shouts. It is rare for him to raise his voice. The words echo in the empty room from which it appears all life has been sucked out. "We were a peaceful, lawful Kingdom, Khaia. Look what we have descended to," he says, his voice trembling.

She feels blood rush to her face—whether from the sting of Rishwa's insinuations or from what she has brought upon the young Queen. She recollects her interactions with Apsara, and Khaia feels surprised as tears well up in her eyes.

Rishwa composes himself. "The people will be repulsed. They are already angry and anxious about our war. We have always been a peaceful people except when we defended ourselves. This is enough," he says, his voice low with exhaustion. "We will have a revolt on our hands."

Khaia's mind conjures an opportunity. She could abandon Egypt—after all, the Egyptians had no navy to attack the Atalanni.

But now she needed help here. Help to quell any rebellion or revolt. Khaia would eventually find a way to rid herself of the King. She needed an effective and respected military commander, while Phaistos guarded Kaftu. She required a general by her side, and the ones still on the Island were ineffective and useless. She turns to Rishwa. "I wish to lend a hand to bring peace, Rishwa; perhaps it is time for us to recognize our situation."

"What do you suggest?" asks the Prime Minister.

"I propose we declare Prince Nimmuruk the King of Egypt and order Teber to conclude his mission in three moons and return, no matter what. He can control the security of this island. The Prince can continue for another summer."

# CHAPTER 48

## LOWER EGYPT – PERKHURE

Our campaign has ground to a halt. The season is dry again. Hot winds flow from the west and kick up dust. The fine grains of sand get into our eyes, noses, mouths, and torment us. My men are exhausted. We have conducted many skirmishes that have only eroded our manpower and reserves. Morale is low, and our one major confrontation with the Egyptians after the death of the Prince resulted in a stand-off with no victors.

I have determined that this war is a lost cause; without a continuous supply from Kaftu, we are in no position to mount a potent offense. This war of attrition will grind us down to nothing. The Egyptians have a significant advantage—this is their land, and their supply is endless. The Pharaoh of Egypt has proven to be a formidable adversary, and his general is exceptional. They have sent us emissaries, but they only demand our surrender. We have tried many times to convey to them that the death of their Prince was an accident and that their Princess may still be alive, but our words have lost their honor. Too many stories have circulated about how the Egyptian died in our court— that he was tortured, set on fire, left to starve, thrown to beasts, hung by a post, stabbed by an aide, dismembered by the guard, thrown off a cliff, drowned in a ceremony, thrown in an arena to fight without weapons, or beheaded by the priests—they are endless. The Pharaoh has no interest in negotiations, and we will not surrender. I believe this travesty results from the wickedness of the Prince and our unbridled ambition. But now he is dead, and I hope that our offers of peace will appease the gods of Egypt and also make our divine see reason!

Our exceptional weapons are too few and poorly supplied for us to make a genuine difference. To add to our injury, a substantial portion of the weapons was ferried away to the secret enclave in the desert for reasons I have never understood.

There has been no news from our King. I do not care for what he says, but I worry about my land. About Apsara. I do not want to die here—alone, away, and under the baleful watch of foreign gods. But there is one final plan: a strategy for one last great push that will either result in breaking the Egyptian resolve or ending in our annihilation. If I die, I hope it is in glory, and I hope Apsara will find a way out of her pain.

They are just hopes.

I look at the leathery faces and hard expressions of my most senior commanders who sit in front of me, preparing for our ultimate battle. Two days ago, we received news that Ahmose had rejected our truce, and his army was moving towards us again. They are now within our visual distance—just ten miles away and camping.

"Bansabira, describe our plans to the men."

Bansabira nods. My most capable officer has recovered, and his loyalty to me has multiplied a hundredfold. I have named him my successor if I die, and he knows how I think. My men have told me more than once that they are still alive because of my maneuvers, and I hope they are not lying.

"We will use a new formation suited for this terrain," Bansabira says. "General Teber calls it the Temple. We will have a wide wedge in the front, with the slopes of the wedge made of spearmen. The archers will form the front lines. The wedge will punch through their center. Behind the wedge will be what we call the Phalanx. We have never tested it, but we believe it is the best way to withstand the Egyptian hordes and advance."

He walks up to the wooden table and the clay bed upon it and draws the formation. The men stand around, and one of them asks, "What is the Phalanx?"

I am excited to explain what it is. I nudge Bansabira aside from the table, place my arms on the table, and lean. "We will create blocks sixty-four men wide and sixty-four deep. They will all place shields in the front and use their spears. They will move forward as an immutable unit and act as a wall. As the front line of the block tires, I have devised a way for those behind to move forward and take their place. This way, the unit remains fit and continues to advance." I use a stick to draw a representation and describe to them how it had worked brilliantly in several practice runs held in secret.

They nod in admiration. "It is brilliant!" says one man, parting the long hair on his wide-set face and rubbing his beard.

"Do you think it will work, General?"

"I have studied their formations many times. The Egyptians are not innovative in their strategy. Their strength lies in numbers and resolve, but this time, if we hold our ground and smash them, I think they will finally give up. It is our best hope."

"What is the situation with our *Daivoshaktis?*"

"All our supplies are depleted. The powders and poisons that power the weapons have all run out," says the weapons controller. "If we had a steady supply, we would be in Thebes with the Pharaoh at our feet by now."

The commanders are frustrated. We had everything we needed to win, and yet poor decisions have placed us at a severe disadvantage. I secretly no longer believe our gods hold sway over the Egyptians, and I suspect the Oracle has other motives. Apsara's words before we left in a hurry remain in my memory, and I have not yet made full sense of what she was implying.

"What is the attack plan, General?"

"We move in three days. This time, we will not wait. We march at night in two days and launch our ultimate attack at dawn. With the blessings of our gods, we will destroy the Pharaoh's army and begin our march to—"

A messenger rushes into the tent and interrupts the conversation. I turn to him, irritated. "Why are you—"

"We have a senior messenger with news and orders from the King."

We scramble to our feet, and I walk out. In a few minutes, seven haggard-looking men appear from behind the guards. The leader, a gaunt, tall man with silver hair and rough stubble, salutes me. "Sinaruk, Chief Messenger from the Palace and servant of his Majesty King Hannuruk, with orders to you and the Prince, sir."

I eye him. So, they do not know about the Prince's death, and no one has told them yet.

"Verify your identity—that you are who you say you are, Sinaruk," I say.

Sinaruk nods at one of his men. They produce an intricate seal with a series of etchings. I study the disk—I am trained to decode these seals. There is no doubt this is an authentic seal bearing the name of the King, the Oracle, and symbols that allude to the time when the order was created.

"How did you find us?"

"We took all precautions," he says, smiling and pointing to his attire. They appear like poor peasants.

"State the orders."

"We must deliver them in the presence of the Prince, sir."

There is some nervous shuffling around me.

"Do you not know?" I ask Sinaruk.

"Sir?"

"The Prince is dead. Felled in battle."

The men gasp. Sinaruk's eyes search mine for more answers.

"Come inside; let us speak," I order them. Sinaruk's men hurry into the tent, and we all sit in silence as they drink and eat to nourish themselves. They are hungry, and there is not a word until they finish their meals.

"How did he die, sir?" Sinaruk asks.

"Bravely," I lie. "The battles have been intense. We underestimated the Egyptian resolve and capability."

Sinaruk pauses. "I will state the original orders, sir, but things have changed here."

"Go ahead."

"The King and the Supreme Council have ordered that Prince Nimmuruk be declared King of Egypt and that you conclude the campaign in three moons and return, no matter the situation."

"What?"

Sinaruk stammers. "Prince Nimmuruk—he, he was to be declared King, sir. But since he is dead, we have to discuss what must be done. Those are the orders. The Prince was supposed to continue until we secured victory, or he too would be ordered to return."

"The Prince is dead, and I am now the commander of the Atalanni forces in Egypt. Do they think I am a supreme magician to conjure a victory out of nothing?"

Sinaruk shuffles uncomfortably. "They are no longer demanding victory, General. I am only the messenger—"

I hold up my palm, silencing him. "We do not know how long we will be here. The Prince made some tactical errors that caused us great harm," I say, and he avoids looking into my eyes. "What I need to convey to the King is that we urgently need supplies and more weapons if we must secure victory. The Pharaoh is weak, but he has a supply line that will replenish their bodies and spirits, and we do not. We have lost much, and it is preposterous to abandon now when we can seize victory with some support from home!"

"I will certainly convey that, sir," he says unhappily. He knows he will be the recipient of a severe tongue-lashing, or worse, from the Council.

I pace around the tent, flabbergasted. My men look deflated at this turn of events. "What else is happening there? Why are we rushing to conclude the campaign now? Or did you come here empty-handed to hand down useless orders?" I ask. I must know more, especially about Apsara, but I cannot make it obvious.

Sinaruk looks offended. "This is the first time since the invasion that we are contacting you. No one from here came to Kallistu—no one there knows what is happening here."

"Then answer my questions. What is the situation there?"

Sinaruk rubs his palms and scratches his neck. "The situation in the capital is rather delicate, sir."

"How?"

His eyes dart around the room. "If I may speak to you in confidence? What I say was reserved for the Prince," he says. I am about to resist sending my men away, but then realize that if Sinaruk keeps his mouth shut, I may not learn things that are worth knowing.

I turn to Bansabira. "Prepare the men for our final advance." He bows, and the rest of the men leave with him, leaving me alone with Sinaruk.

"What is it? Leave nothing unsaid. I must know what we are facing."

Sinaruk looks deeply troubled. He gulps some more water. "Things are getting much worse back home, General. Far worse than you can imagine."

"Tell me," I say, my heart beginning to thud—what is happening?

"First, the King has executed many of his nobles, architects, engineers, and governors. He accused them of treason."

It takes minutes for Sinaruk to explain—this savagery unsettles me, but I am unsurprised, knowing the King's slow descent into madness.

"You bring joy, Sinaruk," I say, and we smile sadly. "What else?"

"The tremors have increased. They now occur once every few days. There are vents of steam all around the central temple complex and the causeway. Cracks are appearing everywhere. Many sections of the inner cliffs are collapsing. The main buildings are still standing, but signs of worry are everywhere. The administrators think we will have a revolt on our hands. People are upset about the war, the executions, and the King has refused to evacuate the populace."

I shake my head. "I no longer know if the gods are angry because of what we did or what we failed to do."

"The King no longer relies on the counsel of the Oracle," he whispers, as if fearing that Khaia will magically materialize and smite him. "There is much tension between them."

"She is quite the woman," I say, without elaborating further. I begin to think that Khaia is far more than formidable—she is dangerous.

"Besides, there are rumors that the King has faced a far greater shame," he says conspiratorially.

"What rumors?"

Sinaruk suddenly looks extremely uncomfortable. "Well, it is not for me to further royal rumors, sir. It is nothing of importance..."

I am about to dismiss the conversation, but a royal rumor? "No one from the Council is here, Sinaruk, and we've been in the mud and rut for a long time. A little gossip wouldn't kill you," I say, smiling.

He grins. "Even so, who am I to comment on the King's marital woes?"

My heart palpitates. I do not know if Sinaruk caught my expression, but I control my reaction.

"What of it?"

He leans forward. "It turns out—pardon me, for I am only relaying hearsay—the Queen spread her legs for someone else!"

Blood rushes to my face, and I turn away as if to cough— but I am trying to catch my breath, for it feels as though a foul ghost has thrust itself into my mouth and sucked the air from my lungs.

"That is unfathomable!" I say, faking outrage.

"Not only that—the harlot is pregnant and has been sentenced to death with *haimskaia*. She has another fifty days to reveal her lover, or she dies," he says, narrowing his eyes and shaking his head in admonishment. "The woman has refused to tell who she is fucking!"

I almost feel like vomiting, and my head spins.

Pregnant.

Sentenced to death.

My love and my child!

Here we are, fighting a fruitless war, and there she is, alone, imprisoned with my child, and soon to die.

"What is *haimskaia?*" I ask, dreading the answer.

Sinaruk lowers his voice. "It is an ancient, ruthless punishment reserved for the greatest outrages against the King, sir," he whispers, as if the very name of the punishment must not be uttered.

"What is it?" I ask, a little more sternly.

"She will be tied naked to a post in front of the people. An executioner will break the bones of her hands, legs, and waist, slowly and one by one, with a heavy club. He will then sever each of her limbs and let her bleed to death," he says, his eyes fixed on the floor.

I pretend that my cough is worse—I walk out of the tent and throw up violently. My body shakes with guilt, terror, anxiety, and anger. I take a while to recover and think about what I must do. When I return, Sinaruk has a puzzled expression on his face.

"This is far worse than I thought. Does the Council not realize what they must do before we lose the capital?" I ask, doing my best to appear serious and angry.

He looks confused. "What do you mean, sir?"

"Think, Sinaruk! Tell me about the state of our reserves and security in the capital, and it might strike you as obvious."

Sinaruk thinks for a while, his deep brows furrowed. Then he says slowly, "Phaistos is struggling to contain Kaftu and maintain a semblance of control. Kallistu has bare reserves for security; the troops there are not well trained—

we never expected this situation to arise so quickly. The senior officers are either here or dead. The Supreme Council does not seem to trust anyone in Kallistu anymore, and you may have guessed by now, general, that they no longer see Egypt as a priority. They want you to achieve a quick victory—they want to leave this behind."

Why am I not surprised? But this gives me the opening I seek.

"We might not have a capital to return to if we lose control there, Sinaruk. I must go back and restore order before there is a civil war. The Queen's execution will hasten it! I must keep the Council safe."

Sinaruk looks horrified. "General, you cannot leave—"

"When is the Queen scheduled for execution?" I interrupt.

He thinks for a moment, still looking concerned. "Fifty days if they stay true to the order, but—"

"Did you not hear what I said?" I tell him. "What is the point of fighting for Egypt if we lose Kallistu?"

"We will not lose Kallistu or Kaftu, General," he says, his voice now hostile. "It seems you are trying to find an excuse to run from the battlefield!"

"How dare you accuse me of trying to leave?" I roar at him.

"Phaistos can be recalled to support the reserves in the capital, and I am here to issue the King's order to you! You will pay for insubordination and defying royal orders!" he shouts, his face etched deep with anger and resentment.

"Do not—"

He raises his palm in front of my face. "The King will hear of this! Follow your orders, or it will be your head, Teber," he says and turns to leave.

I lean and grab Sinaruk by his throat. I pull my dagger out and stab him in the chest. I squeeze his throat to prevent him from shouting and hold him until he slumps against my chest.

His blood is all over me.

I lay his body on the floor and go outside. I tell a commandant to bring Bansabira and the remaining commanders to my tent. My temple throbs violently, and it feels as though a giant crab is wringing my guts from the inside. I calculate the situation—Bansabira must hold firm, and I must return.

For Atalanni.

For Apsara.

It is time for me to take control when they are weakest. Once they are all gathered, I first take Bansabira into my confidence. My story is that Sinaruk threatened all of us regarding the Prince's death and that the delicate situation in the capital requires me to return immediately to prevent a revolt and regain control. It takes some convincing, but Bansabira is proud to carry the mantle of the general of the forces in Egypt, and his commanders agree to his leadership. We arrest the rest of Sinaruk's aides and assign them to peripheral duty.

The plan is for the Atalanni forces to hold firm, to the extent possible, until I return. But deep in my heart, I know Ahmose will not wait, and my men face annihilation.

I will return and bring this all to an end.

# CHAPTER 49
## LOWER EGYPT – PERKHURE

I bid farewell to Bansabira and my men. My final speech is one of hope and duty, and I instruct them to remain faithful to the attack plan. They receive the news of my departure bravely; they express many kind words about my leadership.

They are unaware of the immense turmoil within my mind.

I select Itaja and one hundred highly experienced soldiers to accompany me on my return. I cannot bring more men, as we are already depleted, and I must leave enough capable men for Bansabira. As I walk north from the camps, we ascend a small hillock and gaze back at my army. A vast assemblage of tents and ditches stretches in the distance, while men scurry about to prepare for the next battle. A gentle morning mist obscures the view. I stand there for a while, observing the fine clouds gradually conceal our forces, and I ponder whether this army will fade into oblivion.

With a heavy heart, I turn and depart. I survey the ancient land surrounding me, still beyond my grasp. They say my journey will take thirty to forty days due to the weather. The wait will be agonizing, but that is my penance for leaving Apsara alone. I have informed the captains that we will veer away from Kaftu and proceed directly to Kallistu. I am unaware of the situation in the Kingdom and who may be hostile; Phaistos is in Kaftu, and I do not trust him.

I pray for favorable winds and skies.

Along the way, I intend to prepare my men for the possibility of staging a swift coup and seizing control if necessary.

Once peace is restored and the dancers return to the courtyards, I will be reunited with my beloved Queen.

# CHAPTER 50

## KALLISTU

Khaia finally has gained access to Apsara in the dungeon. The pretext is that the Oracle must bless the Queen, and the priestesses must conduct last prayers.

There are only twenty days until the deadline expires, and so far, Apsara has remained resolute and refused to speak of her paramour, much to everyone's frustration. The King is going mad—he rages most of the day, screaming at everyone, lamenting the dire situation on the island and the lack of news from Egypt. Rishwa has twice dissuaded the King from torturing Apsara, and Khaia has lost most of her access to Hannuruk. The inner ledges of the northwestern part of the island bleed molten rock into the sea, a spectacular and frightening sight. The liquid causes the water to boil and hiss. The sounds carry on the chilly winds of the night as if the goddess whispers ominously. Khaia has her bodyguards and a protection force, for it is now unclear what might happen. There have also been isolated incidents of revolt, with people trying to flee only to be arrested and executed on the spot.

She hopes that once Teber arrives, she can gain control of the island and eliminate the King.

She paces along the cobbled pathway to the stairs of the underground prison. It is dark and damp as they descend deeper. Khaia shudders; it is as if she is walking down the stairs to a well of despair. The walk is long, and the cracked stone corridor becomes narrower.

The dim lamps are not enough to fight the darkness that enfolds them.

Guards allow her through the thick wooden doors to a long pathway—on both sides are doors to the cells. She thinks she hears crying and shouts of despair. Two men from the King's Guard accompany her.

She finally reaches the end of the corridor. In front of her stands a bronze-studded stone door with a small peephole. Two men guard the door; they salute the officers from the King's Guard and kneel before Khaia.

"Open it," she commands.

A foul stench greets her as the door creaks open. It is dark inside, and it takes Khaia time to adjust her eyes. There are two small lamps on a ledge, and the room is sparse.

Khaia finally sees her.

Apsara sits with her back to the wall on her bed, atop a stone platform, which has a flimsy sheet for comfort.

*This is the Queen!*

Khaia turns to the King's Guard behind her. "Stay back. It is time for the ceremony."

"Sacred Khaia, we have been instructed to—"

"Get out! Do not interfere in sacred duties," she admonishes them. After some hand-wringing, the two men step out of the room, leaving only Khaia and her two priestesses, who carry some bread, buckets of water, scented cleaning herb extracts, and medicinal salves.

Khaia walks toward Apsara. The lamps reflect off the Queen's face—her hair is dirty and disheveled. She wears a filthy, half-torn rag, and her once-smooth skin bears scabs—wounds healed from itching.

"Apsara, listen to me," she says as she kneels before the bed. She lays a gentle palm on Apsara's withdrawn knees. The Queen flinches at first but does not move away. Khaia caresses Apsara's shoulders. There is a gasp, and the Queen cries. Khaia allows her to be.

Eventually, Apsara calms down.

"Why are you here?" she asks feebly.

"I may have my differences with you, but I had no hand in this and no desire to see you treated this way," Khaia replies.

"Then why did you not stop that monster?"

"He is beyond reason now, Apsara. We have tried."

Apsara gently removes Khaia's palm from her shoulder. "Why are you here, then?"

Khaia does not answer. Instead, she turns to her priestesses and nods. The two women come to either side of Apsara and gently hoist her to her feet. "They are not here to hurt you," Khaia assures.

Apsara says nothing. The women remove her robes and pour warm water over the Queen. They cleanse her. Apsara's chest heaves throughout, and suppressed sobs are the only sounds along with the noise of water sloshing in the bucket and dripping to the floor. Her belly shows a child growing there, Khaia thinks, but that child will never see life. Once the Queen is clean, they apply perfume and dress her in fresh linen. The priestesses chant prayers as they circle the Queen.

Once the ceremony is complete, Khaia orders them to stand outside. The senior man from the King's Guard watches as he leans into the room from outside.

"Are you preparing me for execution?" Apsara asks. There is no fear in her voice, only acceptance.

"Not yet. There are ten more days. Tell them who your lover is. Make this easy. I cannot protect you from your betrayal of the King, but I can lessen the pain of punishment."

Apsara scoffs. "As if I have not suffered enough."

"Apsara," Khaia says urgently, "listen to me, child. You do not want the death the King has announced if you do not reveal the father."

"My death is guaranteed. My child will never experience air, water, or blue skies. I will not add the name of the man who loves me to the King's death list. Besides, how do you know he is not already dead?"

Khaia sighs at the stubbornness of youth. "You are a fool. That man who loved you could not control his lust, and you will die because of it. How reckless could you be?"

"Love. Not lust. What do you know about love? I have only seen venom from you."

The Queen's words sting Khaia. "Do not lay the blame at my feet. It was you who fucked someone behind your husband's back, and you make it seem as though I had something to do with it. You are a Queen, not a market whore. Duty comes first, and love later, for those designated to rule kingdoms."

Apsara retreats to the back of her bed. Khaia does not give up and sits by Apsara's side. "Things are dire. You feel the rumbles. The people are restless. We have inadequate security," she says, hoping her candid assessment will help Apsara trust her more. "We have sent a messenger to Egypt to find General Teber and tell him to bring victory."

Khaia hears Apsara take a sharp intake of breath. The Queen goes still for several moments. "General Teber will know what is happening here?" she asks.

Khaia finds the question distracting—why does the Queen care? "Yes, if the messengers have reached him, he is alive, and the winds are favorable," she replies.

In the flickering light of the lamps, Khaia notices Apsara sit straight, and there is a sparkle in the Queen's eyes.

"Thank you for telling me," Apsara finally says. "The island is in trouble, and you set all this in motion, Khaia," she says, "and you are partially responsible for my death."

*This child!*

"I will accept your anger at me. I had my reasons to do what I did, but this—" she sweeps her hands around. "This I did not cause. Listen to me, please; take my words as the message from our gods," she implores.

"Your gods abandoned me long ago," Apsara says. Her voice is gentle, without recrimination. "I thank you for coming here. I feel fresh. I am better. Your visit has given me a new resolve. I am ready to die when the time comes. I know Indra will welcome me to heaven, and I will greet my father and brothers there. When the time is right, in the afterlife, I will embrace the one man who was more a husband than your King. I will die a Queen. Let your people see what they did to their daughter," she declares, her voice resolute and final.

Khaia cannot understand her stubbornness. Something nagging in her mind eludes her grasp.

"My decision is final," Apsara states.

Khaia sighs. She reaches into her waistband and unsheathes a glistening obsidian dagger.

# CHAPTER 51
## LOWER EGYPT – PERKHURE

Pharaoh Ahmose surveys the carnage before him. Thousands of bodies lie on the battlefield. The ground is slick with the blood of the dead and the dying. Smoke rises from hundreds of funeral pyres. His soldiers walk about, executing those who still writhe, while hundreds of prisoners wait to hear their fate. A deathly stench lingers in the air, and the hellish landscape, with blue smoke and green-maroon earth, appears sinister as the sun descends toward the horizon.

General Wadjmose and Baba walk beside the Pharaoh. The General is cut and bloody; some of his skin is singed from contact with the fire weapons of the Atalanni. Wadjmose limps, and Ahmose slows his pace to accommodate his brave and brilliant general.

"What are the surveyors saying?" asks the Pharaoh.

"Very few escaped, Your Majesty. We have destroyed their army."

"Are all of them dead or captured?"

"Most are dead, and some are captured," Wadjmose replies.

"What of the rest?"

"They ran toward the western deserts. Someone told them to go to the sea of sand where no one shall pursue them."

Ahmose shakes his head. The sea of sand lies on the western edges of Egypt—an unforgiving, hostile, lifeless expanse of fine yellow sand. The Pharaoh has no intention of pursuing men who are merely fleeing to their horrible deaths.

"What about us?"

"We have lost more than half of our men as well. It will take us time to rebuild, but for now, the threat from the Atalanni is over."

"You are exceptional, Wadjmose," Ahmose says, placing his arm on the General's shoulder. "If only you had children! They could one day serve a glorious Egypt."

Wadjmose bows in reverence. "It is your divine presence and encouragement that leads us to victory, Your Majesty," he states. "I have no desire for a wife or children, but perhaps my name will live on."

Ahmose understands that this battle was a close call. The Atalanni had adopted a new formation that countered the Egyptian Horus. The Egyptian forces had nearly collapsed. It was Ahmose's resolute defense of the center and Wadjmose's exploitation of a weakness in the Atalanni flank that shifted the tide of the ultimate battle.

The dancers, he thinks derisively, fought well. However, they were outnumbered and fatigued. More surprisingly, Ahmose had learned that the formidable commander of the Atalanni had abruptly departed a few days ago. There was also news that the Atalanni troops had rebelled against the crown prince and murdered him.

Why?

The Atalanni had attempted to negotiate with him— they had insisted that Binpu's death was an accident and that Sitkamose was alive. It seemed the general was truthful, unlike his deceitful, cowardly rulers. But Ahmose would entertain no truce. They had struck Egypt in their court, and retribution was the only response. Why did these imbeciles embark on such a disastrous invasion?

"You are confident that they have no other forces in the vicinity?"

"We are, Your Majesty. Our scouts have spread far, and there is no news of other forces."

Ahmose removes his headgear and hands it to an attendant. He then reaches out to another man who pours scented water into the Pharaoh's palms. Ahmose wipes his sweaty and grimy face and pours some water on his neck.

"What do we do with the prisoners?"

"I do not think they share the same greed as their King, Your Majesty," Wadjmose replies. He knows that the lowest man only cares about a full belly and a safe family.

Ahmose ponders for a moment. "Line them up. Ask who will subject themselves unconditionally to serve Egypt in the army—as menders, cleaners—and soldiers if they prove their trustworthiness. Execute anyone who wavers and recruit the rest."

"A sound suggestion, Your Majesty," Wadjmose agrees.

"Take the corpses of their commanders and hang them on the Thebes city walls."

"Yes, Your Majesty."

"Then find out where their Navy is. Burn it. I will have no sign of their existence."

Wadjmose hesitates. "We could use the timber, Your Majesty."

Ahmose considers his General's response. "Fine then. Dismantle every boat and burn what we cannot take."

"Yes, Your Majesty. We will leave no trace of their Navy by the time we are done."

Ahmose glances at the battlefield once more and shakes his head. "They had peace. Their trade was valued. Their art was beautiful. But they were like a diseased dog that came to attack a pack of wolves," he declares as he finally turns away to return to his tent.

# CHAPTER 52

## KALLISTU

Apsara caresses the smooth and deadly dagger that Khaia handed to her just before she left.

"Use this, my Queen. Do not subject yourself to the humiliation and pain of the punishment," the Oracle had said. It almost felt as if she meant it. Khaia had had her washed, cleaned, and the Oracle had prayed for her. Before leaving the dungeon, Khaia even held Apsara's hands and kissed her forehead. Apsara sensed remorse, but one would never know.

The edges are sharp; she has already cut herself by accident as she felt the elegant weapon. It would be all too easy to pierce herself in the heart and bid goodbye.

But she will not.

She attempted to die once, and the shame of running away from her troubles still haunts her.

Not again. The daughter of Mitanni will not go to the afterlife by her own hand.

She has only heard vague descriptions of her punishment, but she has been informed that death will come in hours, if not sooner.

Let it come. Let the citizens of this land see what their King does to a Princess of a foreign land and their daughter. One with a child. Yes, she had sinned, but it stemmed from abandonment by her husband—a vicious, incapable man who never once treated her as anything more than an alliance due to his physical failures.

Let the council and the people watch as their beloved Queen is tied, beaten, and murdered before their own eyes.

Let their deeds shame them for eternity. Let their name be sullied. Apsara is certain their gods will never forgive them, even after her death. If nothing else, her demise will cause an uprising that dethrones the King.

Teber. Oh, Teber. Where is he? Khaia said that there was no news from Egypt but that they had sent a messenger to Teber. That news renewed hope in Apsara—if Teber knew what had happened, he would return in time. There could be a chance to escape. If not, her death would compel him to rise against the madness.

She places the dagger back in a crack in the wall. She scratches the severe itch on her palms and elbow, and the skin ruptures again, leaving a trail of blood. Apsara then caresses her swelling belly, feeling a light kick. She smiles and taps on her stomach in response. There is a gentle rumble beneath her feet—as if the Goddess Mother of Earth approves of her decision.

# CHAPTER 53

## KALLISTU

Apsara completes her morning prayers to Indra and the Atalanni Mother Goddess of the Earth. She washes with the scented water placed before her and wipes her face with fresh linen towels. She dresses in sheer white fabric that drapes around her, from her shoulders to her knees, exposing her pregnant stomach. Her hair hangs loose, and her hands and legs are devoid of any ornaments.

Outside the room, she can hear the chants and bells of the ceremonial group.

*May your sins wash away.*

*May there be mercy for your poison.*

*The pain shall absolve your shame.*

*The goddess will welcome you to her arms.*

*The heavens will say your name.*

*May you walk quietly to the gates of the sky palace.*

They treat me with respect before torturing me to death in front of a thousand, she thinks. Do the gods not see the wickedness?

Finally, the door creaks open. The hinges make a torturous sound as the gravel beneath the door rubs against the wood. Outside is a contingent of the King's Guard, along with three more priestesses.

Apsara's knees feel weak.

Her skin grows hot with stress.

Her heart beats as if it will break her ribs open and explode from her chest.

*It is time. May Varuna give me the strength to endure the pain before I make my eternal journey.*

Unsteadily, she walks to the center of the group. One guard gently asks her to bring forward her arms. He then binds her wrists with a maroon-stained cotton rope. A priestess kneels before her and applies a red pigment to her exposed belly.

They lead her down the dark pathway—it is the first time in many moons that Apsara has been out of her cell. She loses her balance more than once on the uneven, cracked floor, and the priestesses steady her. When she emerges from the corridor to the open ground, the world around her is not as she expected it to be—there is no blue sky or a crisp, cool breeze. Instead, the air is heavy with haze and a pungent smell. The column marches on a narrow pathway along the edge of the cliff. Apsara sees high columns of steam rise from various vents in the black rock below her, and also from the sides of the cliffs.

*What is happening?*

*Are the gods angry with me?*

*Or are they angry at the Atalanni greed?*

People watch her on either side of the path.

Some look fearful.

Some look ashamed.

Some curse her.

"Harlot, you bring shame to this land!" shouts a man, grabbing his crotch.

"You are the reason our land bleeds fire," says an old woman as she stabs the air with her bony fingers.

"Forgive us, Princess," whispers another woman, leaning forward.

But most others treat her with silence, and many bow as she passes them. Worry is writ large on their faces. Apsara hopes that the Atalanni gods spare their citizens.

*What I did was wrong, but do the gods not see why?*

Apsara flinches when a vent near her erupts with a sharp, acrid column of steam, and one priestess screams in fear. They move away from the hazard and continue to the public amphitheater near the Palace. Most of the surrounding plants—olive, palm, cactus—appear to have dried or burned. She wipes her eyes to ease the sting.

They ascend several steps of a walled compound and finally arrive at the place of her execution.

The four-ringed amphitheater is full of people.

Armed guards stand along the back. People sit on cracked stone benches. There is silence—she senses a reluctant audience. Below, in the amphitheater's front, is a stone bed with four poles on each corner.

A rope hangs from each pole.

A heavyset man in a featureless black mask and loincloth stands beside the platform.

He holds a short, heavy club.

At the opposite side of the stone bed is a raised dais—in the center sits King Hannuruk, and beside him are Phaistos, Rishwa, Khaia, and a host of other officials. Apsara walks down the steps with her head held high. Some people stand, while the rest watch quietly. This is a spectacle that the peaceful people of the land have never seen in their lifetime. Officials have used this stage previously for executions—but they were mostly low-life criminals and war captives.

*What must they be thinking?*

*What have they been told?*

She finally arrives in the center and stands near the edge of the stone bed. She defiantly stares into the eyes of those who have condemned her. Hannuruk looks back at her. He appears putrid and foul; his stomach droops below the belt, and his face is puffy and red. Rishwa looks like he could be sick and avoids her eyes as he stares at the floor. Phaistos briefly meets her eye—but there is no expression in those eyes—and he turns away to look at the audience.

But Khaia? She stares straight ahead—her face deathly pale, as she blinks away tears. Uppiluliuma stands by the King in heavy armor, a bronze helmet, and a long sword.

A hush descends on the amphitheater.

Hannuruk, slouching on his side, waves his hand dismissively at one of his officers. The man steps forward and faces the crowd. He beats a drum to command attention, and soon there is no sound in the air except the hum of the agitated world outside.

"This Queen is a sinner. She has brought shame to this land. To the great King," he says, dramatically pointing to Apsara. She watches dispassionately. "The King has been generous. He has afforded her freedom like no other ruler on earth, for we the Atalanni are gracious in our conduct, generous in our treatment of women, respectful of their wishes and desires, and see the divinity in our Queens, for we are blessed by our Mother Goddess of Earth and our sacred Oracle."

Many in the audience shout their agreement.

Hannuruk looks agitated.

"But this woman, a woman wedded to be the Queen of this glorious empire, the one who had the honor and duty to worship the great King and her husband, has shamed herself with her conduct and abuse of our generosity."

A wave of restlessness passes through the crowd. "She has plotted to kill the King!" the man theatrically shouts. "Once a queen, now just a common whore from a foreign land!"

*He does not mention the illegitimate pregnancy.*

The crowd murmurs, but a roar of anger is absent.

*They know the truth. Tongues wag. People speak.*

The speaker looks flustered, discouraged by the lack of robust response. "The King has been most merciful, showing the benevolence of the Atalanni, for we are not barbarians. We follow our law. And the King, while well within his rights to execute this harlot and spill her blood on the palace floors, granted her a hundred days to expose the vermin that conspired with her," he says, raising his voice to elicit a stronger reaction. "And she has not divulged the truth behind her sins!"

The response remains muted, with a smattering of angry cries of "Whore! Harlot!"

*The citizens see the King for what he is and what he has put them through already.*

"The time for his mercy is over. The tremors, the steaming vents, the crying cliffs, the rising heat—these result from this wickedness, and our Oracle says that the gods demand justice!" he declares.

He then turns to Khaia and bows.

Khaia appears displeased. She nods half-heartedly and sits back, leaving the announcer confused. The King is angry, but he gestures for the man to continue.

"The King, our glorious ruler, said there should be no secret from the people. Let them know what their Queen is. Let them know he has swallowed his pride for this betrayal and yet granted mercy, but this sinful swine has maintained her silence."

The people watch on. Apsara feels a warm breeze caress her cheeks. Tendrils of smoke waft over their heads, and some people use their clothing to clear the air.

The announcer steps up onto the dais and puffs up his chest. "Apsara, one who has disgraced her land, has been sentenced to *haimskaia*. An ancient punishment reserved only for Queens who plot the King's death. May you witness this, and let this be a message from the King that the Atalanni are merciful, but may no one test our limits. May the punishment begin."

Two priestesses circle Apsara and chant prayers. They then lift her wrists and untie her. Suddenly, a hand grips her jaw and wraps a firm band of cloth around her mouth.

*Not even the courtesy of allowing her to speak her last words.*

Apsara fights rising panic and the acrid taste of bile in her mouth. She trembles as a priestess leads her to the stone bench, and someone steadies her when she swoons.

The audience watches in absolute silence.

Apsara's eyes dart towards the dais and the periphery, hoping for a miracle.

The executioner, his eyes black as coal, reaches forward and rips Apsara's garment. In a humiliating instant, she is exposed for all the world to see—a Queen once loved, desired, admired, and now naked and shaking in front of a thousand eyes. She tries to cover her modesty, but two men hold her arms apart. They lift her and lay her on the rough stone bed. Apsara glimpses the dais—Khaia is looking down at the floor, and Phaistos is arguing something with Rishwa. Suddenly, Khaia gets up and walks briskly towards her, swatting away the hands of a guard who tries to stop her. The Oracle kneels beside Apsara, looking into her eyes. She pretends to pray but whispers into Apsara's ears, "I will order the executioner to hasten the process and minimize your suffering. May you and your child find happiness in the palace of heavens."

Apsara nods.

Khaia says something to the executioner.

Then she vanishes from Apsara's vision.

The surface of the granite slab feels cold against Apsara's burning skin.

The guards tie her hands and feet to the ropes.

She is spread-eagled for all the world to see.

Once a Princess.

Once a Queen.

Her stomach feels heavy. Her baby stirs as if in protest.

She looks up at the skies as tears fill her eyes.

Then there is a loud sound of the trumpet and the beat of drums that lasts for what feels like an eternity. When the noises stop, and there is deathly stillness, the executioner looms into her vision.

His terrifying masked face looks down at her.

His hand raises the club.

Apsara's ears fill with the roar of a mighty waterfall, and her heart beats wildly.

And then there is a powerful blow to her right wrist. Pain shoots up her arm like a million needles in her palm as the bones shatter.

Apsara's scream dies in the rag that covers her mouth as she kicks in a haze of red-hot agony. She chokes on her vomit and feels the burn in her throat, and her wrist goes limp.

*Help me, Indra, my father, my brother! Teber!*

And yet there is only stillness in the air.

# PART V

*"A King has an obligation to contain his ambitions for his actions alter the fate of not only the slaves and courtiers before him, but a great many that live far away from his eyes, never seen..."*

## DAIVOSHASTRA CH. XIV: "DUTIES"

# CHAPTER 54

## KALLISTU

We disembark and assemble on the dock. It is a surreal scene around us—smoke rises from hundreds of vents, and the central temple island bears a million cracks. Cliff walls spew gas, and the air is putrid with the smell of something rotten.

*What is happening?*

It has taken us forty-five days to reach this place, and along the way, I have done everything to ensure that this band remains loyal to me and will obey my every command, including attempting a coup if the situation is dire. They see that the King has failed and has put the entire Kingdom at risk.

A small contingent guarding the dock approaches us. I am desperate to rush past them and lead my men to find Apsara, but I know that a foolish move now could jeopardize the entire mission. I decide to curb my impulses and remain calm.

I hope I am not too late.

"General Teber, greetings. We are relieved to have you back," he says, saluting. The man looks wary and unhappy. He is disheveled, dirty, and his eyes are puffy from lack of sleep or too much drink.

"What is happening here?"

"We are cursed, General," he replies, looking around pathetically. "We no longer know whether our gods favor us. We have been enduring endless tremors. We cannot even sleep soundly at home at night."

"Why have we not evacuated yet?" I ask. The man looks around uncomfortably.

"The King will not allow it. A fleet carrying a few hundred of our peasants and artisans left, but then the King ordered a blockade and even scuttled trade boats. We are to await evacuation orders."

I curse under my breath. "What is the King waiting for?" I mutter. I am anxious to reach the Palace. Sometimes it is more helpful to learn what is happening by speaking to the men on the ground rather than those who dwell in the clouds.

"I must get to the Palace to assume my orders," I say, turning to my small but capable force.

The captain clears his throat, and his men fan out in front. They are outnumbered and look fearful, but they still block our way. "Your orders are to stay here, sir, and prevent anyone from accessing the docks. We will be sent word when you are to go to the Palace."

"Are you joking, Captain? I bring news from Egypt. The Supreme Council has recalled me with explicit purpose. I am not to serve as a dock guard," I snap at him. He shuffles on his feet and scratches whatever hair remains on his head.

"I know, General; those are my orders, sir. I bow to you, but those are my instructions. I can verify—" he says, and he looks miserable.

"By whose orders?"

"The Oracle's, sir."

"I do not take orders from the Oracle," I say, puzzled. In the distance, I hear clangs and chants—another ceremony, I wonder, to appease the gods who are livid with us.

"The Prime Minister and the Oracle are issuing security orders, sir. The King is preoccupied."

The clangs and chants grow louder in the distance. We spread around the small unenclosed area, and I hear more clamor and sounds again from above. While the Palace amphitheater is quite far and high above, the sounds carry well at this time of day and according to the direction of the wind.

"Captain," I call, and he comes running. "What is happening? Is there another joyous celebration to welcome more tremors?"

"Do you not know, sir?" he says, dropping his voice. "It is time for the Queen's execution."

A heavy rock lands in my stomach. "The sounds—"

The captain looks up the cliff and points. "It is being carried out right now."

*No. No. No.*

It is time to act. I turn to my men, who are now clustered close to me. "This is it," I shout, the strength returning to my being, "A public execution of a Queen on a pretext and another pointless spectacle for the gods by this mad King. Let us put an end to it all. It is time to depose the tyrants!"

This is something we have discussed on our journey home, but now is the time to test their commitment. The dock guards, of course, look perplexed.

There is some consternation, but a few of my closest commanders—Itaja, Kilonas, Eluminnas—raise their hands and swing their swords in the air. "We are with you!" they announce, and soon the entire band supports me. My forethought has paid off—these men have always spoken fondly of the Queen and share a universal disdain for the King and the Oracle.

"We will fight to the death if need be, but the King must go," I shout, with little idea if any of this will work. None of us know how large a force still remains on the island to confront us. But if I must die trying, I will. "Come with me!" I urge the bewildered dock guards, and soon they too shout their approval and join me. We are now a band of about one hundred and twenty-five.

It is a coup, even if it starts small.

We rush up the winding stone and mud steps of the cliff.

My lungs burn, and my calves feel on fire.

I pray I am not too late. We dodge the steaming vents and acrid smoke but make progress. My skin feels as though I have been submerged in hot water for hours. The chants grow louder as we near the amphitheater, and just as we ascend a low swell, the external compound comes into view. We face ten more guards. They recognize my attire and salute, but the leader says urgently, "You are back, sir? You are to—"

My men quickly surround them, swords and spears drawn. The dock captain speaks to the man, "General Teber wishes to bring peace back to our island, brother. Let us not wait until it is too late!"

"I cannot, I mean—" he stutters in fear and anxiety.

I lean over and place a hand on his shoulder. "You have been lied to, and soon we will have nothing if I do not put an end to this disgrace. Now step aside, or join us, because we cannot wait. Do you want the blood of an innocent Queen on your hands, enraging our gods beyond what they already are?" I ask rhetorically.

I hear someone making a speech, but I cannot discern what he is saying.

Then the voice halts.

There are horns and drums.

The man looks around. The smoke, the cracks, the blackened ground—none bode well, and by now they have witnessed the cruelty of their rulers. "We will join you, sir!" he says and nods to his men. One man protests. I thrust my sword into his chest, and he collapses, surprise etched on his face. I then nod to the others. "We have to go."

My heart thunders in my chest, and I do not know what I will witness. I pause and speak to an archer, asking him to join me. Suddenly, the chants and trumpets stop, leaving nothing but silence.

*Is it over?*

We arrive at the entrance, and a few people seated on the rear benches look back. I point my sword at a guard posted at the gateway, and he retreats without resistance. I rush into the corridor that leads down to the focal area.

The benches are full. In the center lies the execution bed, and there—

My heart explodes.

*Apsara!*

Spread-eagled, naked, her body shaking and legs kicking against the ropes that hold her to the poles. These wretched vermin have even bound a rag around her mouth to prevent her from screaming.

An executioner in a mask slowly walks to the other side of the stone bed on which the woman of my life writhes in agony. He wields a thick club.

*Breaking her limbs?*

*Beating a queen to death in front of the citizens?*

I only briefly glimpse the nobility.

Rage consumes me.

My vision blurs.

I scream at the archer, and I watch him raise his bow and draw back on an already hoisted arrow. Then, I rush down the steps with my men screaming from behind.

# CHAPTER 55

## KALLISTU

Her legs shaking and kicking, and her body wracked with agony, Apsara tracks the masked executioner as he walks to her other side. In the haze of her pain, she realizes what Khaia meant when she had asked Apsara to end her life instead of enduring this punishment. The executioner will break every joint first, and she thinks, if this is just the beginning, how long will it be before she embraces merciful death?

Just then, she hears some commotion. She raises her head and looks up—she sees a large group of soldiers rushing down. She cannot make out who they are because of the tears and dust in her eyes, and she turns to her executioner, who is now looking up at what is happening.

From the corner of her eye, she sees a glint streak through the air—and the executioner's skull ruptures. Blood erupts like a fountain, and the man collapses.

*What?*

A great roar and clamor rise, and the surrounding scene descends into chaos. A blur of men fighting fills her vision. The sound of blades and spears fills the air. There are screams, orders, and shouts, and yet she remains fixed where she is.

She wonders if someone will come and kill her quickly. Instead, she feels something at her feet; someone is hacking the ropes.

Suddenly, all her limbs are free.

Her broken wrist falls to the side and strikes the stone bed, and she doubles up in agony. A hand holds her face and rips the gag away, and she gasps for air. But before any other sounds escape her mouth, she feels a powerful hug—and even in the frenzy of the moment, she recognizes the touch and the smell.

*Teber!*

It is as if all the gods smile down on her, and her pain is forgotten, even if just for a moment. She looks up at his face.

He smiles. Love and rage reside in his eyes.

His hair is matted with blood and hangs down in curls at the front.

"No one will ever hurt you again," he assures her.

Someone drapes her with a garment. Apsara releases a loud gasp and a sob of relief. She shivers but feels the warmth of his embrace for a moment longer before he addresses her again. "Stay with Itaja. I am right behind you," he instructs.

"Do not leave me—" she starts, but he is gone, and his soldiers surround her and usher her forward into the descending corridor. She takes unsteady steps, and they enter a darkened passage. Suddenly, a sturdy resolve grips her, and she taps Itaja's shoulder.

"Tie my right hand; my wrist is broken," she says, struggling with every word and pointing to her limp hand. "Give me a knife."

Itaja grunts and inspects her wrist. Apsara cries out again in pain as he manipulates the bones and sets them before placing her hand in a basic harness. He holds her until she stops shaking and hands her a sharp bronze knife. She grips the handle and takes a deep breath.

"Keep going!" She hears Teber's voice from behind; he is a blur as he moves to the front. They are now on a semi-dark path that opens to another room. It is one of the audience chambers of the Palace, and Apsara is familiar with this place.

"Stop, wait!" she hears Teber's voice, and they all come to a halt. Apsara knows why.

Before them stand soldiers.

King's Guard. Loyal only to the King.

# CHAPTER 56
## KALLISTU

I observe them. The room is dark and depressing—only a small stream of light filters through an opening in the stone roof. In front are the King's Guard—I know Uppiluliuma—the tall, powerfully built captain of the guards, not a native Atalanni but from distant lands to the north. He has no loyalty except to the King. I do not know his history, except that this savage will not yield.

"Stand aside, Uppi. The rest of your guards are dead or with us. It is time to end this madness and restore a semblance of normalcy."

Uppiluliuma scoffs. He waves his sword.

"Sedition. General Teber. I accuse you of sedition, treason, and disloyalty. You may lay down your weapons, and we will consider a merciful end for you and everyone with you."

What a fool. The world comes down around him, and he speaks of loyalty to a senile, vicious bastard. His men, at least three visible layers deep, slowly fan across the room, spreading from corner to corner. I signal my men to do the same. I turn back to ensure Apsara is protected. She is defiant and tries to argue with one of my men.

*Brave, yet foolish.*

I turn back to Uppiluliuma. "You are blind to what you see around you. What use is loyalty if it serves to protect a vicious King who seeks to destroy the very Kingdom that trusts him to keep them safe?"

Uppiluliuma scoffs. "My loyalty and oath are to the King, Teber. What he does is of no concern to me. What good is an oath if it bends based on convenience or circumstance?"

"The oath is to the land and its laws, not to a man. If that man fails in his duties, then your oath is no longer binding," I reply.

He cranes his neck and laughs. "Is that your way of justifying the treasonous scoundrels that hide behind you?"

Itaja shouts, "Shut your fucking mouth, you foreign donkey. You have no sense of an oath because you have no loyalty to the people, just to the King who pays you to be a savage and rape as you will."

That riles Uppiluliuma. "I am a greater citizen than you bastards ever were. You plot behind the King and lose every battle," he says, spitting on the floor.

There is no sense in arguing with this brute. I give him an ultimatum. "Step aside, or you will all die," I say, addressing the surrounding men. "Your master will die. He is no Atalanni, but you are. Lay down your weapons or run away."

They do not move.

A gentle vibration tickles our feet. Everyone looks around in fear. We are in a closed space, and it is risky to remain here. "Kill them!" I shout, and we attack the heavily armored guards with the full force of our anger. I rush the group, and Uppiluliuma charges at me. He is a big man, a full head taller than I, but he has spent his life walking behind the King, while I have spent mine fighting our wretched enemies. I let him push my sword back, and he loses his footing due to his forward momentum. I pull a short knife from my belt and stab him in the shoulder. He yelps, but it does not stop him. I jump back as one of the King's Guards stumbles and falls in front of me, his neck hacked away and blood gushing out in spurts.

Uppiluliuma recovers and swings his sword hard, connecting with mine. A jolt of pain shoots up my shoulder, and I stagger back. Just then, the floor shakes again, and pieces of the ceiling drop. I worry we will all suffocate and die. There are more screams, and I realize the corridor we came from is shut off due to the collapse of the ceiling. We have only one way forward—to kill the King's Guard and run until we exit this subterranean complex.

The air is thick with dust.

Some cough as they fight.

I make out Uppiluliuma fighting one of the dock guards. He smoothly severs the guard's head and meets my sword just in time.

This time, I will not let him stop me.

I pirouette with my sword held out in one hand and my knife in the other. He awkwardly tries to stop the arc of the blade. Just then, I thrust the sword forward and slice his thigh. He grunts, and before he can act, I upward thrust my knife right under his chin and yank it forward. Uppiluliuma shudders and falls. He clutches his throat and thrashes about. I leave him and attack the others—but the situation is dire. I can see the wall of the King's Guard pushing my men back. The King's Guard is desperate, and even as we hack them down like sacrificial animals, their greater number takes a toll on us. I quickly glance back to see Apsara still guarded in a corner, but I do not know how long we can hold out. I jump forward with renewed effort, exhorting my men, shouting encouragement.

The floor is already slick with blood and flesh, but we are tiring. I flinch twice as blades cut my shoulder and forearm—just enough to slice the skin and draw blood.

*Help us, Goddess Mother of Earth. Whose side are you on?*

Suddenly, a horn sounds from the corridor behind the wall of the King's Guard. Everyone stops after a few moments of skirmishing. It is as if every soldier hopes for a truce.

From the darkness emerge more armored soldiers.

I struggle to recognize them.

*Phaistos!*

Rishwa follows right behind him.

There is much confusion now. Will they join the King's Guard to kill us? I take a defensive stance, and my men do the same.

Swords drawn, shields in front, helmets back in position.

"Everyone, stand down," says Phaistos. "The Prime Minister orders."

The King's Guard is unsure what to do. Many look down at the pile of bodies on the floor, and their leader, Uppiluliuma, is still twitching, his face smashed in as men run over it. I doubt he can issue more orders.

"Stand down." This time the voice is Rishwa's. The remaining King's Guard lower their weapons and look back for further instructions. Rishwa parts the men and gets to the front—but a clear gap remains between them and us, with the bodies of the dead and dying acting as a boundary. The tremors have stopped, for now, and I know we must hasten.

"Put your weapons down, Teber," Rishwa says. "We can end this amicably."

"You put the Queen on display like an animal and let them torture her to death!" I shout.

Rishwa searches for answers but chooses not to respond. "We must all file out in an orderly way before these corridors collapse on us," he states.

"Then tell your men to leave and not come in our way. Join us, Prime Minister; it is time to end this savagery."

"You should—"

"No! Look around you. What do you see? Join me, and let us bring peace back to the citizens of Atalanni."

Rishwa is silent, eventually conferring with Phaistos. I do not know what Kaftu's new governor's intentions are, but I am surprised that so far he has not tried to kill me. Finally, Rishwa speaks. His voice is tired. "Do what you must. I will go oversee evacuations," he says and signals his men. After some hesitation, all the King's Guard and the rest of the men with Rishwa and Phaistos file out. Soon, the large room is empty. I wait for the corridor to clear, aware of a potential ambush.

We cautiously move through the corridor until we reach higher open ground.

There is no one around. The Palace terrace looms ahead, and it presents a dark and ominous landscape all around us. Many of the buildings, including the Palace, bear signs of great violence. The air is thick with the smell of anger and open earth. We regroup to rest—it has been intense, and I am thankful that many of us are still alive. We take a quick count, and I realize I have lost thirty of my men and about half of the dock guards.

I walk to Apsara. She watches me with a tearful smile as I near her. My men observe quietly; I know what they are thinking—that I will bow to the Queen and seek orders.

That I was here to preserve royal dignity.

Instead, I envelop her in my arms, much to everyone's shock. No one protests, and Itaja looks at me with a half-curious grin on his face.

Apsara relaxes and weeps.

I wait for her to regain her composure, then bend down and kiss her deeply. I hear shouts of approval and surprise around me. Finally, Itaja, his weary eyes full of mirth and his leathery face breaking into a full grin, cannot help himself. "You bastard! It was you who made her pregnant!" he exclaims. Most others laugh. I do not. Instead, I step aside and gently caress her belly and thump my chest.

Itaja is astonished. "I said that as a joke. You, really, sir!" He lets out a roaring laugh, and others join him.

"No wonder the old man was going mad," someone else chimes in.

"General Teber seduces the Queen in the corridors of the Palace. You designed the corridors yourself, sir?"

There is much laughter, and after a long time, I let myself laugh. Apsara, who has her face hidden in my chest, finally emerges, smiling.

"Shouldn't the soldiers behave themselves?" she asks, and her voice is music to my ears. The men continue to make ridiculous jokes. I know that this is a release of pressure because there is much to be done.

The King is alive, somewhere.

And I must know what the Oracle is up to.

Just then, a figure emerges from a broken wall.

Rishwa.

"Phaistos has left to make plans for evacuation. If he cannot muster enough boats, he will leave for Kaftu to plan," he states.

I nod to him. "We must talk, Prime Minister."

His face has aged. There is great sadness in those wise eyes, and his gaunt features show signs of immeasurable fatigue. He takes tentative steps toward Apsara, and she shows no hostility toward him.

Rishwa cradles her, and she sobs again. "My child, my child," he says softly, wiping his tears.

Once we settle, I ask Rishwa and Apsara to walk with me for a conversation. They provide a succinct account of all that happened in my absence, detailing the forces behind various decisions. I am relieved to learn that Khaia tried to prevent Apsara's ghastly execution order. But I am livid that she pushed Apsara to end her own life.

I finally broach the subject. "The King must die."

Rishwa nods imperceptibly. "He has nowhere to go. He is probably hiding somewhere in the Palace with his remaining guards."

"He has turned mad and dangerous. I can understand his following the Oracle's demand of the gods to wage war on Egypt, Prime Minister, but everything else? He is unfit to rule," I continue.

Apsara gently touches my forearm. I turn to her. "You do not see what is in plain sight, Teber," she says, smiling.

"And that is?"

Apsara looks at Rishwa. "I have always wanted to ask you, wise Rishwa, but never found the right moment," she says.

"Yes, my Queen," he replies.

"What do the laws of the Atalanni say regarding succession?"

"Succession?" Rishwa looks uncomfortable.

"Yes, who can succeed to the throne upon the King's death or invalidity?"

Rishwa smiles, his eyes twinkling as if he appreciates a gifted child's remark. He sees something that I still do not.

"Explain that to Teber," says Apsara. Rishwa bows to her again and turns to me.

"Atalanni laws are quite clear on succession. Circumstances do not always allow a king to have a child who can succeed," he says.

"I have some awareness of our succession laws, but not all," I reply. My shoulder and forearm ache with a dull pain, but my mind is clear now. The sun shines on our backs, and vapors cloud the skies.

"The laws are exhaustive but clear. The king's firstborn male is the rightful successor to the throne when the king dies or abdicates. If the successor is not of sound mind, then the king can declare that child invalid for succession, as Hannuruk did with his firstborn. The succession then passes to the next child, and so on. If the child is a girl, she assumes the role of regent until she reaches marriageable age, at which point her husband assumes the role of king. Hannuruk's father came to power that way. You may not know this, Teber, but King Hannuruk's father was not born of this land or Kaftu; he came here through an alliance with an Eastern Kingdom."

Hannuruk's physical features differ slightly from those of most Atalanni citizens.

"But what happens if the queen dies and the king is invalid?" I inquire.

Rishwa clasps his hands and nods appreciatively.

"If the queen is dead, and the king develops a disability or dies without a valid heir, then the lawful succession would be to the man declared king of Kaftu."

I see where this conversation is headed. "In our case, just as an example, Minos would be that man. But he is dead. So does Phaistos assume kingship?"

Rishwa shakes his head. "Not Phaistos. The king has only appointed him temporary governor. Only a man declared king of Kaftu could take that position, and only Minos was ever appointed that way."

"And Minos is dead," I reply. My mind is churning.

Rishwa and Apsara continue to look at me, saying nothing—as if expecting me to have a divine insight.

"So?" I ask again, and Apsara shakes her head.

Frustrated, I take a few steps to clear my mind. Kneeling on the dark-gray, matted grass, I rub my hands in the dust. It is then that a realization dawns on me.

If the king is invalid or dead, his son is invalid or dead, he has no daughter, his wife is dead, and his appointed governor is dead, then who becomes king? It all falls into place with breathtaking clarity, and the audacity stuns me. I turn to Rishwa. "Does the Oracle take the throne under any circumstance?" I ask.

"It seems you have come to the same conclusion as we have, General," Rishwa replies, approvingly. Apsara, her face still white as a sheet from pain and exertion, manages a smile. "The constitution gives the throne to the Oracle when the king is invalid or dead, and his issues, queen, or king of Kaftu cannot take possession."

As the stunning betrayal and deception sinks in, the ground rumbles and shakes beneath us. I turn to my men, who wait patiently, even as the landscape around us shifts. "We are running out of time. The gods are not angry because of what we were supposed to do, but for what we did!" I shout. "Come with me. We must find Hannuruk and Khaia."

We jog toward the palace, making steady progress, and I ensure that Apsara can follow. Her eyes burn with fierce determination.

# CHAPTER 57

## KALLISTU

———————————⚭————————————

Pressure builds deep within the bowels of the earth. Large sections of cliffs collapse, taking homes and places of worship down to the churning sea, which now swells and shakes as if it is within a bowl. The priests and commoners have long abandoned the central temple complex, where the ground has turned black.

Many vents spew toxic vapors.

But now those vents grow larger.

The great temple of the gods, damaged long ago, now tries to withstand the quakes and powerful waves beating against it.

Slowly, in pieces and blocks, the stones shift and collapse.

The grand colonnade topples like a stack of sticks. The beautiful statues of the Goddess Mother of Earth and the God of the Seas, adorned in jewelry and chiseled to be lifelike, break into a thousand pieces. After an hour of violence upon this complex, with all its structure in ruins, the central mound of black rock opens up like the jaws of a hungry hippopotamus.

Just as the sun dips its toes into the western waters, the central mound explodes. Dark red liquid rock springs like a glorious fountain. The vent also ejects fine gray and yellow ash, darkening the vista and hiding the sun in bands of gray and black. If a man could fly, the view would seem like one not of this world—a glowing stream of red, like bloody tears of an angry god, flows from the wound in the middle of a circular gray and black island. Dark blue waters churn within the inner confines of the ring.

The molten rock flows into the lukewarm waters, causing a roaring hiss of steam. The half-submerged causeway is now a river of fire, surrounded by blankets of ash and vapor.

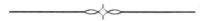

Deep in the subterranean caverns, more than a hundred council members hide in quake-proof chambers.

They sit in a large dark room lit by fish oil lamps.

Comfort has long vanished. It is now suffocating. The pits are just a hundred feet in front of them, and a bright glow emanates from the edge.

"I cannot breathe," an elder complains. "Should we not go back to the surface?"

"It is poisonous near the pits, and we have no way to go up. Besides, we do not know the situation outside. These structures are built to withstand the tremors," says another man. But his voice shakes, betraying the lack of confidence in his own words.

"Our gods will protect us. The Oracle maintains that this is just a display of their displeasure in stronger terms. They love us," rasps a woman as she wipes her face and makes signs of supplication.

"Calm down, Goddess Mother, show us your mercy and love. We have always sought to do what pleases you!" says another man as he gasps for air. All that is now visible in the darkness is the mesmerizing glow from the pit.

"Sacred Khaia, where are you? Save us!" someone shouts, and a chorus of implorations dissolves in the hot, smoky air.

They watch the orange hues from the pit turn yellow. There is an audible gasp as suddenly an immensely bright blob of molten rock bubbles from the pit onto the floor. They scream in panic as the liquid rock advances towards them—spreading and filling up the chamber.

The molten mass pulsates as the earth vomits increasingly into the chamber with brute force.

There is no time for them to react.

With nowhere to run, some fall to their knees to pray. It takes barely a minute before their skin singes, and the screams of terror die in their throats as their molten lips glue together. Death fills the room, burning every man and woman and liquefying their flesh and bones.

And just like that, most of the Divine Council, blessed by the gods themselves—a vast body of knowledge, wisdom, and brilliance of the Atalanni—vanishes from this earth.

Outside, in Enniru, the southeastern town of craftsmen and traders, an elderly man runs along the street, exhorting his fellow residents to get out of their houses. The pavements are cracked, many homes have collapsed, but so far, no one has died. A small part of the population had evacuated before the embargo on evacuations. But the rest are now streaming into the streets as fine ash descends on them from the skies. They have hunkered in their quake-resistant clay and plaster dwellings for days, hoping for the air to clear, but it appears everything has gotten worse. A woman hides her precious gold ibex statue under her floorboards and rushes out to the street to join her people. An artist looks longingly one more time at the beautiful painting of girls picking saffron—a ritual of entry into womanhood. He has loved this stately home since his childhood, for his father bestowed it upon him. Then he joins the others.

Another nobleman looks at the masterful painting on his wall. It depicts a procession of boats traveling between towns as people watch from the terrace. His nephew was the artist behind this lovely work of art. He wonders if things will ever return to normality again.

Someone is leading them from the front as they all head north to a tunnel entrance—one dug hundreds of summers ago, they say, by their wise forefathers who knew of the rages of the gods. The tunnel leads down deep into the bowels of the island's inner-southern edge.

"Are these tunnels not too close to the erupting fountain of fire in the middle of the inner sea?" asks a teenager, his face covered by the fine grains descending from the skies. He blows some of the ash off and spits to clear his tongue.

"The fire is in the middle. We are far away; do not scare the others," scolds his father, an expert tradesman of tables, chairs, and fine pottery. He has not evacuated because he believed that war would help expand his trade into the conquered lands.

Most have already surrendered their treasures for transportation to a secret enclave they have only heard about, leaving them little to abandon. With their meager belongings and leather skins of water and food, they jog through the gentle undulations of the ground, forsaking their comfortable and wealthy homes in search of safety. Two hours later, they come upon the entrance to the tunnel. Only a few feet ahead, the land ends in a cliff. Beyond the cliff, in the inlet, is a raging and angry center that still spews tall columns of bright red along with copious amounts of smoke, ash, and steam from the seas. To the last man and woman, they watch this scene in awe and take tentative first steps into the dark tunnel. A frightened silence falls over the crowd as they descend into the unknown, praying, hoping, desiring safety, and praying for an end to these terrible times.

# CHAPTER 58

## KALLISTU

The palace is ruined. The frescoes are shattered. The statues cry silently on the floor.

There are even signs of looting in some rooms—treasures stripped, pulled, and ripped in a frenzy of greed and desperation. We have rested for a day before pursuing Hannuruk, knowing that the situation in the water and around us would prevent his escape. Since morning, we have been combing the palace and its hidden rooms and tunnels. We encountered resistance thrice, but in short and violent skirmishes we killed the King's Guard, a sign that the King was somewhere, though no one knew where.

We must proceed cautiously, for the walls are shaken, and the roof is fragile in many places. We avoid delicate areas—I need to find Hannuruk, alive or dead. Apsara is much better, refusing to stay behind and rest. She travels with us, resolute in her opinion that she will accompany me everywhere.

By now, Rishwa knows of my affair with Apsara.

He admonished me and also wished us well. Finally, late in the afternoon, we arrive at an administrative office at the back of the palace. The King sometimes spent his time here discussing mundane administrative matters. We approach a large cedar door and surprise the armed guards. The leader is a stout, hairy man, adorned with a heavy bronze helmet and gauze armor.

"Halt," he says, "Proceed no further."

I move slowly towards them, showing the mass of armed soldiers behind me. Apsara steps forward. "Let us go ahead," she says calmly.

The man is confused. "Your Highness, you are no longer, I mean, you must not—" he stutters, unsure whether to act on the Queen's authority or even to treat her as a Queen.

"Do not fight us, Captain. Look behind me. You and your men will die in vain," I say. "Tell your men to put down their arms and leave. Find safety."

"Why are you here?" he asks, still pretending to be brave. But his men seem unsure—two of them quietly lay down their swords.

"Our purpose is not for you to know or decide. I ask you one last time, Captain. Step aside."

"We are the King's Guard, and we have the authority—"

I flick my finger.

The twang of a bowstring rings in my ear.

The Captain clutches his throat and collapses. His men quickly drop their weapons and stand with their backs against the wall. I tell them all to come forward carefully and walk through the parting in our lines. They take tentative steps, fearfully, and I assure them that no harm will come to them. They file in a single line, and once they pass us, they run as if they have never run before.

It is now us and the door.

Two men open it with some effort. My shoulder throbs because of my wounds. We take careful steps inside, knowing there is a risk of ambush.

No one charges us.

About fifteen soldiers await in a fighting stance, and there is Hannuruk, cowering behind them, comically holding a sword in his hand and standing unsteadily.

"Kill them! Kill them! What are you waiting for?" he screams.

The men charge at us like fools. One of them trips on the cracked alabaster and sprawls on the floor. Soon it is close combat again. We outmatch and outnumber them, hacking them down ruthlessly. I have no patience for the feeble minds that still follow this mad king and will lay down their lives for him. I stab one soldier and behead another, letting the white floor turn crimson. The melee subsides quickly.

"They are all dead, General. Fools," Itaja says, shaking his head. He is splattered with gore just as I am. I wipe my face and look around.

Hannuruk stands behind a table, waving his sword.

I advance towards him.

The King's eyes are wide like a lunatic. His face and large belly shine with sweat. His flabby chest heaves heavily.

"Stay where you are, Teber. Such betrayal! You bastard," he shouts.

"You call yourself a King, yet you have destroyed the very people you swore to protect," I say.

"I have done no such thing, you young treasonous fool! I will have you hanged. My son will be home soon and put an end to you swine," he says, swaying from side to side.

"Your son is dead, Your Highness," I say calmly. "I dragged him into a pit of fire and watched him burn."

Hannuruk flinches. "You liar! How dare you lie! Rishwa, do not stand there like a coward. Tell this liar to shut his mouth and lay down his weapons," he screams at the Prime Minister. I turn to Rishwa, who stands with no expression on his face.

"Your son is dead, Your Majesty," Rishwa finally says.

"You scoundrel!" Hannuruk bellows and lunges at me.

I lean back and swing my blood-drenched sword with great force.

The impact knocks his sword down and severs multiple fingers. Hannuruk howls in terror and pain. It is a deep, beastly, guttural sound. The King has happily sent many to their deaths and destruction, and now it is time for him to experience what it means to be helpless and in agony. He stumbles to the floor, clutching his injured hand. I advance towards him, and he looks up fearfully as he pulls himself back, using a pillar as a backrest.

"All you had to do was rule wisely and treat your land well," I say, "and treat your Queen as she deserves."

He stares at me intently, and something flashes in his eyes.

"That whore. So, the harlot was sleeping with you. No gods will forgive you both, you dirty scum," he says, his hate burning through his dark, bloodshot eyes.

"If only you had treated her with kindness and as a husband," I say, refusing to take his bait. "And yet you listened to a manipulative woman, sent your citizens to a fruitless war, murdered those who were loyal to you when they were unarmed and helpless, refused evacuation to the desperate, sent a worthless, incompetent, sadistic son to fight a war, and you tell me I am unworthy!" I shout back.

Hannuruk shakes his head vigorously as he tries to stem the blood from what remains of his fingers. "I am King. King of the Atalanni. Do you know what Atala means?" he splutters, drool flowing copiously from his livid mouth. "It means the greatest. What I did was for the gods, and my people betrayed me."

His eyes open wide suddenly. "There you are, you lecherous cunt. What kingdom had to suffer such a prostitute for a queen?" he harangues. I realize Apsara stands right beside me.

She says nothing. Instead, she kneels in front of him. I put a hand on her shoulder, but she slaps it away. "Let me speak to him, Teber," she says softly.

Hannuruk stares at her with hatred. "It is my misfortune that I had a prostitute for a Queen," he says again.

"Do you even know what it means to treat someone as a wife and Queen?" she asks.

"You deserved no such treatment," he says, spitting to the side. "You fucked him and violated your marriage, and here you are to lecture me. I am King. I do not answer to you, you wretched courtesan! The Mitanni kings must rear a harem of trollops. Your father must have been a pimp, and now you—"

In a smooth, almost dancer-like grace, Apsara arcs a glistening obsidian dagger and slices Hannuruk's neck.

A spurt of dark red drenches his thick, silvery beard.

Hannuruk gasps and clutches his throat with his bleeding stumps. His eyes widen in shock and surprise, but nothing emerges from his mouth except blood that glistens in the dying light.

Air bubbles from his throat.

He flops around like a fish on the beach. Apsara steps back as the King kicks and flails about, and I watch him dispassionately. Rishwa turns away—I cannot blame the man; he has served his ruler for decades.

We all watch as King Hannuruk's twitches subside, and he slides on the slickness of his blood. He eventually stops breathing, dying with his face turned to the side in a grotesque expression. I briefly feel bad for the King—he had ruled the land with relative peace for a long time before he lost control and his mind to the words of a priestess. Apsara buries her face in my chest and cries, and I hold her for a long time until she recovers.

"May I give him a quiet farewell and set up a funeral pyre?" Rishwa asks, looking at me for approval. I realize I am now in charge of decisions.

"Of course, Prime Minister. And free his family immediately," I say, referring to the King's forgotten first wife and their mentally incapacitated son.

Rishwa sighs and looks away as if searching for words in this dark, depressing room that smells of death and misery. "They are long gone, Teber," he says, without meeting my eyes. "She died a while ago, and they quietly killed the boy on the orders of Prince Nimmuruk. I do not think the King even knew—he had forgotten their existence."

"Do you know for certain that it was on the orders of Nimmuruk?" I ask.

Rishwa does not answer.

It is as if we both are guessing the same thing.

"I have to find Khaia," I say finally. "This saga ends with her as it began with her. Meanwhile, Prime Minister, take some of my men, declare that I now control the capital, lift the evacuation embargo, and find means to evacuate all citizens. But wait outside for now, as I must speak to the Queen."

"Yes, General Teber," he responds. I sense pride and affection in his voice. I ask Itaja to gather ten of his best men and wait for me outside the room. The rest clear the room and take Hannuruk's body away. In a few minutes, the room is empty. It is just the woman I love so deeply and me. I must have this conversation.

"The gods have smiled kindly upon us," I say.

She smiles, but there is sorrow in those glassy eyes. "We do not yet know if the gods are with us or against us, Teber, for their intentions are unclear. They saved me, brought you back to us, and yet so many have died in the wake of their fury," she says. I nod. The powers of the divine are beyond my understanding, though I try to reconcile their actions with their impact, and it makes little sense.

I hold her gently, carefully avoiding her secured wrist. "You must leave. I must finish what I started."

She shakes her head. "I will never let you go, Teber. We have been separated for too long," she says.

"I know, my queen. But you know as well as I that this saga is not over until I find the Oracle. I need answers, and it is my duty to bring peace to our land and appease the gods."

"I will come with you."

"Where I am about to go is not a place for my beloved with my unborn child," I say gently, placing a palm on her stomach. The baby kicks with great force, sending bolts of delight up my hand.

I laugh loudly, and she does as well.

"I know you seek to find the Oracle, Teber. As your Queen, I order you to take me along," she says, her face stern and her eyes unwilling to let go. I smile at the audacity. She is strong—immensely strong—to withstand a torturous marriage and to protect me while being willing to die of torture. The gods bless me. I know I cannot talk her into leaving me.

"You are stubborn," I say admiringly. "Come with me. But if I sense great danger, you will leave with Rishwa."

She agrees to that, and we leave the chamber.

Rishwa is still outside, waiting. The Prime Minister hugs me, and finality lingers in his eyes and tone. "A great boulder never stops until it faces a greater obstacle, Teber, and you are the largest boulder I have seen," he says cryptically, then turns and walks away.

# CHAPTER 59

## KALLISTU

The situation in Atalanni has steadily worsened. I look at the churning water below, and the land where I stand juts down to the water like a fist. The air has cleared slightly this morning, driving away the haze, but the entire area bears a fine layer of yellow and gray ash from the still-raging fountain of lava in the central temple complex and the surrounding connected island. I am covered in the fine powder, but none of that matters.

Itaja puts a hand on my shoulder. "We must return before it is dark, sir," he says.

I come back to reality. It has been two days since Hannuruk's death and quiet funeral, and we have not yet found Khaia. But today, there was a sighting on the eastern high point of the inner ring; she was there with her child and a retinue, along with a small protection force. Nothing that could stop us.

It will take me a day to return, for we must loop around the northern edge and turn south again because the inner sea is now impassable.

"Let us go," I say, and we silently descend.

It is time to meet the supreme priestess of the Atalanni Kingdom and seek answers.

We climb steadily up a steep incline that rises behind the Palace. We finally reach the eastern cliff edge of the inner ring and walk a narrow pathway that is now barely visible under the layers of ash. All the shrubs, trees, and plants are gray, lifeless, and sorrowful. The air is black and gloomy, and the glorious blue skies are just a memory. The inner sea is visible to our right as we walk north. It is a vast, churning mass of ash and detritus from collapsing cliffs and deposits from the multiple fountains of lava that continue to hit the water and explode with fierce power.

Even hundreds of feet above the water, we can feel the heat and the violence below. The temple complex has all but vanished, burned, and buried under thick layers of black rock that oozes blood from the earth. Rivers of lava flow along the canals and the collapsed causeway.

No man can question the fury of the divine around me, and no one can provide the reason for their anger.

We eventually come to a point where the path evens for a short distance and angles sharply up a steep incline with steps. This was once a back garden to the Palace, but no garden exists anymore. I jog up the steps and reach a platform—a stone platform with wooden railings that looks down the cliff. There are three benches on the platform, and Khaia sits on one of them, holding her child in her lap.

*No guards.*

Her face is dark and barely recognizable—the strain, dust, ash, and dirt have dimmed her radiance and reduced her to an old, haggard woman worn by the weight of life. She wears a diaphanous kilt, and her hair is tied in a hasty bun, with some curls still falling down her neck.

Once the most powerful woman in the Kingdom.

I brush away my feeling of sorrow for her. I have many questions, many things to tell and ask before I decide what to do with her. She is said to possess a divine connection to the gods.

I approach her slowly, and she looks back and smiles, as if expecting me. Dark smoke rises from the abyss in front of her, and, while we cannot see, a violent river of lava flows right beneath.

"You are everything I expected you to be," she says, half-heartedly waving her hand to beckon me closer. I do not know what she means, and I care little for her words now. "I am glad you saved her," she adds, her eyes pointing to Apsara, who stands behind. I have asked Apsara to allow me the chance to speak to the Oracle first.

"I have questions," I say, still respectful of her stature. But deep in my belly, anger burns at her actions and treatment of this land, its citizens, and Apsara.

"And I am glad you do, General, for I wanted to say much before you kill me."

"It depends on what you say."

Itaja steps forward, and I place a hand on his chest and push him back. "Stay back, Itaja; let me deal with this."

"She is the bringer of dark magic," says Itaja, both fearfully and angrily. "Kill her before she brings more misery to our homes."

"Step back," I admonish him. "We will decide her fate once I have a chance to speak to her. What greater misery can she bring us than what she already has?"

He glares at her and steps back unhappily, leaving us alone.

"What do you wish to know?" she asks. There is no fight left in her. Her child wriggles in her lap and protests the confinement in her mother's arms. I walk closer to Khaia and look down at her. She is frail. Her once eyeliner-decorated eyes hold a faint light as she looks up at me. But there is no fear in her face.

"Why?" I ask.

"Why what?"

"Why did you push us to war with Egypt?"

"The gods—"

"Enough! The time for lies and deception is over. We have trusted and worshipped your words, but they carry no weight anymore. Tell us the truth and unburden yourself," I tell her sternly.

She smiles. "You were always intelligent and inquisitive."

I dismiss her words. "It does not matter what you think. Please answer me."

She stands up slowly and with some effort. I notice scrapes and scratches on the side of her bare breast and waist. She kisses her child several times and lets her stand on the ground while still holding those little palms and not allowing the babe to run around in this dangerous area.

"You must have realized it by now, Teber. What do you want me to say?"

"I wish to hear it in your words. Tell us why."

"The Atalanni were a proud nation. A peaceful nation. But peace exists only if the rising powers around you respect your strength. We maintained a policy of restraint and trade when the lowly kingdoms around us pursued conquest. What happened to us? We were confined to a few islands while all the great lands of the earth were ruled by the brutes of the East or the uncultured of the North. It was time for us to assert our greatness."

"The gods told you nothing?" I ask, half-heartedly, knowing the answer.

She scoffs. "Gods? The gods say nothing to men, Teber. Those are fairy tales you hear. The gods granted us the faculty to understand the nature of earth, water, and fire, and it is up to us to forge and shape the world as we wish. All the backward kingdoms around us behave as if the divine is at their disposal."

She strolls toward the barricade and looks down the edge.

"You made up a story to send us to war," I say.

"The king has always been a coward. Apart from sending you and the others to defend us from the aggressive Mycenaeans, he has done little. He blamed the Divine Council for our policy of restraint, and yet we rescinded that policy long ago. The hints, the discourses... nothing worked. The barbarians from the North would have never stopped. The attrition would wear us out to extinction."

"And Minos?"

Her eyes flicker. I sense an emotion. "Minos was an out-of-control brute. He could have done remarkable things for us, but he threatened to go to the King with lies about me."

"He was not struck by the gods then."

She laughs, but without mirth. "If you believe the gods guided my hands."

"Your ambition and greed brought us to this," I tell her, sweeping my hands.

"I did what was right. It was time for us to shine on the theater of earth. Our ruler was a coward, and I saw it as my duty to act."

"You sought the throne! You led us to ruin. Why could you not fulfill your obligations as our chief priestess and maintain peace?"

"I could have made a great ruler. The Divine Council, while it has the greatest minds bestowed upon this world, has never had a member sit on its throne. Think about it, Teber! Would the Atalanni not benefit from our brilliance? We would be the masters of the earth."

"Your brilliance destroyed us, you witch! You would only seek bloodshed if you became a ruler," I scream at her. The hubris and the delusion are astonishing. I draw my sword and point it at her. "I should cut off your head right here."

Khaia turns and walks toward me. There is no fear in her eyes. She places her neck on the edge of my blade and looks at me. She has an imperial face—bright eyes, a sharp nose, and an oval face. The stress of recent days has given her a stern, intimidating look. I waver for a moment; this woman held sway over the King and the Supreme Council for a long time, so I would not underestimate her.

"You would not kill me," she says, and there is a hint of a sparkle in her eyes.

"Why not?"

"You could still support me, and one day become King yourself, my son," she says.

# CHAPTER 60

## KALLISTU

*What?*

"What—" My mind refuses to believe what my ears just heard.

"You have made me proud, my son," she says, lifting her palm to caress my face. I recoil as if a scorpion has stung my cheeks. I look around to see if anyone else has heard this, but they are out of earshot. The impact of Khaia's words suppresses the roars of nature around me.

"Don't call me your son. I am not your son!" I say under my breath.

She smiles sadly. "The laws of the land took you away from me, but I always watched over you, my child," she replies. Everything in her demeanor suggests that she is telling the truth. I look back and see Apsara watching me intently—curious, afraid.

The Oracle of the Atalanni.

She who drove us to war and countless deaths.

She who killed the formidable Minos.

She who suggested to my love that she take her own life with our unborn child.

Khaia.

Mother.

My legs feel weak from the revelation. What other unkind surprises do the gods have for me?

I look around. Many gray, ash-covered bushes are on fire, and the seeds explode in the heat. Dark smoke rises, ash descends from the skies, and the raging fires roar below us.

The Palace lies in ruins, and parts of it now rest in the waters below after a collapse. It is as if the world around me reflects my soul—broken, burned, deceived, and devoid of life.

"Why should I believe you?" I ask. "All you know is deception!"

"What do I gain by lying now? Not much. Have you never wondered why I resisted sending you to Egypt?"

I pause to reflect. People have often joked that I resemble the manly version of the Oracle.

Her eyes.

Her expressions.

It all comes together.

*She really is my mother.*

But that is no excuse.

"You tried to kill my baby," I say flatly, searching her eyes for a reaction.

Her mouth scrunches in confusion. "What—"

Then it registers with her—a mind clouded by ambition and desire. Her eyes widen in surprise, and she covers her mouth with her palm. To my surprise, tears spring and roll down her cheeks, and she cries.

The little girl picks up on her mother's distress and howls.

Little girl. My sister.

Khaia—no, my mother—holds her tightly as she tries to recover. A gust of hot wind laden with black soot blows over us. Itaja comes forward again and asks me, near my ear, "What is going on, sir?"

"Wait for me," I tell him. "She is revealing what I needed to know, but I must speak some more."

Itaja is unhappy. He wants a quick execution so we can leave.

"Step back. Let me complete my conversation," I command him more forcefully. He finally retreats to the men.

"I did not know. I vaguely suspected, but I dismissed the thought," she finally says, her voice trembling. I believe her.

She continues, "I never intended for her to be tortured. We tried to dissuade King Hannuruk. I tried to—"

"You tried to have her kill herself!" I hiss at her.

"Yes," she replies. "I did not know. A merciful death was better than the horrific punishment. You came on time, but imagine if you had not!"

I follow her reasoning. "But you pushed—"

"Do not lay this on my feet, my son. I had nothing to do with Apsara's difficulties with her husband, your dalliance with her, or imposing her punishment by the King."

I am conflicted. What she says is true. And yet, a corner of my mind insists that my mother is not telling the entire truth—but I decide not to pursue it further. I turn and beckon Apsara.

She takes tentative steps and approaches me. I can see that Apsara has guessed what is happening.

My mother does not embrace Apsara; she looks at her and says, "You would make a magnificent wife, Apsara. Beautiful and bold. What a fool I was not to see this."

Apsara does not respond.

"If there had been peace, would we have reached this situation?" I ask her, changing the subject.

"I thank divine blessings that your child grows within her," she says wistfully, not answering my question.

I realize the gods never sought what the Oracle said they did. It seems the wrath of the gods is directed at us for reasons we might never fathom, or for what we did at Khaia's behest.

"You will never see your grandchild," I say firmly. It is as if I am compelled to be cruel.

She nods.

"Her name is Akhi," she says, looking down at the little girl—no, my sister. She is a beautiful child, and yet her cheeks are wet with tears and her face is dirty with ash and soot as she stands here with her mother. She lifts the girl, kisses her again, and hugs her tightly. Khaia then presents the child to me. "Hold her. Take care of her," she says. There is a finality in her voice. I am a raging cauldron of emotions. I grew up without my parents, or so I thought, and here I stand face to face with the woman who once bore me into this world and saw to my well-being. She actively resisted sending me to Egypt; she again resisted sending me the second time, and she had, from time to time, inquired about me, even as I grew up. I only saw it as interest from the head of the Divine Council.

I take Akhi in my arms.

She resists and reaches back to her mother.

I hold her firmly to my chest—and after a struggle where I realize a toddler poses a greater challenge than an enemy on the battlefield, I beckon Itaja to take her. Khaia touches her daughter's hand as Itaja takes the thrashing girl away.

Tears roll freely down my mother's cheeks, and she wipes them away. "This is not what I foresaw, Teber. I hoped that one day I would rule to make us the greatest empire that ever was and that you would succeed me."

I shake my head. "We could be happy in peace, mother."

She gasps at my utterance.

She reaches out and gently feels my cheek.

I do not stop her.

She comes forward and holds me. She stays that way for a while, and I dare not disturb her—even with all the anger I feel toward her, I cannot help but marvel at the embrace of a mother.

*This is how it feels.*

Apsara surprises me by gently placing her arms around Khaia. My mother turns to her. "May you live a thousand summers," she says. "And may the gods forgive me for my treatment of you."

She then places both her palms on Apsara's cheeks and kisses her forehead. Then she steps back. She fiddles with her gold bracelet—it shines even in the ash-ridden haze. She gently removes it, kisses it, and drops it to the ground.

"Why was I given away?" I ask her. "Where is my father?"

"The laws required that the one anointed to be Oracle must relinquish their child before the child is three and must never reveal themselves. The punishment is death to the child, no matter the age. Your father was a soldier in the army, and he died during a fight with the Mycenaeans—you never knew him."

I wipe ash from my face and clear my eyes. I have the answers I need.

It is time.

"We must end this, mother," I tell her. She nods and gently clears her eyes and face with a linen napkin. She looks up at me once more and leans forward to kiss my forehead.

"Teber. My son. My handsome, powerful son. May you live forever. Look at what I have wrought," she says.

She walks to the edge of the cliff near the barricade. I decide to give her some time to prepare herself. This is a job for eager Itaja.

I step forward to look below.

Far below the cliff, the land burns with fury, and the remaining temple walls cry tears of molten rock. The fountain of lava has grown in size—it is taller, wider, and the grievous wound in the black earth pumps out bright red-orange liquid rock in prodigious amounts. Toxic fumes assault our senses, and fine ash coats every living and non-living being. There is a demonic hum in the air—like a nest of vipers hissing and a million bugs of the night buzzing around our ears.

Another gust of hot wind rustles our hair. Khaia holds the barricade and leans forward to look at the spectacle below.

Then she looks at me.

And then my mother leaps over the low barricade in one swift motion and disappears.

"No!" I scream and rush forward. I lean to look and glimpse only a speck of her sheer blue fabric as she impacts the terrifying heat below us. She burns away like a dry leaf in the raging fire and vanishes.

As if on cue, the central vent roars—it is a sight I have never imagined. A forceful jet of red lava erupts, creating a gigantic column of black ash. Astonishingly, bolts of lightning shoot within the black cloud—it is as if the Great God of the Seas himself rides the clouds and hurls fiery bolts from his Trident.

"Run!" I scream, and I turn to the men still waiting. I hold Apsara's hands, and Itaja has my sister. We rush from the cliff edges as the enormous column rises in the air. We feel the heat on our backs. We run across the undulating fields, hopping and jumping over obstacles, reaching the flatter areas where there are no constructions. Behind us, the earth rages on, and my lungs burn with exhaustion as we strive to distance ourselves. My sister is now in my arms, bewildered and quiet, terrified by her surroundings.

We try to make distance, but the world darkens quickly, and the heat grows.

But I know a secret place, though it is half a day away under these conditions. There are a few boats we can commandeer.

I pray fervently to the gods to let us go.

# CHAPTER 61

## KALLISTU

We finally make it to the bottom of the cliffs to access the secret place—a small cove on the western edge of the inner ring, close to the harbor. I know it contains fifteen fast boats with sails, each capable of holding eight to ten people. An internal tunnel runs directly under the island and emerges at the outer western edge into the open sea. Therefore, the boats do not need to traverse the turbulent inlet to escape the maelstrom.

But the path is treacherous, and Apsara is exhausted. She sweats profusely in the heat. The non-stop shower of fine ash and soot harasses us, and we must frequently clear the coating from our bodies. Even this brief journey has claimed its casualties; I have lost seven more men, leaving us with just forty-five. Some have collapsed during the trek, some fell from the cliffs, and one man ended his life.

Itaja has been my rock.

We finally arrive at a narrow pathway at the bottom of the southern edge. The fountain of fire is away from us, to the northeast, now a little calmer than just a few hours ago. A small hope grows like a plant within me—are the gods accepting Khaia's death and intending to calm? But I cannot take any chances.

Muddy, debris-filled seas slosh to our right. We have only a few leather skins of water left.

"How far is it?" Apsara asks, her breathing heavy and her face almost unrecognizable. I allow her to pause for a while to catch her breath. A pregnant woman should not be enduring these travails.

"Not too far, my love, just there," I say, pointing to a spot ahead where the path turns inward, revealing a small overhang from the cliffside. Beneath the overhang are multiple pathways, one of which—a rocky stone bridge—leads to the secret cove.

"Itaja, take ten men with Apsara and proceed ahead," I instruct him. "You know where it is and what to do."

He nods. Apsara resists leaving, but I insist. "I will be right behind. There is one more thing I must do," I tell her, overriding her protests. She argues further, but I finally chide her for putting herself at risk with my child. "It is your duty to care for yourself for the sake of this land and our child," I say, firmly ending the argument.

"Promise me you will follow us soon," she says, her eyes moist. I hold her face and kiss her deeply. I taste the salt of her tears mingled with the sweetness of her lips. They taste like heaven amidst the surrounding hell. She then removes her necklace—the only possession she was allowed to keep during her imprisonment—and gives it to me. It is a beautiful piece—thin gold thread adorned with green and blue gems.

I kiss the necklace and place it into my waist pouch. "I will be right behind. I just have one more thing to take care of."

We embrace again for what feels like an eternity. I watch her walk away slowly with Itaja and the soldiers surrounding her, and she continues to turn and look at me until her silhouette vanishes in the cave's darkness. If all goes well, she will be on an evacuation boat soon, and I will follow.

There is just one more thing.

With the remaining men, I sprint up the steep incline, dodging burning bushes and gusts of smoke and ash. These men have refused to leave my side despite my exhortations and orders. "No soldier worth their value or the mercy of their gods would abandon their general," one of them says, and I embrace him in gratitude. The dungeons are near the palace. We progress through the cracked quadrangles, collapsed compounds, and arenas. No one remains here anymore.

I have heard that most people, including former guards and soldiers, are hiding in quake-proof tunnels, hoping for calmer days.

I ask most of my men to take shelter. I descend the steps of the prison with two lieutenants. The roof has not yet caved in, but the ground is littered with sharp, upturned slabs of stone and jutting masonry from broken walls. The cell doors are empty—few were held here, as this was not a general prison.

I finally find a closed cell. The door is locked—a large padlock holds firm. I peep through the small opening on the door, and once my eyes adjust to the darkness, I find a figure lying on the floor.

*It is her.*

With the help of one of my men, I use a hammer to break the lock and rush inside.

Sitkamose lies still. I place a finger by her nose and realize she is still alive. The princess is emaciated, and if it were not for the bread and a jug of water placed in her cell, she would have starved to death. I lift her and place a water bladder to her lips. We remain that way for a while as the life-giving fluid enters her, and she finally stirs.

Once she comes to her senses, I hush her from speaking and give her some bread. Strength is critical as we prepare to evacuate. The earth is mercifully quiet—there have been no quakes in the last two days, yet the eruption of fire in the inlet grows stronger by the minute. I do not understand the meaning of it all.

"General Teber," she says flatly. I am surprised she remembers me. "Why come to save me?" I am glad I can converse in broken Egyptian.

"Atalanni do not seek your incarceration or the death of the prince," I reply, hoping that if she returns to Egypt, she might persuade the Pharaoh to show mercy to the Atalanni who may find their way to Egypt.

She nods. "Your land. Ruined. Warned you."

"Time to leave."

Once she steadies herself, we make our way out.

She keeps pace with us, even amid her stumbles.

"Much worse than imagined," she says, looking around as she pauses to catch her breath.

"So we must hurry. Darkness soon and rush of tides."

"Where go?" she asks.

"Egypt," I answer.

Sitkamose appraises me shrewdly. "Me hostage? Bargain?"

"No. Only to right the wrong. Return you."

She takes a deep breath and coughs as the fine ash irritates her lungs. I let her catch her breath as we watch the growing and raging eruption of fire in the inlet sea, now clearly visible from our location.

"You good man," she finally says. "Could have left me to die."

"This way, princess," I say, and we begin our jog to the secret cove. I ask the men to check their ration packs. We are satisfied that we have enough to last us through a few weeks with tight rationing. The food packs slow us down, but they are necessary. Besides, the escape boats are always stocked with animal oil, fishing gear, water skins, and other implements to aid us on our journey across the sea.

The surrounding air has changed by the time we arrive at the bottom of the cliff, at the narrow path leading to the bridges to the cave. The pulsating eruption at the center has grown larger, and the seas are much rougher. Ash and debris-laden waves lap the shore, swirl in great circles, and wash over the path, making it treacherous.

My heart thunders, but this is no time to ponder.

We line up in a single file and walk briskly, staying close to the cliff wall on our left and keeping a careful eye on the waters to our right.

I feel relieved when the stone bridge leading to the cave overhang appears in the distance.

*Not much longer!*

We quicken our pace, and I urge the men and the princess not to stop now, no matter how much their limbs hurt or their breaths burn. My voice struggles to be heard over the roar of the fires, the wheezing ash-filled wind, and the intense sloshing and swaying of angry seas.

"No!" I hear a scream behind me.

An enormous wave sweeps up from the sea, striking a man and dislodging the earth beneath his feet. In an instant, he vanishes, indistinguishable from the debris—floating branches, clumps of sand and ash, burned wood, dead fish, twigs, tree branches, burning rock—a swirling, terrifying spectacle.

"Keep moving!" I shout. Thankfully, the path widens, giving us more room between the sea and the cliff wall, making it safer. I can feel the intense heat of the inlet fires— it is far, yet its power is unquestionable.

I am frightened by what I see near the bridge. The water here is shallow, with dark rock lurking just underneath. But that also means lava from the eruption can flow over it, and that is exactly what is happening. A fast-moving mass of bright orange-red molten rock, with the consistency of thick honey, rushes toward the bridge from the massive erupting central vent of fire.

"Run, run, run," I flail my arms. We reach the stone bridge under the onslaught of heavy, debris-laden waves, and Sitkamose rushes across to the other side. I have already informed her where the boats are.

"Come on!" she turns to us and shouts. The men ahead of me sprint and jump across the now slowly breaking bridge, landing safely. They urge Sitkamose to come with them, and the group runs.

I leap, skipping across the unstable rocks. Men behind me rush one after another, each reaching safety as the hiss and heat of the approaching molten river increases.

There are two men left. The first jumps, but his foot gets caught in a crack, and he tumbles into the boiling water. His screams are drowned in the frothy hot foam, and he vanishes under the turbulence. I watch in dismay as the stone bridge groans and breaks away under the onslaught of heavy water, followed by the hot, thick, fast-flowing molten rock that now floods the space between me and the cave's entrance.

The last man runs back and watches us from a distance.

I pray for him. We run.

My skin singes from the heat and the blasts of scorching air. We reach the hidden boats and help Sitkamose's crew prepare for departure. I instruct them to navigate until they reach Egypt. They promise to take her to safety, and she assures them she will protect them when they reach the shores of Egypt.

I finally pull the princess aside for one last conversation. "Queen. Innocent. My baby."

Her eyes widen. She gestures at me. "Apsara. Atalanni queen. Your baby?"

"Yes."

She smiles knowingly.

"Ask to escape to Egypt. Hide. No harm?" I tell her. I hope it will never come to this.

"No harm. Protect. She is innocent. I know."

"The king declares torture and death for her. I save. Promise me."

"By Amun and Horus," she says, and squeezes my shoulder. I feel relief.

"You?" she asks me.

"I want to join Apsara. But Egypt?"

"Cannot promise safety. You are general. You fought the Pharaoh. Cannot go against the Pharaoh," she says, and I admire her honesty.

"Understood," I reply. She embraces me and steps into her boat.

I bid goodbye to them, assuring that we will be right behind. We watch them sail through the cool, quiet tunnel and begin our preparations. Our plan is to briefly stop at Kaftu, away from all settlements, and depending on the winds, continue to Egypt or to Cyprus. While this plan is fraught with risk, I still long to be with Apsara.

We take a few hours, and by the time we emerge from the tunnels on the far side of the island, it is already late in the day, and the sun has begun to set. Nevertheless, we feel energized and relieved by the cooler, fresher air.

We turn south to coast along the edges of Kallistu, preparing a course toward Kaftu. It is then that we notice something on the northern horizon.

A flotilla!

I cannot make out much in the haze, but the shapes are enough to tell me that these are Mycenaeans, and this time they come in vast numbers. These sneaky bastards will never give up!

They are in for a surprise.

I look at the men. An understanding glimmers in their eyes. While our capital no longer exists in any manner worth defending, our people have fled to Kaftu and other islands. If the Mycenaeans make their way here, I know they will massacre the weakened Atalanni.

"The invaders from the North," I say.

"They never give up, do they?" Innas, another trusted lieutenant, replies, nodding his head in exasperation. "What do they seek?"

"Our ports. Our ships. Our riches. Our trade connections. Our women. Everything we wanted from someone else," I say. We watch in silence as the full extent of the Mycenaean fleet becomes clear.

The sea remains blue here. The imposing cliffs hide the tumult in the inlet. The haze of smoke and ash is visible in the skies above Kallistu, like a cloud of gnats on a buffalo.

We watch in silence. It will soon be dark, and I know the invaders will wait for morning. I give my men a chance to leave, but not one man agrees.

These are the true men of the Atalanni.

Our eight boats are no match for hundreds.

But then we have something else.

# CHAPTER 62
## KALLISTU

At dawn, we wash our faces with the blue-green waters as the boats sway gently in the unassuming seas. A cool breeze blows from the southeast, pushing the cloud of ash away from our direction. The hum from the fires raging in the inlet has become louder, more incessant, more urgent, as if a great cataclysm is about to be unleashed.

We make our prayers to the gods:

*O mighty Trikaia,*

*Bless us,*

*Give us wisdom to fight darkness,*

*Bestow health, plentiful food, and riches,*

*We bow to you,*

*Protect us and give us eternal life.*

Once the prayers are complete, we place each other's palms on our comrades' shoulders as the boats dance beneath us.

"The invaders are in front of us," I say, looking at each man. "But our gods are behind us," I add with a smile.

One man wipes a tear from his cheek and laughs.

"I am proud and honored to be with you. We will live in the hearts of our families," I proclaim. Well, my family is dead, and the woman I love is out there somewhere, hopefully headed to safety.

"To the general for whom we would all die," announces Innas, and I hear a chorus of "hear, hear!"

"To the man who got between the Queen's legs while the King scratched his balls!" announces Eluminnas, and the group cackles.

We raise our hands and bow to each other.

Eyes shine with mischief.

We huddle to strategize. Then, we get to work.

First, we unfurl the bold and colorful Atalanni flags so they are clearly visible.

Then, we spread our boats in a broad arc so that the eight vessels feel like a welcoming party.

Once in position, we pull out the powerful conches— these are always available in all Atalanni speedboats. These instruments, fashioned from seashells, emanate a powerful battle cry.

I close my eyes, feel the gods smile upon me, and sense Apsara lean forward to kiss me.

In unison, we raise the conches and blow a long, ear-shattering horn into the air.

# CHAPTER 63

## KALLISTU

Draklymaxos, called Drax by his men, squints at the southerly seas. The vessels in his temple throb with a combination of eagerness and anxiety. The powerfully built commander of the Mycenaean forces places a foot on the boat helm and elevates his height to get a better look at the vista ahead.

The cliffs of the island of the Atalanni rise to his left, and Drax and his men have been hearing a strange buzzing sound emanating from within the island for two days. Dark clouds loom in the sky, but they seem to drift away.

Drax does not like what he hears, sees, and smells. It does not feel right, and he does not know why. He is of the mind to halt the advance until further notice—but now there is another development. Far ahead, to the south, the Atalanni military boats appear. They are close to the cliffs, near the entrance to the islet; no doubt they are the welcoming party for the fleet. They raise their customary battle horns—loud, annoying, intimidating. Drax knows that previous battles with the Atalanni have gone poorly for his navy.

"Why have they not met us before with their larger fleet?" he asks his advisor.

The older man squirms. "We do not know, sir. Perhaps it is another trick from these wretched sea-farers?"

"What do you make of the sounds and the strange smells?"

"We have not heard the likes of it before, sir. I only have accounts from far lands that sometimes lofty mountains hum."

Drax looks at the man with irritation and slaps his chest to push him back. "This old fool knows nothing," he mutters.

The conches blow again from the Atalanni boats. The enemy boats then turn away.

"Do you think they are leading us into a trap, sir?" the advisor asks.

"What trap? Even if it is a trap, a few hundred boats are no match for our thousand!" he shouts.

He exaggerates, of course; they have three hundred. "This is not any other invasion, you idiot. Do you not see how great our forces are?"

The advisor shrinks and quietly vanishes behind the other men.

"Kolymos, hoist the masts and prepare to advance at full speed!" he orders. "We will put an end to this farce. Aememnon did not send us here to sit and wait with our cocks tucked between our legs!"

Kolymos raises an attack flag, and the hundreds of boats behind them acknowledge the sign. In unison, the great Mycenaean fleet of King Aememnon slices through the dark blue waters and races along the western cliffs. Their destination is the only passage into the inlet, beyond which lies the great inner harbor and temple of the Atalanni. Drax expects vicious fighting and attacks from the cliffs.

He inhales the salty wind, the exhilarating aroma of seaweed, and laughs at the childish tactics of the Atalanni.

He orders a hundred boats to get ahead of him. Too bad they shall withstand the worst of the first attacks, but it is necessary. It does not take long for them to arrive near the inlet, but the signs are deeply unsettling.

The sea is more disturbed here.

The sky is darker.

The hum is much louder.

There is abundant debris—the inlet does not look beautiful and emerald.

Thick brown, black, and yellow swirl around.

The Atalanni boats have vanished somewhere in the turn, behind the cliffs. Drax ponders: Should they just wait, or send in the first hundred and see what happens?

"Should we wait, sir?" Kolymos asks tentatively, looking worried.

"Have you heard of the legend of King Amaeos?" Drax inquires of his lieutenant.

"No, sir."

"Amaeos was a weakling. When he took his powerful army to fight the Northern rebels, they came to a narrow mountain pass. He suspected ambush and sent small units forward to inspect. The clever rebels massacred the parties just out of eyesight, and then a man would dress himself as one of the unit's men and signal the next batch to come in. This way, he lost a good portion of his best men before his generals realized and intervened. By then it was too late— killed by a thousand cuts—all because of the man's abject stupidity."

Kolymos nods. He does not know if this is a made-up story, for it sounds ridiculous. Why would the king send more small parties after the first one? However, he is too afraid of Drax to protest.

Drax continues, "Maybe the Atalanni planned it! These tricksters surely created an ambush-like scenario to make us pause, think this is an ambush, send small groups that get destroyed, and then wear us down."

Kolymos nods half-heartedly, unconvinced.

"I will not let that happen. Not on my watch!" Drax yells, pumping his fist in the air and twirling his great beard.

He orders the boats to spread wider—into an arc of about fifty boats each, and six rows deep. The rectangular fleet can fit into the inlet, which is about half a mile wide, based on the assessment by previous messengers. This entry, Drax is sure, will frustrate any ambush; the boats are too many, and the formation is too wide and deep.

His boat is in the fourth row of formation.

Ah, to look at their surprised and terrified faces! He fantasizes about the upcoming massacre, loot, and rape—these people would finally experience what they had evaded thus far.

Drax is ecstatic as the wind picks up speed. The closer they get, the harder it is to control the formation. Copious amounts of mud and ash are ejected from the innards of the inlet.

*What is going on?*

"Full speed ahead; let us thrust the mighty Mycenaean cock into the Atalanni!" he shouts, his face red with excitement. The great fleet makes its slow turn into the inlet, with the farthest wings rowing quickly to reach it.

# CH∧PTER 64

## K∧LLISTU

Just as the sun ascends and begins its daily rise in a cloudless sky, the enormous forces beneath the earth's surface conspire. The central vent, now hundreds of feet wide and spurting prodigious amounts of lava, rumbles like an enraged monster from the deep. First, the entire inlet shakes as a massive earthquake bubbles up from the depths. The sea churns with breathtaking ferocity, with waves up to eighty feet high, smashing against the fragile cliffs and causing large sections to break and collapse. The landslides and the quakes cause the rest of the Palace, along with the once-magnificent cliff-facing complexes and homes, to crumble, shatter, and fall into the sea.

The first four rows of the Mycenaean boats that entered the inlet now realize what peril they have embraced after ignoring the obvious signs of danger all around them. Kolymos shouts, "Fire! Their earth spews fire, sir!"

The boats in the front panic.

The captains signal the rest to halt and attempt a turnaround. But it is impossible—stuck in a narrow inlet and with their own fleet clogging the entire width, they have nowhere to go as the huge debris-and-mud-filled waves strike them. The tumult causes the boats to crash against each other as if a giant were banging the heads of weak opponents in the arena.

When the last row of boats tries to turn, the troops see eight Atalanni speed boats racing behind them. The Atalanni commander stands tall as he exhorts his troops.

They blow their conches again, which can still be heard amid the din of crashing boats, waves, rocks, and fire.

The Atalanni boats approach, and the men pull strange metallic orbs from bags tied to their waists.

"What the—" a Mycenaean captain shouts. Just then, the first metallic orb arcs through the air and lands on a boat. It explodes, killing several men instantly and igniting the vessel. The rest yelp and howl as the flames engulf them.

The Atalanni boats flit like bees, dashing from one Mycenaean boat to another.

Several boats in the last row catch fire, inciting further panic. The Mycenaeans hurl their javelins, killing several Atalanni and thinning their numbers until only a few remain, including their colorful leader, covered in ash and soot. However, the last row of the Mycenaean boats has become a flaming wreck, entangled and preventing the escape of those trapped ahead.

Birds create an uproar as they fly around, terrified. The central vent ejects immense columns of fine, superheated ash high into the air, the pillar now exceeding the height of the cliffs and quickly spreading across the island like an enormous mushroom, embracing the land in a deathly hug.

Drax experiences terror like he has never felt before. The spectacle before him, around him, and beneath him makes him realize what he has led his fleet into. "Turn, men! Signal the last rows to turn!" he yells, but it is too late. The inlet churns violently, causing the boats to entangle and many to overturn quickly, prompting shrieks and bellows from men plunging into the poisonous waters.

Then, a loud roar erupts, like an outraged giant from the bowels of the earth, and simultaneously, a tremendous explosion sends huge sections of the inner ring collapsing.

Drax feels as if he is being sucked into a vortex of horror. Powerful blasts shoot pulverized rock into the air with great force.

Drax watches in horror as flying rocks, some the size of boulders, smash into the boats swirling around, tangled in the turbulent waters near the inlet entrance. The powerful vortex, caused by inward rushing waters, draws the entire Mycenaean fleet into its maw.

"Gods have mercy!" Drax shouts, the fire in his belly extinguished and replaced by cold, dreadful fear. No one is there to heed their lament or save their lives. Along with the black, sharp rocks that smash into them, pulverizing many men into mists of blood and flesh, the extremely hot fine ash burns their skin. The collapse of the inner seabed generates great waves, much taller than even the boat masts, flipping most of the Mycenaean flotilla.

The colliding, burning, and overturning vessels annihilate the men. Those who jump into the raging seas drown or boil, without even a moment to scream or pray.

As Drax watches in horror, a fiery black rock flies at him, and his head explodes like a watermelon.

The earth gives little pause.

As the sun rises, the gods engineer the greatest violent eruption from the center. This eruption creates a gigantic column of fire and ash that races toward the sky like a ravenous beast leaping to clutch the sun. The cloud rises and rises until it exceeds the heights of the cliffs, more than twice, more than thrice... until it reaches the edge of the sky.

The massive explosion rains enormous volumes of fine yellow pumice and smoldering boulders. Thick, rapidly moving, extremely hot ash flows in all directions, concealing the lava spurts within. In the eastern inner ring, people still hide in a tunnel. They have been trapped there for days, terrified and unaware of the wrath of the gods outside. Many are already dead, their corpses lying amidst the living. The rot and stench spread sickness among the others. They are running out of water, and the air is fetid and foul. Even as they pray to the gods for mercy, the ground shakes, and a side of the wall collapses.

They cry and embrace one another.

A raging flow of hot pumice envelops them like molten bronze armor in the summer heat, turning them into ash statues frozen in time. The entire tunnel fills within seconds, creating an eternal tomb for the last living Atalanni.

The ferocious eruption continues beyond the setting of the sun, and the night is alive with howls of terrible wind, devastating waves, and roaring fires.

The Mycenaeans vanish beneath the waves.

The entire land that comprised the Palace collapses beneath the rushing waves and flowing molten rock.

The remnants of the vast and spectacular temple complex disappear in the explosions.

And with that, the capital of the Atalanni becomes only a memory.

The beautiful island is now sawed into multiple sections. The rushing waters and eruption create giant waves over a hundred feet tall.

In the northwest, two Mycenaean boats, survivors of the carnage, flee from the destruction behind them. They are safe, for the clouds and waves no longer head in their direction.

They will have tales to tell.

In the southeast, not too far away, a lone boat in the vast sea first feels the swelling waves pass beneath it. Two men lie lifeless, while one man struggles to maintain control of the boat as it sways and plunges with the swells. The fierce waves grow larger. The man kneels during a brief lull. He watches as immense dark clouds rise high above his homeland, resembling the mesmerizing hood of an angry cobra. He pulls a necklace from his waist and kisses it. The golden thread and blue-green gems shine under the waning moon.

He then bows his head and prays.

It appears he is asking for forgiveness and love in the afterlife.

He holds the necklace to his chest.

A great wave looms behind him—it is ten, no twenty, no thirty, no forty, no fifty, no sixty—over a hundred feet high—and the boat disappears beneath the great fist of the God of the Seas.

# PART VI

*"It is the nature of the world that it continues its eternal march with no regard to the acts of men and beasts; their station or travails; their joy or sorrow; their greed or ambition; their love or hate. For such is the world the gods have bestowed upon us..."*

**DAIVOSHASTRA CH. XXII: "RHYTHMS"**

# CHAPTER 65

## KAFTU

Phaistos stands on the hill and gazes at the coastline. The devastation is immense—the important trading ports of Ihnuma, Pennaraya, and Asarata—all extinguished in the monstrous waves from the sea that smashed the towns like an angry fist of the Sea God and burned everything with hot ash and ferocious winds. The water and superheated ash have obliterated the navy. The harbors and the shipbuilding facilities, the lifeblood of their empire, have vanished.

Phaistos despairs—what are the Atalanni without their navy and trading partners?

That was their life.

That was their means to prosperity.

That was what they knew.

The Divine Council is no more, taking immeasurable knowledge with them to the afterlife.

For days, the air has been poisoned by fine ash and dust that rained from the sky, causing all sorts of ailments. After that shameful spectacle of the Queen's execution, Phaistos had obtained the assent of the Prime Minister to take control of Kaftu and await the King and other senior members.

The Grand Palace of Kaftu has survived, but has sustained some damage. However, he does not know how he will resist any attacks from the aggressive Mycenaeans or even the angry Egyptians. So far, there has been no news at all from the capital. Two boats sent out to scout have returned, speaking of how nothing exists anymore and that the island is a flaming wreckage, with the sea a turbulent mass of debris and mud so thick that no boat could venture closer.

Not a hint of life remains, as if Kallistu never existed, they say. Phaistos looks around sadly once again. He rubs his scalp and squeezes his temple.

Will my people ever survive this or vanish from the pages of history? he wonders.

"We will do what we can," says a voice beside him. Phaistos looks at Rishwa and nods sadly.

The two men ponder their future.

# CHAPTER 66

## WESTERN DESERT – EGYPT

Bansabira stumbles and falls to his knees. The sun beats down, and there is nothing but fine yellow sand all around. Of all those who escaped the massacre at the hands of the Egyptians, only twenty remain.

The plan was to hide deep in the western deserts and bide their time. The men who gave them directions had long vanished, leaving Bansabira uncertain whether they had been deliberately misled or if he and his men had simply gotten lost. Instead of a path that supposedly led to a small oasis, they had entered a sandy and rocky wilderness where nothing—not even a shrub—grew. They had one last mission as they escaped from the battlefield: to secure the blueprints, burned in clay and written on papyrus, for the *Daivoshaktis*. Bansabira carries them in his leather bag. Teber had instructed them to protect these blueprints and keep them away from the Egyptians.

Someday, he hopes, the Atalanni will return.

*Teber will return with an army to end the Egyptians.*

One of his men grunts something. Bansabira turns, and at a distance, ominous shadows appear in the sky.

*Sandstorm!*

He finds himself by a cliffside. Dark rocks jut out from the sand, and a small cave is nestled among them. He crawls inside the cave. His mouth is too parched to issue orders, and his body is too weary to escape. Bansabira gently removes his backpack and lies down on the sand.

Far ahead, at a great distance, he thinks he sees a speck of green.

*Oasis?*

But he is tired. Most of his men collapse as well; their bodies no longer willing to move. A few of them stumble onward aimlessly, their legs sinking into the sand.

The wind picks up speed, kicking dust into their faces.

Bansabira wonders if the gods of Egypt have sent a storm after them as retribution. He removes his upper garment and ties it across his face, protecting it from the fine grains of sand that feel like sharp pinpricks.

He hopes to wait until the storm passes.

But the wind intensifies—instead, the storm gains speed and ferocity. Soon, the sky darkens, and dust and sand assault him with brutal force.

He can no longer see or hear his men.

Bansabira turns and lies on his stomach, attempting to shield his face. He closes his eyes and prays to his gods. He feels someone call his name and someone tug at his backpack—but he clutches it tightly until they let go.

Then there are no more human sounds. Only the whispers and songs of the swirling sands.

He dreams of his home and the love of his parents as the storm buries him under massive quantities of fine grain.

The sand feels immensely heavy. It feels as if he is in a boiling pot. Breathing becomes harder and harder.

Bansabira feels as if he floats over a forest while a falcon shields his eyes from the sun.

Then there is eternal darkness.

# CHAPTER 67
## THEBES – UPPER EGYPT

Pharaoh Ahmose observes as the workers erect the great stele. It speaks of a great tempest, storm surges in the Great River, and the destruction of buildings and temples. He has commissioned this stele to recount both the invasion of the Atalanni and the darkness it brought to the kingdom, as well as the mysterious and terrible weather experienced soon after the war with the Atalanni.

Messengers report that the gods have destroyed the Atalanni. There have been scant accounts of an indescribable catastrophe in the far islands of the Keftiu. However, Ahmose has adhered to his word to his nobles, priests, and the military—that the name of the invaders shall never make its way to the written word. His only interest lies in uncovering the secrets of the Atalanni and their fire weapons. But those secrets remain buried.

His aunt, Sitkamose, has returned. She possesses a remarkable story, but one that must not be uttered in public. Ahmose has plainly told her that she will remain hidden for life, and her story must remain on her lips. Sitkamose understands. She pleads for the life of Teber, the Atalanni General. Ahmose has made no promises; besides, no one knows if he even lives.

Ahmose has issued a proscription against the Atalanni and anyone from the lands of the Keftiu. He squeezes his lovely wife's hand and looks affectionately at his baby, Amenhotep, in her arms. Ahmose-Nefertari knows that her young husband's mission has only begun. Now that the Atalanni threat has abated, it is time to turn towards the *Hyk-Khase*. Khamudi still reigns in Lower Egypt—a matter of great shame. The scourge of these invaders must be exterminated.

"The god of Egypt makes his father and brother proud," says Wadjmose, standing by his side.

"And my hand is strengthened by your hands, Wadjmose," Ahmose says affectionately to his general. Wadjmose lost his hand in the last major battle with the Atalanni, but he now serves as the supreme advisor to the Pharaoh. Baba is proving to be a fine commander and is preparing for the fight against the Asiatics.

There is much to accomplish now—to restore the health and spirit of Egypt, to reward those who stood by him in these hours of darkness, and to punish those who obstructed his path. The granaries are stretched; families are despondent over the loss of their loved ones; armament workshops are low on metal and wood; two nomes in the Northern regions threaten to revolt.

Pharaoh Ahmose, He of the Sedge and the Bee, benevolent god of the great people of Egypt, gazes at the magnificent temples and the throngs that adore him.

It is time to prepare for the long struggle ahead.

# CHAPTER 68

## SAIS – LOWER EGYPT

The haggard man and the pregnant woman smile at each other. A little girl holds the man's hand. The high priest of the magnificent temple of Amun at Sais has finally granted them an audience. The attendant beckons them, and they rise to their feet and follow him.

It is a glorious temple—not as great as the one from the land they came from—but it serves as the place of worship. The cobbled, uneven stone floors feel cool underfoot. The painted sandstone walls depict Pharaohs and their wives, mothers, and concubines. Statues of cross-armed Pharaohs gaze down sternly beside the large open doors. The corridor becomes increasingly gloomy as they walk further, illuminated by only a few flickering oil lamps affixed to the walls by crude fasteners.

"Are we safe—" she whispers to him. The attendant, a clean-shaven young man wearing a crisp white tunic and small gold bangles around his wrist, looks back at them. "Quiet!" he admonishes.

The man grips the woman's palm reassuringly and slows his pace to walk beside her as she takes her unsteady steps. They finally arrive at the inner sanctum—the holiest place in the temple.

The attendant whispers to them, "Wait."

The woman nods.

She understands some Egyptian that she has picked up with the help of a kind Egyptian farmer over the last few moons as they made their way here. After some time, two women come and take the little girl with them, enticing her with small thread-dolls. "We will bring her back to you after your audience," they tell the man and woman.

The man and woman stand respectfully by an ornate wooden door that is slightly ajar. Inside, they hear chants and the soft clang of bronze bells striking a plate.

A ritual to the gods.

A lovely fragrance wafts through the crack.

"Come," the attendant says. The man and woman step onto the cold, painted floor. Someone shuts the door behind them. It is dark inside, except for a few lamps that reflect off various objects. In front of a tall pedestal for the god Amun sits a figure heavily cloaked in a black garment.

"Sit down, children," says a gentle voice. The woman whispers the translation to the man, who has not yet grasped the basics of the language. They kneel on the floor, and she struggles to support herself. Someone brings a soft pillow for her to rest on. She bows to the figure.

"A Princess," the figure says. It is an old, gentle, and deep voice of a man.

His observation startles her. She says, "May the gods bless you for your kindness, Your Holiness."

Silence envelops them, punctuated only by the sound of breathing. Then the man speaks in clear, halting Mitanni, "A Princess of the Mitanni."

Apsara scrambles and prostrates with significant effort before the High Priest of Sais. "Yes, Your Holiness," she replies in her native tongue.

"Sit back. Do not exert yourself. Your husband does not speak your tongue," he states.

"He does not."

The old man exhales, his raspy breathing filling the air. "He bears scars of battle, and his land is no more."

Apsara holds the man's palm and squeezes it.

"The wrath of the gods was upon you," continues the high priest. "Pharaoh Ahmose has a proscription on the Atalanni."

Apsara bows again. "And yet here we are to seek your blessings and protection, Your Holiness."

The high priest sprinkles some cool water on them. Apsara calms. "This is a sanctuary, and no harm will come to you. But this is also a temple of ancient knowledge," he continues. "Every traveler tells us a story. You must also perform duties to the temple for three harvests. Is that acceptable?"

Apsara nods vigorously. The man looks apprehensive. She squeezes his palms again. "Itaja," she whispers. He looks at her, love and devotion shining in his eyes.

"Yes, of course," he says, and prostrates before the high priest.

Apsara holds Itaja's hand.

She thinks fondly of Teber.

But there is no news of him. There are already tales of how the gods punished the Atalanni and how, in a night and day of great fires and quakes, the island vanished beneath the sea. Teber's trusted lieutenant had brought her to safety and had unabashedly been besotted by the Queen of the Atalanni. He had agreed to raise the child as his own and had already suggested a few more with him. Deep in grief and yet bound by circumstance, Apsara had stayed with Itaja.

She is slowly growing fond of him.

"The time is now, child. Tell me."

"Do you not want someone to write...?" she asks.

He laughs. "We carry our knowledge in our minds. It has been so for thousands of harvests, and so it will be. From father to son, from priest to his next."

Apsara nods. "What do you wish to know?"

"What you wish to tell," he states.

The priests must light their lamps twice as Apsara speaks of her childhood, her land and family, her marriage, and her life in the Atalanni.

She narrates the greed, the madness, and the destruction.

There are tears, exaggerations, modifications, and omissions, but the high priest listens attentively, asking barely a question. When it is all over, he says quietly, "A tale of greed and hubris."

She nods.

"A remarkable story of the Atalantis," he pronounces, mispronouncing the name, but Apsara does not correct him.

The name means nothing to her anymore.

They rest for some time and eat a sparse, simple meal of bread with beer. She receives fruit for the child and for her womb.

Once that is done, the high priest speaks to her again. "Why have you not gone to your homeland?"

She smiles wistfully. "I know they will not accept me or the man who is with me."

The old man ruffles his garment. "Your child grows of a brave and powerful man."

She smiles and rubs her belly.

"I foresee much greatness for him."

"Is it a boy?" she asks, surprised.

"Yes. And we must name him now, for this is the most auspicious time."

Apsara dithers. She has not thought of a name for the baby. "I have not thought of a name, Your Holiness," she replies. She translates their conversation to Itaja, who haltingly expresses his reservations.

"You have sought the mercy of our gods. You eat our food and drink our water. You will now be Egyptian, seek the blessings of our gods, and live our life, will you not?" the high priest asks sternly.

"Of course," she affirms, and Itaja agrees. They have accepted Egypt. It was not a hard decision. Egypt had done no wrong to them, and the gods had spared their lives.

"Then come forward and kneel," he orders.

Apsara rises with Itaja's support. She kneels before the high priest and moves the fabric covering her belly, exposing it. The old man presses his palm to her stomach.

Apsara feels a powerful kick and winces. The high priest laughs, a deep-throated, joyous laugh. He presses his hand again and feels another kick.

Satisfied, he leans back.

"Your son will bring glory," he states. The lamps crackle on the side, and a gentle breeze drifts through the doors, illuminating the idol of Amun, who appears to smile at them. Apsara feels a great power within her, as if a lightning bolt has infused the strength of the universe into her and her child.

"You will hereafter be known as Seneseneb," the old man declares. Apsara acknowledges his words.

"I am Seneseneb," she repeats.

The high priest places his palm flat once again on her belly. "You say his father comes from the land of profound knowledge and that he possesses strength and intelligence," he remarks.

Apsara takes a sharp breath and nods.

The priest rasps, "Then you shall call your child the one born of Thoth."

"Thutmose..." Apsara whispers.

The priest inhales deeply. His wiry, rough hands grip Apsara's gently, holding them near his chest. He then utters the words.

"...And your son shall one day fight for a Pharaoh and become Pharaoh himself."

# THE END

# NOTES

Where do I even begin? While one could write an entire novel-length history book explaining the historical references (and liberties taken) within this novel, I will cover a few interesting aspects that may have caught the reader's attention. I strive to blend fact with fiction and fantasy in my works, and, where possible, I have used historical precedent as the basis for descriptions, names, and events. In these notes, you can see some of the connections between the novel and the known history of the era. I would ask for your kindness when you see a departure from known history because this is, after all, a thriller and not an academic paper!

I leave the rest of fact versus fiction to your imagination and research.

## TIME PERIOD

The book is loosely set in the early New Kingdom period of Ancient Egypt, circa 1550 BC. Astute readers will no doubt have realized that the Atalanni (Atlantis) are based on the Minoan civilization that thrived in Crete (Kaftu, a name derived from Caphtor or Kaptara, Keftiu per Egyptians), and the volcanic eruption is based on the Minoan eruption (or the eruption of Thera). Be aware that the timelines of practically everything in this period are very murky. We do not know with certainty the actual eruption dates, the rule of Sekhenenre and Ahmose, or the exact reign and sequence of the Hyksos rulers.

Many debates and academic papers have addressed the dating of the Minoan eruption, and yet today we are no more certain than we were decades ago. The eruption certainly occurred sometime between 1630 and 1550 BC. Likewise, the exact time periods of the late Second

Intermediate Period and the rise of the New Kingdom (starting with Ahmose) remain in question as well.

The *Hyk-Khase* (or *Heqa-Khowse*) in the book refers to the more commonly known "Hyksos." The original Egyptian term simply meant *rulers from hill countries*—that is all. At some point, later Greek writers translated it as *Shepherd Kings*. We have no conclusive evidence regarding the origins of the Hyksos, though they were most likely of Semitic origin from the Levant and surrounding areas. At the end of the book, we read the chapter where Ahmose oversees the construction of a Stele. Look up the "Ahmose Stele" for an interesting artifact left behind from the Pharaoh's time that discusses an unusual weather phenomenon. Some have posited that the Ahmose Stele speaks of the aftermath of the Minoan eruption, though many others suggest the descriptions serve as an allegory for the tumult in the Kingdom. Pharaoh Ahmose is considered the first pharaoh of the New Kingdom and the one who drove the Hyksos out of Egypt. His father (or grandfather) Sekhenenre Tao likely began the conflict.

In the book, we encounter a rather revolting scene where Teber is shown severed palms in Khamudi's palace. You might find it fascinating to know that archaeologists have actually discovered palm and finger bones in the Hyksos excavations at Tel-el-Daba (ancient Avaris) (see this interesting link: https://www.livescience.com/22267-severed-hands-ancient-egypt-palace.html), indicating that this was a prevalent practice.

## LOCATIONS

If you have not figured this out already, here is how to map the locations in the book to their modern-day equivalents. Enjoy flying over on Google Maps!

- **Kallistu**—Santorini (Thera). The ancient Greek name was *Kalliste,* meaning "Most Beautiful." Thera was also known as *Strongyle* (The Round One). We do not know its original name prior to the Mycenaean/Greek influence. I have called it Kallistu, assuming that the usage of Kalliste came from an older name that the Mycenaeans may have borrowed.

- **Kaftu**—Crete. Known as *Caphtor* or *Kaptara* in ancient sources. The Egyptians appear to have referred to Crete as *"Keftiu,"* and it is entirely possible that this is borrowed from the original name.

- **Enniru**—Akrotiri on Santorini.

- **Thebes**—modern Luxor (Egypt).

- **Siwa**—Siwa (Egypt).

- **Sais**—ruins of Sais (Egypt).

- **Washukanni**—Unknown (*possibly Tell-Fecheriye, Syria*).

- **Hutwaret**—Avaris/ruins in Tell 'el Daba (Egypt).

## NAMES

We know little about authentic Minoan names. A few names preserved in Egyptian records possibly provide some authentic Minoan names or locations, though we do not know for sure. In the book, Aranare, Bansabira, and Itaja are named after similar potentially authentic Minoan names. It is also worth noting that "Minoan" was simply a term coined by archaeologist Arthur Evans, who excavated ruins in Crete. Upon seeing the labyrinthine constructions in the palace of Knossos, he was reminded of the Greek stories about Minos. Having no way to identify the original name of the people who lived there, he simply termed them "Minoans." There is very little evidence to connect the original Minoans to the Greeks. What is broadly accepted is that at some point after the Theran eruption, the Mycenaeans (precursors to the ancient Greeks) invaded or occupied a weakened Crete, effectively colonizing it. Over time, we lost the original civilization entirely as it was subsumed by the new people. We have also not deciphered the original script of the "Minoans" (we call the script Linear A).

Hannuruk/Nimmuruk exhibit an eastern influence, hinting that the Atalanni could be an amalgamation of people from various regions.

Apsara has an Indo-European/Sanskritic influence, as she is a Mitanni princess. The Mitanni were known to have had Indo-European/Aryans in their ruling class, and some words in their vocabulary are found in Sanskrit. For example, the Mitanni worshipped Indra and Varuna, who remain part of the list of deities in Hinduism!

Egyptian names follow regional styles. An interesting fact is that the word "Mose" simply means "Son of." Today, we see similar applications, for example, in Arabic names (*Ibn or Bin* means *son of*).

### ERUPTION OF THERA

At some point, possibly between 1630 BC and 1550 BC, the volcanic caldera of modern-day Santorini erupted in one of the greatest cataclysms of the ancient world. Possibly a hundred times more powerful than the Pompeiian eruption, this mega-volcano destroyed everything that lived on the island, shattered it into pieces, generated a massive tsunami that radiated outward in all directions, and likely significantly damaged the seafaring civilizations in Crete. The pyroclastic surges buried the ancient city of Akrotiri (named *Enniru* in the book) where spectacular frescoes depicting the ancient people were found. The eruption appears to have happened in three phases.

## ORIGINS OF ATLANTIS

There is only one place in any historical record where Atlantis is mentioned—and that is in Plato's *Timaeus* and *Critias*. Any other reference is derived essentially from Plato's work. I cover the subject of "Was Atlantis Real" in my light-hearted exploration of such topics in my book "Cousin Clay's Confounding Claims."

If there were any other books on the topic, perhaps by the Greek philosopher Solon himself (who apparently originated the story, based on his discussion with Egyptian priests at Sais, as per Plato), they have all been lost.

That Thera/Santorini could be the location of the original Atlantis has been a hypothesis for decades now, based on certain parallels between Plato's story and the geological features of Thera. Once again, as is the case with many aspects of the ancient world, much of it is speculation.

So, the story continues.

# THANK YOU!

———◇———

I would be immensely grateful if you would take a few minutes to either rate the book or leave a review if you enjoyed it. This makes a significant difference to authors like me. You can also visit https://www.jaypenner.com/reviews for easy links.

**What should you read next?**

March with an army of fifty thousand on the way to burn the sacred temple of Ammon in the next exciting novel of the series, The Curse of Ammon, based on the fascinating tale of the **Lost Army of Cambyses**.

If you are a history enthusiast, you will enjoy the flyby that will take you to all the major locations mentioned in this book. Go to: https://www.jaypenner.com/maps

Jay Penner

# About Jay Penner

Equal parts history buff and tech enthusiast, Jay weaves tales of kings, queens, and pharaohs alongside nerds, megalomaniacs, and "smart cookies." His acclaimed Whispers of Atlantis, Cleopatra, and Spartacus, series transport readers to ancient Rome, Egypt, Mesopotamia, Persia, and India, while his Dark Shadows saga spans the globe in the "near future." He is a resident of the beautiful US Pacific Northwest where he lives with his wife and daughter. Jay happens to be an engineer with an MBA (apologies).

Having lived, studied, and worked across three continents and five countries, Jay's deep appreciation for diverse cultures fuels his passion for writing stories that transcend borders and connect people.

Jay's occasional newsletter is a must-read whether you're a fan of his page-turners or an aspiring writer (or both!). With insights into his books, characters, and craft, it also features new releases, deals, and bonus content. Plus, he throws in original write-ups on various intriguing topics, all seasoned with humor.

The Whispers of Atlantis Anthology

*An anthology of thrillers set in the ancient world.*

...

Cleopatra - The Last Pharaoh

*A series on the rise and fall of Egypt's famous queen.*

...

The Spartacus Rebellion

*A trilogy on the astonishing rebellion against Rome.*

...

Dark Shadows

*Techno-thrillers set in the near future.*

...

Cousin Clay's Confounding Claims

*A light-hearted, fact-filled exploration of 'interesting' theories about our ancient past.*

**Follow me on:** The Amazon author page

# REFERENCES

- Tiziano Fantuzzi – Tell el Dab'a and The Interlinked Chronologies of Minoan Crete and Egypt in the Bronze Age – 2013

- Nanno Marinatos - Minoan Religion – 1993

- P. Nomikou et. Al. – Post-eruptive flooding of Santorini caldera and implications for tsunami generation – Nov 2016

- Emily Vermule – The Promise of Thera – A bronze age Pompeii

- Jan Heinemeier & Walter L. Friedrich – Time's up! Dating the Minoan eruption of Santorini – Nov 2007

- Mark Cartwright – Akrotiri Frescoes – March 2014

Made in the USA
Columbia, SC
12 December 2024

48801419R00248